HOUSE OF RECKONING

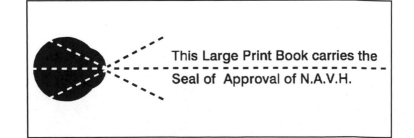

This Large Print Book carries the
Seal of Approval of N.A.V.H.

HOUSE OF RECKONING

JOHN SAUL

WHEELER PUBLISHING
A part of Gale, Cengage Learning

GALE
CENGAGE Learning

Detroit • New York • San Francisco • New Haven, Conn • Waterville, Maine • London

GALE
CENGAGE Learning™

LIBRARY OF CONGRESS CATALOGING-IN-PUBLICATION DATA

Saul, John.
   House of reckoning / by John Saul.
     p. cm.
   ISBN-13: 978-1-4104-2266-8 (hardcover : alk. paper)
   ISBN-10: 1-4104-2266-6 (hardcover : alk. paper)
   1. Teenage girls—Fiction. 2. Foster children—Fiction. 3. Ex-mental patients—Fiction. 4. Art teachers—Fiction. 5. Haunted houses—Fiction. 6. Supernatural—Fiction. 7. Large type books. I. Title.
   PS3569.A787H68 2009
   813'.54—dc22   2009037523

Published in 2010 by arrangement with The Ballantine Publishing Group, a division of Random House, Inc.

For Michael —
Who made it all possible!

Chapter One

Sarah Crane breathed deeply of the Vermont air as she quickly counted the chickens to make certain they were all safe in the coop before she closed the door for the night. Twelve. Perfect. She secured the door against any raccoons or weasels that might be out looking for an easy midnight snack, and with a last backward glance at the barn to make certain she had locked the door, she carried the egg basket up to the house, just as her mother had done every night for the past fifteen years. Fall was Sarah's favorite season; there was something about the light — maybe the way it filtered through the golden leaves of the maples surrounding the small farmhouse, or just the angle from which the sun shone down on her. Whatever it was, it always made her skin tingle and filled her with a sense of pure exuberance. Or at least it had until her mother got sick almost a year ago, and then died six months later. Since then even the fall twilight couldn't quite fill her with the joy of earlier years.

Nor did it help that there were only six eggs in the basket, and with the late September chill in the air, Sarah knew that the hens were about to stop laying until next spring. That, though, was nothing compared to the other thing worrying her tonight: how were she and the animals and the farm going to survive the winter with her father going into what her mother used to call "his cycle," without any preparation at all for the cold months ahead. He hadn't chopped any wood, he hadn't hunted deer, he hadn't even sold the calves, and now they were too old to bring the best price.

Instead he started drinking, and the vague unease Sarah had been feeling for the past few months was blossoming into a gut-churning fear as she scraped the bottom of the feed barrels. Now, with winter quickly approaching, the rats were taking over the barn, the hay was rotting in the field, and the woodpile, which should have been at least four cords by now, was pitifully small.

But she couldn't do it all herself.

The last of her exuberance fading as she stepped back into the warm kitchen, Sarah tried to unwind her worries as she unwound the wool scarf from around her neck. She put the eggs into the refrigerator and began cleaning up after supper, even though her father was still sitting at the kitchen table.

He hadn't eaten any of the corned beef hash she'd made for him; instead he pushed his plate aside and was staring morosely down at a photo album open on the table in front of him.

Sarah quietly cleared the table, careful not to bother him. She scraped the leftover hash into a dish, covered it with plastic, and put it next to the eggs in the refrigerator, then began running hot water into the sink.

"Sarah?"

Her father's voice was hoarse with the grief he'd been carrying for half a year, and the sound of it pulled tears to her eyes. Those tears were never far away, but most of the time she could control them.

Unless her father began to cry.

Then she wouldn't be able to stop them. How many times in the past six months had she and her father held each other on the sofa and just cried together? But when were they going to move away from all that? Her mother had told her — told her over and over again — that she wasn't to spend her life grieving. *You keep living, understand? You have a whole life ahead of you, and I don't want you wasting any of it crying about me going and dying on you.*

"Yes?" Sarah said, in response to her father, gritting her teeth against the cold fear in her heart.

"Bring me another beer, honey."

She felt a fist close in her belly. Before her mother died, her father never had more than one beer, even on the hottest days. But lately the first beer led to the second, and then on and on. And it did no good to argue with him — he'd just tell her to stop worrying. She pulled a beer from the refrigerator and put it on the table, but couldn't keep herself from at least trying to slow him down. "Do you have to, Daddy?" she asked, her voice barely above a whisper.

"Just something to take the edge off, sweet pea," Ed Crane said, putting his thick arm around his daughter and drawing her close.

Every part of her father seemed larger and more powerful than other men, which was why everyone except her mother always called him "Big Ed." He was tall, broad-shouldered, had legs nearly as thick and strong as the trunks of the maple trees, and a grip that could have crushed her if he wasn't careful. But he was always careful, at least with her, and now his arm was gentle around her.

"Look at your mama in her wedding dress," he said, pointing to a photograph. "Wasn't she the most beautiful thing you've ever seen?"

Sarah didn't want to look at those pictures again; they only made her miss her mother even more. She wanted her father to put them away and start living again. But night after night, he didn't eat, he didn't sleep.

He just grieved.

And now he wanted another beer.

She knew how this would end. He'd keep drinking most of the night, and in the morning would apologize and swear it would never happen again. And for a while he'd be her father again.

Until the next time he decided to have a beer, and then another, and then ended up going out and drinking all night.

She squirmed uneasily from his grasp. "I have homework I have to do."

Ed let out a massive sigh. "How am I going to raise a daughter?" he said. "Without your mama . . ." His voice trailed off and his entire body seemed to shrink into a shrug of defeat.

You stay sober and tend the farm, Sarah wanted to say. *I can raise myself if you just take care of the farm. I'm already fourteen and I can handle it.* But she said nothing, and went back to the sink to finish cleaning up.

Just as she was drying the last of the dishes, her father opened the refrigerator and helped himself to yet another of the brown bottles that always sat at the back of the top shelf.

"Please don't, Daddy," Sarah said, unable to bite back the words. "Please don't start." The tears she had struggled to control now slid down her cheeks.

"It's okay, sweet pea," Ed said. "This isn't like last time. Don't you worry now, you go up and do your homework."

"Please?" she begged, a sob escaping her. What if he went off the deep end this time and never came home again? What would she do then?

"Don't nag me," Ed said, twisting the cap off, throwing it at the garbage bag and missing. "Better get to doing all that homework."

Sarah looked toward the ceiling. "Help me, Mama," she whispered. "Please help me. I don't know what to do."

Taking a deep breath, she wiped the tears from her face with the dishcloth, hung it carefully and neatly on its hook, then went upstairs to her room, leaving her father to his personal demons.

Lily Dunnigan was about to cover her husband's dinner plate with a sheet of aluminum foil and put it in the warming oven when she heard a loud crash from upstairs.

"Nick?" she called out, then listened for a moment, heart pounding, for his voice to come floating down the stairs, telling her everything was okay.

Instead she heard another loud bang. And another. Grabbing a bottle of his pills from the cabinet above the refrigerator, she ran upstairs, praying all the way.

By the time she got up to Nick's room, he was yelling, his voice rising by the second. "Stop! Stop it! Stop it *now!*"

Lily pushed the door open without bothering to knock, knowing that right now Nick wouldn't even hear her voice, let alone a rap at his door. Sure enough, his face was contorted into a grimace that hovered somewhere between pain and anger as he smashed the keyboard of his computer on the back of his desk chair. "Stop it!" he howled again, his voice cracking. "Stop saying those things to me!"

"Nick!" Lily cried, then repeated his name

13

even louder: *"Nick!"*

Startled, he looked up at her, but for a moment his eyes didn't seem to focus. A second later, though, he stared down at the broken keyboard in his hands and a look of confusion spread over his features.

Lily's heart sank.

She wrapped her arms around her son, and he carefully set the keyboard back onto his desk, then clung to her, sobbing.

"They won't leave me alone," he said, his voice breaking.

"What is it, darling?" she asked. "What are they saying to you this time?" She gently guided him across the room and they sat on his bed. She smoothed his hair and rocked him back and forth, even though his fourteen-year-old frame was far too large for the easy cuddling that had calmed him in years gone by.

Nick shook his head as if trying to rid himself of some terrible memory. "Awful things," he said. "They talk about horrible things." His gaze fixed on the ruined keyboard on his desk. "I thought they were coming out of my keyboard," he sobbed, pressing his head into her bosom. "But they weren't. They were inside my head." He paused. "I don't even know what they keep saying to me. But it was —"

14

"Hush," Lily soothed. "Just relax. It's all right — it's not real . . . none of it's real."

Nick's sobs slowed as the two of them rocked on the mattress. When he finally spoke again, Lily could hear the fear in his voice. "You won't tell Dad, will you?"

She pulled a tissue from her pocket and handed it to him. He blew his nose.

"I won't tell him," she promised. "Assuming he comes home at all," she went on, then wished she could reclaim the words when Nick suddenly looked even more frightened. "From work, honey," she added. "He's just really late, that's all," she went on, and couldn't resist adding one more word: "Again."

But why shouldn't she say it? It was true — Shep had been working late every night for months, ever since his promotion. And lately he was always in some kind of negotiations over prison expansion plans, as well as trying to keep up with all his regular duties as deputy warden at Lakeside State Penitentiary. And for what? Did he really think that if he just kept on working twelve hours a day instead of his usual ten they'd eventually make him warden? Not likely, given that his boss was five years younger than him, and showed no interest in going anywhere else.

"You took your medication today, right?" Lily asked her son.

Nick nodded.

"I'm going to double your dosage tonight. Maybe it will help you get a good night's sleep."

Nick nodded again, but didn't loosen his grip on her.

Lily rocked him, wishing she could absorb his fears, draw them right out of him and banish them forever. But she couldn't — so far it seemed nothing could rid Nick of the voices in his head and the strange hallucinations he sometimes saw. But she wouldn't tell Shep about this episode tonight, because he'd want to send Nick right back to the hospital in Waterbury, and she would not let that happen.

Not again.

Not after what they'd done to Nick last time.

"You okay now, sweetie?" she asked softly.

"They're quiet when you hold me," he said.

"Then I'll hold you all night," she said.

She felt him smile, but they both knew that holding him, rocking him, was not the answer.

But that hospital hadn't been the answer, either, and neither, apparently, was this latest medication.

Nor had her fervent prayers released Nick from the grip of what she'd come to think of as his demons. And if God couldn't free him, what could?

Maybe if they tried a different doctor.

Or a different medicine.

Or if Shep spent more time with his son.

But since Nick's last hospital stay, Shep didn't seem to have any time for Nick at all, and when the two of them were together, Shep had nothing to say to the boy, and at fourteen, she knew that Nick needed his father far more than he needed her. Yet Shep only seemed more absorbed in his work as each day and each week passed. The thought she tried to hold at bay but that always seemed to escape her control in the darkness before each dawn now stabbed through her like an ice pick driven directly through her heart. *He no longer cares about Nick. My own husband doesn't care about our son.*

Well, it couldn't go on — not while Nick seemed to get worse each day.

She would talk to Shep when he got home. She'd talk to him again.

But for now she would just hold Nick close, hold him and rock him and wish that things — many things — were different.

Big Ed Crane blearily lined up his shot, jabbed the stick at the cue ball and completely missed. For the second time in a row. Dropping the pool cue on the felt table in utter disgust, he made his way unsteadily back to the bar.

"Dude! You owe me two bucks," the kid in the John Deere ball cap called after him.

"Sue me," Ed muttered as he slid onto the corner bar stool and tried to bring Christine, the bartender, into focus. "Boilermaker for the road," he said.

Christine eyed him from her position at the beer tap. "I think maybe you've had enough, Ed."

"You cuttin' me off?" he demanded, belligerence rising inside him like molten lava.

"I'm thinking you could use a cup of coffee," Christine said, sliding the just-poured beer in the opposite direction, then pouring a steaming mug from the pot next to the tap and setting it in front of Ed. "And you need to pay that kid his two bucks. He beat you fair and square."

"Got no money," Ed said, his anger melting into drunken self-pity. "Got nothin' anymore." He ran his hand over his face.

"Used to have . . . everything before Marsha died. Now I got nothin'."

"Man, you don't know how lucky you are," a man two stools away, wearing stained bib overalls, said. "Women are all whores. Take your money, and steal your soul. Wish *my* wife would die and leave me in peace."

Ed pushed the coffee mug aside, swung around on his bar stool, and glowered darkly at him. "Marsha wasn't like that."

"Sure she was," the guy shot back, ignoring the warning note in Big Ed's voice. " 'Course she was — they're all bitches, every one of 'em. Didn't you just say you've got nothin'? That's 'cause she stole it all from you, then left you to rot."

"Not Marsha," Big Ed grated, his eyes narrowing and his right fist clenching dangerously. "She was the bes' woman of 'em all."

"More like was the biggest *whore* of 'em all," the other guy sneered. "And your daughter'll be just like her. Just another fu—"

In one swift movement Ed lurched over the adjoining stool, grabbed the guy's bib overalls, and jerked him close enough so he could see panic in the man's eyes. "You lookin' to get hurt?" he growled.

"Hey!" Christine said, pulling a worn

baseball bat from behind the bar. "Settle down, you guys, or I'll settle both of you down."

Ed gave the guy a shove backward and he teetered for a second before he fell off his bar stool and crashed to the floor. Swearing angrily, the man worked his way slowly back to his feet with the help of one of the regulars who frequented the Fireside in the futile hope of accompanying Christine to her apartment upstairs after she closed the bar.

"That's it," Christine sighed, turning the lights up bright. "Drink it up, everybody." A chorus of complaints arose from the small crowd, but she ignored them, focusing instead on Big Ed Crane. "As for you — out. Now." Her cold gaze shifted to the man who a few seconds ago had been sitting near Ed. "Both of you." She came around the bar and poked Ed in the ribs with the bat. "Out! Out!"

"Hey," the kid at the pool table said. "My two bucks."

"That's your own problem," Christine tossed back over her shoulder as she marshaled both men out the front door. "Go home."

The blast of cold September air slapped Ed in the face, and he stumbled as he fished in his pocket for his keys. He didn't want to go home — home was nothing but emptiness and sadness and terrible loneliness.

The Fireside Tavern — or any other bar — was warmth and distraction.

"She was a whore!" the guy in the overalls yelled at him from a few steps down the block. "You should be glad she's dead!"

In an instant Ed Crane's long-suppressed rage at the loss of his wife flared inside him. Fueled by hours of drinking, the fury erupted and he charged toward the man, again grabbed him by the bib of his overalls and hurled him against the brick wall of the building at the mouth of the alley he'd been passing.

"Don't say that!" Ed said, the words twisted by the alcohol in his blood and strangled by the grief that had overwhelmed his soul. Barely aware of what he was doing, he slammed the man's head into the brick wall.

"Hey, I'm —"

"Don't!" Ed commanded. Then, while smashing the man's head again and again, as if to punctuate every word, he said, "Do. Not. Say. That." The man's knees buckled, and Ed let him sink to the ground. "Idiot," he muttered, barely noticing the blood that began to pool beneath the man's head. "You don't know nothin'."

Ed stumbled back to his old truck, held on to the door handle while he pulled the keys from his pocket, dropped them, groped in the gutter until he found them, and eventually hauled himself into the cab. After a half-dozen tries he fit the key into the ignition and started the truck.

"Idiot," he muttered again, revving the engine. He ground the gears, trying to find reverse, then spit gravel from the tires as he popped the clutch and shot out onto the dark, lonely road that would take him to his equally dark and lonely home.

Sarah Crane woke up with a start, her heart pounding. The image from the nightmare she'd been having since her mother died was fading rapidly, and all she remembered was that in the dream she was in a house — a huge house — and even though it was filled with people, she couldn't see or hear them.

But she knew they were there.

And they were as lonely and frightened as she was.

Now she lay still in her bed, her pulse slowly returning to normal as the last images from the nightmare faded away. She was about to turn over and try to go back to sleep when she suddenly had a feeling that something wasn't right.

She listened, but heard nothing.

The house was silent, as silent as the great mansion in her nightmare.

A clouded moon cast soft shadows across her bed in the stillness.

She hugged the worn plush rabbit that had been her nighttime companion for as long as she could remember, and listened again.

Nothing.

The house was quiet.

Too quiet.

Her mom used to say that her father could snore the paint off the barn, but tonight Sarah heard no snoring from the next room, nor anything from anywhere else in the house.

Which meant one thing: he'd gone out drinking at the Fireside.

Hoping, wishing, even praying that it might not be true, Sarah slipped out of bed and peeked into her parents' bedroom. But the bed hadn't been slept in. She crept quietly down the stairs, but even before she got there, she knew she was alone in the house.

She could actually feel the emptiness.

The sofa, too, was vacant, the crocheted

afghan still stretched cleanly over its back. A dozen beer bottles littered the kitchen table, and a glance out the kitchen window showed her that her father's truck was not in its usual place in front of the garage.

Which told her that he was indeed at the Fireside, where he'd gone more and more often, and drinking more and more every time he went. And last time he'd come home drunk, he almost rammed the truck into the barn, and she'd decided that the next time it happened, she would go to the bar and bring him home herself.

And tonight was "next time."

She didn't have a driver's license yet but had driven the truck all over the farm since she was ten, so she could certainly drive it the two miles home from the Fireside.

She pulled on jeans and a sweater, and tried to imagine herself walking into that bar and trying to convince her father that he needed to give her the keys and get into the truck so she could bring him home.

But she couldn't. She just couldn't picture it at all. But her mother had done it, so she would do it, too. And maybe someone there would help her if they weren't all as drunk as her father.

Sarah wrapped the wool scarf she'd worn to check the chicken coop and the barn a few hours earlier back around her neck, pulled a thick stocking cap down over her head and ears, put on a heavy jacket and a pair of fleece-lined gloves, and went out into the frosty night.

She wheeled her bicycle out of the garage and climbed onto it, riding down the long driveway and out onto the quiet road with only the intermittent glow of the moon to light her way.

She stood up on the pedals and pumped hard, the cold breeze making tears stream from the corners of her eyes, and hoped she'd make it to the Fireside before her face froze.

As she came around a bend in the road, she saw headlights crest a hill in the distance, then disappear as she dropped into a dip and then pedaled even harder up the small rise beyond. When the headlights appeared again, they were on the wrong side of the road.

And far closer than they should be.

Too late, she realized she had not worn the jacket with the reflective stripes that her mom bought for her when she went out at night.

And the generator for the bike's headlight had given up last year. She told herself that when she got to the top of the hill, where whoever was coming toward her could at least see her, she'd pull off to the side of the road and let them pass.

But by the time she crested the hill, it was too late.

The car was still on the wrong side of the road, and it was careening straight toward her.

Blinded by the headlights, Sarah swerved her bicycle across the road to get out of the way, but the driver seemed to see her at the same moment and jerked the steering wheel, slewing straight at her.

She didn't want to dive into the ditch, but had to get out of the car's way. She jumped from her bike and pushed it off the road, intending to follow it into the ditch.

She was a split second too late.

The driver saw her at the last instant and swerved too hard the other way, overcorrected, and slewed back to the left, tires screaming in protest.

Sarah, terror freezing her in place, suddenly realized exactly who was hurtling toward her.

"Daddy?" she whispered.

The single word still hung in the night air when the truck's enormous radiator grille slammed into her.

CHAPTER TWO

Sarah shivered. She'd been caught outside without a coat, and now the cold seemed to have penetrated to her bones.

Then came the sounds, strange beeping noises and something that sounded like squeaking shoes, but very faint, as if they were muffled by a thick fog.

Yet there was no fog.

Only the cold of the air and —

Huge, blinding headlights racing straight toward her!

She gasped, jerked awake, and a bolt of white-hot lightning struck her in the lower back, shot through her hip, and blazed down her right leg.

"Sweet pea? You awake?"

Sarah gasped for breath, searching for something — anything — to drive away the cold and the pain, but everything was wrong. She should be outside, but she wasn't, and if she wasn't outside, she should be warm. But she was still freezing. Panic rose up inside her, but just as she was about to scream she saw — and felt — something familiar: the silhouette of her father sitting at her bedside, and his hand holding hers.

"Cold," she whispered through chattering teeth.

"Would you like a warm blanket?" a strange voice said. Sarah turned from her father as a pretty blond nurse checked a bag of something connected to a tube in her arm. She nodded, and turned back to her father. "Wh . . . wh . . ."

"You were in an accident, honey," her father said, his voice trembling, his features strained. "You're in the hospital now, but you're going to be okay."

Her father was lying. If the pain in her hips and her leg wasn't enough to tell her so, his voice and expression left her no doubt. She struggled to sit up, but white-hot agony seared down her side. She shuddered.

"Can't you give her something?" she heard her father ask, the fear in his own voice reinforcing her own.

A new voice spoke, a man this time. "She's awake? Sarah? Sarah, can you hear me?"

She made herself nod, too tired even to open her eyes. "I'm Dr. Cassidy, Sarah.

We'll be taking you into Surgery in a few minutes to fix your hip and leg. So you just lie back and relax, and let us take care of you. All right?"

She opened her eyes as the nurse wrapped a warm blanket around her and tucked it under her chin. She blinked a couple of times trying to clear the fog, and looked around. She was surrounded by striped curtains, and several people in white coats stood by her bed.

"You're in the emergency room, honey," her father said.

She barely recognized his sunken, un-shaven face. His eyes were bloodshot and rimmed with red, and there was blood all over the front of his shirt. And even from where she lay, she could smell the stale beery odor of his breath.

A new woman slipped through the curtain. "Mr. Crane? I'm Leila Davis from the business office. I need you to come with me to fill out some paperwork. Do you have your daughter's insurance card with you?"

Her father's wince told Sarah there wasn't any insurance, but he patted her hand and stood up. "Do you really need to operate?" he asked the doctor, his voice low, as if he hoped she wouldn't hear.

But every word slammed into her ears like

a death knell.

"If we don't, she'll lose her leg," the doctor said.

What was that she was hearing? *Lose her leg?*

"Thing is," her father said, his voice dropping even further and his eyes studying the floor, "we don't have any insurance."

"I can help you apply for Medicaid," Leila Davis said. "Please come with me."

"Don't leave me!" Sarah cried, the panic she'd fought back only a minute or two ago now gripping her chest. *"Not now!"*

"Shhh, honey," Ed said. "I'm right here." He sat back down in the little orange plastic chair and held her hand. "I'll go take care of that later." He looked at the woman from the business office, who checked her watch and then nodded.

"Through the double doors and to the right," she said.

"Sarah?" It was the pretty blond nurse again. She had a nice smile and there was a little koala bear clipped on her stethoscope that somehow made Sarah feel just the tiniest bit less frightened. "I'm going to give you something that will make your mouth cottony, and you'll get kind of sleepy. You just relax and take a little nap, okay? Soon we'll be wheeling you down to the O.R."

30

The nurse injected something into a tube, and a moment later Sarah felt her eyelids grow heavy.

Now there was another voice, a heavy voice. "Ed Crane?"

"Yes?"

Sarah felt her father's hand slip out of hers, and when she tried to reach for it, she couldn't find it. Fighting the heaviness in her lids as hard as she could, she forced her eyes open far enough so she could see her father, standing just out of her reach, facing two men who wore police uniforms instead of white coats.

"I'm Sheriff Wilson, Mr. Crane," one of the men said. "This is Deputy Clark. We need you to come with us to the police station, to answer some questions."

"Not now," Ed said. "My daughter —"

"I'm afraid it has to be now, Mr. Crane," the sheriff said. He glanced at Sarah for a moment, and she let her eyes drop closed so he'd think she was asleep. "You're under arrest."

"It was an accident," her father said. "You don't think I'd run over my own daughter on purpose —"

Sarah struggled once more against the drugs that were pulling her into blackness.

What was going on? What were they talking about?

She had to get out of bed and talk to them — tell them they were wrong. But she couldn't — the blackness was wrapping around her now, and the voices — and the last of her strength — were fading away.

"It's not about that, Mr. Crane. Mel Willis was found beaten to death in the alley next to the Fireside Tavern, and half a dozen people say you were arguing with him. And from the looks of you, I'd say they're right."

A dream! It had to be another dream! Sarah marshaled the last of her strength and managed to force her eyes open again. Her father's shoulders were slumped in a way that drained her of hope. A single word drifted from her lips: "Daddy?"

He turned and gave her a sorrowful look, a look that made a new pain blossom in her chest, and without another word he followed the two men as they moved out through the curtain.

"Daddy! *Daddy, don't leave me!*" she whispered, struggling to get up in spite of the pain that made flashes of searing light edge the darkness that was still swirling around her, drawing her inexorably toward its vortex.

"Shhh, honey," the nurse said, gently

pushing her back against the pillows. "He'll be back. He'll be here when you wake up."

But she knew that wasn't true, and she knew that the nurse knew it, too.

Nick Dunnigan cracked an eye and looked over at his alarm clock.

Ten minutes before it would go off and he'd have to get up.

The toilet flushed in his parents' bathroom. In a minute his mom would knock lightly on his door as she passed by on her way downstairs to make breakfast.

Nick squeezed his eyes closed and whispered the litany he had developed over the years. "I'm going to be okay today," he said into his pillow. "Okay. Please God, let me be okay." He stopped and listened for the voices in his head.

They were there, but way off in the distance, whispering just around the edges of his consciousness. And this morning it sounded as if they were talking to one another, and not to him.

Or maybe they were still quiet because of the double dose of medication his mother had given him last night.

A shiver ran through Nick as the memory flooded back. The voices had been screaming at him, a cacophony of demons each

33

trying to drown out the others. One voice telling him to do terrible things to innocent little animals, another demanding that he lock all the kids from school inside the church and then set fire to it. And there were others — lots of others — all vying for his attention, all commanding him to do something unthinkable.

All trying to destroy his mind.

The soft knock on his door interrupted his thoughts. " 'Morning," she said.

" 'Morning."

Nick shook his head to clear the last vestiges of the memories away, turned off his alarm, and got out of bed.

The broken keyboard, battered beyond repair, lay on his desk as if he needed further proof of last night's "episode."

And next to it his mother had left the pill bottle. Usually she kept it in the kitchen, high in the cupboard above the refrigerator, as if he were still a little boy who could neither reach nor climb that high, to dispense his medication strictly in accordance with the doctor's orders.

But today she'd left it on the desk, and if two pills worked last night, two might work again today.

Okay, he prayed. I just want to be okay today.

He dressed carefully, listening to his mother empty the dishwasher in the kitchen. She would want to keep him home today and call the doctor about what happened last night. But he wasn't going to give her the chance. The more normal he acted, the more normal she would think he was. They didn't put normal people into psychiatric hospitals. Besides, if he acted normal enough, he might even feel normal.

He took a pill from the prescription bottle and washed it down. Then he brushed his teeth, combed his hair, smiled at himself in the mirror, grabbed his book bag, and headed downstairs.

This was going to be a good day — he could feel it.

Or was it just the medicine kicking in?

Nick handed the prescription bottle to his mom, who shook one out and set it next to his orange juice, then put the medication back in its place in the cupboard above the fridge. "I think you better stay home today," she said, just as he'd known she would. "I'm going to call your doctor."

Nick swallowed the second pill with the orange juice and spread peanut butter on his toast. "But I'm okay," he said. "I feel great."

His mother turned away from the stove

and eyed him appraisingly, her eyes boring into him as if she could actually see the extra pill he'd taken. "Really?"

"Really," he insisted, biting into the toast. "No problem."

"No voices?" She turned off the stove and slid two eggs onto a plate.

Nick shook his head. "None." He busied himself putting some marmalade on the toast so she wouldn't see the lie in his eyes. He could still hear them, but he wouldn't — couldn't — let her know that. He had to look normal, had to pray that the second pill would carry him through the day.

"Maybe doubling your medication last night worked," his mother mused, but he could hear the doubt in her voice.

He shrugged as if he'd all but forgotten last night. "I've gotta go, or I'll be late." He pulled his jacket on, picked up his book bag with one hand, and grabbed his peanut-buttered toast with the other.

Lily Dunnigan wrapped her son in a hug before he could slip out the kitchen door. "I just worry about you, that's all," she said as she kissed his cheek.

"Well, don't," he said. "Worry about something else for a change, okay?"

"Easy for you to say," she replied, but managed to force a wan smile. "I'm going

36

to call the doctor anyway about doubling your medication."

"Whatever," Nick muttered as he escaped her embrace. "I really gotta go, Mom."

"Okay," she sighed. "Have a good day."

"I will," Nick tossed back as he banged out the kitchen door and into the chilly September morning.

I will, he repeated to himself.

But he was no more than a block from his house when the committee in his head began raising their volume, shouting loud enough to drown out everything else.

By the time he got to school, they had his full attention.

Kate Williams drained the last of the cold coffee from her travel mug, dropped the mug into the cup holder between the seats in her car, and turned into the hospital parking lot.

She would see two new clients here this morning. One was a newborn infant abandoned by his mother — left in a Dumpster like so much garbage but found twenty-four hours later, having somehow survived the ordeal of its first day in the world. The baby would be easy to place: his story was all over the media, and her office had already been flooded with offers of foster homes and half a dozen pleas to adopt him.

It was the other one that would be difficult, but Kate hadn't realized how difficult until an hour ago, when she stood in the courtroom watching Edward Crane sentenced to fifteen years in prison on a manslaughter charge.

Nothing about this case had been what she expected. When she'd picked up the file and seen that it concerned a fourteen-year-old girl whose father was charged with murder, she was prepared for the usual tawdry tale of people living on the fringe of American culture — probably in a trailer park — whose tenuous grip on life had finally given way. What she'd found was a description of tragedy: a family that hadn't managed to survive the death of Ed Crane's wife six months earlier. Making no excuses for his drinking problem, he'd merely apologized to the family of the man he killed and pleaded with Kate to take care of his daughter.

"I will," she assured him, but his eyes were so filled with tragedy that it made her own well with tears. Ed Crane was no run-of-the-mill thug who killed someone in a drunken rage and then ran over his daughter on purpose. This was a tragic series of events that began with the death of the man's wife, setting the pieces of his life to toppling over like so many dominoes, landing him in jail and his daughter in the hospital with no place to go when she recovered.

If she recovered.

This one would have been hard if there were no other problem than her age. At fourteen, Sarah Crane would not have an easy time adjusting to the foster care system. But in addition, it wasn't easy to place children in wheelchairs, a situation in which the Crane girl might very well find herself.

Kate parked, grabbed her bricfcase, and stepped out of her car into the cool fall morning. The brilliant color of the maple trees on the hospital grounds gave her an excuse to pause for a moment and bask in the glory.

And steel herself to deliver a large package of bad news to a fourteen-year-old girl who'd done nothing to deserve what had befallen her.

Kate locked her car and walked up the broad steps into the hospital. Resisting the urge to put Sarah Crane off for at least a few more minutes, she checked with the information desk, then made her way to the third floor. Unconsciously sucking in a deep breath, she tapped softly on Room 332, then pushed the door open.

A girl lay in the bed, her face turned away from the door as she stared out the window, and Kate felt a fleeting urge to just close the door, go away, and let her enjoy the morning. That, though, would only postpone the inevitable. "Sarah?" she said.

The girl turned a pale face toward her and nodded. Beyond the sallow complexion, Kate could see sharp intelligence behind Sarah Crane's blue eyes, and though her smile was wan — as well it should be, given what she'd been through — it was friendly and revealed well-cared-for teeth. Other than the scrapes on her right cheek and a bandaged forehead, Sarah Crane was the typical girl next door.

Kate strode across the room, pulled a hard plastic chair to Sarah's bedside, sat down, and pulled the girl's file from her briefcase. "Hi. I'm Kate Williams, with the Vermont Department of Social Services. How are you doing?"

Sarah eyed her cautiously. "I'm okay, I guess."

Kate arched her brows. "That's not what it says here. According to this, you have a broken leg and a broken hip, and they're not sure you're going to be able to walk again."

Sarah seemed to ignore her words. "Do you know what's happening with my dad?"

"I just saw him," Kate said, and though she tried to keep her voice from revealing anything, she saw the instant worry in Sarah Crane's eyes.

"Is he going to be able to come and see me?" Before Kate could formulate any kind of answer at all, Sarah came up with her own. "He's not, is he?"

The girl was looking at her with a forthrightness she hadn't seen in so young an adolescent, and she instantly knew that Sarah had far more strength than her wan smile had revealed. "I'm afraid not," she said. "He pleaded no contest to a manslaughter charge. Apparently, he got into a fight the night of your accident, and the man he was fighting with died."

Sarah bit her lip, and Kate could see her struggling not to cry. She started to reach out to take her hand but quickly thought better of it; Sarah Crane had taken blows before and survived, and she had a feeling the girl would survive this one, too.

"He didn't mean it," Sarah finally said. "He didn't mean to hurt anybody — he just drinks too much sometimes." She looked out the window, then her eyes met Kate's. "What's going to happen to him?"

The words were so direct that Kate Williams saw no reason to try to skirt around the issue. "He's going to be in prison for a while."

Sarah lay motionless, digesting the words. "Well, then," she finally said, her voice strengthening as she took a deep breath. "I guess I need to get out of here, don't I?"

"You get out of here when you're well," Kate replied. "Which means a lot of rehab. Think you can do it?"

"If I could take care of the farm after Mom died, I can learn to walk again," Sarah replied without a hint of self-pity. "How long do they think it will take?"

"They don't know," Kate said. "It'll be mostly up to you. Rehab goes as fast as you want it to go. It's going to involve a lot of physical therapy, but I have a feeling that's not going to be a problem for you."

"Can I do it from home?" Sarah asked. "That way I can at least feed the animals, and by spring I should be able to do the rest of it." She forced a painful grin. "I mean, it's not like the fields are doing anything all winter."

Despite the girl's brave words, Kate could see that Sarah knew she wouldn't be going home. "Someone is looking after your animals," Kate assured her. "And I'm afraid that for now, at least, you won't be able to go home, except to pack some clothes. Once you're out of rehab, you'll be going to a foster home."

Sarah stared at her. "A foster home," she breathed. "For how long?"

Kate saw no other option than to tell her directly. "Until you're eighteen."

"Eighteen!" Sarah echoed. "I can't —" She abruptly cut off her words, seemed to collect herself for a moment, then spoke again. "Is that what Dad wants me to do?"

Kate nodded.

Sarah sank back into her pillows, staring at the ceiling.

"We'll find you a nice home," Kate went on. "With a good family."

Sarah took a couple of deep breaths and wiped her cheeks with the tissue. "Near my dad?"

"Absolutely," Kate said, even though she hadn't yet identified any family — let alone a good one — that would be willing to take Sarah in. "I'm going to try to find people in Warwick, near where your father will be. That way at least you'll be able to see him." Sarah said nothing, and finally Kate stood up. "It's going to be all right, Sarah. I promise you." When the girl still said nothing, Kate pulled one of her cards from her purse, added her home phone number to it, and laid it on the stand next to the bed. "I'll be coming back often," she promised. "And I'm going to find the right place for you. You just concentrate on getting well so we can get you out of here, okay?" Without even thinking about what she was doing, Kate Williams leaned over and kissed Sarah's forehead, then picked up her briefcase and started toward the door.

"Thank you," Sarah abruptly said just as Kate was about to pull the door shut behind her.

Kate turned back, smiled at Sarah, and finally pulled the door closed. But even as she walked down the hall toward her next destination, she realized her card wasn't all she'd left in Sarah Crane's room.

A little bit of her heart had stayed there, too.

CHAPTER THREE

The gray facade of the Lakeside State Penitentiary at Warwick made the chill of the late fall morning feel even colder than it was, and Sarah Crane felt an icy shiver of apprehension as she followed Kate Williams toward the single small door that led from the parking area into the prison itself. How can my father be in here? she wondered, and reached for Kate's hand as much to reassure herself as to steady the painful gait the surgeries on her hip and leg had left her with. Get used to it, she told herself. It's not going away — not ever — so just get used to it.

As if she'd read Sarah's mind, Kate slowed her pace, squeezed Sarah's hand, and gave her a reassuring smile.

A man in a uniform waved them toward the metal detector, and Kate signed them in, put her purse on the conveyor belt, and stepped gingerly through the archway. When the officer motioned Sarah forward, she laid her backpack on the conveyor, then hobbled through the detector, which instantly screamed out a loud beeping sound.

Her hip! Why hadn't she thought of it before she stepped into the detector? But before she could begin to explain, Kate Williams was grabbing her purse from the X-ray machine and opening it. "She has metal plates in her hip and leg," she said, handing the doctor's certificate to the nearest guard, who read it, made a copy of it, then handed it back to Kate.

"I should have given you this earlier," Kate said, slipping the certificate into Sarah's backpack before Sarah proceeded through the detector, then stood still while yet another officer scanned her with a wand. "I can get as many more copies as you need, but you'd probably better keep one with you all the time, given how often everyone gets scanned these days."

"Okay," the guard with the wand said, "go ahead."

Sarah shrugged her backpack on and followed Kate into what looked like a shabby school cafeteria.

A dozen men sat at a dozen round tables, each with four or more plastic chairs. Sarah's heart hammered in her chest and she nervously ran her tongue over her lower lip as she scanned the faces, looking for her father.

A gaunt, thin man in the corner stood up, lifting his hand as if in greeting, and for a moment Sarah thought he must be waving at someone else. But then she realized it was her father, though he'd changed so much she barely recognized him. His hair was gone, so short was the buzz cut they'd given him.

He was much thinner than the last time she'd seen him.

And his face was pale and drawn.

"D-Daddy?" she stammered. Then, as his eyes lit up at the sound of her voice, she hurried toward him, ignoring the pain in her hip and leg.

Ed Crane put his arms around his daughter and lifted her off her feet in a bear hug, and for the first time in months Sarah felt safe.

Safe. Comfortable. Secure.

Loved.

"No touching," a guard warned, and Sarah's moment of security instantly collapsed back into the terrible reality of what had happened.

"I'm sorry," her father whispered as he lowered her gently back to the floor. Steadying her while she got her balance, he guided her into one of the chairs, then sat beside her, his fingers as close to her hand as he could put them without earning another admonishment from the guard.

"Thanks for bringing me my little girl," Ed said to Kate Williams as she joined them at the table.

"I'm just sorry it couldn't be sooner," Kate replied. "But with the rehab —"

"Kate's been great," Sarah cut in, not wanting to waste even a second of her time with her father talking about what she'd been through. She started to slip her hand under her father's but checked herself just in time as the guard's warning voice echoed in her mind. Then, as she saw the word INMATE stenciled on his shirt, her eyes welled with tears.

"Don't, honey," Ed Crane whispered. "Everything's going to be —" he went on before his voice broke.

"I'll be okay," Sarah said, struggling against her tears. "It's just —" Now it was her voice that broke, and she quickly reached into her backpack and pulled out a piece of paper rolled into a tube. "I made you this while I was learning to walk again," she said, handing it to her father as one of the guards stepped closer to monitor what was going on.

"Just seeing you is enough for me," Ed said. "How's your leg? Does it hurt?"

"A little," she admitted as her father unrolled the paper.

"She's doing very well," Kate said, reading Ed Crane's anguish at what he'd done to his daughter. "She isn't even using her crutches anymore."

But Ed was no longer listening. Instead he was staring down at the picture he'd flattened out on the table. It was of Sarah, and her eyes seemed to be smiling up at him with some kind of internal light, even from the thick charcoal lines with which the drawing was limned. "It — It's beautiful," he whispered.

"I did it by looking in the mirror, so it's all backward," Sarah said, but Ed shook his head.

"Couldn't tell by me. It looks exactly like you." He turned the picture toward Kate. "Did you see this?"

Kate nodded but said nothing.

Ed turned the picture back and gently lay a finger on the image's left cheek just the way Sarah remembered him doing to her back when . . . back when . . .

Back when everything had still been all right and her mother hadn't been sick, and her father only drank once in a while and — No! she told herself. Don't start crying and don't start feeling sorry for yourself!

"Thanks, sweetheart," she heard her father say as she jerked herself out of her thoughts. "And thank you, too, Ms. Williams."

"Call me Kate," the social worker said. Then, seeing that both father and daughter were welling with tears neither one of them wanted to give in to, she decided to change the subject. "We've found a family here in Warwick for Sarah to live with," she began. "They're —"

"Isn't that great?" Sarah broke in, seizing on the opportunity Kate had offered. "They've got a girl my age and a boy a couple of years older. And I'll be able to visit you all the time!" She saw a terrible sadness wash over her father's face, and in that split second, all the regrets she knew were inside him. "I-I'll draw you more pictures," she offered, wishing there was something else — anything else — she could do to make him feel better, but knowing there wasn't.

"I'll be all right," Ed whispered. "I'm a lucky man."

"And when you get out," Sarah pressed on, "we'll go back to the farm. We'll . . ." But the words died on her lips as she saw

50

the look that passed between her father and Kate.

We're not going back to the farm, she thought. Not ever.

Angie Garvey finished wiping down the kitchen counters, rinsed the sponge, stuffed it into the mouth of the pottery frog that everyone in the family hated except her, and pushed the button on the dishwasher. Except for a quick mopping of the floor, the kitchen was finished.

Too bad she hadn't gotten around to washing the windows. They were pretty bad. On the other hand, with the sheers dropped, you could hardly notice the streaks.

She pulled the vacuum cleaner from the closet and plugged it into an outlet in the small dining room, anticipating a roar of disapproval from Mitch, who, as usual, was slouched on the sofa watching some sporting event on the television that dominated the equally small living room.

"Mitch," she said. "I have to vacuum."

"Do it later," he said, not even bothering to glance at her.

Angie's jaw muscles tightened, but instead of putting the vacuuming off, she walked over to the couch, picked up the remote and turned off the television.

"Hey!" Mitch glowered up at her. "I was watching that." He grabbed for the remote, but she held it out of his reach.

"Watching what?" she challenged. "Tell me who was playing and what the score was within three points." Seeing the blank look on his face, she twisted the knife. "Forget the score. Just name the teams. Even one of them."

Mitch's glower deepened and his fingers closed around the beer can in his hand, crushing it.

"You don't even know one of the teams," Angie said, not trying to keep the disgust out of her voice. She tossed the remote back onto the couch. "Get up, Mitch. Get dressed. The social worker's bringing the foster kid here in an hour, and I want you to look as good as the house."

"I look fine," Mitch said, "and I don't want no foster kid living with us. They're nothin' but trouble. If they were worth anythin', they wouldn't need people like us."

Angie pulled open the drapes, and Mitch, unshaven and still in the T-shirt and underwear he'd slept in, squinted in the light. "Get dressed."

"C'mon, Ange," he whined. "It's my day off."

"You've got more days off than you work

52

lately," she shot back. "They cut your hours at the prison, remember? And we aren't making ends meet, remember?" She picked up dog toys and tossed them into the corner.

"That's not my fault."

"Did I say it was? Besides, it doesn't make any difference — it is what it is."

"You could get a job," he groused.

"Which is exactly what I'm doing," Angie said as she pulled a pile of old newspapers out from under the coffee table. "I take care of people, remember? You and Zach and Tiffany. And it keeps me plenty busy, believe me. But I'm doing what I can to bring in some extra money by taking care of one more person. We get paid to take care of a foster kid, remember?"

Mitch scratched his belly and drained the last of his beer out of the mangled can.

"Come on," Angie said, swatting his leg with the newspapers. "We need to impress that social worker." She checked her watch. "They'll be here in forty-five minutes. Get up!"

She hustled the newspapers into the kitchen garbage, and when she got back to the living room, Mitch had disappeared. She disposed of the empty beer can, then fluffed the throw pillows and placed them just right to disguise the worst of the stains on the old sofa. She still needed to dust, vacuum, and spray some of that air freshener, but then the living room would be finished. At least it would be if Pepper didn't track in a bunch of the rotting leaves that Mitch hadn't bothered to rake up from the yard. Too bad she hadn't had time to give the dog a bath — if he came in wet, the old cocker spaniel would smell pretty rank.

Angie turned on the vacuum cleaner and was just starting to run it around the living room when Mitch came downstairs dressed in his ragged Warwick High School letterman sweater and a pair of jeans that were at least clean, if almost as worn as the old sweater. "I'm going to watch the game down at O'Malley's," he said. "Got any money?"

Angie had just been to the grocery store, and all that was left in her purse was twenty dollars that was supposed to serve as the kids' lunch money for the week. Still, better to have Mitch out of the house when the social worker arrived, even if it meant spending the kids' lunch money on beer at the local tavern. "In my purse," she sighed.

"Thanks," he said, riffled through her purse, came up with the cash, and opened the front door, letting a wet and muddy Pepper scurry in as he went out.

"Noooo!" she moaned, but the storm door

had already slammed behind Mitch and he was gone. "Come on, Pepper," Angie said, gingerly lifting the filthy dog off its feet and taking it into the kitchen. "You stay in here and I'll clean you up in a couple of minutes."

Perspiration dampened the back of her neck, and if she was going to finish cleaning the house — and the dog — she wouldn't have time to take a shower herself.

Which meant she had a choice: either the house wouldn't look or smell as fresh as she wanted or she wouldn't.

Abandoning the house in favor of cleaning up herself and the dog, she headed back to the kitchen.

She'd do what she could for Pepper and herself, and light a vanilla candle just before the social worker was due.

It wasn't much, but it might help.

"Did you hear me, Sarah? That's the school you'll be going to. Aren't you even going to look at it?"

Kate Williams's voice jerked Sarah out of the memory of her father's gray and haggard face as she made her eyes follow her caseworker's pointing finger. Caseworker, she thought. Where did they get that word? It sounded so . . . so . . . she wasn't quite sure what. Sort of like she wasn't a real person, but just some papers in a file. Why couldn't they just call Kate a counselor or something like that? Of course it didn't really matter, because in a few minutes Kate would drop her off at the Garveys' house, and she probably wouldn't see her much anymore. If only —

If only!

She had to stop using those words. How many times had she thought them over the last two months? A hundred? A thousand? If only her mother hadn't died . . . if only her father had stayed home that night . . . if only she had stayed home that night. But none of that had happened, and she had to deal with things the way they were, not the way she wished they were. Now her mother's voice echoed in her head.

Wishing, wishing, doesn't make it so!

We have to deal with things they way they are, not the way we wish they were.

She was right, Sarah told herself. And that's what I'm going to do.

Finally, she looked out the window and discovered that they were no longer making their way along the narrow road that wound through the farms from the prison to Warwick, but had come into the town itself.

The school Kate was pointing out looked

56

as if it had been there for at least a hundred years, but it was freshly painted in white with black trim, just like most of the houses around it. It was one large building with a big sports field next to it and a tennis court behind the parking lot. There was a flagpole in the center of the front lawn, and as they passed, a bunch of boys in football jerseys jogged around a track while cheerleaders practiced their moves on the infield.

"I hear they've got a good team this year," Kate said, her gaze following Sarah's.

"My dad played football," Sarah said, then wished she could pull the words back.

"You can visit him once a week," Kate said. She turned left, and two blocks later Sarah felt like she was looking at a movie set.

The town of Warwick had been built around a square, and in the center of the square was the kind of gazebo she'd seen dozens of times at the movies, but never before in actual real life. Across the street from the square, a bigger-than-life-size bronze statue of a man holding an old flintlock rifle stood in front of an ancient log cabin with a steeply pitched roof. "That's Jeremiah Bigelow, in front of the first house built in Warwick, back in 1654. It's a museum now."

"It's pretty," Sarah said, scanning the small shops that lined the street. Nowhere could she see a 7-Eleven, or a Minimart, or any of the other chains she was used to seeing elsewhere. And as they passed the corner of the square, she could see an old Carnegie library next to a post office with half a dozen cars parked diagonally in front. "I've never seen anything like it," she went on, her spirits rising at the sight of the town that seemed to have come right out of the past. "Look!" She pointed at two old dogs relaxing outside a coffee shop, waiting patiently for their people. "The dogs aren't even tied up!"

Kate turned left again after they passed a large park with a jogging trail winding through the maple trees, and a large church with intricate stained-glass windows, a simple sign in front proclaiming it to be THE MISSION OF GOD. Then Kate turned right onto a tree-lined block and pulled up in front of a modest two-story brick home. "This is it," she said. "Twenty-seven Quail Run."

All the anxiety that had been slowly easing as they drove through Warwick suddenly gripped Sarah's stomach again.

"Do you remember their names?" Kate asked.

"Garvey," Sarah said, struggling to concentrate. "Angie is the mother, and the kids are Tiffany and Mitch."

"No, Mitch is the father. The kids are Tiffany and Zach."

"Zach. Right." Sarah tried to take a deep breath but couldn't — it felt as if a band of steel had closed around her chest. Yet there was no choice but to get out of the car and face whatever was to come next.

As Kate got her suitcase from the trunk, Sarah tried for the umptcenth time to find the words to the question she'd been wanting to ask Kate for weeks now. But cvery time she practiced it, the whole idea sounded stupid. How could she come right out and say something like, "Can't I just live with you?" It seemed like such a simple question, and Kate probably had a dozen kids a day ask her the same thing.

On the other hand, Kate seemed to truly care about her — she'd visited her in the hospital a lot more often than she had to, and most of those times didn't seem to have any real reason to be there at all. And she'd brought her little things to help her through the rehab, too. Did she do that with a dozen other kids? Sarah wasn't surc she wanted to know the answer to that; besides, she'd already been enough of a burden on Kate.

Sarah opened her door, but when she tried to put her right leg on the sidewalk, nothing happened; all the walking at the prison had stiffened not only her leg, but her hip as well. Using both hands, she lifted her right leg and swung it out and to the ground, then — with Kate's help — hoisted herself to her feet. A moment later she stood unsteadily on the sidewalk, her hip aching.

"Want your crutches?" Kate asked in an anxious voice.

Sarah looked through the rear window at the two metal sticks she'd already grown to hate and shook her head. "No. I'm done with them."

Kate seemed about to argue, then appeared to change her mind. "Tell you what," she finally said. "I'll take them in and leave them with Angie Garvey, just in case. Okay?"

Not wanting to argue — and knowing that Kate was right to insist on leaving the crutches — Sarah slowly limped up the front walk. Then, as Kate pressed the doorbell, she suddenly felt the hair on the back of her neck start to prickle, and a shiver ran through her.

She was being watched.

"You all right?" Kate asked.

Sarah nodded, but the unmistakable feeling that someone was watching her grew stronger, and she glanced both ways down the row of houses facing the street.

No one.

But the feeling was still there. Steadying herself on the black wrought-iron railing that guarded the Garveys' porch, she turned around.

Across the street a boy wearing a parka and a backpack was staring directly at her, but before she could get a clear look at his face, he lowered his head and hurried down the sidewalk and around the corner.

"Already turning heads?" Kate asked, following Sarah's gaze in time to see the boy scurry away.

Before Sarah could answer, the door opened and a tall blondish woman wearing a denim skirt and a bulky sweater opened the door. "Hello," she said, nervously wiping her hands on the apron tied around her waist. "You must be Sarah."

"Yes, ma'am," Sarah said.

"Well, come right in." She held the storm door open. "I'm Angie Garvey."

Sarah's right foot caught on the threshold as she stepped into the house and Kate caught her arm, steadying her before she fell to the floor.

The glimmer of hope that Sarah had

61

nurtured as they drove through the little Vermont village began to evaporate as she took in the Garveys' living room. Though it was at least as large as the living room of the farmhouse — maybe even a little larger — it both looked and felt completely different. No art hung on the walls, the furniture was worn, and the carpet was badly stained. Where the living room at home had been filled with books and magazines, here there was only one small stack of books, and they were being used to prop up a corner of the sofa.

A huge television took up one whole corner, and the furniture had been arranged so every seat had a view of the screen.

Nothing — not one single thing — felt anything like what she'd grown up with, and a wave of homesickness threatened to crash through the thin wall of courage she'd been constructing to get her through the day. But just as she felt herself losing the struggle not to start crying, a small brown and white spaniel came skittering out of the kitchen and jumped up on her, almost knocking her over.

"No, Pepper!" Angie snapped, snatching the little dog off the floor. "You can't just jump all over people, especially our Sarah here."

Kate put out a hand to help steady Sarah, but Sarah stepped forward and held out her hands. "Can I hold him?"

Angie hesitated a moment, then handed the wiggling little dog to her. Sarah let Pepper lick her all over her face, and though Kate laughed, Angie Garvey pursed her lips disapprovingly.

"He likes you," Kate said.

"But you don't know where that tongue has been," Angie countered. "Maybe you should put him down."

But Sarah clung to the warm little dog. If she could just cuddle Pepper every day, maybe she could actually survive four years in this house.

Maybe.

Silence.

The kind of silence Nick Dunnigan could barely even remember.

All the voices in Nick's head had fallen completely silent, and he knew exactly when it had happened: the moment when he'd first seen the girl with the bad limp getting out of the car and making her way slowly up the Garveys' walk.

He'd stopped and stared, and it took him a moment before he realized the voices had stopped. And then he found himself engulfed in a silence so profound, so welcome, so completely glorious, that he'd felt lightheaded, almost dizzy.

He felt as if he'd been touched by something special.

An angel, perhaps, if such things actually existed.

He'd watched as a woman carried a suitcase — one he was sure belonged to the girl — up to the Garveys' house.

The girl would be staying for a while.

Maybe she'd even be going to school here.

And maybe — just maybe — she'd be his friend. Even though he knew he shouldn't be thinking it, memories of the way he'd been teased flooded his mind, and as he watched the girl limping painfully up the sidewalk, he knew that the same kids who had shut him out for as long as he could remember would shut this girl out, too.

He could already hear them whispering to each other, see them pointing at her, and giggling at the way she walked.

Maybe if he was nice to her — tried to befriend her — she wouldn't turn away from him the way all the other kids did.

He was still gazing at her when she turned around on the stoop almost as if she knew what he'd been thinking. Their eyes met for an instant, and then Nick dropped his head and hurried away, ashamed at even hoping the other kids might be mean enough to her that she'd have to become his friend.

But as he started home, the voices began to protest. Yet they were different now. Instead of whispering to him to do the kind of terrible things he hated even to think about, it now sounded as if they were crying out for help.

As if they thought this girl could help them.

Was it possible? Of course not! They were just voices! It wasn't as if they were real. They couldn't be.

Could they?

Unable to stop himself, Nick turned back for one more look at the Garvey house before he turned the corner. The girl was gone; she had already disappeared inside the house, and the storm door was still settling in its catch, its pane of clouded Plexiglas still vibrating.

Then one voice, louder than the rest, shrieked through Nick's head and a great red streak appeared on the front of the Garveys' house.

He blinked, shook his head and looked away, trying to erase the hallucination.

But when he looked again, it was still there. A huge red streak that ran across the

entire front of the house.
A streak the color of blood.

CHAPTER FOUR

"This is where you'll sleep," Angie Garvey said as she pushed open the door to one of the bedrooms on the second floor of the house, and stood aside to let Sarah enter first. "My Tiffany is only a few months older than you, and she's been so looking forward to having you share her room."

Her hip was burning from the struggle to climb the stairs, but Sarah managed to show none of her pain as she stepped into the room, where she felt a chill that belied the words her foster mother had just spoken.

All of Tiffany's stuff had been moved to one side of the room, and Sarah could see that it was done quickly, as if whoever had cleared the other side waited until the last possible minute to do it. Posters of rock stars were taped to the walls around Tiffany's bed, which was heaped with more stuffed animals and pillows than it could even hold; a teddy bear was sprawled face-down on the floor at the foot of the bed, and if her hip hadn't been burning so badly, Sarah would have picked it up and put it back where it belonged. The wall behind the second bed — which would be hers — the empty bed — was as stripped of any decoration as the mattress was of bedding, though Sarah could see the marks on the wall where tape had been pulled off, some strips taking paint with it, others staying, along with the corners of the posters they had recently held to the plaster. The posters themselves were almost hidden behind the dresser, where someone — probably Tiffany — had shoved them after pulling them off the walls, and even now Sarah could almost hear the argument between Tiffany and her mother when she was told she had to make room for the new foster child.

The girl's anger was palpable enough to make Sarah shiver despite the heat in her hip. Well, maybe once Tiffany got to know her, it wouldn't be so bad. Besides, who wouldn't be mad at losing half their room to a total stranger?

Angie put Sarah's suitcase on the floor. "The bathroom's across the hall, and I cleared out the second shelf of the medicine cabinet for you." She smiled, but Sarah had the feeling it wasn't easy for her. "I'll leave you to your unpacking. Tiffany and Zach should be home any time."

Sarah nodded as Angie left the room, closing the door behind her. The moment she was alone, she started toward the bed, wanting nothing more than to throw herself onto it and sob.

Which, she knew, wouldn't change anything. Hauling the suitcase off the floor, she maneuvered it onto the bed while doing her best to ignore the pain in her crippled leg. Besides, maybe she was jumping to conclusions. Maybe she and Tiffany could become friends. "Give it a chance, honey," she remembered her mother saying more than once when she was little and trying to avoid something — anything — unfamiliar. "Things are never as bad as they seem at first." Her mother had always been right back then, and it might be true now.

No sense expecting the worst.

She opened her suitcase, took out a pair of shoes and her slippers, and put them carefully under her bed. Then she shook out her best white blouse and opened the closet door.

The closet was stuffed so full of Tiffany's clothes that there wasn't so much as an empty hanger, let alone room to add any more clothes.

She was still trying to decide what to do with the blouse — and the rest of her clothes — when she heard voices downstairs, then the sound of feet pounding up the stairs. A moment later the door burst open and a girl who looked at least two years older than her came into the room.

"So you're the girl we have to take care of," she said, closing the door and leaning against it as she glared darkly at her. "I'm Tiffany, and this is my room. Not 'our' room. Mine. Get it?"

"I — I'm sorry," Sarah stammered. "If there's another room —"

"If there were another room, do you think you'd be in here?" Tiffany cut in. Finally, she left the door, pushed some of the stuffed toys on her bed aside and sat down. "Let's get things straight right from the beginning."

"Okay," Sarah said carefully.

"I don't want you here. I don't want your clothes in my dresser, or in my closet, and I don't even want your bed in my room. You're only here because we need the money from the county, and as soon as my dad gets more hours at the prison, you're gonna be out of here."

"I — I don't want to be any trouble," Sarah said softly, struggling to keep her

70

voice from trembling.

"Good. Then just don't touch my stuff. Mom says you can have the bottom drawer in the dresser, but the rest of it's mine." Tiffany got off the bed and used her forefinger to draw an imaginary line between the two beds. "Just stay on your side of this line," she said. She moved to the door and opened it. "And leave my dog alone, too."

Then she was gone, slamming the bedroom door behind her.

Give it time, the echo of her mother whispered. *Nothing is ever as bad as it seems at first.* Taking a deep breath and ignoring the pain in her leg, Sarah leaned over, braced herself on the dresser with her left hand, and used her right to work the bottom drawer of the dresser open. She peered down into the empty drawer, then over to her full suitcase, and found herself smiling. There wasn't going to be a problem at all — everything she owned would easily fit in the single drawer, and the suitcase itself would go under the bed. Maybe her mother was right: maybe things wouldn't be so bad after all.

Ten minutes later everything was folded and in the drawer, and Sarah was working the suitcase into the space under the bed when she heard the front door slam and a voice shout out.

A man's voice.

Mitch Garvey was home.

"Sarah?" she heard Angie call up the stairs. "Come down and meet your new father."

My new father? Sarah silently echoed. I already have a father. A father who loves me. "Just a minute," she called back.

The man's voice — an angry voice — roared up from below. "Not in a minute, young lady! Now. Come down right now. Don't make me stand here waiting for you. Not ever."

Moving as quickly as she could, Sarah started for the door, but it seemed to take forever just to limp across the room. Finally, though, she was there, pulling the door open and lurching toward the top of the stairs, where she hung tightly to the banister for a moment, both to steady herself and let the pain in her hip and leg ease slightly before she started down. At the foot of the stairs, two faces were tipped up, two pairs of eyes were looking at her.

Angie Garvey was smiling that same not-quite-warm smile Sarah had seen earlier.

Mitch Garvey was scowling, his face red.

Grasping the handrail, Sarah took the first awkward step down, then another.

"Jesus Christ," Mitch Garvey said, his voice grating with anger he didn't even bother to conceal. "They sent us a damn cripple!"

Sarah's fingers trembled under her foster mother's critical eye as Angie straightened every one of the five forks, centering each on its perfectly folded napkin. "Better," Angie declared, looking pointedly at Sarah. "Anything worth doing is worth doing right." She turned to Tiffany, who sat curled up on the chair in the living room, watching TV. "Dinner's ready. Go get your brother and your father."

Tiffany jumped up, ran to the bottom of the stairs and called out, "Dad! Zach! Dinnertime!"

Sarah took an uncertain step back from the table, not knowing which place was hers, while Angie wiped the top of the pepper shaker with the palm of her hand.

Moments later a teenage boy, a little older than Tiffany, but with the same dark eyes, came down the stairs dressed in a T-shirt and jeans.

"Sarah, this is your foster brother, Zach," Angie said.

"Hey," Zach said, giving her the barest of

glances before he pulled out a chair and sat down.

"Hi," Sarah said, her voice weaker than she intended. She cleared her throat.

Moments later Mitch Garvey took his place at the head of the table, and Tiffany sat next to her brother.

Sarah pulled out the remaining chair and was about to sit when Angie said, "You may serve now, Sarah."

Sarah froze for a second, then realized there was no food on the table. She moved into the kitchen as quickly as she could and brought back bowls of mashed potatoes and string beans, setting them on the table and waiting for some sign of Angie's approval.

When Angie said nothing, she went back for the platter of chicken breasts, and by the time she uncovered them, put a fork on the platter, and limped back to the table, Mitch was saying, "Amen," and as she set the platter down, everyone began to fill their plates.

Sarah finally took her seat, but just as she was starting to relax, she heard Mitch Garvey say, "Bread and butter."

Sarah looked up to see Angie peering at her, one eyebrow arched accusingly, and suddenly the entire scope of her role in this household was crystal clear.

She was the help.

The maid.

The foster child who was paid for her work with room and board.

She pushed back her chair and struggled to her feet. In the kitchen, she found butter in the refrigerator and a loaf of bread in the cabinet. She put five slices on a small plate and set them in front of Mitch. Then, stifling the sigh that rose in her chest, she sat down once again and slid her napkin from the table to her lap.

By the time the dishes were passed to her, Sarah had to scrape the sides of the bowl for a spoonful of potatoes, took the last four green beans — three of which looked like they'd been starting to rot when they were cooked, and the half chicken breast that was left after her new foster father took the other half to add to his already filled plate. She started eating, waiting for the chatter that always filled the farmhouse kitchen at dinnertime to begin. But the Garveys ate in a silence that dragged on until finally Tiffany held up her glass and looked accusingly across the table at her. "Water?"

The single word sent Sarah back to her feet. Her hip and leg stiffening from the long day that still hadn't come to an end, she took Tiffany's glass and limped to the kitchen. As she filled the glass from the pitcher of cold water in the refrigerator, she heard Zach's voice.

"Kickoff."

By the time she'd put the pitcher back in the refrigerator and returned to the dining room, the table was empty.

Empty except for all the dirty dishes.

The family had moved into the living room to watch the game, and Sarah, without being told, knew exactly what was expected of her. She set the water down by Tiffany's abandoned plate, then sat down at her own place and silently finished her meal.

Forty minutes later Sarah gave the spotless kitchen one final inspection and hung up the damp dish towel. She'd never minded cleaning up after dinner; she always did it at the farm, while she listened to her parents talking farm business as they lingered over their coffee. And when she was done, it always made her feel good to have the kitchen fresh and ready for the next morning.

She turned off the light and slowly made her way though the living room. Everyone but Zach was still staring at the television, while Zach himself was nowhere to be seen.

No one so much as spoke to her as she

passed them on the way to the stairs.

The climb to the top seemed longer than she would have thought possible, and it seemed as if fire were coursing through her hip and leg with every step. Gritting her teeth against the pain, she clung to the banister with both hands and slowly made her way up, pausing at the top to catch her breath.

Zach was in his room, talking on his cell phone. Sarah glanced at him lounging on his bed as she passed his open door a moment later.

"Hell no, she isn't hot," she heard him saying. "She's a crip." He glanced up at her, then quickly looked away again. "And an ugly one, too." He reached out with his leg, caught the edge of the open door with his toe, and slammed it in her face.

Four years, Sarah thought as she brushed her teeth and put on her nightgown a few minutes later. How was she going to get through four years in this house, with these people? Then, even before she could formulate an answer to her question, she remembered how her father would be spending the next four years, and a lot more as well. Finished in the bathroom, she made her way back to the bedroom, put the linens onto the bed, and slipped between the sheets.

She turned out the nightstand light.

And thought once again of her father.

If he could get through the next four years, so could she.

And she'd do it without the crutches that were still standing by the front door downstairs in case she needed them, and she'd do it without complaining.

And tomorrow, she told herself, would be a better day.

Her father was smiling at her, a sad smile, his face lined and gray. It was the same smile he'd given her at her mother's funeral. But they weren't at the graveyard — they were somewhere else. She tried to look around, but everything was cloaked in a damp gray fog.

Slowly, the fog began to lift, and Sarah knew where they were.

The mansion — the enormous house she'd dreamed about before, the one that was empty but not empty, that was filled with voices she could not hear, people she could not see.

But this time she wasn't alone. Her father was with her, and someone else, too.

Her mother?

She turned, searching the shadows around her, but saw nothing. And when she turned back, her father was walking away from her. She wanted to cry, and reached out as if to touch him, to pull him back, but just as she was about to reach him something happened and —

Sarah woke up, a sob rising in her throat.

The dream had been so real that the tears she'd tried to hold back in her sleep now ran from the corners of her eyes.

She wiped at them with the sleeve of her pajamas, then took a couple of deep breaths and tried to calm her heart.

And tried to remember what happened at the very end of the dream, what happened that jerked her awake.

Tiffany breathed softly in the bed by the closed window. The bedroom door was closed, too, and the room felt so hot and stuffy she felt as if she were suffocating. She threw off the quilt, but that barely helped — she wasn't quite so hot, but there was still no air in the room and she could hardly breathe.

A drink. That's what she needed.

Maybe she should go to the bathroom and get a glass of water. But what if someone woke up? What if she ran into Zach, or Mrs. Garvey?

Better to simply try to ignore it all, relax back into the pillow and go back to sleep.

Where the terrible dream would be waiting for her.

Her stomach growled.

If she were at home on the farm, she'd just go get a glass of milk, then turn on her nightstand light and read for a while. If her mother was also awake — as she'd been so often during those last months — they'd snuggle under an afghan on the couch, wrapped up together, and just talk for a while. Not about anything.

Just talk.

Suddenly missing her mother so badly she knew she wouldn't be able to go back to sleep, Sarah slid out of bed and carefully tested her injured leg. It was sore but not so bad that she couldn't stand it. She slid her feet into her slippers and silently left the bedroom.

Even the air at the top of the stairs was fresher than in the bedroom. Maybe tomorrow she'd ask Tiffany if they could sleep with the door open. Or at least the window. At home they'd always slept with the windows open, even in the middle of winter.

She paused at the top of the stairs, which seemed somehow to have become steeper and longer than when she climbed them earlier. What if she stumbled? What if she wound up at the bottom in a heap with her one good leg broken? She wouldn't — she couldn't. Steeling herself, Sarah made her way slowly down to the kitchen. Pepper got up from his bed in the corner of the mud room, stretched himself, then trotted over to lick her ankles.

Very quietly, Sarah poured herself a glass of milk. She was tempted to put it in the microwave for a few seconds, but the silence in the house seemed so complete that she was sure even the sound of the machine's fan would waken somebody else.

She opened the kitchen window just enough to feel the cool draft, and stood for a moment, sipping the cold milk as the stream of air blew across her flushed cheeks.

Suddenly, the kitchen was flooded with light, and Sarah whirled to see Mitch Garvey standing in the doorway, clad only in his underwear, scratching his belly. "What the hell's going on?" he demanded.

"I — I — I just came down for a glass of milk," Sarah stammered, trying to look anywhere in the room except at her foster father's nearly naked figure.

"You!" Mitch said. "Back to bed."

Startled, Sarah looked up to see him pointing at the mud room, and Pepper, tail down, slinking back toward his pile of old towels. With the dog banished, Mitch reached across her and slammed the window shut. "Think we can afford to heat the whole planet?" he demanded. "It's November, in case you hadn't noticed."

"I'm sorry," Sarah breathed, shrinking away from him. "I couldn't sleep, I was too hot, and I just —"

"You just thought you'd come down here and steal milk?"

"Steal? No, I —"

He took the glass from her hand. "Milk is expensive, and Angie's a good planner. She knows what she's gonna use this for, and there isn't any extra."

Sarah's cheeks burned. "I — I'm sorry, I didn't know."

"If you're thirsty, drink water," Garvey told her, pouring the milk back into the carton, then pulling a beer out of the refrigerator before closing its door. "Better for you, anyway." He twisted the cap off the beer and took a long swallow, his eyes steady on her.

Sarah crossed her arms in front of her chest, and wished she'd put on her robe.

"You better go back to bed," Mitch said.

The smell of beer on his breath brought back the memory of that last terrible night on the farm when her father opened one beer after another, and Sarah suddenly wanted to be as far away from Mitch Garvey as she could get. She ducked past him through the kitchen door, but he followed her through the living room and stood at the bottom of the stairs, drinking his beer and watching every painful step she took as she made her way back up to the second floor.

The bedroom seemed even stuffier and hotter than when she awoke from the dream, but there was no way she would leave the door open, not given how she'd felt as her foster father watched her climbing the stairs a moment ago. Even if it meant she'd lie awake for the rest of the night, tossing and turning, and be a wreck for her first day of school, it would be better than having Mitch Garvey staring in at her as she slept.

Then she remembered her pain pills. She hadn't taken any for almost two weeks, because whenever she did, they instantly made her drowsy.

Which was exactly what she needed right now.

With a glance at Tiffany's still form in the bed by the window, Sarah quietly opened the bottom dresser drawer, shook one pill out of the prescription bottle, put the bottle back under her clothes, then went to the bathroom and washed the capsule down with a glass of water. Hoping the pill would allow her to sleep well enough to let her get through her first day at her new school, she crept back into her bed, pulled the covers up to her chin, and drifted into sleep.

Tiffany waited until she heard Sarah's deep, regular breathing, then slipped silently out of bed, opened Sarah's dresser drawer and felt around until her fingers closed on the prescription pill bottle. Using the tiny flashlight she kept in the drawer of her nightstand, she studied the label on the plastic bottle. She didn't recognize the name of the drug, but the red sticker warning that it could be habit-forming told her all she needed to know.

Whatever they were, someone at school would be willing to buy them. Maybe she'd try to remember the drug's name to look it up on the Internet, but that part didn't really matter. She could sell anything that might get someone high.

Tiffany shook out a half-dozen pills, then put the bottle back, stashed the pills in a little zipper pocket in her backpack, and went back to bed.

Tomorrow, after school, she'd be going shopping.

CHAPTER FIVE

Sarah sat in the front row of her biology class, holding her emotions firmly in check. She wanted to cry, but not because of the pain in her leg and hip. She was used to that; in fact, most of the time she could almost ignore it. What she couldn't ignore was that everyone was looking at and whispering about her.

But not talking to her.

And it was only third period.

At home, she'd loved going to school. School was easy and fun and everyone was a friend and it was the best part of the day.

Here, finding her locker and her classrooms had proved almost impossible when she got caught up in the swirling rivers of students that flooded the hallways of Warwick High School between classes.

At home, the school was small, and all on the same floor. Here, she'd already gone up and down the big marble staircase in the center of the building four times. And either they hadn't been teaching her anything at her old school or she simply hadn't learned it, since most of the morning she had no idea what her teachers were talking about.

But worst of all, she had no friends.

She'd known she was going to be the new girl.

But she hadn't realized that she would be the weird, gimpy girl.

The girl whose father killed someone and was in the penitentiary just outside of town.

The girl whose father had run over her.

Tried to kill her.

She'd heard it all as the morning dragged on, heard the bits of conversations as people passed her, felt eyes watching her, then seen people quickly look away when she turned around.

And now she felt like crying, which wouldn't help at all. In fact, it would only make it worse. She chewed on the side of her thumb to keep the tears at bay and tried to listen to the teacher, and when the bell rang, she consulted the little printed schedule they'd given her at the office that morning.

Lunch period. Was it really possible? Was she going to have an hour when she didn't have to sit in another classroom wondering if she'd ever be able to catch up with the other kids after the weeks she lost in rehab?

She found her locker, dropped off her heavy biology book, put the literature book she'd need in the class after lunch into her backpack, then followed a stream of kids to the cafeteria.

The three dollars Angie gave her that morning bought a small carton of milk, an egg salad sandwich, and a bag of chips. The change from the three dollars safe in her backpack, she balanced the tray carefully and scanned the room for an empty chair, already starting to feel her bad leg threatening to give out.

She spotted Zach Garvey, but there were no vacant seats at his table, let alone any girls. Besides, even from where she stood, she could feel their eyes on her, and when she finally limped by Zach's table on her way toward an empty place at the table where Tiffany sat with her girlfriends, she heard someone whisper a few words: ". . . killed some guy, then ran over her . . ."

She shut the words out, quickened her pace as much as she could, but just before she set her tray down one of the girls plopped a book bag onto the vacant chair. "This seat's taken," she said.

Sarah stopped abruptly, staggered, almost

lost her balance, and lurched against Tiffany rather than risk letting go of the tray to grab the chair for stability. "Sorry," she said.

Tiffany glared at her but said nothing.

Now two tables full of kids were staring at her. The noise level in the cafeteria dropped as conversations died away and everyone watched her limp around looking for a place to sit.

Way in the back, a boy sitting alone watched her, too. There were plenty of empty seats at his table, but as soon as she made eye contact with him, he averted his eyes and looked down.

Sarah got it — he didn't want her to sit with him, either. Yet the way he ducked his head seemed familiar, as if she'd seen him somewhere before.

Then, in the far corner of the cafeteria, she spotted four students sitting at one end of a long — and otherwise empty — table. Her face burning as everyone watched, she hobbled through the maze of tables and chairs, almost tripping over a book bag someone shoved in front of her as she passed. Finally she set her tray at the opposite end from where the other kids were sitting and let her backpack slip off her shoulder onto the floor.

The other kids at the table instantly rose

to their feet, picked up their trays, and walked away.

Sarah glanced around and saw that everyone in the cafeteria had seen what happened.

She sat down but couldn't make her trembling fingers open the milk carton.

Then, after what seemed an eternity, the hum of conversation began to rise again as people found something else to do besides watch her.

Except that now, she was sure, instead of staring at her, they were talking about her.

It doesn't matter, she told herself.

Shutting out the hum of the chatter around her, and refusing to look anywhere but at the table in front of her, Sarah finally took a small bite of her sandwich.

It tasted almost as bad as she felt.

The perpetual storm inside Nick Dunnigan's head fell suddenly quiet as he took the first bite of his lasagna, and for a moment the unfamiliar calm inside his head unnerved him. Then, without even looking around, he knew that the girl he'd seen at the door of the Garveys' house yesterday had walked into the cafeteria.

How did the voices know before he did?

Nick felt a sudden urge to run to her, to

cling to her, but all he managed to do was glance up from his solitary table at the back of the room. She looked every bit as awkward as he always felt as she struggled with her tray and her backpack while everyone else in the room just stared at her and wouldn't even let her sit at their tables.

The voices in his head began their mumbling again, and at first Nick couldn't quite understand what they were saying. But as the girl went from table to table, searching for a place to set her tray down, and was being turned away from seat after seat, the voices began to whisper to him about what he should do to all the kids who were shutting her out.

Nick's palms began to sweat.

And then she looked over at him, almost as if she knew he was watching her.

And knew what was going on in his mind.

Their eyes met and every nerve in Nick's body tingled as if a jolt of electricity had just run through him.

The voices in his head quieted, too, as if they as well as he had been shocked into silence.

Shamed, he looked down, but prayed that she would come sit with him.

She didn't, of course.

And the voices began discussing among

themselves what they would do to each of the kids sitting at Tiffany Garvey's table.

Nick looked over at Tiffany, and her face seemed to melt before his eyes.

Bonnie Shupe burst into flames and her agonizing screams tore through his mind as the flesh on her skull charred and flaked off.

Across from Bonnie, Beth Armstrong's head — severed by an invisible machete — toppled onto the table and rolled between the lunch trays, her blank eyes wide open and staring at the other girls.

And inside Nick's head the terrible voices screamed in glee at the mayhem they were showing him.

Nick clamped his eyes closed, bent over so his head was as low as he could get it, and squeezed his temples with both hands.

Stop, he silently begged. Leave me alone!

He wanted to rip his hair out, but knew it wouldn't help.

He wanted to scream back at them, to order them to silence, but the last time he did that, his father had taken him to the state hospital, where things were even worse than what went on in his head.

He opened his eyes, staring down at his cold lasagna, wishing himself invisible to everyone around him, when another sound, sharp and intermittent, slashed through the cacophony in his mind.

The alarm on his cell phone.

Nick groped in his pocket for his phone, silenced it, then turned his attention to his backpack, struggling to keep his eyes from wandering even for an instant to the horror going on around him. His fingers closed on a pill bottle, he shook one out and washed it down with milk.

"Taking your crazy pill, Nick?" someone yelled from across the cafeteria.

"Wouldn't want you to miss your pill," someone else said. "You might become normal."

"Nah," came an instant rejoinder. "He'll never be normal."

Once it started, the mocking only grew worse as everyone around him fed on one another's insults.

Get out!

He had to get out before the new girl heard them, before she understood what they were saying, who they were talking about. He couldn't let her see him the way the rest of them did. Nick grabbed his book bag, picked up his tray, and started toward the door. He kept his eyes straight ahead, ignored the taunts, tried to ignore the hallucinations, but all around him blood was spurting from torn arteries, faces were dissolving as if doused in acid, and maggots tumbled from empty sockets where the eyes that were watching him should have been.

He dropped his tray on the counter next to the kitchen door, then fled to the library, where at least he might hide in the stacks until his medicine kicked in.

But one of these days the medicine wasn't going to work anymore.

And then his only hope might be the girl whose mere presence seemed to calm the voices, if not completely silence them.

Sarah paused at the door of the art room, steeling herself against the glare she'd receive from the teacher for being five minutes late for the last class of the day. Then would come the stares of her classmates. But she'd moved as fast as she could, and as she pushed her way into the art studio, her whole body ached.

Instead of glaring at her, though, the teacher actually smiled, pausing in the midst of distributing oversized sheets of drawing paper to the class. "Come on in. You must be Sarah Crane."

"Sorry I'm late," Sarah muttered, sliding as inconspicuously as she could into the closest empty chair to the door. She shrugged out of her heavy backpack and let it drop to the floor next to her seat.

"You've all read the textbook about perspective," the teacher said, laying a sheet of heavy drawing paper on the table in front of Sarah. "Today we're going to put that theory into practice."

But Sarah hadn't read the textbook and knew nothing about perspective. So here was yet another class for which she was completely unprepared. She gazed down at the blank sheet of paper the teacher placed in front of her and wondered what she was going to do. But then the teacher was speaking again, and Sarah felt a twinge of hope — she was giving the class a quick review of the text, and though she seemed to be talking to the whole class, Sarah had a feeling the words were being spoken just for her.

She stole a look at her class schedule to remind herself of the teacher's name.

Philips. Bettina Philips.

"Things that are closer are larger," Ms. Philips was saying as Sarah looked up again. "If you draw a road, the telephone poles closest are tallest and biggest. For the picture to appear real, everything in it must be focused on a vanishing point somewhere in the picture. You also have to consider the point of view of the artist. Where is the artist — or photographer — situated in order to capture the scene? So now I want all of you to think of something to draw, and concentrate on showing it from your perspective."

Sarah closed her eyes and an image of the huge house that had haunted her nightmares rose in her memory. But today, with a blank sheet of paper in front of her, the details of the structure were far clearer than they'd been in her dreams. It was a stone house with a gabled roof, and she tried to imagine it with morning sun throwing shadows on the angles of the roof. And if she were farther from it than she ever was in her dreams, looking at it from maybe a hundred yards from its southeast corner . . . She opened her eyes, blinked at the bright fluorescent lights, and picked a medium brown oil pastel crayon from the box on her table.

Her hand moving quickly, she began to draw.

A few minutes later she felt someone behind her, and twisted around to see the teacher looking down at what she was drawing. As if she sensed how difficult it was for Sarah to move in the chair, the woman crouched down so their heads were on the same level. "Hi," she said quietly. "Welcome to the class. I'm Miss Philips."

Sarah found herself looking into a kindly pair of blue eyes in a face framed by light brown hair that flowed straight down her back. She was wearing exactly the kind of clothes an artist should wear: a long skirt, a brightly patterned blouse, and a purple velvet vest. Exactly the kind of thing she herself would have worn if she hadn't grown up on a farm. "Hi," she said, instinctively liking Bettina Philips.

"You're doing a good job there," Miss Philips whispered, tapping a forefinger on Sarah's paper. "Keep at it." Then she stood up and continued making the rounds of the classroom, murmuring suggestions and encouragement as she moved from one student to another.

Sarah looked back at her drawing, but suddenly couldn't concentrate as she remembered the warmth in Miss Philips's eyes. She tried visualizing the house again, tried to remember how the walkway went up from the circular drive to the double front doors, but somehow couldn't quite bring back the image as clearly as she had seen it before the teacher stopped to talk with her. She looked up to see that Miss Philips was now bent over the drawing of one of the other students, but as if sensing her gaze, the teacher looked up and gave her a smile.

Sarah's face warmed, and she went back to her drawing, and the image of the old rock house was once again clear in her mind. It had big shutters on the front and the side, and she quickly sketched them onto the paper. As her hand transferred the image from her mind to the paper, she worked faster, quickly losing track of the time.

When the bell rang, everyone around her scrambled to pick up their things and get out of the classroom as quickly as possible. "Don't forget to put your name on your drawings," Miss Philips told them, raising her voice above the rustling of the class. "And the pastels go back in the cabinet."

Sarah waited until everyone else was out the door before she hauled her backpack from the floor to the desk, then finally pulled herself to her feet, holding on to the table for support.

"You've got a lot of talent," Miss Philips said, seeming not even to notice how hard it had been for her to rise from the chair. "But then I'm sure you already know that, don't you?" she added, grinning at Sarah without so much as a hint of pity.

"I just like to draw," Sarah said, signing

her name and handing the sketch to the teacher. "Usually I draw people, but this was fun."

Bettina Philips laid the drawing flat on the table and looked at it. "Do you know this house?"

"No," Sarah said. "It just sort of came into my mind."

"Really? You just imagined this?"

Sarah nodded, and struggled with her backpack.

Miss Philips added the drawing to the stack of paper already on her desk, reached over and lifted up the bottom of Sarah's backpack so she could slip the straps over her shoulders.

"Thanks," Sarah said, settling the weight evenly.

"I'm glad you're in this class," Bettina said. "You'll do very well."

She looked up at the teacher one more time and felt an easy warmth flow through her.

Seventh period art had just become her favorite class of the day.

CHAPTER SIX

Bettina Philips turned her battered Mini Cooper onto the rutted driveway and through the ornate wrought-iron gates that hung rusted and crooked from two once-proud granite columns that were now so covered with moss and lichen that the inscription carved into them when they were new was now illegible. Sighing softly at the decay, Bettina downshifted and gunned the little car up the long curving driveway toward the house she'd lived in all her life.

When she was little, a gardener had been employed for almost half the year in an attempt to keep the grounds of the old mansion up to her grandfather's exacting standards, but after he died, the gardener was the first expense to be cut, but hardly the last. And Shutters — as the house had always been known — fell into worse disrepair every year since. Bettina did what she could to try to keep the place up, but just paying the heating bill in the winter was beyond her meager salary, and when the shortest and coldest days came, she retreated to the kitchen and her studio, letting the rest of the house freeze.

Someday the historical society would make her an offer she couldn't refuse, hopefully before the manse was beyond repair.

She parked in the garage, entered the house through the kitchen door, and called to her two dogs and three cats, but as usual none of them came to greet her. That was all right; one by one they'd eventually show themselves, eyeing her suspiciously and looking vaguely guilty, as if they had been up to no good while she was at work.

She moved on through the big kitchen and through the huge dining room and the salon beyond, coming finally to the north side of the house, where she had turned her great-great-grandfather's old conservatory into an art studio.

As was her ritual, Bettina took a moment to look out the back windows, across the terrace, and down the broad lawn to the shore of Shutters Lake. The waterfowl had long ago flown south, but the lake still held its ethereal beauty, looking different every day of every season. Now, in late fall, the lake was rippled with a northern breeze, a precursor of the bitter cold to come. What was left of the cattails drooped in the fading afternoon sun. Soon, the lake would be frozen over and snow would cover everything, and the eerie silence of winter would fall over not only the lake, but the house as well.

Bettina took a deep breath, unzipped the portfolio containing her students' work for the day, and laid its contents on her worktable. The top drawing was the one done by Sarah Crane, the new girl with the crippled leg.

Sarah had done a study of a stone house, using a single brown pastel crayon, which gave the drawing an old, sepia-toned mood. Her talent was evident in every stroke of the sketch. Her perspective was precisely correct, from the artful shadows on the gabled, multilevel roof to the corresponding aspects of the roofline with the shutters on the front and side. She'd accomplished a lot in a very limited amount of time, even adding touches — more like indications, actually — of landscaping and shading on some of the stones around the heavy, double front door.

The door.

Bettina stood back and looked at the

101

drawing again.

Shutters?

She moved the drawing under the light and looked more closely. Sarah's drawing looked much like a smaller version of her own house. The house in the drawing had a gabled roof and a circular drive similar to hers and oversized shutters very much like the ones that had not only given her house its name, but the lake upon whose shores it had been built as well.

But Shutters had a carriage house — now her garage — to the east, and servants' quarters to the west. An enormous maple tree, the leaves of which were now falling fast and blowing into the angles of the house and roof, stood in the center of the circular drive.

Still, despite the differences, the similarities could not be denied.

Bettina looked up through the conservatory's enormous roof of glass. Daylight was fading, but if she went out now, she'd still have time to see the front of the house clearly before it was obscured by dusk. She hurried across the large marble-floored foyer, an orange tabby cat scuttling out of her way and ducking under the massive round table.

Bettina opened the great front door and

took the drawing out into the cold twilight. Crisp brown leaves swirled around her ankles in the wind and she shivered in her light sweater, but there wasn't time to go back for a jacket.

Holding the sketch high, she backed away from the house onto the big driveway and began working her way toward a point of view that might duplicate the one in Sarah Crane's drawing.

There wouldn't be one, of course, since Sarah's house existed only in her imagination, but even in the face of this impossibility, Bettina had a feeling she would find something close.

Something very close.

She found herself in front of the garage, the old servants' quarters on the other side and to the rear of the house hidden by the house itself. Again she held the drawing up in front of her, blocking off the view of the garage, and there it was.

With the leaves stripped from the enormous trees, she could see that the complex, multilevel roofline on Sarah Crane's drawing perfectly matched that of the old house. The windows were all in the same place, and though there were different details on the double front door, the shiver that ran up Bettina's arms was not caused by the chill November air.

Still, this couldn't be; surely she was only imagining the similarities in the fading light. She went back in through the double front doors, started back down the length of the foyer toward the conservatory, then heard Rocky whining softly. The mottled terrier mix had been brought in from the woods as a tiny puppy by one of the cats half a dozen years ago. Now, he sat facing the door to her grandfather's study, twisting his neck so he could look back at her.

Bettina moved toward the conservatory again, and Rocky barked, just once, but as he always did when he intended to get his way. And right now, apparently what he wanted was to get into her grandfather's study. "Oh, all right," she muttered, turning back. "God, I am such a pushover." Rocky stood up as she approached, his tail wagging, and he slithered inside as soon as she opened the door.

The room still smelled like brandy and cigars.

Suddenly, Bettina felt like a little girl, looking around at book-lined walls, the leather chairs, and enormous desk. Not only did her grandfather's spirit still seem to be in this room, but so did those of Harold Philips's own father and grandfather. Rocky was now sniffing at the double doors of a cabinet below one of the bookcases, and Bettina, her curiosity aroused, knelt down and pulled open the cabinet's doors.

Dozens of identical dark leather photograph albums stood lined up on the shelves. Bettina pulled out the first one, took it to the big desk, turned on the desk lamp and opened the album as the dog curled up at her feet. The first few black pages held yellowed newspaper clippings from the *Warwick Sentinel,* announcing the appointment of Boone Philips as the superintendent of Shutters Lake Institute for the Criminally Insane, followed by formal photographs of her great-great-grandfather as a middle-aged man. In succeeding pages there were photographs of him in front of what the townspeople referred to as the old "retreat."

Bettina kept turning pages, and then, there it was: a sepia-toned photograph of Boone Philips standing next to the door of Shutters as it was when he'd first moved in.

The enormous maple tree, then no more than a sapling, grew from the center of the circular drive.

The photograph was taken from the west side of the driveway, and there were no servants' quarters on that side of the house. If there was a carriage house on the east side, it was out of sight, but she could see nothing that indicated a roadway to that side.

So the servants' quarters had been added later, and most likely the carriage house as well.

Bettina lifted the photograph from the little corners that held it to the black album pages and set it on her grandfather's desk, next to the drawing by the young student.

Sarah had even included the sapling.

A chill ran up Bettina's spine.

Today, the enormous shutters that protected the fragile windows and occupants of the old stone house from the nor'easters that roared down the lake in the winter sagged on their hinges. But they were still operable, and Bettina occasionally employed them when the winds were bad enough.

But in both the photograph and the drawing, the shutters were the same — square and even.

New.

The front doors in the drawing and the photograph were the same, and different from the current front doors, which Bettina's mother had replaced before she had even been born.

Somehow, Sarah Crane — new to Warwick — had plucked the image of her house out of thin air, and drawn it in her classroom not as it was now, but as it had been when it was new.

Bettina unconsciously rubbed the goose bumps that rose on her arms and turned to look at Rocky, who now sat quietly at the doorway and gazed at her with calm brown eyes.

"What do you think?" she asked him.

The dog merely kept looking at her for another moment, then stood up and trotted away, probably in search of the cat who had been the only mother he'd ever known.

"Spooks me, too," Bettina said softly to the now empty room. As she leaned in to turn off the desk lamp, she looked one more time at both the photograph and the incomprehensible drawing.

Sarah Crane would get an A for the assignment.

And she would keep a close, watchful eye on the girl.

Sarah waited until everyone was seated and everything was as perfect as she could make it at the Garveys' dinner table before she slipped into her seat and put her napkin on her lap, then checked to make sure everyone else had already helped themselves to the tuna noodle casserole before putting a single small portion on her own plate.

And she made sure there was plenty left for both Mitch and Zach to have second helpings, even though her own stomach was begging for more food. But already she'd learned that the more invisible she could make herself, the better off she'd be in the Garveys' house.

Almost as if she'd heard Sarah's thoughts, Angie Garvey's eyes fixed on her. "How was your first day at school, Sarah?"

Now all four of the Garveys were looking at her, and Sarah sensed some kind of trap being set. But how could such a simple question — a question her own mother must have asked her thousands of times — be a trap?

Maybe it wasn't — maybe Angie really was wondering how she'd liked school. "Good," she finally said.

Everyone kept looking at her.

"Fine, I mean," she hurried on. "I liked it. School was really good." Her eyes darted from Angie to Mitch, and she could see she still hadn't said enough. "Lots of home-work," she ventured.

Without taking his eyes off her, Mitch drained his beer and tipped the empty bottle toward Zach, who took it and immediately jumped up to get his father another one.

"Homework's good," Mitch said. "Trouble with schools nowadays is not enough homework. When I was your age, we didn't have time to hang out and get in trouble — we had work to do. Lots of it." Then his eyes bored into her. "And when we were asked a question, we answered it. Didn't make folks pull every word out one by one."

Sarah took a sip of water and sucked in her breath, thinking fast. What did her foster father want to hear? What was she supposed to say? "Well," she finally began, "I found all my classrooms without too much trouble, and my locker is in a really good place, practically in the middle of the whole school."

Mitch went back to his meal, and as if they had been signaled, so did the rest of the family.

Sarah relaxed slightly. "I really like my art teacher, Miss Philips."

All four heads snapped up, and once again the family was staring at her.

"D-Did I say something wrong?" Sarah stammered. What was going on? What had she said?

Angie Garvey sipped from her own glass of water, then dabbed her napkin at the corners of her mouth. "Bettina Philips is not someone you should be associating with," she said, the distaste for the woman's name clear on her face. Then she added, "She is a witch."

Sarah's mouth dropped open. A witch? What on earth was Angie talking about? But before she could ask, her foster mother answered her unspoken question.

"This is a Christian community," she declared. "And there is no place in it for the likes of Bettina Philips."

Sarah's eyes flicked toward Mitch, but his expression was as implacable as Angie's.

"Outside of class, you must never speak to her," Angie went on. "In this house — in every good house in Warwick — we do our best never to speak of her at all."

Sarah could barely believe what she was hearing, but her foster mother was still not finished.

"On Sunday," Angie Garvey continued, "you'll have a chance to cleanse your spirit in church."

"I — I don't understand," Sarah began, finally setting down her fork as her appetite deserted her. "She's my teacher. All we talked about was . . ." Her voice trailed off, but now everyone's eyes were fixed on her again and she knew she had to say something else. "We talked about art," she said, her voice coming out in a whisper that sounded desperate even to her own ears.

"Then let me make it real clear," Mitch said, jabbing at the air with his fork. "You don't speak to that woman except to do whatever you need to do to pass her class. Not one extra word. You don't talk to her, you don't talk about her, you don't even look at her. Got it?"

Sarah put her hands in her lap. "Yes, sir," she whispered.

"Jesus Christ, Angie," Mitch said, still glowering at Sarah. "All we need is for this kid to be getting ideas from Bettina Philips!"

Angie put a calming hand over her husband's, and a moment later he shook his head in disgust and returned to his meal. But Angie's expression told Sarah that she was in total agreement with her husband and that she had better pay very close attention to what Angie had just said.

She chanced a look at Tiffany, who only shook her head and looked away.

The message was more than clear.

She was now forbidden to speak to the one and only person in Warwick who had been nice to her.

Lily Dunnigan tried to work the crossword puzzle while her husband read the evening newspaper, but the house was quiet.

Too quiet.

She couldn't concentrate.

And Nick had been unusually cheerful at dinner. He'd eaten everything she served him, then disappeared up to his room to do his homework.

And she hadn't heard a peep out of him since.

No wonder she couldn't concentrate: usually by this time of day the voices in his head were so out of control that he was upstairs sobbing or banging his head against the wall — anything to shut them out. But not tonight.

Could they finally have hit on the right medication? Was it actually possible? She set her crossword aside. "I'm going up to check on Nick."

Shep Dunnigan barely glanced up from his paper. "He'll never be normal if you don't start treating him like a normal kid."

"I'll just go see what he's doing."

Shep sighed loudly and rattled the paper as he turned the page.

Lily walked softly up the stairs and tapped on Nick's door.

"Come on in," Nick said.

Lily opened the door and peeked in. Nick sat at his desk, writing in a spiral notebook. "What are you doing?" she asked.

"Chemistry," Nick said. He made a couple more notations, then set his pen down. "Done."

"All finished?" She moved into his room and perched nervously on his bed. Though it seemed as if she'd been praying for a sight this ordinary all Nick's life, actually seeing him act like a normal teenager with no worse problems than too much homework was difficult to believe.

"I wish," Nick said as he put his heavy chemistry book into his backpack and pulled out a tattered paperback. "Still have to write a book report on this."

Lily hesitated, wondering if she should just leave well enough alone, but before she could stop herself, the question leaped from her lips as if of its own volition. "No voices tonight?"

Nick swiveled his chair so he was facing her. "They're actually leaving me alone."

"You mean it's working? We've actually found the right dose of the right medicine?"

Her son shrugged and his eyes shifted away from hers.

There was something he wasn't telling her. "What is it, Nick?"

"Nothing." He began swiveling back and forth in his chair, a nervous tic that put the lie to his answer.

"It's something." She reached out and took the arm of his chair to stop the swiveling. "Are you taking some other drugs?"

"No," he said, but his eyes still avoided hers.

"Then what?"

Nick hesitated, but then finally spoke, his eyes turning quizzical. "Well, a weird thing happened."

Lily steeled herself for whatever he was about to tell her.

"There's this girl."

A girl? Whatever she had expected, it wasn't this. "A girl?" she echoed. "You've met a girl?"

"Well, I haven't really met her yet. She's new. She's staying with the Garveys. Her name's Sarah Crane."

Lily had heard that Angie Garvey was getting a foster child. "So what was weird about it?"

Once again Nick hesitated, and for a moment Lily thought he might just close down. But then he actually grinned.

"The voices stop when she's around," he said.

Lily let out a breath she didn't know she'd been holding. "What do you mean, they stop?"

"Just that — when she's around, they just

stop bugging me."

"Well, I don't call that weird," Lily declared. "I call that wonderful. So tell me about her."

He looked up at her. "There's nothing to tell. I don't even know her yet."

"Well, whatever makes you feel better makes me feel better," she said, standing up. "So get to know her, okay?" She leaned over and kissed the top of his head. "I'll let you get back to your homework."

"Okay. Good night."

Heading back down to the living room, Lily picked up her crossword puzzle, but now, instead of the silence, it was an overwhelming feeling of hope that kept her from concentrating. "Guess what?" she said to Shep, putting the puzzle aside once again.

Shep glanced disinterestedly in her direction. "What?"

"Nick's found a girl."

Shep lowered his newspaper and looked at her.

"Which isn't the best part," she went on. "The best part is that his voices go quiet when he's around her." As Shep looked at her in disbelief, Lily finally let her face break into the grin she'd been holding back.

"You're kidding," Shep said.

Lily shook her head.

"What's her name?"

"Sarah Crane. She's a new girl at school."

A shadow passed over Shep's face, and he was silent for a moment, then stood up. "I think I'll go have a talk with him."

Lily's belly clenched. If her husband went upstairs and started pressuring Nick —

But what could she do? Shep was Shep, and she could only do so much to shield her son from him. So she held her tongue as she watched him walk up the stairs.

Nick tried to focus on the words on the page in front of him, but he couldn't. He hadn't quite lied to his mother, but he hadn't told her the whole truth, either, and he knew she'd been happy at what he had told her. He hadn't told her just how weirdly the voices had reacted to Sarah Crane, and he sure hadn't told her about the horrible hallucinations he had in the cafeteria when the other kids were being nasty to Sarah.

He hadn't told her because he knew she'd never understand.

She'd think he was getting worse, and he wasn't.

He was getting better. He could feel it.

He took a deep breath, went back to the book, and focused once again on the words on the page.

But before he got through the first paragraph, his bedroom door opened simultaneously with a single loud knock.

"Hi," his dad said. "Studying?"

"Yeah." Nick couldn't remember his dad having been in his room more than a couple of times in the last year, and now that he was here, the voices were suddenly muttering again. He should have known his mom would tell his dad about Sarah Crane; he should have kept his mouth shut. Now he was going to have to listen to one of his father's pep talks on how to act like "a real teenager."

By which he meant "a normal teenager."

Sure enough, his dad was wandering around the room, touching his printer, looking at the books on his shelf, picking up a CD.

Stalling.

"Hear you've got a girlfriend," he finally said.

"Not really a girlfriend," Nick replied, keeping his eyes on the book in front of him.

"Sarah Crane," Shep said, and now Nick could feel his father's eyes on him.

He finally looked up and nodded.

"She's the daughter of one of my prisoners."

Nick nodded again. "I heard something about that. She's staying with the Garveys."

"Look, I'm all for you having a girlfriend," Shep said, and now his eyes began wandering around the room again. "I mean, it's time, you know? All boys your age need a girlfriend. But kids whose parents end up in prison can get kind of screwed up in the head, know what I mean?"

Nick said nothing. His father didn't know anything at all about Sarah Crane.

"High school is for having fun, Nick," his dad said.

"I know," Nick said.

"So have some fun, okay? Just make sure you don't make any lifelong mistakes."

Nick nodded, feeling his face burn with embarrassment. Why couldn't his father just leave him alone to do his book report?

"Use your head," his father pressed on, then offered him a leering wink that made Nick want to squirm. "And stay safe, you know?"

Nick nodded again.

"Okay, sport. I'll let you get back to your studies."

" 'Night, Dad."

As his father closed the door behind him, the mumbling voices quieted.

Giving up on his desk, Nick turned off his

computer and study lamp, undressed and got into bed with the paperback book, but all he could think about was Sarah Crane.

Why hadn't he defended her in the cafeteria, or at least offered her a place to sit when the other kids kept turning her away?

She needed a friend — that was for certain — and maybe he could be that for her.

Tomorrow he'd find the courage to talk to her.

He turned off his nightstand lamp and discovered that he was looking forward to that.

Talking to Sarah Crane.

Tomorrow.

The voices in his head blissfully mute, Nick closed his eyes and drifted off to sleep.

CHAPTER SEVEN

Bettina Philips was still three blocks from school the next morning when she saw Sarah Crane walking slowly down the sidewalk. Her backpack was heavy enough that she was bent forward, her bad leg keeping her pace to a limping walk no more than half as fast as the other groups of teenagers who were converging on the school with no sense of urgency.

Bettina slowed the Mini Cooper, watching as two girls — Heather Smythe and Jolene Parsons — caught up to Sarah, then passed her.

Passed her without so much as a glance, let alone a word.

As if she didn't exist.

But Sarah, obviously not yet used to the role the kids had already cast her in — that of outcast — had looked up eagerly as Heather and Jolene came abreast of her, only to fall back into a slump as they hurried past.

Bettina moved the car forward, then slowed to a stop alongside Sarah.

She rolled down the passenger side window.

"Hi," she said. "Hop in and I'll give you a lift."

Sarah paused, her breath condensing in the cold air. But instead of hurrying toward the warmth of the car, she hesitated, looked both ways up and down the street, then shook her head. "No, thanks."

No, thanks. The words echoed in Bettina's mind, and she knew instantly what had happened.

Someone — probably Angie Garvey — had told Sarah all the rumors. For an instant Bettina was tempted to stamp on the accelerator and send the car flying away, but she suppressed the urge just as quickly as it rose inside her. No sense taking her own anger out on Sarah. So she stayed where she was. "C'mon, you're freezing," she urged.

Once again Sarah hesitated, and again looked up and down the street as if to see if someone might be watching. Then, as Bettina glanced in the rearview mirror and saw Tiffany Garvey turning the corner from Quail Run, Sarah looked Bettina squarely in the eye. "Thank you," she said firmly, "but I can't. I really can't." Turning away from the car, she started once more toward the school.

"Okay, then," Bettina called after her. "I'll see you in class."

But Sarah Crane didn't so much as lift her hand to wave, let alone look back to acknowledge Bettina's words, and finally Bettina put the window back up and drove on, past Sarah, past Heather and Jolene, and on toward the school.

Bettina knew perfectly well what so many people in Warwick said about her, especially those who gathered every Sunday at the old white-clapboard community church whose congregation had grown since the new pastor came to town five years ago and found out that Bettina Philips was not only an artist, but dabbled in fortune-telling with tarot cards, palmistry, and astrology, as well as medicinal herbs, homeopathics, and everything else that interested her.

The terrible disrepair of her house hadn't helped; even when she'd been Sarah's age, many of her classmates wouldn't come near the old mansion on the lake, given the stories not only about the house, but the long-closed "retreat for the criminally insane," which had been told and retold until most of the children "knew" that the house was haunted and that she was a witch.

Then, when Reverend Bradley Keener came to town, he began convincing the parents as well, and though Bettina hadn't yet lost her job, she knew it wasn't for the lack of the minister trying to get her fired.

Rather, it was the fact that she did her job well, and no one ever had cause to complain about her.

And now they'd told Sarah Crane about her, and either Sarah was afraid of her or had been told to stay away from her.

But Sarah was different.

As Bettina turned into the school's parking lot, she decided she would set the record straight with her, perhaps today.

Sarah Crane had a talent.

A very special talent.

And she would do her best to help Sarah make the most of her gifts, just as she herself had always tried to make the most of her own.

Normally, Kate Williams would have called to make an appointment to check up on a foster child, but when she found herself in Warwick on another case that morning, she suddenly thought of Sarah Crane.

Maybe she should just drop by and see

how things were going.

Why not? After all, her office encouraged drop-in visits, and she always tried to stop in unannounced at least once early in every placement. Besides, letting her see what the home was like when there was no notification that she would visit also served notice on the foster family that she was watching. Angie Garvey would certainly be within her rights to refuse to let her in the door, but most foster parents never exercised that right. After all, if someone refused her a look inside a house where one of her kids lived, it would send her back with a warrant until she found out what was going on.

Her mind made up, Kate pulled to a stop in front of the Garvey house, picked up her shoulder bag and strode quickly up the walk. Shivering in the cold morning air, she rang the bell.

The look of surprise on Angie's face when she opened the door seemed genuine, and when the woman immediately opened the door wide, Kate was already sure she would find nothing amiss.

"Kate! What a surprise!" Angie said as she stepped back to let Sarah's caseworker in. "Come in. The house is a mess, but I think I still have some coffee."

"I was in the neighborhood," Kate said.

"So I just thought I'd drop by."

"I'm so glad you did," Angie said, picking up a jacket and hat from the sofa and hanging them on the coat tree by the door. "Do you have time for a cup of coffee?"

"I wish I did," Kate said, her eyes quickly appraising the room and finding it no messier than the last time she'd been there. "I just wanted to see how Sarah's doing."

Angie shrugged. "Well, all things considered, I think she's doing pretty well. Would you like to see her room?"

Another good sign, Kate thought as she nodded and began following Angie up the stairs. Most foster parents — especially the bad ones — couldn't say enough about how well their charges were doing. The really good ones recognized that nothing was going to be perfect, especially at the beginning, and Angie Garvey certainly seemed to be aware of it. "She's doing all right with these stairs?" Kate asked as they came to the top.

"Well, they're not easy for her, but she won't use her crutches and she insists she's fine, so I let her get the exercise and try to keep an eye on her in case she trips." Angie opened the bedroom door and Kate followed her into the girls' room.

Both beds had been made and everything

was orderly. The bed by the window was covered with stuffed animals, and the other bed was bare, with only a clock and light on the nightstand, and the sight gave Kate a little pang. She should have thought to bring a stuffed animal for Sarah's bed. "Very nice," Kate said. "Actually, it's a lot neater than most teenagers' rooms I see."

"Mitch and I insist on it," Angie said. "We bring our kids up right, and we'll do the same with Sarah."

"How's she getting along with Tiffany and Zach?"

Angie sighed. "As well as can be expected, I think. Needless to say, Tiffany isn't quite used to sharing her room yet, but she'll get over it. At least they're not tearing each other's hair out."

"Has she talked about school yet?"

"I think she's a little bit behind in her studies," Angie said, "but she's smart and should catch right up." Angie paused. "It's the social part I'm more concerned about."

Kate felt the first pang of concern since she'd arrived at the Garveys', but thought she knew what was happening. "It's her leg, isn't it?"

"Well, that's probably part of it, I suppose," Angie mused. "But she's a troubled girl." She offered Kate a wan smile. "But then, that's why she's here, isn't it?"

Kate turned Angie's words over in her mind as she looked again at Sarah's side of the bedroom, bare of any decoration at all. She had never thought of Sarah as "troubled," at least not in the way the Protective Services people defined it. On the other hand, the girl had not only been torn out of her home, but away from everything else familiar to her as well. Why wouldn't she be having some adjustment problems? At least Angie Garvey seemed to understand what Sarah was going through.

"It'll all be just fine," Angie assured her. "We'll introduce her to the whole community in church on Sunday, and our family is one hundred percent committed to bringing her into our love. Don't worry — she'll be lucky if we don't just smother her with love."

Kate followed Angie out of the bedroom and back down the stairs, deciding she had, indeed, made the right choice in picking the Garveys for Sarah.

"You just pop in on us any time," Angie said as Kate walked toward the front door. "Any time at all."

"Thanks," Kate said. "I don't usually come unannounced."

"Doesn't matter to me," Angie said, smiling broadly. "I'm usually here."

Kate returned Angie's smile, then headed back to her car. For a moment she considered dropping by the school to check up on Sarah personally, then changed her mind. Better just to let Angie handle things for now. She could spend some time with Sarah by herself later.

Whatever fears she'd had about Sarah's placement well allayed, Kate started her car and headed back to Burlington. Her caseload was overwhelming right now, and each placement seemed harder and more complicated than the last. If Sarah Crane was happy and adjusting well, it was at least one case she didn't have to worry about.

At least for now.

Sarah Crane filled her lunch tray, steeling herself against the words she could already hear being whispered and the mocking eyes that were watching her limp through the cafeteria line. She paid for her macaroni and cheese and a tiny dish of fruit with the three dollar bills Angie had given her that morning, pocketed the change, then took a deep breath and turned around to face the crowded lunchroom.

Just like yesterday, almost every chair in the room was already taken. But now her backpack was starting to slide off her shoulders, and if she didn't find a place to put her tray down within the next few seconds, it might slide all the way down her right arm, bang into her bad hip, and throw her off her feet. She turned back toward the cashier, but another student was standing there, paying for his meal.

Maybe over by the busing station.

Now there was someone behind her, probably trying to put his own tray away.

Or getting ready to trip her.

Sarah stiffened, leaning her good hip against the metal cabinet to steady herself, getting ready for whatever was about to happen. But instead of feeling an "accidental" bump or feeling a foot at her ankle, she heard a soft, uncertain voice.

"Can I help you?"

Was it a trick? Was someone just setting her up? But when she turned around to see who it was — sending her backpack sliding down to the crook of her elbow — she saw a face she recognized.

The boy she'd seen watching her from across the street the day she arrived at the Garveys' house.

The boy who sat alone at the back of the cafeteria yesterday.

The boy who looked down when she

looked at him.

Now, instead of waiting for her to answer his question, he simply took the tray away from her. "You can sit by me if you want," he said, flushing a deep enough red that Sarah knew he was expecting her to refuse the offer.

Hoisting her backpack onto her shoulders as soon as her hands were free, she followed the boy through the maze of tables and chairs, ignoring the whispers and snickers — and a single wolf whistle that she would have known wasn't meant as a compliment even if it hadn't been followed by a wave of laughter. After what felt like an eternity but couldn't have been more than thirty seconds, they were at an empty table in the back of the room, and the rest of the kids finally seemed to find something else to talk about.

Sarah sat down across from the boy and pulled her tray close enough to move the food and utensils off it. "I remember you," she said. "I saw you on the street the day I moved into the Garveys'."

He nodded, blushing again, but not quite as badly as before. "I wasn't staring," he said. "I'm Nick Dunnigan."

"I'm Sarah Crane." She tipped her head toward the tray. "Thanks for the help. I was afraid I was going to fall."

"Actually, you don't need to fall for them to make fun of you. All you have to do is —" His words were cut off by a series of loud beeps coming from his shirt pocket. He quickly silenced the cell phone, blushing again.

"Thanks for reminding us again, Nick," someone yelled from across the room. "We wouldn't want to forget you're a fruitcake, would we?"

So that was it — at Warwick High, Nick was in the same boat she was.

"Meds," Nick muttered, fumbling a pill bottle out of his pocket, shaking two into his hand and washing them down with a swallow of milk.

"How come the alarm?" she asked. "They might not tease you if you didn't beep."

Nick shrugged. "They'll tease me anyway. And I can't trust myself to remember to take the pills."

"Even if it's the same time every day?" Sarah asked, frowning in puzzlement.

He nodded, his lips twisting into a wry grimace that Sarah was pretty sure was meant to be a smile. Should she volunteer to remind him herself, the way he'd volunteered to carry her tray? Or would that make him feel even worse? She picked up her fork and began to poke at her macaroni and cheese, but Nick just sat silently, staring at the hamburger and fries on his tray. Sarah paused, her fork hovering in the air.

"Aren't you going to eat?"

He nodded, but made no move to pick up his fork.

Sarah glanced around, but no one seemed to be looking at them. "What is it?" she asked quietly. "What's wrong?" He glanced up at her, and she could see the fear in his eyes. "Just tell me," she pressed. "Maybe I can help."

Nick looked at her again. "Promise not to laugh?" he whispered.

Sarah rolled her eyes. "Oh, sure, I'm going to laugh my head off, just like you did when I couldn't even hold on to my tray any longer."

Nick still hesitated but finally leaned closer, and when he spoke, his voice was so soft she could barely hear him. "I see things sometimes. Things that aren't there. That's what the pills are for."

Saw things? What did he mean? What was he, some kind of a nu— Sarah cut off the thought even before it was fully formed, but still felt a wave of shame — she wasn't any better than the other kids in the room.

Except that at least she hadn't said what

she'd thought out loud, and from now on, she promised herself, she wouldn't even think it. "So are you seeing something right now?" she asked, keeping her voice as level as if they were just talking about the weather.

Nick nodded.

"What?" Sarah asked, her own lunch forgotten for the moment. "What do you see?"

He hesitated, but then looked straight at her. "Worms," he said. "I know there's supposed to be french fries on my plate, but that's not what I'm seeing."

Sarah glanced at Nick's plate and saw the tangle of skinny fries. Reaching over she picked one up. "Mind if I eat one?" she asked. "I always used to like worms with my mud pies when I was little." Without waiting for an answer, she popped the fry into her mouth, chewed it, and swallowed. "Pretty good — tastes exactly like french fries. Looks sort of like worms, though, doesn't it?"

"But it's not, right?" Nick asked.

"It's not," Sarah promised. "It's just french fries."

Nick took a deep breath, nibbled a fry, then picked up his hamburger and bit into it. As he chewed, Sarah finally took her first forkful of the macaroni and cheese, then pulled all but the first taste back out of her mouth. "You sure it wasn't this that looked like worms?" she asked.

Nick just shook his head. "That always looks like maggots." Abruptly, he grinned. "But I'm not sure that's a hallucination at all."

Staring at the lunch she now knew she wasn't going to finish, Sarah decided she liked Nick Dunnigan.

At least she liked him a lot better than the macaroni and cheese.

CHAPTER EIGHT

Sarah sat quietly at her table in Miss Philips's room as her classmates disappeared out the door into the corridor.

What had she done?

Why had Miss Philips told her to stay after school?

Had she done something wrong today? But there wasn't even an assignment — all they'd done was listen as Miss Philips talked about still life drawings and how the really good ones were so carefully composed they didn't look composed at all. And Sarah knew she certainly hadn't done anything wrong — in fact, she hadn't done anything at all, except take notes.

When the room was finally empty except for the two of them, the teacher pushed the big door closed and perched on the edge of her desk. Sarah's heart began to pound.

Witch.

Her foster mother's words from last night

rose in Sarah's mind, and she glanced at the window in the door to make certain Tiffany and Zach weren't peering in, ready to tell their mother that she had stayed after school.

"What did you think of the class today?" Miss Philips asked. "It must have seemed pretty simple, given your talent."

Sarah shrugged, saying nothing.

The teacher paused, shifting her weight, and then Sarah knew that whatever this was about, it wasn't today's class. Sure enough, Bettina Philips's next words confirmed it.

"Sarah, did I embarrass you when I stopped to offer you a ride this morning?"

Sarah felt the color rise in her cheeks, but shook her head.

"Then what was the problem?" Miss Philips went on.

Sarah cast around in her mind for something that might sound reasonable, then remembered the kids in the cafeteria. "You didn't offer the other kids a ride," she said quietly. "Just because I can't walk very well doesn't mean I need a ride. And if the rest of the kids had seen me taking it, things would have just gotten —"

She cut herself off — if she started complaining about the kids who were teasing her, Miss Philips might go to the principal, and the principal might go to the kids' folks, and then things would get really bad.

"You're sure that was it?" Bettina asked. "There wasn't anything else?"

Sarah hesitated, then decided there wasn't any reason not to tell Miss Philips the truth, even if it did make her foster mother look — "Stupid" was the word that came to mind, but she quickly rejected it. Anyway, it didn't matter how it made Angie Garvey look — she wasn't going to lie about what her foster mother had said. Sarah cleared her throat and looked directly at Bettina. "My foster mother says I can't spend time with you except in class."

Bettina gave her a rueful smile. "That's what I figured. Did she call me a witch?"

Sarah flushed, looked down again, but nodded.

"You're not going to tell me you believe in witchcraft, are you?"

Sarah decided this had to be the most uncomfortable conversation she'd ever had. "I guess not," she whispered, her eyes on the table in front of her.

"Good," Bettina said. "I just wanted to set the record straight. You have a lot of talent, and I'd hate to see it wasted because of what people say about me."

Sarah's head came up, and the face she

saw was hardly that of some kind of witch, but a perfectly normal one, with soft eyes and a kind smile. Why on earth would anyone talk about this woman the way the Garveys had?

As if she'd read Sarah's mind, Bettina Philips began answering her unspoken question. "I live in an old mansion called Shutters that's seen better days. A lot of better days. So naturally all the kids say it's haunted. It isn't, of course, but it was built a hundred and fifty years ago, and my family has lived in it for generations."

Her gentle smile broadened into a grin. "But living in a haunted house is just the beginning. I'm also 'different.' " She pronounced the word in a way that turned it from a simple adjective into an insult. "I'm an artist," she went on, and then her voice dropped so it sounded almost conspiratorial. "But it's even worse than that: I'm also interested in tarot cards and astrology and all kinds of religions, especially the more mystical ones. I've studied the medicinal properties of various herbs, and grow them in my garden. And worst of all, I don't go to church, and in Warwick that alone would make me suspect. I also don't lunch with the ladies, or serve on the right committees, or attend the right fund-raisers. I also tend to dress the way I please, and mind my own business. All of which, as I'm sure you would have come to find out even if Angie Garvey didn't tell you so, makes me different. In fact, I've always been different, even when I was your age."

She paused, and Sarah suddenly understood exactly what Bettina Philips was saying: that when she herself was a student at this school, she was the one everyone whispered about and laughed at. When Bettina had been her age, it was probably Angie and Mitch who sat in the cafeteria making fun of the girl who wasn't quite like them.

"And here's the best part, Sarah," Bettina said, moving to a chair on the opposite side of the art table. "Those same people who are always gossiping about me are the ones who always come to me when they're in trouble. Would you believe it? They actually come and knock on my back door and ask to have their fortunes told."

Sarah stared at her. "Seriously?"

"Seriously," Bettina repeated. "And I do my best for them. I'm nice to them. I lay out the tarot cards and try to tell them what I think they want to hear, and they go away grateful. Sometimes they come to me for herbs, thinking I might have some magical potions. And often my herbs work for them, but it's not because of any magic — it's just that I know what I'm doing with medicinal herbs."

"Does Angie Garvey come to see you?" Sarah whispered.

Bettina shrugged. "I never say who comes to see me. The point is that you shouldn't listen to the rumors. You're fourteen years old and smarter than most of the kids around here. So when you hear things about people, you should weigh all the evidence and make up your own mind about them."

"Except," Sarah reminded her, "that I still have to live with the Garveys."

"Very true," Bettina agreed. "And I certainly don't want to cause you any trouble. I just didn't want to lose you as a student because of what amounts to nothing more than medieval nonsense. And I don't want you doing the bare minimum to get by in my class, either. I see exceptional promise in your talent, and I think I can help you hone your skills."

Sarah smiled. "I'd like that."

"Me, too," Bettina said, pushing back from the table. "But I can't do it if you're afraid of me. So have a nice evening and I'll see you tomorrow." The teacher turned back to her desk and began shuffling a stack of class drawings into a zippered portfolio.

Sarah picked up her backpack and left the art studio, suddenly feeling better than she had in a long, long time.

Nick Dunnigan was in love.

At least he was pretty sure it was love as he moved down the hallway toward the school's front doors. After all, what else could it be? He felt sort of light-headed and had a sort of hollow feeling in his stomach, and just thinking about sitting across from Sarah Crane in the cafeteria not only made his heart start to pound but also plastered what he knew must be a really stupid-looking grin across his face. Until lunch-time, he'd had no idea, really, what love was, but now he knew.

It made you happy, and it made you want to dance, and it made you feel funny.

But most of all, you knew you had some-one you could trust.

Someone you could tell everything to. Absolutely everything.

How could it have happened so quickly?

And how was it that when Sarah Crane was close to him, his voices went quiet?

Profoundly quiet.

Unimaginably, astonishingly, joyfully quiet, as if she had the same effect on them that she did on him. They hadn't even objected when he started telling her about the hallucination. And that was weird, too — he never talked to anyone about the hallucinations except his mother and the doctors. But today he'd been able to tell Sarah Crane about it and she hadn't laughed or made fun of him.

He pushed through the heavy doors into the crisp outside air and paused on the steps. Maybe he should wait for Sarah and walk her home. But what if she didn't want to walk with him? What if she'd thought about what he told her at lunch and decided he was crazy?

He didn't even want to think about that possibility, and suddenly the whole idea of waiting for her seemed stupid.

Really, really stupid. How was a girl as beautiful and nice as Sarah Crane going to feel the same way about him that he felt about her? Taking the steps two at a time down to the sidewalk, he turned right, then headed diagonally across the football field toward home, his footsteps crunching on the nearly frozen grass.

He was passing the bleachers on the far side of the field when a movement from under the seats caught his eye. Then he heard a voice that made his stomach clench.

Conner West.

Conner got away with everything because his father ran the Warwick police department, which consisted of three deputies, including Conner's dad.

"Hey," Conner said.

Before Nick quite realized it had happened, Conner and two of his friends had surrounded him, and the euphoria of the hours since lunch drained out of him in an instant.

He was back to being crazy Nick Dunnigan.

"So the lunatic has a girlfriend, huh?" Conner said, his lips twisting into a sneer. "What do you think it'd be like, screwing a crip?"

Bobby Fendler edged closer and leered at Nick. "At lunch we thought you two should have gotten a room."

"Gonna go find someplace to make out now?" Elliot Nash chimed in. "You and the gimp?"

The voices in Nick's head roused from their silence, gabbling angrily among themselves.

"Can we watch?" Conner demanded. "It'd be neat watching Lunatic Nick try to stick it into his gimpy girlfriend."

"Oh, God, I could puke just thinking

143

about it," Elliot said, clutching his belly and bending over as if about to vomit all over Nick's shoes.

"Their kids would all be hunchback psychos," Conner said, jabbing at Nick's chest.

Nick stood perfectly still. They'd get bored in a few minutes and leave him alone.

They always did.

But then the committee in his head began howling at him to fight back, to lash out at them, punching, gouging, kicking, even biting and clawing at them until they were lying in the street, writhing in agony, bleeding and dying. The howling rose until the voices were so painful, he felt like his head was about to blow up, and something was happening to his eyes, too.

Now he could barely see Conner and Elliot and Bobby.

"Quiet," Nick cried out, his voice choking. "Be quiet. Please be quiet."

"Be quiet?" Conner said, jabbing him in the chest again. "You don't tell me to be quiet. Get it?"

A blaze of agony exploded in Nick's brain, and his vision abruptly cleared.

The flesh of Conner's face was falling away in strips as blood ran down his neck and dripped onto the ground.

Elliot burst into flames, his mouth wide-

144

open in a scream drowned out by the demons in Nick's head. "Stop!" Nick yelled. "Stop it!"

"Shut up, loser!" Bobby Fendler shoved Nick hard to punctuate his words.

Now pieces of Bobby were flying off as if caught in some great wind, hanging like gory Halloween decorations in the naked branches of the leafless trees.

Meanwhile, Elliot Nash still burned, his flesh melting off his bones.

And Conner West's tongue hung by a thread, flapping grotesquely with every word he spoke.

"Quiet!" Nick screamed, suddenly lashing out, flailing at the air around him with a viciousness that made all three of his tormentors step back. "Leave me alone! I don't want to see this anymore!"

"Hey, cool it," Conner said. "We haven't done anything to you."

Conner's voice sounded like nothing more than warbling static to Nick, whose head felt like it would burst with the pressure of the shrieking voices he was hearing and the horrors he was seeing, even when he clamped his eyes shut. Now he put his hands over his ears and began turning slowly around. "Please, please, please," he said, turning ever faster until he was whirling violently, as if under the impetus of some unseen force.

"Jeez," Conner whispered, grasping Elliot Nash's elbow. "Let's get outta here — I think Nick's about to take a dive over the edge for good."

"Crazy," Bobby Fendler said, but couldn't resist a final shove at the spinning boy.

Nick lost his balance and tumbled to the ground, and his three tormentors stepped back, glancing around to see who might have been watching the scene on the football field. Then, seeing no one, they turned and fled.

Nick covered his head with his arms and pleaded in a choked voice that seemed lost in the cacophony of the demons in his head who were still screaming for their revenge.

The voices finally calmed.

Nick sat up, groped in his backpack for his knit cap and put it on his head, pulling it down to cover his freezing ears.

From the corners of his eyes he thought he could still spot scraps of Elliot Nash caught in the twigs of the trees, and for a moment he thought he saw blood still running in rivulets in the gutter in front of the bleachers.

But he could see real things again, too.

146

Only a few steps away from the football field were houses and the sidewalk, and after a few blocks he would be home.

He stood up, brushed the dirt and gravel from his pants, and started homeward.

Her backpack stuffed with more books than she would have thought she could carry, Sarah paused on the sidewalk outside the school and looked around for Nick. They hadn't actually talked about meeting up after school, and even if he'd hung around waiting for her, she was late because of her meeting with Miss Philips. Still, when she didn't see him, she felt a pang of disappointment that was almost as painful as the twinge that went through her hip with every step she took.

Well, maybe tomorrow.

She started along the sidewalk and was just passing one of the gift shops in the middle of the block on Main Street that faced the village square when something in the window caught her eye. It was a large — and way too colorful — map of Warwick, with all the historic buildings and churches prominently displayed, if not quite as prominently as the Chamber of Commerce–affiliated businesses that had contributed to the creation of the map.

She stopped to study it more carefully, located the high school, the Garveys' house, and, of course, the shop in front of which she stood. At the edge of the map was the prison that held her father. And just a mile from where she was, on the shores of Shutters Lake, she saw something else.

The site of an old prison, which had apparently been replaced by the new one.

Sarah cocked her head, eyeing the small drawing of what had once been the warden's mansion and was all that was left of the prison.

She cocked her head, looking at the drawing more closely as she realized it sort of resembled the house she'd drawn in art class.

The house she'd only seen before in the nightmares that sometimes haunted her. She frowned. The resemblance was definitely there, but how many big old stone houses were there in New England? Hundreds? Probably thousands. And in one way or another, they'd all have some similarities.

Then another thought occurred to her: Could that be the house Bettina Philips lived in?

Deciding the exercise would be good for her leg, she concentrated on the map, memorizing the streets that would take her to the old prison site. When she was certain she wouldn't get lost, she set off down the sidewalk, came to the end of the block, and turned north. Then as the streetlights suddenly came on, she hesitated. But the sun was still shining and it wasn't very far.

She had time.

Fifteen minutes later Sarah gazed up the long curving driveway that led toward Shutters. Ornate, rusted wrought-iron gates hung crookedly on their hinges, entwined with frost-covered bindweed. She shrugged out of her backpack and let it fall to the ground, then stretched her sore shoulders.

Gates were meant to keep people out. If she went farther, would she be trespassing?

But they weren't closed, so maybe Miss Philips didn't mind if people came up her driveway. Besides, she'd only walk far enough to get a look at the house.

She stashed her heavy book bag behind the gate and walked slowly up the drive, which turned out to be longer than she'd expected.

And then, as she came around one more crook in the drive, there it was. Bettina was right: it really did look abandoned. Its shutters hung as crazily as the wrought-iron gates at the bottom of the drive, and the gutters around the eaves drooped loosely, some of them hanging so far away from the roof they couldn't have caught any water at all.

And all of them were bent and rusted.

Stones were missing from the walkways, and a big fountain in the front looked like no one had cleaned it out in decades.

The place really did look haunted.

Haunted, and strangely familiar.

Sarah closed her eyes and pictured the art paper on her table and the brown pastel crayon.

She saw the image of a stone house, with an intricate roofline complicated by gables and shadows.

She opened her eyes and there it was, standing before her. Shabbier than she had drawn it, but still the same house.

A shiver crept up her arms, then the skin on her back was crawling, too.

She should leave before Bettina Philips looked out a window and saw her trespassing.

Then a black dog, the fur around its neck up and its head lowered, slunk around the corner of the house and crouched low to the ground, staring at her.

Sarah froze. The last thing she needed was to be confronted by a watchdog. If it jumped at her, she wouldn't be able to fend it off before it knocked her over.

Now it started down the driveway toward her, moving very slowly, the strip of fur along its spine still raised, its head still lowered.

Sarah stood quietly, her breath loud in her ears, her heart pounding.

They both heard the slam of a car door, and the dog, startled, crouched, took one last look at her and vanished into the woods as quickly and silently as if it had never been there at all.

A car engine started.

Sarah stepped off the driveway and into the shadowy trees. The sun, very low in the sky now, shone right on the driver's face, and Sarah saw her clearly as the car passed her. It was a lone woman, her hair bound severely to her head, but smiling as if she'd just heard something good.

Was this one of the gossiping women from town who passed rumors about Bettina Philips, then came to her for advice?

Sarah waited until the car disappeared around the first curve in the driveway, then emerged from the shelter of the trees and took one last look at the house.

Suddenly she wished she could see the inside. She could hardly even imagine how Bettina lived in that enormous house. Did she live there all alone or at least have some pets? Were the furnishings in as bad shape as the house itself?

A thin line of smoke now trailed out of one of the chimneys. Dusk was coming on, and Bettina Philips was building herself a fire.

Sarah realized she'd have to walk quickly to get home before dark and even then would have to tell Angie Garvey something about where she'd been.

The library — that was it. She'd just say she went to the library, and to keep it from being a lie, she'd actually stop there on her way home.

And she wouldn't say a word about Bettina Philips.

Not one word.

CHAPTER NINE

Sarah made her way along the frozen sidewalk as fast as she could, the cold of the Sunday morning making her hip ache with every step as she tried to keep up with the Garveys. Yet even walking as fast as possible, the family was well into the next block by the time she turned the corner and the Mission of God church came into view.

Sarah stopped dead in her tracks.

An icy chill — far colder than that of the late fall morning — filled her body as she gazed at the building that proclaimed itself the house of God.

But if it truly was God's house, why did she feel an overwhelming sense of darkness and evil as she beheld the simple frame building adorned only by a tall steeple spiking into the sky?

"Come on," she heard Tiffany calling, "keep up."

But the dread that flooded over her was

so dark that she felt like even the wrath of Mitch Garvey might be preferable to being drawn through the doors of that church.

"Sarah?" Mitch said, his voice sharp and his eyes boring into her so deeply she was afraid he might have heard her thought.

She put her head down and kept going, but the closer she drew to the church, the colder she felt.

And now she felt eyes watching her.

Evaluating her.

Condemning her.

She wanted to turn away and run, wanted to find someplace — anyplace — that would shelter her from the strange cold that was invading her.

But there was no place.

Besides, she told herself, you've survived worse. It's only a church and there's nothing to be afraid of.

The pastor, wearing a long white robe and a black stole embroidered in silver, stood on the front step, nodding to each of his parishioners as they streamed through the door.

Sarah's palms went clammy as she waited, shivering, behind Zach and Tiffany on the step while Angie Garvey leaned in to the pastor's ear for a private word.

The pastor's eyes fixed on Sarah as Angie

whispered, then he nodded, and one by one the Garvey family filed into the church. Mitch introduced her to Reverend Keener, but Sarah tried to evade both his gaze and the touch of his proffered hand until Mitch squeezed her elbow hard enough to hurt as the pastor's cold fingers closed on hers.

She peered up at the minister's thin, deeply lined face, and his ice-cold eyes pierced into her as if he were looking into her soul.

Looking into it, and hating what he saw.

"Welcome," he said.

She drew her hand back and slipped it into her pocket, even though she had a feeling it would never be warm again. Then, as Mitch steered her to the doorway, Sarah balked. "I . . . I don't feel well," she said.

"Come *on*," Tiffany said, grabbing her arm and pulling her through the small anteroom and into the sanctuary.

Light seeped in through two tall and narrow stained-glass windows that flanked the altar, their leaded panes casting a tangle of shadows onto a thin metal cross suspended over the altar.

Hanging on that cross was a skeletal Christ, his mouth sagging open in a perpetual moan of helpless agony.

Sarah shivered and lowered her eyes.

A low and throbbing chord of organ music rolled out of unseen speakers, and then the choir, clad in black robes, appeared through a side door and took their places, sitting silently as Sarah followed the Garveys to their pew. She recognized some of the faces in the choir, which seemed mostly made up of the girls who sat with Tiffany in the cafeteria.

Now, as they had in school, they all turned their heads to stare at her.

Sarah took a deep breath, decided to ignore them, and glanced around to see if maybe Nick was here.

The church was filled, but Nick was nowhere to be seen.

But everywhere she looked, everyone seemed to be looking back at her.

And whispering to each other, their eyes remaining fixed on her.

She recognized some of her teachers, and the gym coach, and even the woman she'd seen in the car coming down Bettina Philips's driveway.

That woman was sitting next to Conner West, one of Zach's friends.

And they all knew who she was — the newcomer — and wanted to see her for themselves.

Some of them smiled at her, but their

smiles felt cold, and even as they smiled, they kept on whispering.

Where is she from?

Who is she?

She's the Garveys' foster child.

Her father is a murderer.

Her father tried to kill her, too.

She stays after school in Bettina Philips's room.

"Straighten up," Angie whispered harshly, and Sarah jerked around, fastening her eyes on the back of the pew in front of her.

It's only church, she told herself. It's no big deal.

As if in response to an invisible signal, the entire congregation stood and opened their hymnals. Lagging behind the rest of the worshippers, Sarah pulled herself to her feet, found the hymnal, and tried to mouth the words of the two dark dirges that followed. Then the pastor took his place in the small pulpit high above the congregation and began to speak.

Sarah tried to follow what he was saying, but her mind kept drifting back to the little country church where all her old friends back home were right now, singing joyful music, swaying together, smiling, and anticipating the great potluck feast that always followed Sunday services.

Her belly cramped with homesickness.

Then Reverend Keener's voice rose in volume and turned strident, and Sarah looked up just in time to see him slam his hand down on the pulpit with enough force that she jumped even in her pew halfway back in the church.

Then his eyes fixed on her, drilling deep inside her. "Satan is among us," he said. "Right here in Warwick. Some of us would hold with him —"

"No," the congregation cried.

"But I say unto you right now," the minister roared, his right arm rising and his forefinger pointing directly at Sarah, "you'd best steer clear of those who personify Satan's evil."

Sarah shrank down into her seat.

"Cleave ye to God Almighty!" he shouted.

"Amen!" the congregation responded.

The pastor let the word hang in the air, then drew in a deep breath. "Amen," he said quietly, his eyes still on Sarah. After a moment that seemed to Sarah to go on forever, the choir rose to sing the recessional, and the pastor turned his back on his flock of faithful to make his way down the small circular staircase from the pulpit.

Sarah drew her coat collar up around her

burning face, wishing she could simply disappear.

But what had she done?

Why had she been singled out and accused with consorting with the devil?

But of course she knew: it had been Angie Garvey whispering to the preacher about Bettina Philips.

Now the heat of indignation began to burn away the embarrassment of a moment before. Bettina Philips was her friend — her only friend, except for Nick Dunnigan.

No one — not even Reverend Keener — was going to change that.

Sarah sat quietly in the front seat of the old Pontiac as Angie backed out of the driveway. The dashboard clock read 2:07, and the prison visitors' center let no one in after two-thirty. If she wasn't inside by then, she wouldn't get to see her father.

"Stop fidgeting," Angie said as she turned out onto Quail Run and proceeded down the street at what seemed to Sarah to be more the pace of a snail crawling than a quail running.

"The visitors' center closes —" she began, but Angie cut her off.

"At two-thirty. I know. And I also know I've got better things to do on a Sunday afternoon than to ferry you back and forth to the prison. From now on you can take the bus."

Which would have been fine, except no buses ran out to the prison at any of the times she could possibly use them.

She'd already checked.

"And there better be a whole column of A's marching down your report card, too, missy," Angie continued, lighting a cigarette. "Hanging out at the prison is not the right thing for a young lady, and it's the first privilege you'll lose if your grades aren't up to snuff."

Sarah sat silently, determined to do nothing that might give Angie an excuse to turn around and go back home, but the dying landscape of autumn flying by outside the car's windows looked almost as bleak as she felt.

At 2:24, Angie pulled into the circular drive in front of the visitors' center. "I'll be back at four o'clock sharp," she said, barely even glancing at Sarah. "Don't make me wait — not even one minute."

Sarah hurried into the visitors' center, signed in, and caught up with the last of the visitors as they were going through the metal detector.

She'd made it.

But when she saw the man who stood up to greet her in the cavernous visiting room, she almost didn't recognize him, and for a moment thought her father wasn't there at all. Then, when he came a little closer, she did recognize him. In only a week, Ed Crane had lost more weight than Sarah would have thought possible. His cheeks had taken on a sunken hollowness, and his skin had turned a sickly looking yellow.

"Hey, sweet pea," he said, a small flicker of light glimmering in his tired eyes.

Sarah ached to run into his arms, to hold him, to comfort him, but one glance at the guard standing nearby told her that she'd better do nothing more than sit in the molded plastic chair across from him and hold his hand.

But at least she was here, and she could see her father, and he could see her, and no matter how cold and bright and horrible it was, it still felt better than being back in the Garveys' house.

"You okay?" her father asked. "How's school?"

Sarah searched her mind for a way to keep the truth of how bad it was from him, but already knew he'd seen some of her misery in her eyes. She forced a shrug. "It's okay, I guess. You know — I'm new — I limp —

they think I'm a geek."

Her father's eyes clouded with anger. "You're not a geek."

She managed a smile. "I know that and you know that. Now all we have to do is figure out how to convince everyone in Warwick."

Some of his anger seemed to fade. "How's the family you're with?"

What was she supposed to say? If she poured her heart out to him about how horrible her life was, she'd only make him feel worse than he already did. "They're all right, I guess," she said. She could see he knew she was holding something back, so she forced a small smile. "They're just different."

"I'm sorry —"

"It's okay," she interrupted, deciding to toss one of her father's favorite sayings back at him: " 'Life throws you some fastballs, some sliders, and the occasional changeups,' right?"

Ed Crane smiled. "Right."

"What about you?" Sarah asked, trying to change the subject before he could ask more questions about the Garveys. "Are you taking care of yourself? You look kind of skinny."

"Now you sound like your mother," Ed

retorted. Then the flicker of humor in his eyes died away. "Hey, I'm fine. I just don't have much of an appetite in here," he said. "The food's not like what you and your mom used to make."

"Well, make yourself eat it," Sarah told him, realizing that she was now repeating words her mother used to speak to her. "You're going to get out of here in a few years, and I'll graduate and we'll go back home again, right? We'll be together again, like it used to be. So you have to be strong — you have to get through this."

"And I will," Ed Crane said, suddenly understanding just how much Sarah wasn't telling him, and knowing that no matter how much he asked, she wouldn't tell him. And if she could get through what she was going through, so could he. "Stop worrying about me," he went on. "We're both going to be okay." It seemed, then, that Sarah might start crying, and Ed knew he'd never be able to get through that. If she started crying, it might just kill him right here, right now. "Tell me about your art," he said, leaning closer and taking her hands in his. "Does the school have a good teacher?"

Sarah seized on the question, forcing back the tears that had been about to overwhelm her. "A really great one," she said. "Her name's Miss Philips. But —" She cut the word off as quickly as possible, but not fast enough.

"But what?" her father asked, cocking his head the way he did when he wasn't going to give up until he had an answer.

Sarah tried to make it sound like no big deal. "I don't know — the Garveys — the people I live with — they don't like her."

"Why?" Ed asked, frowning. "Is there something wrong with her?"

Sarah hesitated, then decided there was no point in not telling him the truth, at least about this. "The people at their church don't like her, either. They all think she's a witch."

Ed stared at her for a second, and she could see that whatever he'd been expecting, it wasn't that. Then, when her expression didn't change, he suddenly laughed out loud.

It was a huge, rich, booming laugh that transported her back to the home she'd grown up in and the way things used to be.

"A witch?" he cried out, then laughed again, and finally wiped the moisture from the corners of his eyes. "That's quite a church they've got you going to. How do you even keep a straight face?"

Sarah bit her lip. "If you'd been there, and

heard the minister, you wouldn't think it was so funny."

Her father's laughter finally died away, and he reached out and took her hand once more. "You can't listen to nonsense like that and take it seriously, sweet pea. You've got a solid head on your shoulders, and you're perfectly capable of making up your own mind about things like what people might and might not be."

"That's what Miss Philips said."

"Well, good for her. Sounds like she's all right to me." He shook his head. "A witch. That's a good one."

It got easier then, and for the next hour Sarah found herself talking with her father almost the way they used to at home. And for a while the sterile visiting room in the state prison might as well have been the kitchen in the little farmhouse outside of Brunswick. But soon — too soon — the big clock with the cage over its glass face read three-fifty and it was time for her to go.

Away from the coziness of being with her father in the prison, to the prison of being in the house with the Garveys.

"I'll be back as soon as I can, Daddy," she promised, refusing to ruin the visit at the very end by bursting into tears.

"I'll look forward to that, honey."

"So you eat your vegetables, okay?"

He nodded. "Okay."

Before her tears could overcome her, she hurried away, suddenly terrified that she might be even a few seconds late to meet Angie Garvey.

That could cost her a visit with her father, and no matter what she had to do, she wasn't going to let that happen. And the next time she came to visit, she'd bring him another drawing.

Maybe she'd do a portrait of her mother. She'd never tried to do that before, and it might be kind of fun, even if it didn't turn out very well.

Not that it mattered how bad it came out.

Her father would love it anyway.

Sarah eyed the object on the counter in front of her as warily as if it were a cobra rather than merely a carrot, knowing that if she didn't cut it exactly as Angie had shown her a moment ago, her foster mother would strike out at her with a venom that might not be fatal, but would sting every bit as much as a serpent's bite. Now, as she held the knife over the carrot at what she hoped was the same angle Angie had demonstrated, she felt the woman's cold gaze over her shoulder. "Presentation is everything,"

Angie reminded her when she was done, reaching over and rejecting two chunks that failed to meet her standards. "Especially for Sunday dinner. Remember that any job worth doing is worth doing well."

Sarah tried not to think about the fun she and her mother used to have cooking dinner together, laughing and joking and sometimes dancing around in the kitchen, paying no attention at all to the size or shape of carrots. Here, there was no temptation at all to break into song, let alone dance around the Garveys' kitchen.

"Hey," Tiffany said as she came in and opened the refrigerator door.

Sarah stiffened. "Hey," she replied, carefully keeping her eyes on the work in front of her.

"So, what's it like to visit someone in prison?" Tiffany asked with an exaggerated innocence that immediately put Sarah on guard. She glanced over at Tiffany, who was now leaning against the doorjamb, a Coke in her hand.

"It was kind of hard the first time," Sarah said, choosing her words carefully.

"Keep working while you talk," Angie reminded her.

Sarah reached for another carrot. "But I love seeing my dad."

"Your dad the *murderer?*" Zach asked, suddenly appearing in the doorway next to his sister. Sarah felt a twinge of anger at the emphasis he put on the last word.

"It was an accident," Sarah said quietly.

"I thought running over *you* was the accident," Tiffany said. "That's two too many accidents, if you ask me."

Sarah's face burned, but she said nothing, keeping her eyes on the carrot as she quickly sliced it into the exact pieces Angie demanded.

"He's going to Hell, you know," Zach said. "So visiting him is kind of a waste, isn't it?"

Sarah glanced over at Angie, who stirred the boiling pasta and seemed not even to have heard what her children were saying.

"Seems like maybe you should spend your time trying to save your soul instead of hanging out with him," Tiffany said.

"He's my father," Sarah whispered, her voice sounding weak and small even to herself.

"But he's going to Hell," Zach repeated.

"You should be in church, praying for your own salvation," Tiffany said.

Sarah's fingers tightened on the knife. "If I'm in church, I'll pray that my father gets out as soon as he can, and when I'm not in church, I'll go visit him as often as I can," she said, her voice trembling.

"Keep chopping," Angie said. "If you don't get your work done, you won't be visiting him at all. And when you finish the carrots, you can cut up the broccoli for the salad."

So that was it — soon they weren't going to let her visit her father. No matter what she did — no matter how hard she tried to please them — it wasn't going to be enough.

And the punishment would be keeping her from visiting her father.

She took a deep breath and turned to face Angie. Out of the corner of her eye she could see the smirk that twisted Zach's lips and the brightness in Tiffany's eyes as she waited to see what was about to happen. "You can't keep me from visiting him," Sarah said, struggling to keep her voice under control. "I have a right."

Angie turned around to face Sarah, drying her hands on her apron. "You have no rights at all," she said, her cold eyes fixing on her. "You're here because you need to be brought up properly in a good Christian home, and that's exactly what we are going to provide. Your father is a sinner, and your mother died of sin, and you're headed in that same direction unless you straighten up and start working and praying for your own salvation. Now stop arguing and get back to your work."

Sarah's fingers tightened on the knife and she struggled to keep her fury under control. "My mother did not die of sin," she said quietly. "She died of cancer."

"Same thing," Zach said, and reached over for a handful of chopped carrots.

It was all Sarah could do to keep from driving that kitchen knife right through his hand, pinning him to the cutting board.

"Cancer is evil made manifest," Angie said, draining the pasta into the sink amid a billowing cloud of steam. "All illness is caused by evil and sin, and if your mother had cancer, it was because she had fallen from God's grace. Hand me that bowl."

For a moment Sarah gazed mutely at the blue bowl Angie was pointing at. Was it possible she'd heard her foster mother's words right? But she knew she had — what Angie Garvey had just said wasn't much different than what Reverend Keener had said only this morning at the church.

And Angie had just called her mother evil.

She'd called a woman she didn't know — a woman she'd never met — evil!

The fury she'd been holding in check began to erupt inside her. How could she live with these people? How could she even sit at a table and eat dinner with them?

She couldn't.

Dropping the knife on the cutting board, she walked past Tiffany and Zach, through the door to the dining room, then on through the living room. Ignoring Angie's demands that she come back and finish her work, she took her hat, her thin coat, and a scarf from the coat tree by the front door, and walked out.

By the time she got to the corner of the block, where she paused to pull on the coat, wrap the scarf around her neck, and pull the knit cap over her ears, she already knew where she was going.

Indeed, there was only one place she *could* go where she knew she would be welcome.

Shutters.

Shutters, and the "witch" who lived within its walls.

CHAPTER TEN

The looming mass of the ancient stone house looked even larger against the fast graying sky than the last time Sarah had seen it, when at least there was sunlight to wash away some of the mansion's air of gloom. She paused, gazing at the gabled roof, and for a moment wondered if she'd been wrong.

If instead of making her way up the long and winding driveway through the woods, she should have turned back.

Turned back, returned to the Garveys', and made her peace with Angie and Tiffany and Zach.

But even as the thought formed, she found herself moving forward, closer to the old stone house. And even though it still reminded her of the house from her dreams, it didn't seem frightening now that she was awake. Indeed, the house tugged at her as if it had a gravity of its own, and oddly, instead of fear, she felt a strange familiarity — almost a feeling of homecoming, as if something buried deep inside her had always known that this place was more than just something from her dreams, but was a real place that was waiting for her, patiently waiting, until she came back to it.

Yet she'd only been here once before, and never set so much as a foot inside the house.

She wiped her nose — running from the chill in the air — on a scrap of tissue she found in her coat pocket, then climbed the front steps and pressed the bell next to Shutters' enormous oak front door.

A solitary dog's bark echoed from deep inside.

Moments later Bettina Philips opened the door. "Sarah," she said softly, neither looking nor sounding surprised to see her. "Come in."

Sarah stepped through the door and into the cavernous foyer, and immediately a feeling of warmth enveloped her, banishing the cold that had invaded her body as she made the long walk. And with the cold, all her doubts, nervousness, and anxiety drained away as well.

And the house, too, seemed to change as she took another step. Though she knew it could be nothing but an illusion, the lights seemed to grow a little brighter, and the flames from the fire burning on the great hearth set into the wall of the entry hall halfway between the foyer and the far side of the house seemed to leap higher and throw off more heat.

Bettina glanced into the fast-fading light outside before closing the door, then took a closer look at Sarah. "Are you all right? What's happened?"

Suddenly, all of Sarah's anger at her foster family dropped away and for a moment she felt completely disoriented. *Why had she come here? What force had drawn her?* She shook her head and felt her face burn with embarrassment. Maybe she should just leave.

But she didn't want to leave.

"I'll make us a pot of tea," Bettina said. "Take off your coat."

Leaving her cap, scarf, and coat on a great oaken tree surmounted with an ornately carved owl that stood just inside the foyer, Sarah followed Bettina through an enormous dining room, then a smaller room lined with sideboards that were filled with dusty crystal goblets of more shapes and sizes than she'd ever seen outside a department store, and into a kitchen at least six times the size of either the Garveys' or the one back home on the farm.

As Bettina pulled the teapot from the cupboard over the sink, put four tea bags into it, and filled it from the kettle that was already steaming on a huge eight-burner range, she tilted her head toward a table where a plate of sliced banana bread was already waiting. "Something must have happened," she said. "You didn't just decide to walk all the way up here for no reason at all, did you?"

"They were telling me my father's going to Hell," Sarah replied. "I didn't want to start yelling at them, and I didn't know where else to go." She paused for a second, then went on. "You've been so nice to me." Then, as Bettina brought the pot and two mugs to the table, Sarah's body trembled with a sense of déjà vu: she had been here before, sat on this very chair, eaten a piece of banana bread off this same Franciscan-ware plate.

Sipped tea from that blue stoneware mug.

But instead of fading away, the déjà vu grew stronger, and as she looked around at the high ceiling, the scrubbed wooden table that could easily seat twelve, the old wavy-glass-fronted cabinets that lined the kitchen walls, Sarah felt as if she had eaten countless meals at that table, read a hundred books while curled in that window seat by the door to the side entrance.

This was her house.

She cast around in her mind for something to say that wouldn't betray her strange certainty that she had been here — even lived here — before. "D-Do you live here all by yourself?" she finally asked, unable to keep from stammering. But Bettina Philips didn't seem to notice.

"My great-great-grandfather moved in here when he was the first warden of the old prison. Then when he retired, he bought the place from the state, since the prison was closing. I grew up here."

"It's huge."

Bettina's brows arched. "Huge heating bills, I can tell you that." Then she picked up her cup. "C'mon, let's go have a look at my studio — you're going to love it."

Sarah followed Bettina back the way they had come until they were once more in the mansion's great central hall, the walls of which were studded with half a dozen heavy mahogany doors, all of them closed. "I keep these rooms shut up tight during the winter," Bettina said. As they moved toward the north side of the house, the teacher pointed to the doors they passed. "That goes to my grandfather's study, that one to the formal parlor with the music room on the other side. Up the stairs" — she gestured at the curving staircase to the second and third floors — "are more bedrooms than you'd think possible, but only two bathrooms. And above that, on the third floor, is a ballroom. Just what I need, right?"

And as Sarah passed each of the closed doors, she was certain — *absolutely certain* — that she knew exactly what each of the invisible rooms looked like. Even the music room, which she knew contained not only a grand piano, but a harpsichord as well, upon which someone — *who?* — used to play Vivaldi on a spring morning.

And she could name each of the upstairs bedrooms and describe how each of them was decorated.

She peered up at the crystal chandelier that hung twenty feet above her head, then gazed down at the intricately inlaid marble floor. The shapes of the crystals and the patterns of the floor were as familiar as her face in the mirror.

Then the black lab mix that Sarah had seen on the driveway the other day stuck its nose through the spindles on the staircase and looked down on them. This evening, though, it did not bark.

"That's Cooper," Bettina said. "Sometimes he's friendly, but not often."

As if to prove her point, Cooper backed away and soundlessly disappeared.

Bettina moved on to the last pair of big doors on the left, slid them aside into their pockets. "And this," she announced, "is my studio."

Sarah's breath caught in her throat as Bettina switched on the lights in what had once been a conservatory. Glass walls soared to a glass ceiling nearly as high as the one in the entry hall. For a split second Sarah saw it exactly as it had once been, filled with tropical plants, a potted palm and ficus tree, a riot of flowers and foliage that could never have survived a Vermont winter. Then the vision faded and she gazed at the worn area rug at the far end, with a sofa, two chairs, and a coffee table arranged around a freestanding gas fireplace, along with books, teacups, notepads, and woolen throws.

The rest of the space was mainly occupied by a drafting table, several easels, and makeshift brick-and-board shelving, every square foot of which was jammed full of paints, brushes, pencils, books, and papers.

Beyond the windows, Sarah could still barely see the sweep of overgrown lawn that stretched all the way down to the shores of the lake whose waters were shining silver in the cloudy twilight.

And this, she knew, was where she belonged.

Here, despite the house's rotting facades and overgrown grounds, and peeling wallpaper and faded upholstery.

Not in the Garveys' house, despite its neatness and its tidiness, with nothing ever out of place.

Then her eyes were drawn to one of the easels and the fresh sheet of thick paper that seemed to be waiting for someone to draw on it.

For *her* to draw.

The stub of a charcoal stick lay in the tray, and without thinking, Sarah walked over, picked it up, and drew a dark vertical line.

Her fingertips began to tingle, and she set her mug down and drew another line.

The tingling increased, moved up her fingertips to her hands, and as her hand moved with increasing certainty, as if guided by some unseen force, she let herself drift into a warm and welcoming world of inspiration.

"Good, Sarah," Bettina whispered. "Keep going. Just let it happen."

Sarah barely heard her. The drawing consumed her — she *was* the charcoal —

she *was* the image. It was as if she were a mere medium that allowed the image to emerge from the paper of its own volition.

Every mark seemed preordained, as though the paper, with the image already hidden inside it, had been waiting for her to show it to the world.

Then it was finished.

There was not another stroke to be made.

The tingling began to recede, first from her fingers and hands, then her arms. Finally it seemed to drain out through her legs and feet, vanishing into the floor like lightning going to ground. Sarah's cramped fingers relaxed, and the charcoal stick dropped to the floor.

She blinked, disoriented, as if awakening from a dream.

She looked at what she'd done.

On the easel she saw a charcoal drawing of a room.

A small, dark room, filled with skeletons.

But the skeletons were still wearing clothes — nothing more than tattered rags.

And they still stood, as if supported by some unseen force.

She looked down at her hand; her fingers were black with charcoal dust from smudging shadows and lines.

She looked over at Bettina. "Did I do that?"

Bettina nodded slowly.

Sarah backed away from the horrific image. "No," she whispered, her hands trembling now as much as her voice. "I couldn't have."

"Sit down and drink your tea," Bettina said. "We need to talk."

Nick Dunnigan fixed his eyes on the perfectly browned rib roast, and willed the voices in his head to keep silent. But even as he tried to deafen himself to them, he knew it was useless; they'd begun whispering before he even came downstairs, and though he tried to ignore them, their chatter grew steadily louder, demanding more and more of his attention. "Roast looks great, Mom," he said too loudly, but though his mother shot him a worried glance, his father seemed not to have heard.

Shep Dunnigan was gazing hungrily at the beef as he shook out his napkin and placed it on his lap while his wife sliced off a thick slab, placed it on a plate, and passed it to him. "Smells as good as it looks," he said, scooping into the bowl of mashed potatoes, then ladling gravy over everything.

Nick was about to take the first bite of his

own meal when a dark line — as thick and black as if it had been drawn with charcoal — slashed across the left side of his vision.

No, he thought. Not now. Not with Dad sitting right here.

He made himself stay perfectly still as he waited for the dark line to fade away, and after a moment or two it did.

But so also had his appetite.

Nor, he was certain, was it actually over. How many times had he been given a flickering hint of what the demons were about to show him, only to be lulled into thinking the hallucination was over when it actually was only beginning?

"Honey?" His mom's face filled with concern. "Are you all right?"

"I'm okay," Nick said, but the words rang hollow even to his own ears, and his fork rattled against his plate as his heart began to hammer in his chest.

He carefully set the fork down and tried to will his heart back to normality. But it was no good — things were getting worse. The hallucinations had become so dark lately — so violent — that he was starting to worry about what he might do to himself.

Or to somebody else.

What if they got so bad he couldn't find his way back to reality?

What if he got trapped forever in some unspeakable horror that might not be real but might as well be?

But he already knew the answer to those questions: his father would take him back to the hospital, and they'd never let him out again.

And he'd never see Sarah again.

The thought came unbidden into his mind, and for a moment the voices actually fell utterly silent. When had the idea of never seeing Sarah Crane again become even more frightening than the thought of going back to the hospital? he wondered. Then there was another flicker at the edge of his vision — another great, thick, dark line.

The medicine! Take another dose of the medicine!

Even as the thought flashed into his mind, he was sliding his chair back. "Excuse me," he mumbled. "I need to go to the bathroom."

His mother frowned worriedly but nodded and didn't ask him any questions.

Nick ran up to his room, tore open his backpack, and retrieved the pill bottle. He shook out one of the pills, but before he could even put it into his mouth, let alone wash it down with a swallow of water, his vision narrowed, then darkened.

A moment later he could see nothing at all.

But he could hear the voices rising, hear the moaning and wailing growing louder.

So loud it would soon consume him.

His hands shaking uncontrollably now, he somehow managed to force the pill between his lips and to swallow it with what little saliva he could muster in his suddenly bone-dry mouth.

Now he began feeling his way toward the bed, knowing that if his parents found him on the floor, they'd call an ambulance. At least if he made it to the bed they might just let him sleep.

If he could sleep.

He found the bed, crept onto it and lay still. After a few moments, points of light began to appear, then spread. He was in a room, a dark, fetid, stinking room, with —

"Help us!" The voices erupted in his brain and began to shriek. *"Save us."*

Nick whimpered, but his brain was no longer his to command, and he lay writhing on the bed watching helplessly as the visions rose before his eyes and the howling, pleading demons filled his ears.

Corpses!

There were rotting corpses everywhere!

Corpses that were still standing and gazing at him and —

Nick shoved a corner of his quilt into his mouth to keep himself from screaming at the vision of the dead and the dying howling in their agony in the dank prison where they were mired in their own filth.

The visions grew more lurid, and the screaming rose, and now he could smell the putrefaction in his nostrils and taste the rot on his tongue, and all he could do was lie on his bed, listening, crying, mutely begging for them to stop, for the horror finally to pass.

But it didn't pass, and when he was finally exhausted, he lay still, trying desperately to hold on to whatever might remain of his sanity.

Or was it already gone?

Was he already lost forever?

Time no longer had any meaning, and he didn't hear the sound of his parents entering his room. But at the touch of his mother's hand, he jerked spasmodically upright and clung to her, his moans echoing those of the creatures in his head.

She held him and rocked him as he sobbed, and slowly he began to feel her tears on his cheeks.

But he never felt the needle that slid deep

185

into his arm, and barely noticed his consciousness begin to fade away before a quiet darkness enveloped him and he relaxed into an exhausted, dreamless sleep.

CHAPTER ELEVEN

I should make her stay, Bettina Philips thought as she stood at the front door of Shutters, watching Sarah make her slow way down the driveway, until finally she vanished into the darkness. But she'd tried, and Sarah Crane had brushed aside every argument she offered.

She had seen how upset Sarah was by what she'd drawn, but just as she began explaining that an artist can't always know what's hidden inside them until the image finds its own moment of expression, Sarah caught sight of the clock and insisted that she had to go home, upset or not.

She wouldn't even accept another cup of tea, let alone the ride Bettina offered. But Bettina understood that: if anyone saw Sarah getting out of her car, there was no telling how her foster parents might punish her.

So Sarah had walked out into the wintry

night wearing a jacket barely heavy enough for fall, and now she was gone, and as Bettina finally swung the heavy oak door closed she felt something she hadn't experienced in a long time.

She felt lonely.

Trying to shake off the feeling, she returned to the studio to gaze once more at the drawing that still stood on the easel. Perching on the stool in front of it, she studied the way Sarah had used a combination of light and shadow to indicate total darkness. And the angle of the beams in the dark chamber's ceiling perfectly indicated the tight proportions of the space.

The beams . . .

Bettina leaned forward, cocking her head.

There was something familiar about those beams.

A chill began to crawl up her spine.

Sarah had drawn Shutters sight unseen on her first day in class. And not as the old manse currently was, either, but the way it had been when it was first built.

Was it possible this was another view of her house from sometime in the past? Could a room like this have ever existed within these walls?

No. Of course not. And yet . . .

She knew those beams.

Bettina unclipped the drawing from the easel and took it out into the entry hall, scanning the ceiling and the way the walls joined, but knowing even as she gazed upward that the beams in the picture would be gone in the opposite direction.

Grabbing a sweater from the coat tree in the foyer and turning lights on as she went, she carried the drawing down the steep flight of stairs that led from the kitchen into the cold basement that never seemed to warm up, even in the midst of the hottest summer.

Tonight it felt even colder than it ever had.

The musty smell felt choking in her throat, but she ignored it as she moved among the shrouded furniture and the old filing cabinets that held so much of her family's history. Tonight, though, she ignored everything but the beams overhead, eyeing not only the angles at which they ran, but the way they connected with one another.

The enormous timbers that had supported the house for nearly two centuries still held, now chalky white with age and cobwebs, but never painted or covered with plaster or drywall.

But nothing matched Sarah's sketch, at least not nearly as perfectly as the drawing of the house had hewn to the original. Still, there were probably areas in the basement that she had never seen. The old coal chute and bin and furnace that took up so much room long ago had been torn out and replaced by the oil-burning furnace that was now installed in a tiny portion of the area the coal-fueled system had required.

How many other areas of the basement had been reconfigured over the stretch of decades that had run their course since the foundation was laid?

And where to begin to look?

Furniture and ancient machinery were stacked high at the far end of the chamber in which she stood, blocking her from even reaching the pull chains on the series of ancient lightbulbs that someone had strung among the joists somewhere in the far distant past.

Nor could she get close to the far end without moving what looked like several tons of things past generations had consigned to the darkness, and she wasn't about to go fumbling through it until she could reach the lights.

But she could see nothing that looked even close to the small dungeonlike chamber Sarah had drawn.

But if there really were such a room down here, wouldn't it show on the original plans?

Of course! And when her parents built the garage forty years ago, they had found the original plans in her great-great-grandfather's study.

Yet as she took a final look at the huge timbers in the ceiling — timbers whose proportions seemed perfectly to match those that Sarah had drawn — Bettina suddenly realized that she didn't need the plans of the house to know the truth. Already she had little doubt that in the long-ago past someone had stored things somewhere in this basement that they intended to keep hidden forever.

And Sarah had drawn them.

Bettina pulled the sweater close around her neck and hurried back upstairs, turning off the light and firmly closing and locking the door.

The kitchen, still smelling of warm spiced tea and filled with bright light, seemed a safe haven, but Bettina moved straight through it, across the inlaid marble floor of the hall, and pushed open one of the heavy mahogany doors to the room that had not been used since it was her thrice-great-grandfather's study.

Instead it had been left exactly as it was when Boone Philips died, the one room in the house that was always closed, and never used.

The one room that she herself had never played in as a child.

It had always been a cold room, but tonight it felt even colder than the rest of the house.

Bettina switched on the overhead chandelier and surveyed the glass-fronted cabinets, the floor-to-ceiling bookshelves with the brass library ladder on a rail, the leather chairs and massive desk.

Where to begin to look for a set of two-hundred-year-old plans?

Where had her parents found them?

The desk was as good a starting place as any.

Bettina perched on the cracking leather of the big desk chair, and the smell of old leather, and even older books, enveloped her.

She opened the front drawer of the desk, glanced at its jumble of pens, pencils, and paper clips, and closed it again.

The top drawer on the right-hand pedestal held Boone Philips's personal engraved stationery, now yellowed and crisp.

The deep file drawer below that was filled with folders, but none of them thick enough to hold a series of house plans.

Still, she flipped quickly through them; they looked like old inmate files from the time when her ancestor was the last warden of the old prison. Maybe someday she'd donate these and the contents of the cabinets in the basement to the historical society. At least she'd be rid of them, and maybe the historians would find some use for them.

Then, just as she was about to close the drawer, she noticed something odd.

The drawer's face seemed to be a few inches taller than the drawer was deep.

She closed the drawer and looked at the front of it, measuring its depth with her fingers, hand, and forearm. Then she opened it again and repeated the exercise. Sure enough, the bottom of the drawer was nearly three inches higher than it needed to be.

And when she felt the exterior bottom of the drawer, it was nearly even with the bottom of the drawer's face.

The drawer had a false bottom.

Bettina lifted the files out of the drawer, stacking them on the desk.

Barely visible at the back of the drawer, she found a small notch in the drawer's bottom. Taking a paper clip from the top drawer, she straightened it out, bent it so it formed a right angle, then fit it into the notch.

It came up without so much as a squeal.

And there, hidden away in the secret compartment that had been built into the desk, was a sheaf of handwritten pages.

A manuscript?

Bettina carefully pulled the papers out of the drawer.

AN HOMAGE TO E. A. POE
BY BOONE PHILIPS

Her thrice-great-grandfather was a writer? What had he written?

She quickly replaced the false bottom, put the files back where they'd originally been, and closed the drawer.

The house plans — even if they were here — could wait.

Leaving Sarah Crane's drawing on the desk, she took the manuscript back to her studio, curled up on the chaise with a thick wool throw, and began to read.

With her coat buttoned up tight, her scarf wrapped around her mouth and nose, and the knit cap pulled well down over her ears, Sarah made her way slowly down the last few yards of the driveway, feeling each step out carefully.

The last thing she needed to do was trip in the dark.

And with her hands plunged deep in the warmth of her pockets, she might not be able to pull them out in time to catch herself if she fell. Then what would she do? There was no way Bettina Philips could hear her from here, and even if a car passed on the road, its windows would be closed. But if she pulled her hands out now, her fingers would freeze.

At last she came to the road, turned left, and started down into the village. For the first part of the long walk back to the Garveys', all she'd been able to think about was the macabre drawing she'd made at Shutters. Where had it come from? And why couldn't she remember drawing it? Was it possible that she *hadn't* drawn it? That was certainly how it felt: like some strange force had just taken over, moving the charcoal all by itself. But as she came to the bright streetlight across from the town square, her mind shifted from where she'd been to where she was going.

What would it to be like to face the wrath of Angie Garvey?

A cold that was different from the icy chill in the air penetrated deep into her, making the night seem almost warm by comparison.

What was she going to say when her foster mother demanded to know where she'd been?

Should she try to lie and say she was at the library?

But she wasn't very good at lying, and Angie would know right away that she wasn't telling the truth.

Just walking out had been bad enough; if she lied about where she'd been —

She didn't even want to think about what Angie might do. Not letting her visit her father would only be the beginning of it.

Five minutes later she turned the corner onto Quail Run, and stopped for a moment, still trying to think what she might say. The Garvey house was dark except for the bluish cast from the big-screen television that showed through the draperies. Still uncertain what she was going to say, Sarah took a deep breath and crossed the street. A moment later she climbed the three steps to the front porch, steeled herself, and opened the storm door.

The front door was locked.

Sarah moved to the window, peered through the sheer curtains, and saw Mitch Garvey's foot propped up on the coffee table as he lay sprawled on the sofa that faced the television.

She knocked on the glass, but his foot didn't even twitch.

She rang the bell and waited, shivering in the cold, but there were no answering lights, no sound, no movement of any kind.

Maybe they'd left the back door open for her.

Sarah closed the storm door, went around to the back of the house, and was about to try the back door when she saw a rolled up sleeping bag standing on its end right next to the dog door. Sitting on top of it was a small plate — not even covered — that held half a sandwich.

There was a note pinned to the bread with a toothpick.

Sarah's heart faltered as she began to understand her punishment.

She unpinned the note and held it up to the glow of the porch light.

```
You don't storm out in a
temper tantrum and come back
whenever you want to. Good
night.
```

She read the note again, barely believing that someone would lock her out of the house, leaving her to sleep on a porch in

197

November.

Even the dog got to sleep in the laundry room.

But what else could she do?

Maybe she should go back to Shutters. Bettina would let her sleep there — she'd already offered.

But the cold was penetrating deeper and deeper into her, and her hip was throbbing and her leg aching so badly she'd barely made it the last couple of blocks before she got back to the Garveys'.

She'd never make it all the way back to Shutters.

Sighing, she unrolled the heavy down sleeping bag and kicked off her shoes. Then, still wearing her coat, knit cap, and scarf, she wriggled into the sleeping bag and pulled it close around her.

She reached out a hand into the cold and picked up the sandwich from the plate.

She nibbled at it, and then, as the cold began to ebb out of her body, quickly finished the rest of it.

She stretched out flat on her back, and felt the throbbing in her hip begin to ease, despite the hardness of the porch. As her body warmed, exhaustion flowed through her, and suddenly even the wooden floor of the porch didn't seem so bad.

Better, anyway, than trying to keep on walking through the cold and darkness. Letting the last piece of bread crust fall from her fingers, Sarah gave herself up to sleep.

Tiffany smiled in the darkness of her room when she heard the doorbell ring, and a tingle of excitement ran through her as she waited to see if her parents were really going to make Sarah sleep outside all night.

She'd never seen her mother as furious as she'd been when Sarah just walked out of the house before dinner. Her mother hadn't even been that mad when she had to pick Zach up at the Morganton police station after he took her car for a joyride with Conner West.

And the best thing was that her mother's fury had only gotten worse as the evening went on and Sarah didn't come back and apologize. Still, even given how angry her mother was, Tiffany couldn't quite believe she'd actually make her sleep outside. She'd probably let Sarah shiver out there for a little while longer, then let her in and start yelling at her.

The doorbell turned into a couple of knocks, but Tiffany knew it didn't matter how hard she knocked — her mother had gone to bed — or at least disappeared into the big bedroom at the end of the hall, and her father would be asleep on the sofa.

Except he wasn't really asleep — he was passed out, and no amount of ringing or knocking would wake him up.

So it was true — nobody was going to let her in until morning.

Then an ugly thought occurred to her: What if her mother did the same thing to her?

Behave, or you'll sleep on the porch.

No. Doing it to Sarah Crane was one thing, but her parents would never do that to her. Sarah was no more than a way for her folks to get some extra money, and the way she'd acted, she needed a good slap in the face to learn her place in the family.

Which was no place at all.

Suddenly, Tiffany wanted to actually see what was happening, to witness it with her own eyes, so she could relate every detail to everyone at school tomorrow. If people were snickering about Sarah already, just wait until they heard this one — they'd all die laughing.

She slid out of bed, put on the robe she'd tossed over her desk chair, and silently slipped out of her room on bare feet. She stepped over the creaky step on the stairs just in case her father wasn't quite as passed out as she thought he'd be, but when she went through the living room, he didn't so much as twitch.

Pepper was in his bed in the laundry room, and he got up and wagged his little stump of a tail when she came in, and she crouched down and petted him for a second just to make sure he didn't start whimpering or barking.

Then she peeked out the back door window.

Sarah was in Zach's sleeping bag.

Lying on the porch.

Still wearing her hat.

Perfect! Exactly what she deserved.

And for tonight, at least, she had her room all to herself again, the way it should be.

Which gave her another idea.

Giving Pepper one more pat on his head, Tiffany quietly retraced her steps until she was safely back in her room, then locked the door, just in case.

She crouched down in front of the dresser and opened the bottom drawer.

Sarah's drawer.

The bottle of pain pills was right where she'd left it when she took a few last week. She'd earned enough money from those to buy a new sweater, and now she wanted a skirt to go with it.

She even knew who her best customer was going to be: Conner West, who'd bought one of the pills last week and asked her for more.

Now she had more.

Silently, she closed the drawer, then unzipped her backpack, put the pills in her makeup kit and buried it in the bottom of her pack.

Then she took off her robe, slipped back into her warm bed, and snuggled down into her soft mattress, thinking of Sarah shivering out on the porch.

Whatever happened tomorrow, tonight at least had been a great evening.

No Sarah, and plenty of pills to sell in the morning.

CHAPTER TWELVE

Nick stamped his feet against the cold and flexed his fingers inside the mittens his mother had knit for him. He knew he'd be warmer if he kept moving but decided to try to walk to school with Sarah this morning, so for the last twenty minutes he'd been hanging around the corner closest to the Garveys' house, trying to keep an eye out for her while not appearing to wait for her. By now he was freezing, and if she didn't show up soon, he knew they'd never make it on time.

Maybe she was sick.

Maybe she wasn't coming at all.

Tiffany and Zach had left the house at least ten minutes ago and were probably inside the school building by now.

The nice, *warm* school building.

When Conner West drove by — flipping Nick the bird as he passed — Nick glanced at his watch. He'd give her another minute and then —

The Garveys' front door opened and Sarah appeared, gripping the railing tightly as she made her way down the three steps of the front porch.

And then the voices in Nick's head — the voices that had begun babbling angrily as Conner West lifted his finger at him a minute ago — fell silent as Sarah caught sight of him and waved.

Nick hurried toward her. Maybe if he carried her book bag they could still get to school on time, but when he caught up to Sarah, he stopped short. She looked as if she'd barely slept at all. "Hey," he said. "Are you okay?"

"Fine," she said, but the way she kept her eyes down told him she wasn't telling the truth.

"You don't look fine," he said, then realizing how that sounded, felt his face burning and tried to find better words. "I mean, you look great — really pretty, but —" He reached for her backpack. "Let me carry that, okay?"

Sarah stopped long enough to let him slip it off her shoulders. "I didn't get much sleep."

"What happened?" Nick pressed.

Sarah hesitated, then offered Nick a careless shrug that he didn't believe any more than he'd believed her words when she told him she was fine. "They made me sleep outside," she finally admitted.

Nick stopped short, staring at her. "They made you sleep *outside? Why?*"

Instead of answering his question, Sarah pulled the collar of her coat tighter and started down the street. "We have to hurry or we'll be late."

"It's November! They can't make you sleep outside." Nick tugged on the shoulder of her coat until she stopped walking. "You should tell someone. Don't you have, like, a social worker or something?"

"No!" Sarah looked up at him with such fear that Nick took a step backward. "If I tell anyone, the Garveys won't let me go see my father."

"How can they do that? I mean, he's your father! Will you please tell me what's going on?"

Sarah kept walking, but finally began telling Nick what had happened yesterday, starting with going to church, then recounting everything right up to coming home and finding the note on the sleeping bag.

They were just across the street from the school when she abruptly stopped walking. "There was one more thing, too," she went on. "I drew this weird picture up at Miss Philips's house. It showed this dark room filled with skeletons." Nick felt a tingle at the back of his neck, and on the edge of his consciousness he thought he could hear the voices whispering among themselves. "It was like I was possessed or something," Sarah finished, her voice dropping to a whisper so low he could barely hear it.

"Like I feel," he said softly. "Only I feel like that most of the time." As they started across the street, Nick finally told her what had happened to him last night. "It was really awful — I mean, I think my dad wants to send me back to the hospital."

"What were they about?" Sarah asked, stopping at the foot of the steps leading to the school's front doors. "I mean, the stuff you saw. What was it?"

Now it was Nick who shrugged, but the voices in his head were murmuring a little louder. "Just weird stuff — really thick black bars . . ." He groped for a better word. "Like huge beams or something, you know? Like —"

"What time was it?" Sarah cut in.

Now the voices were getting louder, but they weren't shouting at him, and they weren't screaming or howling in fury or pain. It seemed they wanted him to tell her about them. "It started while we were eating dinner," Nick said. "Then I went upstairs, hoping my dad wouldn't see how bad it was, but I guess I started throwing things or something, and they finally came up and gave me a shot."

"What time?" Sarah pressed. "I mean, what time did they give you the shot?"

"About eight, I guess. But I don't really know."

"That's about when I left Miss Philips's house," Sarah said. "And the room I drew while you were seeing something has really heavy rafters on the ceiling."

The voices sounded even more excited now, and suddenly in the periphery of his vision Nick caught a glimpse of something.

A skull?

But it was gone as quickly as it had come, and he couldn't be sure. "I don't remember exactly — it was really dark, and the voices were screaming like they were people being tortured or killed or —" He shook his head. "I don't even want to think about it." He moved up the steps and pulled open the heavy door just as the bell rang. "You want to meet up after school?"

Sarah hesitated only a second, but that second seemed to Nick to go on and on. Then she nodded. "Sure."

By the time Nick slid into his seat in his first class — a moment too late to escape a glare from his teacher — he had decided on two things.

For the first time in his life, he would struggle to remember the hallucination he'd had, instead of trying to forget it.

And second, no one — not the Garveys or anyone else — would ever treat Sarah Crane as she'd been treated last night.

Never.

Conner West gazed dolefully down at the big red F on the corner of his English test, then wadded it up and tossed it expertly into the trash can that stood fifteen feet down the hall from his locker. If English were basketball, he'd ace the tests every time. As it was, the only way he could keep from flunking the course was to write a book report tonight for a few extra credit points. Or he could do a class presentation on one of the authors they were studying, but even Mrs. Roselle knew he wasn't going to do that. So it was the book report or nothing, and he couldn't just chuck his quarterly report card into the trash like he had the test.

Crap.

Now he'd have to eat lunch fast and spend

half the hour on one of the computers in the library trying to find CliffsNotes on the Internet for one of the books on the list Mrs. Roselle had handed him. Not that using the CliffsNotes was cheating — even old Mrs. Roselle knew he wasn't going to actually read the book.

"But you will do the writing, Conner," she'd told him when she held him after class a few minutes ago. "And don't think you can just copy and paste something — I've seen them all, and I have a program that will find anything new and compare your work to it. Even a little decent paraphrasing will do you enough good to get you a D. Okay?"

What was he supposed to say? If he didn't pass English, he might not graduate.

Even worse, his dad would take away his car keys.

"Mac and cheese for lunch again," Bobby Fendler said as he opened the locker next to Conner's.

"Swell!" Conner said, slamming his locker door and spinning the dial on the lock. "Just freakin' *swell! If* it's like yesterday's, I'll hurl in study hall."

"Hey, Conner," a voice he recognized as Tiffany Garvey's said from behind him. Suddenly things were looking up.

And things were looking even better when he turned around, saw the look in Tiffany's eyes, and remembered the pills she'd been selling last week. If she had more —

"Want to take me to McDonald's?" Tiffany asked, twirling a lock of her blond hair around a finger and running her tongue over her lower lip in a way that drove any thoughts of spending part of the next hour in the library out of his mind.

"Sure," he said. But even as he spoke, he remembered the condition of his wallet and glanced at Bobby Fendler. Bobby always had plenty of cash. "Want to go along?"

"Beats mac and cheese." Bobby was about to toss his backpack into his locker, but then eyed Tiffany speculatively. "We comin' back?"

Tiffany shrugged. "Depends."

"On what?"

"On what you buy," she replied. She glanced around to see who might be listening, then patted her own backpack. "You guys buy what I'm selling, and I'm going shopping after lunch."

Grabbing Elliot Nash on their way to the parking lot, Tiffany slid into the front seat next to Conner while the other two boys piled into the backseat. Conner floored the accelerator as he turned out of the parking lot, laying a strip of rubber that would take at least a thousand miles off the rear tires.

Ten minutes later they'd shouted their orders into the little speaker and waited for the carhop to bring their food.

"So," Tiffany said, leaning back against the passenger door of Conner's car and getting right to the point. "I've got more of those little blue jobbies."

"How much?" Conner asked.

"Ten bucks each," Tiffany said.

"Ten bucks?" Elliot Nash complained. "Oh, man, I don't have any money."

"Bobby does," Conner said, and glanced at Bobby in the rearview mirror. "Loan me twenty bucks, dude?"

"You haven't paid me the last twenty I loaned you."

"I will," Conner said. "I've got money at home. I'll pay this afternoon."

"Liar," Bobby grumbled, but still fished out his wallet and handed Conner a twenty.

"Can I borrow ten?" Elliot pleaded. "Please."

"This is why I stock the shelves at Wal-Mart?" Bobby demanded, but handed Elliot the ten. "But you guys are going to pay me back this time," he added. "Both of you." His eyes bored into Conner West's reflection in the mirror, but Conner only shrugged.

"Didn't I just tell you I would?"

Tiffany took the money from Bobby Fendler, tucked it deep into her backpack, then doled out four blue capsules, two for Conner and one for each of the boys in the backseat.

The food arrived, but suddenly Conner wasn't hungry anymore — the pills in his hand were already talking to him. Tiffany seemed to read his mind.

"Don't even think about taking that until after you drop me at the mall out by the prison," Tiffany said.

"Whatcha going to do after the mall?" Conner asked.

Tiffany rolled her eyes. "Nothing with you — you'll be so stoned you won't even be able to get in trouble."

Conner grinned, and dropped the pills into his shirt pocket. Maybe he wouldn't be able to get in any trouble with Tiffany Garvey, but so what? Who needed Tiffany?

There were plenty of other ways to make trouble.

Sarah sat at her art table and eyed the still life Miss Philips had arranged on the table: a crystal ball, fruit, a silver teapot, and a black-and-white china teacup edged in silver on a matching saucer, all laid out on a checkered cloth, the monochromatic pattern reflected in the mirrorlike polish of the teapot. A spotlight that Bettina Philips had set up to the right of the arrangement cast shadows and reflections everywhere, making the exercise one in executing light and shadow as well as portraying the still life itself.

Sarah decided she'd start by sketching the crystal ball, since it was totally in the foreground as everything else was slightly hidden behind it, but her fingers refused to pick up the charcoal pencil. Instead they hovered over the oil pastels, and without thinking about it, she picked up the medium brown.

With broad strokes, she centered the tabletop two-thirds down from the top of the page, but as she looked at the paper, she realized the light didn't come from the side as Miss Philips had indicated; it came from the big windows to the south, behind the man —

Wait a minute.

What man?

And what windows?

She looked up, and the still life was exactly as it had been a moment ago.

Nothing had changed at all.

But when she looked back at the paper —

It was as if there was an image inside the paper itself, trapped beneath its surface, struggling to get out.

Or trapped in her own mind, projecting itself onto the paper, demanding that she give it form and expose it to the light.

No longer thinking about what she was doing, Sarah let her hand move as if by its own volition, losing herself in the strange world she was creating.

Except she wasn't creating it — it was real; it existed somewhere, or had existed, or would exist, or —

Her hand moved faster, picking up one color after another, filling the paper with shapes and colors in bold, sure strokes, the classroom around her fading from her consciousness as her mind focused solely on the image that was quickly taking shape on the paper.

In his math classroom on the second floor, Nick Dunnigan's knuckles turned white as his fingers clamped the edges of his desk while he tried to keep the pain in his head at bay. But it wasn't working.

And this afternoon it wasn't just the voices raging at him, but something else as well.

A dog!

A dog that was howling in either fury or in agony or both. And one of the voices was growing, rising above the rest, erupting with a hideous laughter that slashed through Nick's mind like a ripsaw.

As the screeching laughter built and the dog's howling grew along with it, Nick saw a flicker of motion at the periphery of his vision and felt his guts twist in fear at what might come next. A second later it was there — a huge yellow dog, leaping toward him out of a strange blackness, its mouth gaping, its fangs dripping with saliva, its fury still boiling from its throat.

As the howling grew and the maniacal laughter reached a crescendo, the throbbing in Nick's head threatened to explode his skull, and the yellow mass that was the dog exploded into a blaze of crimson that wiped everything else from his sight.

Whimpering against the hell into which he was quickly descending, Nick Dunnigan offered up a silent prayer of deliverance.

Deliverance for himself, and for the howling dog as well, for now, as his vision began to fade, the fury in the dog's fading howl drained away into nothing more than a dying gurgle.

Sarah's head snapped up as Bettina Philips

rose from the chair behind her desk and clapped her hands twice. "All right, we only have a few minutes left, so let's start cleaning up our tables and putting things away."

Sarah's eyes shifted from the teacher to the clock on the wall — was it possible the class was almost over? But it couldn't be — she'd only been working for a few minutes! Yet there it was: in four more minutes the final bell of the day would ring.

Then her gaze shifted again, to the sheet of paper spread out on the table in front of her.

No, she thought. I couldn't have drawn this — I couldn't!

Silence dropped over Nick like a shroud, wiping away the hallucinations as completely as it cut off the voices in his head. Yet even with his eyes closed, he could still see the image of the dying dog, etched into his memory forever. He tried to close it out, banish it as he was banishing the tension that had strained every muscle in his body. He sat unmoving, his spine ramrod straight, his eyes focused on a spot directly ahead. He could feel his classmates looking at him and starting to whisper among themselves, but he didn't care. All he wanted was one thing.

He wanted to see Sarah Crane.
He *needed* to see her.

Sarah stared at the drawing in front of her, the shock of what she had done hitting her with the force of a baseball bat.

Barely able to breathe, her eyes fixed on the sepia-brown image of a screaming man, his arm in the jaws of a pain-crazed dog whose intestines had exploded from its belly and were spilled across a table in a swath of crimson-tinged gore. In his hand, the man held a scalpel still dripping with blood and glinting in the sunlight refracted from the tall windows behind him.

A terrible numbness began to spread through her. How could she have done this? And worse, what would Bettina Philips think when she saw it? Quickly folding the drawing in half before anyone else could get even a glimpse of it, she thought quickly.

"Any questions?" Miss Philips asked the class.

The bell rang and everybody stood up, eager to get out of the building for the day.

"Put your drawings on my desk," she said over the growing din of the students already preparing for their release from school. "And don't forget to put your names on them."

As the students started making their way toward the front of the room, Sarah hung back, folded her drawing again and slipped it deep into her backpack.

Nobody — nobody at all — was going to see this drawing.

Except that even as the thought formed in her mind, she knew it wasn't true.

One person would see the drawing.

She needed to find Nick.

She needed to find him now.

Nick knew something was wrong as soon as he saw Sarah coming down the main staircase. Her face was ashen and her limp even worse than usual, but he said nothing until he pushed one of the school's heavy front doors open and they were both in the bright sunlight outside. "What's going on?" he asked, relieving her of her backpack as they started down the stairs. "Are you sick?"

On the sidewalk, Sarah shook her head, taking a deep breath of the frosty air. "I just had a weird experience in art class — I mean, like, *really* weird! Remember how I told you about getting so lost in drawing a picture that I hardly even remembered doing it?" Nick's pulse quickened but he only nodded, saying nothing. "Well, this afternoon the drawing was even worse than the one last night," Sarah said as they crossed the street. "It was awful," she went on, and shuddered as they kept walking. "I mean, *really* awful."

Nick stopped and turned to face her, and Sarah stopped, too. "Did you turn it in?"

She rolled her eyes. "Are you kidding?"

"So where is it?" he asked, and when Sarah hesitated, he knew she had it with her. "Let me see it."

Her eyes met his for a moment, and he thought she was about to refuse. But instead of shaking her head she tilted it toward her backpack, looped over his shoulder. "It's in there — way down at the bottom."

Nick unzipped the top and pulled out a folded piece of heavy art paper, then hesitated, no longer sure he actually wanted to see it. But he knew that whether he wanted to see the drawing or not, he had to.

He had to know.

Struggling to keep his fingers from trembling, he unfolded the sheet of paper and looked at the image.

"Oh, jeez . . ." he whispered, his voice trailing off as he took in the nightmarish image of an eviscerated dog attacking its tormentor. When he'd taken in every detail, he folded it up again and shoved it back into Sarah's backpack.

She stared at him, waiting for him to say something, but instead he just began walking again. She fell in beside him, and for several minutes neither of them spoke. Then, when they were three blocks from the school, Nick broke the silence. "I saw what you drew," he said softly. Then: "I even heard the dog."

Sarah gazed at him, thinking she knew what he meant but hoping she was wrong. "What are you talking about? What do you mean, you saw —"

"I heard a dog howling. I mean, really screaming. And then I saw it, too. This huge, yellowish dog, coming right at me and —"

"When?" Sarah broke in. Again she was certain she knew and tried to cast around for something else.

Something other than the truth.

"You mean last night?" she went on.

Nick shook his head, as she knew he would. "Just now," he said, his voice low. "My last period — math class. I had this horrible hallucination. At least I thought it was a hallucination. But —" He hesitated, trying to find some other explanation, but found nothing. "It was like I was seeing and hearing what you were drawing. *While you were drawing it!*"

Sarah stopped walking, his words hanging

between them. "I — I don't understand," she said quietly.

He opened his mouth to speak, but before he could say anything there was a screeching of tires, and then a car slammed to a stop in the street next to them.

Conner West was behind the wheel, and Elliot Nash and Bobby Fendler rode with him. The way Conner was leering at them told Nick he was stoned.

Or drunk.

Or both.

He was just reaching out to take Sarah's hand, to lead her away, when Conner slid out of the driver's door, slammed it, and came around the front of the car and on to the sidewalk, to stand facing them. Conner's shoulders were slouched, his hands on his hips. "What are you two doing here by my house?" he demanded.

At the sound of Conner's voice, a big German shepherd came bounding around from behind the house Conner was pointing at, barking wildly, then ran back and forth along the cyclone fence between the house's front yard and the sidewalk.

With the dog's first loud bark, the voices in Nick's head came alive, chattering as insanely as the dog was barking, but he couldn't understand a word they were saying.

There were too many of them, and they were too loud, and the dog was howling now and —

Elliot Nash and Bobby Fendler got out of the car too, and Sarah shrank back as they started toward her, their eyes glazed, their lips twisted into dangerous smirks.

Nick struggled against the chaos rising in his head, but before he could formulate a word, Sarah took him by the arm. "C'mon," she whispered. "Let's just go."

His hand in Sarah's, he took a step forward, but Conner moved to block him.

"Just leave us alone," Sarah said to Conner.

"Why should we?" Conner snarled back. "I'm asking you again. Who said you could be here, next to my house?"

The dog was still racing along the cyclone fence, barking furiously.

Sarah hesitated, but as she gazed at the three boys, she suddenly decided she'd had enough. "Do you own the sidewalk?" she asked.

"We all own the sidewalk," Elliot Nash shot back. "And there's more of us than there are of you, and we don't want you on our sidewalk. Get it?"

Nick's voices began to howl as he heard Elliot's words.

"And if you don't get it, my dog will teach you all about it," Conner said. "He's a police dog."

"You wouldn't —" Sarah began, but Conner West was already calling out to the dog.

"C'mon, King! C'mon boy — sic 'em!"

The dog lunged against the cyclone fence, then dropped back and abruptly stopped barking. He crouched low to the ground, his lips curling back to expose long, sharp fangs.

A dangerous growl emerged from the animal's throat, and Elliot Nash backed off a step. "C'mon, Conner," he said, sounding nowhere near as confident as he'd been a moment ago. "Maybe —"

As the snarling dog tensed, backing up to hurl itself over the fence, Nick squeezed Sarah's hand so tightly she thought her bones would break. "The barking," he whispered. "The howling. It's all happening again." The voices were screaming in his head now, but one of them was rising above the cacophony of the others.

"Kill it!" the voice screamed. *"Kill it now!"*

Then Conner West was screaming, too: "Get 'em, King! Sic 'em!"

As the chaos in Nick's head began to

blend with reality, his life went into slow motion.

The snarling dog took a great leap and cleared the fence, launching itself at Sarah, teeth bared in a snarl.

She froze as she recalled her drawing. The dog she'd drawn — *was it a German shepherd?* — had its mouth agape exactly as did the beast that was hurtling toward her!

But this animal wasn't dying — it was attacking, its fangs dripping with saliva, its eyes glittering with fury. Yet it was the same dog.

She *knew* it was the same dog.

And there was nothing she could do to stop it. In another second its jaws would close on her neck, its fangs slash through her skin to tear at her flesh, its —

Nick's eyes, too, were fastened on the huge shepherd cresting the fence and plunging toward Sarah, but its snarl was overwhelmed by the voice rising in his head, with more fury even than that of the dog.

"Kill it — kill it — kill it now!"

Nick's right hand rose, but it wasn't just his hand he saw reaching to protect Sarah, to fend off the attacking dog. Now there was a knife in it, a great, glittering blade, curving upward and ending in a dagger point.

As the dog dropped toward Sarah, Nick held the knife out, and a second later he jerked it upward, twisting it as it slashed into the dog's belly, then ripped upward into its chest. A howl of pure rage rose from Nick's throat, and he jerked on the knife once more.

As the dog's torn body dropped to the ground only inches from Sarah's feet, and blood began gushing from the great gaping wound that had torn its entire torso open, Nick's eyes fixed on the knife in his hand.

But there was no knife.

His hand was empty.

And the voices in his head were now gone.

Conner West was staring at the dog he had only a moment ago commanded to attack Nick and Sarah. Now, so fast he could barely believe it, the animal was sprawled on the sidewalk, its intestines spilling out onto the cement, its feet flailing, faint snarls emanating from its throat. *"What did you do?"* he screamed, dropping to his knees next to the dying dog. As he reached out to touch his pet, the dog's eyes suddenly fixed on him, and then it lashed out, sinking his fangs into his master's forearm.

Conner's scream of rage dissolved into agony as he tore his arm loose from his dog's jaws.

A moment later the dog lay dead in the fading afternoon sunlight.

"You killed him," Conner said, holding his bleeding arm and gasping for breath. "You killed my dog!"

Bobby and Elliot were backing away as Conner rose up from the dog's carcass and moved toward Nick.

Elliot Nash grabbed the sleeve of Conner's jacket. "Don't, man — let's just get out of here." He tried to pull Conner back, but Conner wouldn't move as he glared at Nick.

"You killed him, you little fu—" he began, but before he could finish, the front door of the house next door opened and a woman stepped out on the porch, a telephone pressed to her ear. "It's Conner and those friends of his, and Nick Dunnigan," she said, raising her voice so none of the teenagers on the sidewalk could mistake what she was saying. "I don't know who the girl is . . . The dog looks like it's dead . . . I don't *know* how they did it . . . I'll be here." Now she came down the steps of her porch and started toward them. "And so will they. None of them are going anywhere."

As the woman approached, Sarah barely even saw her, let alone heard what she was saying.

She couldn't move, couldn't speak.

That dog had bitten Conner exactly like the one she'd drawn in class had bitten its tormentor.

Except in the drawing, the man held a scalpel.

But Nick Dunnigan's hand had been empty.

He'd held it up to protect her, but he had no weapon.

He'd had nothing at all.

But now the dog lay dead, its belly laid open clear up to its throat.

It wasn't possible.

And yet, it had happened . . .

CHAPTER THIRTEEN

Angie Garvey drove the four short blocks to Dan West's house, her hands gripping the steering wheel so hard her knuckles were white. The last thing she needed on a busy Monday was a call from the sheriff, asking her to come and pick up Sarah Crane.

No, not asking her to. *Telling* her to. Maybe taking in a foster child had been a mistake.

She pulled to a stop in front of the house next door to the Wests' just as Lily Dunnigan was getting out of her car and crossing the street, where a knot of people — and Angie could see both Sarah and Nick Dunnigan among them — were gathered in front of the Wests' house. And there was something on the sidewalk, covered with what looked to Angie like a bloody towel.

"Thanks for coming, Ange," Dan West said. "We've had . . . ." He paused for a second, as if searching for the right word.

". . . an incident here, and I'd like your permission to search Sarah and her backpack." He turned to Lily Dunnigan. "And Nick and his book bag, too."

Angie's lips compressed into a tight line. What could Sarah have done? Unless, of course, it was Nick Dunnigan who was responsible for whatever led Dan West to call her. Well, this was the last time Sarah would be having anything to do with Nick — everyone in town knew they never should have let him out of the mental hospital. "Search anything you want," Angie said. "But I still want to know what . . ." Her voice trailed off as she saw the four canine feet sticking out from under the blood-soaked towel. "Did someone run over a dog?"

"My dog," Dan said. "And nobody ran over him — his belly's slit open."

Angie's eyes shifted to Sarah, but it seemed that Sarah hadn't even noticed she was there. She was just standing like an idiot, staring at the ground.

"I don't believe it," Lily Dunnigan said, moving to slip her arm around her son's shoulder. "Nick would never do anything like that."

Nick tried to shrug his mother's arm off. "Conner sicced him on us. He jumped over

229

the fence like he was going after Sarah, then started bleeding. Then he just sort of fell onto the sidewalk and . . ." Now it was Nick's voice that trailed off as he couldn't bring himself to repeat what he'd seen.

Lily looked over at the cyclone fence that surrounded the Wests' property, taking in the sharp ends of twisted wire that ran the entire length of its top. "He must have cut himself on the fence."

Dan West shook his head. "There's no fur or blood on the fence. And the wound looks more like a cut than a tear, but we'll leave that for the vet to determine."

"I went to nursing school," Angie said. "Let's just take a look." She lifted the towel, then quickly dropped it again as her gorge rose. "Oh, my sweet Lord."

"*He's* the one who did it," Bobby Fendler said, jabbing a finger in Nick's direction.

"Okay, just cool it," Dan West said, putting a hand on Bobby's shoulder and squeezing it hard enough to give the boy a warning that was a lot stronger than his words. "We've all heard what you think." He turned to Lily and Angie. "The thing is, there's no blood on anybody except Conner, and he says the dog bit him while he was trying to help it. Must have been so far gone, the dog didn't even know him. But

230

nobody could do this without getting some blood on them."

"Where *is* Conner?" Lily asked.

"My wife took him to the hospital."

"So what are you looking for?" Angie asked.

"Don't know," Dan West admitted. "But I figured I should get permission from you and Lily before I went through their stuff. I mean, since it's my dog and my son involved, I didn't want anyone saying I planted anything on any of these kids."

Angie snatched Sarah's backpack from her and thrust it at Dan. "Search whatever you want," she said. "If Sarah had anything to do with this, I want to know about it, too."

"I should start with Nick," Dan said, shifting his attention to Lily Dunnigan. "I mean, since Elliot and Bobby say they think he —"

"Elliot and Bobby would say anything if it kept them out of trouble," Lily cut in. "And they'd blame Nick, too, if they thought they could get away with it. So take a look — whatever you're hoping to find, Nick won't have it."

Nick stepped over to the sheriff.

"Spread your legs and put your arms out straight," Dan said. "Do you have any weapons on your person or in your back-pack?"

"No," Nick answered.

Dan felt each of his pockets, patted him down, then opened Nick's backpack and emptied the contents onto the sidewalk. Except for his books, a notebook, some pens, and a half-empty water bottle, there was nothing.

Satisfied that Nick held nothing incriminating, Dan West turned his attention to Sarah's backpack, and a few seconds later was unfolding the picture Sarah had drawn less than an hour ago.

Angie took one look at the image and knew instantly that whatever had happened to the sheriff's dog, Sarah Crane — the child of a convicted murderer — had something to do with it.

The girl was a bad seed — Angie knew it!

Dan's face paled as he took in the carnage depicted on the paper — carnage matched by the remains of the dog on the sidewalk. Then he turned to Sarah. "Did you draw this?"

Sarah nodded. "In art class," she whispered.

"In *Bettina Philips's* art class," Angie added, her voice trembling with fury.

Right away, Sarah knew that Angie would

somehow try to blame her teacher for what had happened. "But she's never even seen it. I didn't turn it in — she didn't have anything to do with that drawing, and I didn't have anything to do with —"

"It's devil worship," Angie said, pointing to the drawing Dan West was still holding in his hands. "Animal sacrifice — that's what they do! They sacrifice innocent animals so —"

"Let's just take it easy, Angie," Dan said. "Instead of making wild accusations, why don't you let me get to the bottom of this?"

"You won't find a bottom," Angie said, her voice hard, her eyes fixed on Sarah. "Evil is bottomless. Inexhaustible."

Dan took a deep breath and finished searching Sarah's backpack, finding no more than the same collection of books and pens that he'd found in Nick's.

No knives, no bloody rags they might have used to clean blood off themselves, nothing.

"Okay," he said, his eyes moving among the four kids, looking for something — anything — that might give him a hint as to what had happened here. But as with the backpacks and Conner's car, there was nothing. "You can all go home, but you all need to understand that this investigation is not over. It's just beginning, and you can be certain that I will find out what happened to our dog."

Elliot and Bobby began to walk away.

"What about them?" Lily Dunnigan demanded. "Why didn't you call *their* parents? Why didn't you search *their* backpacks?"

"Because nobody accused them of anything," Dan West replied, making no effort to keep the impatience out of his voice. "And you can believe I searched Conner's car and everything that's in it. Even Nick and Sarah said Elliot and Bobby didn't do anything, but Conner and Bobby both say that Nick did it, and Elliot said Sarah was close enough to the dog to have done it, too."

As Lily Dunnigan led Nick to her car, and Dan West opened the trunk of his cruiser, took out a tarp, and began to wrap up the dog, Sarah put her things back into her backpack. Angie watched, her blood pressure rising, and when Sarah was finally ready, Angie wordlessly marched back to her car, starting it before Sarah even got in beside her.

Her silence lasted no longer than it took her to pull away from the curb. "Where did you go last night when you stormed out of the house like a spoiled brat?"

"I just went out walking," Sarah said.

"Walking," Angie repeated, her voice dripping with sarcasm. "With that leg and hip, you went out walking for hours when it was freezing."

Sarah looked up and met her gaze squarely. "I haven't done anything wrong," she said with infuriating calm.

Angie's blood pressure spiked, shooting into the red zone, and her temper along with it. "So far you've lied and been disobedient and disrespectful, and now you're dallying with the devil." She paused to take a deep breath. "I know what that picture means," she went on. Then she turned to look straight at Sarah, her eyes as cold as the air outside. "God will judge you, young lady," she said. "But before He does, Mitch will. And so will I."

Sarah didn't know which was worse — listening to Angie Garvey's tirade about the "evil" she was "carrying inside her like the seed of the devil," or the ominous silence that fell over the house as she sat at the dining room table waiting for Mitch Garvey to come home. When he finally came through the back door at five minutes before six, the first thing he did was pull a beer out of the refrigerator, crack it open, and start through the dining room on the way to the living room, where his couch and TV were waiting.

"What's your problem?" he growled as he glanced at Sarah. "How come you're not settin' the table or workin' on dinner?"

"Family meeting," Angie announced before Sarah could say a word. Then she yelled up the stairs for Tiffany and Zach to come down.

Mitch, looking annoyed even before Angie told him what had happened that afternoon, sat at his usual place at the table, his eyes fixed balefully on Sarah. "What'd you do to piss your mother off this time?" he demanded.

Sarah bit back the first words that rose to her tongue. What good would it do to remind Mitch that Angie wasn't her mother at all, that her mother was dead? That would only make him madder. Deciding a noncommittal shrug was her best option, she said nothing, and a moment later Zach and Tiffany came pounding down the stairs. One look at the tableau in the dining room told them Sarah was in trouble, and they slid eagerly into their chairs.

"Dan West called me this afternoon," Angie said, her eyes boring into Sarah. "Someone slashed his dog. Slashed him to death. And Conner's at the hospital."

Sarah saw Tiffany stiffen and her eyes flick anxiously, first toward her mother, then toward her father, but she didn't say anything.

"So why did Dan call you?" Mitch asked.

"Because," Angie announced, once again fixing Sarah with a cold gaze, "our little Satan-worshipper here was involved. Dan had to search her backpack right there on the sidewalk for the whole town to see. I hate to think what everyone must be saying."

Sarah didn't need to look up to know that all eyes were now on her, and she could actually feel Angie's fury and Tiffany and Zach's hatred closing around her until it seemed she was suffocating.

"It was humiliating," Angie spat.

"So what did Sarah do?" Zach asked. "She really kill Conner's dog?"

"Dan doesn't know yet," Angie replied. "But she did do this!" She threw Sarah's drawing on the table, and Sarah could hear Tiffany's gasp as she caught sight of the bloodied dog she'd limned on the paper.

"Holy crap," Zach whispered. "That's too weird!"

"I'm not letting her sleep in my room anymore," Tiffany said, her eyes moving from the picture to her mother. "You can't

237

make me!"

"So what was going on?" Mitch asked, ignoring Tiffany, at least for the moment. "Who else was there?"

"Two friends of Conner's," Angie replied, then paused for a moment. "And Nick Dunnigan."

"Nick Dunnigan?" Mitch echoed. "He's kinda nuts, but I never heard of him hurtin' anything but himself. And what's this picture got to do with it? Sarah draw it after whatever happened happened?"

"She drew it *before* the dog died," Angie said. "And then the dog got torn open, just the way our little Sarah here drew it!"

"So who had the knife?" Zach asked. "Sarah?"

"That's the thing," Angie said, her eyes fixing yet again on Sarah. "There was no knife. At least not that anyone saw or anyone found."

"C'mon, Ange," Mitch said, draining half his beer. "If no one had a knife — or a scalpel like in the picture — how'd the dog die?"

Angie Garvey's features darkened. "Witchcraft," she pronounced.

"Aw, Ange, come on . . ." Mitch began, but Angie cut him off.

"She drew this picture in *Bettina Philips's*

238

class, and half an hour later it all came to pass! Just like she drew it!"

"Isn't that what we said?" Tiffany spat. "Didn't we say just last night that the same kind of evil that got her mom and dad would get her, too?"

"That'll be about enough —" Mitch began again, but this time it was his daughter who brushed his words away.

"It won't be enough until she's out of here," Tiffany raged. "I'm not living in the same room with someone like her, and you can't make me!"

While his sister went on talking, Zach turned the picture toward him for a closer look. "Jeez, that looks exactly like King — how'd she know what he looks like? And how'd she get crazy Nick to —" He cut off his own words, snickering. "Never mind — he's crazy, right?" He looked up at his mother. "So what are we 'sposed to do with her?"

Sarah felt like she must have suddenly turned invisible. How could he talk that way, like she wasn't even here? But she said nothing, waiting to hear what would come next.

"I'm going to call Kate Williams," Angie said. "She can come get Sarah right now."

Sarah's heart leaped with unexpected

hope. Was it possible — actually *possible?* — that she might not have to spend even another night here?

"Now just hold on," Mitch said. "Everybody needs to just slow down."

"Dad!" Tiffany screeched. "How could you let some — some *thing* like this live in our house? After what she's done?"

"You think money grows on trees?" Mitch asked, then turned from his daughter to his wife. "You know that big-screen TV we talked about for the bedroom? Well, it was supposed to be a surprise, but it's being delivered tomorrow. And that county money's gonna pay for it." Angie silently crossed her arms in front of her chest, her furious eyes fixed on her husband, but Mitch didn't flinch in the face of his wife's anger. "We knew goin' in that we were gonna have a problem child living with us. I don't know why you're so surprised that something happened."

Please call Kate Williams, Sarah prayed silently. *Please call her.*

"Now, I don't like having her here any more than any of the rest of you, but we planned our finances based on what the county pays us for her housing, so we're just going to have to suck it up and deal with it."

Tiffany rose from the table. "You've *got* to be kidding!"

For the first time, Mitch squirmed a little. "Maybe she can sleep in the attic or something," he offered, but Tiffany only turned away.

"I'm locking my door," she announced. "And I don't care where she sleeps, as long as it's nowhere near me!" She marched out of the dining room, and a moment later Sarah heard her pounding up the stairs.

The bedroom door slammed.

And Sarah suddenly felt dizzy. What was happening? Where was she going to go? If they'd only call Kate —

"You can get your stuff when Tiffany's in the bathroom," Angie said, and Sarah felt a flash of hope. "And then I'll show you where you're going to sleep from now on."

Sarah's brief moment of hope crashed down around her as she realized everything had been decided.

She wasn't going anywhere.

Something in the house had changed.

Bettina felt it the moment she opened the back door of Shutters and stepped into the mud room. Yet what could have changed? Maybe she was tired — it had been a long day at school.

And yet . . .

Maybe it was the silence — usually when she opened the door, Rocky, the half-terrier, half-everything-else mutt she'd rescued from the woods five years ago was there to greet her, barking happily, rolling around on his back hoping to have his tummy rubbed.

Today there was no sign of him, nor were any of the cats staring pointedly at their empty food bowls. In fact, none of the cats were around at all.

Bettina set the portfolio of her students' work on the folding table next to the washing machine, took off her coat and unwrapped the scarf from her neck, and hung them on the hooks by the back door. Then she pulled on the bulky wool cardigan that was always waiting by the door to ward off the chill of the house until she got at least the kitchen warmed up.

And today the house seemed even colder than usual.

Cold, and something else.

What?

She stood still, listening.

Nothing.

But even the silence didn't reassure her, for as she moved toward the kitchen, the sense that the aura of the house had changed grew stronger.

Was someone here? Had someone come into the house while she was gone?

No.

It wasn't that — it was something else. It was as if the house itself had somehow changed since she left for school this morning.

She was inside the kitchen now, and had just picked up the teakettle to freshen its water, when she felt the skin on the back of her neck tingle.

She was not alone in the kitchen.

Someone, or some*thing,* was watching her.

"Wh-Who is it?" she said, her voice sounding preternaturally loud to her own ears.

Nothing.

She started to set the teakettle down, then changed her mind. It was still half full from this morning, and though it wasn't much, it was something.

Something to fend off whoever was behind her.

Bettina gripped the kettle's handle harder, steeled herself, then spun around.

And saw nothing.

Nothing except Cooper, the black mostly lab that had stumbled out of the woods a week after she'd taken Rocky in, knocked over three easels and a table within the first hour, and never left. Now he was sitting quietly in front of the door that led to the basement, staring at her.

"What are you doing?" she asked him. "Guarding the basement? Is something down there?" She started toward the door, and a low rumbling issued forth from the dog. Bettina took a step back and the dog seemed to relax. "Coopie?" she went on. "What's going on? I rescue you, feed you, I let you move in with me, and now you won't even let me go down into my own basement?" But even as she spoke, she realized that she didn't want to go down to the basement — didn't want to at all. Suddenly, just the thought of the steep narrow stairs, the dank walls, the musky smell, and cobwebby beams . . .

Those beams . . .

The beams Sarah had drawn. A shiver ran though Bettina, and she looked at the dog again. What was going on? Had he read her mind?

Or did he, too, feel the change in the house?

The teakettle began to steam, and she made a cup of tea, telling herself she was being silly. This wasn't the first time she'd felt strange in the house — even afraid. But all those other times were different; she'd been alone, watching the kind of movie that was designed to instill terror even in people in crowded theaters, let alone single women living by themselves in exactly the kind of house those movies depicted so well.

But tonight she wasn't watching a movie, and things just didn't feel right.

And Cooper, who usually lay at her feet wherever she was, was still at the door to the basement steps, sitting quietly and watching her.

And where were the other animals?

As if on cue, Pyewackett, the orange tabby cat she'd named after a cat in an old movie she watched the night she brought him home, padded in through the door to the butler's pantry and wound himself around her legs.

Stupid. She was just being stupid — everything was fine!

With Pyewackett trailing along behind her, but Cooper staying at his self-appointed post in the kitchen, Bettina took her cup of tea and her portfolio into the studio. But rather than ignoring the gloom of the rooms she passed — and escaping paying for the electricity it would take to light them — this evening she switched on every light she came to, driving the darkness as far away as she could.

Thick fog pressed up against the enormous conservatory windows, and instead of seeing the vast expanse of near-frozen lawn sweeping down to the icy lake, all Bettina saw in the windows was a reflection of herself that, for a fleeting instant, almost seemed to be someone else altogether — a woman she recognized as herself, but who was no longer safe inside the house. Instead she was vanishing into the mists outside.

Stop it, she told herself. Don't get started. Just do what you came in here to do.

She laid her portfolio on the drafting table, unzipped it, and pulled out the work her students had done that day. Those from her last class — Sarah Crane's class — were on top, and Bettina flipped through them, looking for the best student's contribution to her evening workload.

And found nothing.

Nothing but the usual collection of sketches ranging from uninspired to barely recognizable, but nothing from Sarah.

What had happened? Sarah had been in class, and while the still-life arrangement was obviously a challenge for many of her students, Sarah would have had no trouble with it.

But she had turned nothing in at the end of the period.

Bettina was halfway through the stack of drawings when she suddenly jerked upright.

An instant later there was a crash from somewhere above, and Pyewackett dashed off to investigate.

But her reflex — the sudden contraction of every muscle in her body and the flush of adrenaline surging into her blood — had happened *before* the crash.

Only an instant, but still, she felt the shock before she'd heard the sound.

How was that possible?

Pulling her cardigan closer around her, she started after Pyewackett, then hesitated. Maybe she should call the police, then wait right where she was until —

Until what? What was she going to tell the police? That the house didn't feel right and that she'd heard a crash from upstairs like something falling? She lived with five animals, and everyone in town knew it — was she expecting them to come out and investigate a broken vase simply because she was too frightened of her own house to do it herself?

Besides, if something was truly amiss — *if someone was in the house* — both Cooper and Rocky would be barking their heads off.

Rocky!

Of course — that was it. Rocky — who had turned out to be even clumsier than Cooper on his worst day — had probably tried to jump up on her bed and succeeded only in hitting the nightstand.

Still, before she went upstairs to investigate, she went back to the kitchen, where Cooper was still at his post by the basement door. "Come on, Coop — let's go see what Rocky's gotten into now."

The big dog didn't move.

"Please?"

Cooper hesitated, casting one more suspicious look at the basement door, but then rose to his feet and followed Bettina to the foot of the stairs. But instead of bounding ahead of her as he usually did, this evening the dog lagged behind, staying a step or two back and seeming ready to change his mind when they reached the landing.

Had he heard something?

Bettina paused, too, and listened.

Nothing.

Nothing except a tendril of cold air that seemed to be wafting down from above, bringing with it a chill that made her skin crawl and brought a low growl to Cooper's throat. "Come on!" Bettina demanded, but wondering even as she issued the command whether she was directing it at the dog or herself.

She mounted the second half of the flight, but now there was something else: the air smelled dank and musty.

Like the basement.

Bettina's heart began to hammer in her chest. What was it? What was going on? "A window must be broken," she whispered out loud. The words didn't even sound convincing to herself.

At the top of the stairs, Forlorn, the gray tabby with one ear and no tail, and an expression that had given him his name the moment Bettina first saw him, sat staring at one of the walls with such intensity that she involuntarily followed his gaze.

Again, nothing.

Just a blank wall, unadorned with anything that might have caught the cat's attention. She scooped him up and held his warm body close, but even the cat's heat couldn't penetrate the cold that filled the long corridor.

None of the doors were open.

And two of the animals were still missing.

She started down the corridor, listening at every door before she opened it, then reaching in to switch on a light before pushing the door wide.

All the rooms were empty.

Nothing seemed to be wrong.

And yet nothing felt right.

She had just pulled the door to the blue bedroom closed when the silence of the house was shattered by Rocky's yapping bark, and a second later the little terrier came running down the stairs from the third floor. Charging down the corridor, he hurled himself into Bettina's arms, nearly knocking her over, and garnering a furious hiss from Forlorn.

"What is it?" Bettina demanded as she put the dog back on the floor. "What did you do?"

Rocky only tried to scramble back into her arms.

The temperature in the hallway seemed to drop even further, and the musty smell grew stronger.

Then, as Bettina watched, the last door on the right swung slowly inward, its hinges creaking.

Cooper's body stiffened and he pressed up against Bettina's legs.

A whimper emerged from Rocky's throat as Forlorn uttered a low hiss.

A terrible fear began to engulf Bettina, a terror that seemed to emanate from the room whose door was still creaking open.

Her mouth went dry. She wanted to turn and bolt back down the stairs, flee the house and go —

Go where?

Anywhere! She wanted to be anywhere but here, with the house feeling all wrong and the animals behaving as they never had before and doors opening by themselves and —

And then suddenly Houdini, the ancient — and stone-deaf — white cat who had been living with Bettina for almost twenty years, emerged from the room at the end of the hall.

And Pyewackett was right behind him.

Suddenly, with all the animals back around her, the spell seemed broken.

The house felt almost back to normal, except for the strange smell. Dropping Forlorn to the floor to join the rest of the menagerie, Bettina strode down the wide hallway to the last door, reached in to switch the chandelier on, then looked around.

Inside, a lamp lay broken on the floor — a big, ugly, old midcentury TV lamp in the form of a leaping wolf whose eyes glowed when it was turned on. Bettina had been terrified of it as a child and hated it as an adult.

Well, it was gone now, and good for Hou-

251

dini for having finally smashed it!

Mystery solved.

She switched off the light and pulled the door closed, shutting off the musty odor. She'd clean up the broken lamp and air out the room over the weekend.

It wasn't until she was back downstairs and in the kitchen that she wondered how Houdini — and Pyewackett, too — had gotten into that room in the first place. Even she hadn't been inside it in years. Too many years, actually, given the smell that had built up in it.

On the other hand, getting into closed spaces was what Houdini had always specialized in, which was exactly how he'd gotten his name.

Still . . .

Stop! Bettina told herself. Don't freak yourself out.

Shutters, after all, was just a house.

Wasn't it?

As the clock in the niche under the main stairs chimed nine, Bettina headed back up the stairs, this time to go to bed.

Houdini lay curled up on top of the pages of her thrice-great-grandfather's manuscript, which was mostly still on the bedside table where she'd left it.

But at least fifty pages were strewn over the floor around the table.

As the other four animals began settling themselves into their usual places for the night — all on her bed — Bettina stroked the white cat, who began to purr. "Whatcha been doing, sweetie? Reading the old man's tales?" Giving the cat another scratch, she stooped down to gather up the pages the cat had scattered as he made himself a little nest.

The pages in hand, Bettina perched on the edge of the bed, and began to re-assemble them, tapping them back into alignment. But when she tried to brush Houdini off the manuscript to return the stray pages to their place, the cat wouldn't go. And when she reached out to pick him up, the cat lowered his ears and hissed, lightning-fast claws slashing out and narrowly missing her hand.

Bettina jerked reflexively back. "Okay," she said. "You win."

She set the fifty-odd pages in her hand next to those the cat was lying on, and moved into her dressing room to get ready for bed. When she returned a few minutes later, now clad in her flannel pajamas and a thick robe, Houdini had shifted position.

Now he was lying on the stack of pages

he'd rejected when he first decided to turn the manuscript into a bed. And when Bettina tried once more to move the cat to the bed, Houdini narrowed his eyes again and snarled.

"What the hell is going on with you?" Bettina demanded. Then her eyes shifted to the rest of the animals, all of whom were sitting up and watching her intently, rather than curling into their usual nighttime balls of fur. "What's going on with *all* of you?"

Forlorn blinked innocently.

Rocky and Pyewackett twitched their tails.

Cooper jumped off the bed and went to the door, but instead of scratching to be let out, he only sat down, apparently planning to continue the sentry duty he'd been performing downstairs earlier.

But what was he standing sentry against?

Bettina put the thought out of her mind, certain that if she didn't, she'd scare herself out of any sleep at all. Besides, despite all her worries earlier — *oh, all right, her outright fear* — nothing had actually happened.

Nothing except an ugly lamp getting broken.

She slid into bed and tentatively reached for the manuscript, bracing herself against an attack from Houdini, but the cat simply sat where he was, watching her.

She picked up the manuscript and gazed at the top sheet. By chance, Houdini had knocked the pages off at the beginning of a story — if that's what the collection was — entitled "Carnivore."

Apt, considering how many of that exact kind of animal she was currently surrounded by. She hesitated.

Maybe this wasn't the best night to read any more of her ancestor's strange fantasies. So far the ones she'd read weren't like any kind of stories she'd ever come across, but more like graphic depictions of some of the terrible things perpetrated by the kind of people who had once been incarcerated on the property.

Yet her ancestor had made no mention of them being case histories or even being based on case histories.

He had presented them as fiction.

His own fiction.

Bettina started to flip through the pages, wondering if there wasn't something she might want to read other than something called "Carnivore," but the minute she began, Rocky growled, and Pyewackett lashed out at her bathrobe, his claws extended.

Even Forlorn hissed and showed his fangs.

What was going on? she wondered once again.

These were not her pets. Or at least not the same ones she had left in the house that morning.

They, like the house, seemed to have changed.

It was as if there were a presence within the walls of the mansion that she had never felt before — a menacing presence.

And clearly the animals felt it, too.

"Which is all ridiculous," she said out loud, but her voice sounded like a tiny whisper in the vastness of the old house.

Her robe still on, Bettina slid under the covers, then drew the collar of the robe snug around her throat. Suddenly certain that she no longer had any choice in the matter, she began to read. Soon she was lost in the story, fascinated by the tale of a man and his dog.

Not just a dog.

A German shepherd, large, and lithe, and perfectly trained, and utterly obedient to its master.

Bettina Philips tried to stop reading when she came to the passage where the man bound his pet to a table and picked up a scalpel.

She tried to stop, but she couldn't.

Either the animals — or the strange presence in the house — kept her turning page after page after page.

CHAPTER FOURTEEN

Shep Dunnigan didn't have to listen to the warden as he droned on with the standard politically correct speech about sexual harassment. He could have given the speech himself, he'd heard it so many times, but it never hurt to show the boss that he was a team player. Most of the rest of the guards and administrators of the prison that were gathered in the big meeting room seemed to feel the same way; most of the people around him were either checking their e-mails on their BlackBerries, texting someone with their phones, or doing anything other than listen to one more pile of P.C. crap handed down by the state, like calling the prison a "correctional facility." Who'd thought that one up? The same clowns who had tried to call prisons "penitentiaries" for a few decades? And when had the same people decided to call the guards "correctional officers"?

Who was kidding whom? This was a prison, and most of the people in it were neither penitent nor interested in being "corrected." They were interested in getting out, and that was pretty much all they were interested in. Shep, on the other hand, was interested in keeping them in, as were most of the rest of the people around him.

Including Mitch Garvey, who had plopped himself down in the chair next to Shep, and was even less interested in what the warden was saying than Shep. On the other hand, Shep knew Mitch didn't like him any more than he liked Mitch, so why had Mitch sat down next to him?

It didn't take more than a second after the warden finished his talk before Shep found out.

"So," Mitch said, pulling the top off his paper cup of the stale coffee the prison cafeteria seemed to specialize in. "What did you and Lily do about that kid of yours?"

Shep flipped through his memory of the previous evening. Nick had done nothing that required disciplinary action. Not that he knew about, anyway. "What do you mean?"

Mitch's eyebrows went up and his lips curled into a hint of a smirk. "You don't know?"

"Know what?" Shep asked, wishing Mitch would just get to the point. But he never did; instead he strung you along, paying out information like fishing line, a little bit at a time, doing whatever he could to make himself seem more important than he was.

"About the dog?" Mitch said, looking Shep square in the eye. "You don't know about Dan West's dog?"

Shep wanted to shake Garvey, but kept his placid expression carefully in place. "No," he said calmly. "What about the dog?"

Mitch leaned closer than Shep would have liked. "Seems like Nick and our foster kid killed the sheriff's dog."

"Are you nuts?" Shep demanded, pulling away from him.

"Ask Dan," Mitch said, the smirk on his lips starting to spread across his face.

Shep could barely believe it. Lily would have said something.

Wouldn't she?

No, she wouldn't. Not if she thought it might mean Nick would be sent back to the hospital. Shep stood up, nodded to the warden, and left the room. The minute he was back in his office, he picked up the phone and dialed the sheriff's number.

"Results from the vet aren't in yet," Dan

West told him after confirming that his dog had, indeed, died yesterday and that Nick and Sarah Crane seemed somehow to be involved, but so, apparently, were a few other people, Dan added, his own son among them. "Don't know what happened yet. Looked to me like a clean slice that cut the dog wide open. Conner and his friends say they had nothing to do with it, but there's no evidence pointing at Nick or the girl, either."

"Weird," Shep said.

"Very," Dan responded. "And you better believe I'm going to get to the bottom of it, whatever it is."

"Keep me posted, okay?"

"Sure thing."

Shep hung up the phone and leaned back in his desk chair.

Maybe Lily was right — Dan didn't seem to have Nick under any serious suspicion. On the other hand, she knew just what he thought of Mitch Garvey, and the least she could have done was give him a heads-up so he wouldn't look like an idiot in front of one of the guards, especially Mitch.

He'd have a talk with Nick when he got home.

He'd talk with Nick, and then he'd have a little chat with Lily.

■ ■ ■ ■

Mitch waited until the last possible moment before finally crumpling up the paper coffee cup, tossing it into the trash barrel by the door, and heading back to work.

Except he wasn't going back to the cell-block he normally worked. He was going to pay a little visit to Ed Crane.

Mitch crossed the yard with his usual swagger, checked with the supervisor in the block housing Crane, then headed down the long line of cells on the second tier until he came to the last one.

Ed Crane was lying on his bunk staring into space with a closed library book on his chest, but stood up as Mitch approached.

Mitch walked into the neat cell and looked around for something that would give him an excuse to write the son of a bitch up, but it seemed that Crane was the kind of prisoner he hated most — took care of his cell, didn't make trouble for anyone, and didn't even bother to claim he shouldn't be there. Finally, Mitch settled on the charcoal portrait of Sarah that Ed Crane had taped neatly to the wall above his bed. "Your daughter draw that?"

Ed nodded.

"Some artist, huh?"

Ed nodded again, but more slowly this time. What was going on? Why was this guy talking about Sarah?

Mitch moved closer to the portrait, leaning in as if searching for something in Sarah's face. Then, his back still to Ed, he said, "Tell me, Crane — does your little girl get as violent as you?" Ed said nothing until Mitch Garvey turned around, his eyes narrowing with menace. "Asked you a question, Crane. Smart cons answer when they're asked a question. Especially by me."

Ed's lips tightened, then he shook his head. "Sarah's a sweetheart. Hardly ever even gets mad about anything."

"How about religion?" Mitch asked. "You put the fear of God into that girl?"

Ed Crane's eyes sharpened. "What business is it of yours?"

Mitch smiled. "Oh, it's my business all right. Don't you know who I am, Crane?" Not waiting for an answer, Mitch leaned closer, and his voice dropped to a dangerous whisper. "I'm her new daddy, Ed. I'm her father now, and I think you screwed up raising that girl. Something's wrong with her, Ed. Seems like she's following in the footsteps of Satan."

Ed stared at Garvey. "Satan?" he repeated.

"What the hell are you talking about?"

"See?" Garvey said. "See what I mean? You curse like that in front of your daughter?"

"I don't know what you're talking about," Ed said.

Mitch could see the fear that was starting to come into the man's eyes. "Seems she killed a dog yesterday," Mitch said. "A helpless dog."

"Bullsh—" Ed began, but cut himself short before giving Garvey an excuse to write him up. "Sarah wouldn't do something like that."

Mitch moved toward the door. "Believe it, Ed. It happened. But thanks to me and my family, your little girl's still got a chance."

"She doesn't need a 'chance,' " Ed insisted. "She's already as good as kids get!"

"Maybe she is — maybe she isn't," Mitch said. Then his voice turned hard. "And you'd better make sure you behave yourself around here, if you get my drift. We wouldn't want anything to happen to Sarah that she didn't deserve, would we?" Mitch stayed in the cell just long enough to watch the color drain from Ed's face as he realized exactly the threat his daughter was now under. Then, chuckling softly, he headed back down the cellblock. Just seeing the look on Crane's face had been worth the walk over here.

Sometimes this was the best job in the world.

Bettina Philips moved slowly through the classroom, handing out the students' graded drawings from yesterday and offering encouragement and suggestions as the class worked on today's assignment. When she paused at Sarah Crane's place, the girl actually seemed to shrink away from her, and when she finally looked up, she didn't meet Bettina's gaze.

"I'd like to see you after class," the teacher said, but even though she'd done her best to keep her voice warm and welcoming, Sarah still looked as if she might actually bolt from the room.

What was going on with the girl?

But finally Sarah nodded, and a moment later the bell rang. Bettina began to straighten up her desk and load her portfolio with that evening's workload while the classroom quickly drained of students. In less than a minute only Sarah was still at her place.

"You didn't hand in a drawing yesterday, Sarah," Bettina said. "What happened?"

Sarah kept her eyes on the table in front

of her. "I didn't like what I did."

Bettina eyed her quizzically. "You not liking it doesn't necessarily mean I wouldn't have liked it."

Sarah opened her mouth to say something, then seemed to change her mind.

"I'd really like to see all your work," Bettina pressed. "Otherwise, how can I tell if you're making progress?"

Sarah shifted uneasily on her stool and once again seemed about to say something, but again didn't, and Bettina was sure that it wasn't just that Sarah hadn't liked whatever she'd drawn yesterday. Then she recalled the scraps of murmured conversation she'd been hearing all day, not only among the students, but some of the teachers, too.

"Do you want to tell me what happened with Nick Dunnigan and Conner West yesterday, Sarah?"

Now Sarah's head snapped up. "I don't *know* what happened, Miss Philips. Conner tried to get his dog to attack Nick and me, and the next thing we knew, something happened to it." Sarah haltingly tried to describe what occurred, but it didn't make any more sense to her today than it had yesterday, when she'd actually seen it. "Anyway, I don't know how it got cut, but it fell onto the sidewalk and — and —"

Bettina saw Sarah's body shudder as her voice failed her, but her own mind was already reeling.

From what Sarah had told her, it sounded like Dan West's dog died exactly as the one in the strange tale she'd read last night had.

"What a horrible thing to have to see," she finally said. She moved closer to Sarah, sitting down on one of the stools on the opposite side of the table. Picking her words carefully, she went on. "I — I guess I'm not sure what you mean when you say the dog was cut wide open. You mean it was a deep cut?"

Sarah nodded. "So deep everything was —" Once again she fell silent for a moment, then took a deep breath. "— everything was falling out of it," she finished.

"My God," Bettina breathed. A long silence hung in the room as she tried to suppress the next question, wanting neither to ask it nor to hear the answer, but knowing she had to do both. When she finally spoke, her voice was trembling. "Sarah, can you tell me what kind of dog it was?"

Sarah looked up at her. "A German shepherd. A really big one. And it was really weird — it was coming right at me, and then Nick held up his hand and then —" She shook her head as if trying to shake off the memory itself. "Then its stomach just opened up and its guts fell out. But nobody touched it! Nobody!"

Bettina felt a terrible cold spreading through her. "You mean it looked like it had been cut open with a scalpel or something?"

Sarah nodded. "And the strangest thing is —" Again the girl faltered, and Bettina could see she was struggling, as if she didn't want to go on but couldn't hold it inside herself.

And as the silence stretched out, Bettina realized what it was that Sarah didn't want to tell her.

"The — The drawing I made in class yesterday?" Sarah finally managed, her trembling voice reduced to a nearly inaudible whisper.

"Yes?"

Sarah finally looked straight at Bettina, meeting her eyes squarely. "I drew the whole thing. I — I meant to draw the things you set up for us to draw, but something happened. I sort of just started drawing, like I did before at your house. And when I was finished, I'd drawn a man with a scalpel, and a German shepherd was lying on a table with its intestines all —" Unable to go on, Sarah covered her face with her hands for a moment, but then regained control of herself. "I couldn't show it to you," she whispered, taking another deep breath.

Bettina laid her hand on Sarah's forearm. "You can show me anything," she said. "And tell me anything, too." But even as she spoke the words, she wondered if she truly meant them. How was it possible that Sarah had drawn what she herself had read only a few hours later?

"Thanks," Sarah whispered. "But —"

Again she seemed about to say something more but changed her mind. Then Sarah was off her stool and heading for the door, slinging her book bag over her shoulder. "I've got to go — if I'm late, Angie'll ground me for the rest of my life."

"Sarah . . ."

Sarah, at the door now, suddenly turned back. "Angie thinks I'm worshipping the devil," she said, her voice turning harsh. "She actually said it! And she thinks you're the one that's teaching me to do it!"

"Sarah, wait," Bettina began, but it was too late. She was alone in the art studio, her mind churning with the imagery from the story she'd read last night, the story whose darkest moment Sarah had faithfully depicted even though she'd never seen the story, just as she had drawn Shutters as it used to be.

Just as she'd drawn a dark and secret room that Bettina was starting to believe must surely exist somewhere in the basement of her home.

For the first time in her memory Bettina Philips wondered if she wanted to go home that night.

But where else was there to go?

Nick walked slowly away from school, dragging his feet in hopes of hearing Sarah's voice calling him to wait so they could walk together, but still not in violation of his mother's dictum: "I want you to come straight home after school, Nick. *Straight home.* Don't wait for anyone at all. Understand? I don't want you getting into any more trouble."

Not that he had ever gotten himself into trouble on purpose, and he knew perfectly well that by "anyone" his mother had meant Sarah Crane. But if he didn't wait for her, and she should come out, surely there couldn't be any harm in walking with her, at least for a block or two.

Could there?

But she didn't come out, and the second he turned the corner toward home and away from school, the voices in his head began to mutter.

"Shut up," he said out loud, suddenly not caring who might be listening. "I'm sick of you. Get it? Sick of all of you."

But the voices didn't shut up, so he did his best to simply ignore them, which wasn't too hard since today they seemed to be whispering to each other more than trying to make his life miserable.

He was barely two steps past the entrance gate to the park when the hairs on the back of his neck began to prickle.

Someone was watching him.

He could feel it.

And he was pretty sure the committee in his head felt it, too, because their babbling abruptly grew louder.

"Quiet!"

Though he hadn't uttered the word out loud, it still resounded in Nick's head with enough force to startle him. And, at least for a second, it worked. The voices fell silent, and he listened for footsteps, or voices, or any evidence that he was being followed.

Nothing.

The voices started up again.

He looked behind him, but saw only a couple of kids he didn't recognize crossing the street way down the block.

It was just his imagination. It had to be.

Nobody was following him, nobody was watching him.

Still, Nick walked a little faster, repeating over and over to himself that nothing was wrong, that he was just being paranoid. But the feeling of someone watching him, *stalking* him, did not go away. Goose bumps coursed down his arms.

Suddenly, Conner West stepped out of the bushes directly in front of him, his mangled arm heavily bandaged and held in a black sling.

His eyes glittered with a cold anger. "Well, look who's here," he said, putting his hands on his hips so the sidewalk was entirely blocked.

Nick turned around to head back the way he'd come, already starting to break into a run, but he saw Elliot Nash there, moving toward him, though still on the far side of the park driveway.

His heart hammering, Nick shifted toward the street itself, only to see Bobby Fendler moving toward him.

He saw only one option and ran through the gate into the park, realizing his mistake a second too late: once he was in the park, he was out of sight of anyone on the street — or anywhere else — who might help him.

Now the voices in his head were screaming, and the only thing he could think to do was run — run fast — run as hard as he could down the jogging trail.

Run, and pray that there was someone else in the park besides him.

Even before he'd gone twenty yards, he could hear pounding feet coming closer and closer behind him, and then he felt someone grab his backpack. Whoever it was jerked hard, but somehow he managed to stay on his feet. He twisted around far enough to recognize Elliot Nash, then began struggling, trying to rid himself of the backpack.

Too late. By the time he got his arms loose from the straps, Conner, Elliot, and Bobby had surrounded him.

"If I had a knife," Conner West said, barely even winded by the short chase, "I'd cut you open and rip out your guts, just like you did to my dog."

"I didn't kill your dog," Nick said.

"You wish!" Conner shot back. His foot lashed out then, the toe of his shoe catching Nick's kneecap and sending Nick sprawling to the ground, clutching at the injured knee.

"Want to see how it feels?" Conner said, lashing out again as Nick tried to squirm away. "Where's the knife? Want me to cut you with it?" Another kick. "Huh?" Another. "Come on, asshole, where is it?"

The voices in Nick's head were screaming at him now, telling him to fight back, to kick Conner, or trip him, or —

But it didn't matter what the voices were saying; every time he tried to get up, someone kicked him again.

Nick curled into a ball, praying for one voice to rise above the others the way it had yesterday when the dog was about to attack. Where was that one voice that had somehow given him the power to stop the dog with nothing more than a single desperate slash with a hand that held no knife?

But no voice rose above the rest. The cacophony in his head and the taunting from the boys who kept on kicking him swirled into a nightmare of chaotic sound and searing pain.

Nick curled tighter and held his arms over his head, shielding himself as best he could, but the blows kept coming, raining down with ever-increasing force.

They were going to kill him.

He gritted his teeth, refusing to give them the satisfaction of crying out, but then someone — he couldn't even see who — picked up a rotting branch and slammed it down on him so hard that the world around him reeled, spinning black with shooting points of light.

The voices, the sounds, the pain, all of it began to recede into a tunnel of calm, quiet darkness. But before he gave in to the quiet and the darkness, he heard one last thing.

Conner West's voice.

"You think *you* hurt? Wait'll you see what we do to your crippled girlfriend!"

Sarah!

Nick struggled to stand, but his arms and legs wouldn't respond. He slumped onto the frozen ground and slipped gratefully into the darkness.

CHAPTER FIFTEEN

Sarah pushed through the heavy school doors, hoping Miss Philips hadn't made her so late that Nick would leave without her. But the sidewalk and lawn around the school was empty, which meant she was even later than she thought. Nick had already gone, and Angie would be furious.

She made her way down the steps, but as she started to cut across the lawn to the left, she found herself going in the other direction instead.

But why?

Why wasn't she going directly home, just as Angie had told her to?

All she had to do was turn around and —

But she was no longer near the school. Instead she was at the gate to the park, with no memory — none at all — of walking in that direction. In fact, she had no real memory of going anywhere at all — it felt as if she'd taken only a few steps, but the park was more than two blocks from the school.

How had she gotten here? What had brought her?

She looked around, but nothing seemed out of the ordinary. Yet she was certain there was a reason she was here. She took a few steps into the park, listening for anything other than the sporadic traffic on Main Street, heard nothing, and was about to head back to the sidewalk when she saw something lying in the middle of the jogging path.

Nick's backpack.

Sarah's heart began to pound as she moved closer and clumsily stooped down to pick it up. "Nick?" she called out as she straightened up. "Nick, are you here? Nick!"

She heard a faint groan from off to the left, dropped the backpack and ran. Nick, unconscious and covered with blood, lay on the frozen ground half hidden by a bush, a bloodied tree branch next to his head. "Help!" Sarah called out. "Someone help me!"

Ignoring the pain in her hip, she dropped to the ground. "Nick? Nick!"

For a moment it seemed he wasn't going to respond at all, but then his eyes opened a crack. "S-Sarah?" he said, his voice barely audible.

"What happened?" Sarah asked. "Who did this to you?" But even before Nick could start to form the words, she answered her own question. "It was Conner, wasn't it? Conner and his friends!"

"I — I tried to s-stop them," Nick whispered. "Like I did . . ." His voice trailed off, then he spoke again. ". . . yesterday."

Yesterday? What was he talking about? Yesterday the dog had come at them and —

Her thoughts were interrupted by a groan as Nick tried to sit up, failed, and dropped back onto the ground. "Where's your phone?" Sarah asked. "I'm going to call 911."

"P-Pocket," Nick managed. "But not 911. Call my mother."

"You can't even stand up," Sarah said, fishing the phone out of Nick's pocket as carefully as she could, but still seeing him wince as she pulled it from his pants. "And if your mom tries to move you, it could make things even worse."

"They hit my head," Nick said. "And kicked me. But I don't think anything's broken." But when he tried once more to get up, and failed again, he shook his head. "Okay. But call my mom, too."

In less than a minute Sarah had made

both phone calls, and when she started to slide Nick's phone back into his pocket, he pushed her hand away. "Keep it," he said. "That way I can call you."

"But it's your —"

"Just keep it for now, okay?"

She started to argue with him, but already she could hear the siren of the approaching ambulance, so she dropped the cell phone into her backpack. "They'll be here in a minute," she told him. "You're going to be okay."

Nick managed a nod. "I — I'm glad you weren't with me, but —"

"If I'd been with you, maybe they wouldn't have tried anything."

Nick shook his head, wincing at the pain even that slight movement caused. "W-We could have stopped them," he said. "Like yester—" He broke off as the siren, which was blaring so loudly that Sarah could barely hear him anyway, abruptly fell silent. "You better go tell them where I am," he said, but Sarah was already getting to her feet. Then, as she started back toward the path, he spoke again. "I'll call you," he said. "Tonight, after my mom's gone home."

No more than thirty seconds after the ambulance arrived, Lily Dunnigan pulled up behind it and ran into the park. Sarah watched as the EMTs quickly went over Nick, then loaded him onto a stretcher and carried him to the ambulance. If Lily Dunnigan even noticed Sarah, she gave no sign, but simply followed the EMTs, brushing past Sarah as if she hadn't seen her.

The fading light of the afternoon made Sarah glance at her watch as she stepped out of the park, and she hurried her step as she started home. Angie was going to be angry, but maybe when she told her why she was late —

No. Not Angie. It wouldn't matter why she was going to be late.

Angie was going to be angry, and she was going to be punished.

Sarah lay down on the old camp cot in the attic that now served as her bed and wondered what Angie would do if she knew that the person she thought she was punishing would far rather be right where she was than downstairs with the Garvey family. Angie had been so angry at her late return from school that instead of listening to what had happened, she simply banished her to her "room" without dinner. Sarah had seen no reason to tell Angie that the banana in her backpack — left over from lunch — would do just fine for supper, let alone that she'd rather be up here by herself than sitting at the table with the family. Nor was the attic nearly as bad as she suspected the Garveys thought it was.

She had found an old table to serve as a desk and rescued a piece of clothesline and some old wire hangers from one of the drawers of an old dresser she suspected the Garveys had forgotten was even up there. After stringing the clothesline between two of the rafters for a makeshift clothes rack and hanging most of her clothes on the hangers, she put the rest of her things in the dresser drawer without having to worry about Tiffany complaining that she was taking up too much space.

The naked lightbulb hanging from the rafters was a little glary, but all in all, the attic was a whole lot better than sharing Tiffany's room.

She was just finishing the banana when Nick's cell phone vibrated in her pocket.

Swallowing the last of the banana, Sarah sat up, fished the phone out of her jeans and started to open it. But then she hesitated. What if it wasn't Nick? But even if it wasn't, what did it matter? He'd given her the phone, and even Angie couldn't get mad at her for answering it. Well, maybe Angie could, but not anyone else. Still, she turned her head away from the attic door just in case someone was out there listening.

"Hello?"

"It's me," Nick said.

A flood of relief flowed through her. "Are you okay?"

"They gave me a bunch of painkillers," he said, his voice tired. "I have a couple of cracked ribs and some other stuff, but they're letting me out tomorrow."

"Did you tell them who beat you up?"

"Are you kidding?"

Sarah frowned, then understood. "So if they get away with it, why won't they just do it again?"

"They probably will," Nick said. "But it's not just me — Conner said something about you, too. So just stay away from them, okay?"

"Why don't we just tell the police?" Sarah countered.

"Because Conner's dad *is* the police, remember? Besides, maybe this way Conner will think we're even."

"Even?" Sarah echoed. "For what?"

"Killing his dog."

"You didn't —" Sarah began, but Nick broke in.

"I think I did, Sarah," he said. "I mean, it sounds crazy, but while they were beating me up, I tried to do the same thing to Conner that I did to his dog yesterday."

"What are you talking about? Neither one of us did anything!"

Nick was silent a moment, and when he spoke, his voice had dropped as if he didn't want anyone else hearing what he said. "I think maybe we did. Or at least I did. Remember how I had the hallucination of the dog being cut open at the same time you were drawing it?"

Every nerve in Sarah's body began to tingle, but she said nothing.

"Well, when Conner's dog came at us, one of the voices in my head started yelling at me, and I knew what to do. I mean, I just *knew.* I just remembered that hallucination and —" He hesitated, then plunged on. "— and I knew I could do it! I just held up my hand like I had a knife in it, and — and . . ." His voice trailed off. There was a long silence, and when Sarah didn't say anything, Nick finally spoke again. "I mean, you were there — you saw what happened."

Sarah shuddered at the memory. "You didn't do anything," she insisted.

"I think I did," Nick replied. "I saw the whole thing while you were drawing it, and then when Conner's dog came at us, I just did what the voice in my head told me to do. And I tried to do it again today."

Sarah's fingers were gripping the phone so hard her knuckles were turning white. What was he talking about? He couldn't have done what he said he'd done. "But it didn't work, did it?" she said, the trembling in her voice belying the confidence she was trying to project.

"I think it was because you weren't there," he said. "I think I could have stopped them if you'd been there with me."

"No," Sarah said. "What happened to Conner's dog didn't have anything to do with us."

"I think it did," Nick said. Then, before Sarah could say anything else, he added, "The nurse is here. I've got to go. Talk to you tomorrow."

And the phone went dead in Sarah's hand.

For several long minutes she sat where she was, trying to make sense of what Nick had said.

It was the drugs they'd given him for the pain. It had to be!

Without thinking about it, Sarah rose from the cot and moved to the grimy attic window. Rubbing some of the dirt away, she peered out into evening darkness.

Out there in the shadows of the gathering night was someone — one person — who might be able to tell her what had happened.

And she had to talk to that person.

Tonight.

Now.

Sarah listened to the house.

Mitch's TV was blaring through the surround-sound speakers, barely even muffled by the full floor separating it from the attic. Sarah unlocked the window and pushed up on the old wood frame.

It was stuck fast, glued in place by layers and layers of paint.

She pressed harder and pushed upward again, but not until splinters and paint chips had dug into her palms did the window finally move, giving way with a protesting screech but only opening less than half an inch.

She pushed again, but the window held fast. Yet if she was going to go see Bettina Philips, she had to get it open. Turning back to the attic, she searched for something she could use to pry the window open. It didn't take long to find the near perfect tool: behind a cracked mirror was an old set of wrought-iron fireplace tools.

Perfect. She took the poker back to the window, wedged it into the opening and pushed down.

Slowly — and protesting loudly — the window opened far enough so she could get a good grip on the bottom of the frame.

She raised it as quietly as she could, inch by inch, every screech and scrape sounding loud enough to wake the dead, let alone summon one of the Garveys, but finally the opening was large enough to squeeze through, and no one arrived at the attic door to stop her.

Now all she had to do was wait for everyone else to go to bed.

At ten the television finally fell silent. At ten-thirty loud snoring began wafting up through the floor from Mitch and Angie's bedroom directly beneath Sarah's cot. As the snoring settled into a steady rhythm, she put on her parka, stuffed gloves into her pockets, wrapped her scarf around her neck, and pulled her wool hat down around her ears.

One leg at a time, she climbed out of the window and stood shakily on the steeply pitched roof outside. She held perfectly still for a moment, staring down at the yard below and wondering if she wanted to risk breaking her leg again — or even worse — just to get to the ground, only to still be faced with the long walk up to Shutters.

What if Bettina wasn't even home?

But she would be — Sarah knew it.

And if she didn't talk to Bettina, she wouldn't sleep at all.

Slowly, testing every step before she trusted her weight to it, she moved down the roof until she could steady herself against a large branch of the maple tree that overhung the roof. Then she was in the tree itself, climbing down the branches until she was at the lowest one. Once again she paused. It still wasn't too late to turn back, to climb back up, creep across the roof, and slip into the shelter of the attic. She looked down at the ground, which now seemed much farther away than the seven or eight feet it actually was.

Two feet, she told herself. That's all it'll be when I let go of the branch. But what if she broke her hip again?

Don't think about it!

Steeling herself, she lowered herself from the branch until only her hands were clinging to the bark, offered a silent prayer to whatever god might be listening, and let go.

Her good leg hit first, catching most of her weight, and there was just a small jolt of pain from her bad hip. She took a couple of deep breaths and limped toward the fog-haloed streetlight, away from the ugliness of the Garvey household and toward the sanctuary of Bettina Philips's mansion.

The fog rolling into the village had turned the quiet of the night into an eerie silence, and her ears strained to catch the slightest noise as she moved through the mist. The main street and the village square felt utterly abandoned, but a few moments after she passed the town's lone tavern she heard it.

The sound of feet.

Someone was behind her.

She stopped short, listening, but there was nothing.

Except that she could still feel it.

Should she turn around?

No! Just keep going.

She moved on, quickening her pace, but now she could hear something behind her as well as feel it.

More footsteps.

Following her?

But why? Even if someone was behind her, it didn't mean they were following her.

Unless it was Conner West. Nick's words echoed in her head: *Conner said something about you, too. . . .*

Stupid! She was just being stupid and letting her imagination run away with her. There was nothing behind her — no one was following her. And even if there was, better to face it straight on than stand here in the thickening fog doing nothing.

Steeling herself, willing her heart to stop pounding, Sarah suddenly whipped around.

Nothing! No one! The sidewalk behind her was as empty as it was ahead, and the silence of the night was undisturbed.

All she'd heard was the echo of her own footsteps bouncing off the storefronts.

Or maybe nothing at all.

But just as her pulse was slowing to normal, a car turned the corner a block ahead and began creeping slowly toward her. Sarah shrank into the doorway of a pottery shop, pressing as deeply into its shadows as she could and pulling the hood of her parka over her head. But if it was Mitch or Angie out looking for her — or even Conner West — what would she do?

She couldn't run . . . there was no place to hide —

Panic began to rise in her again, and her heart was thudding so loudly she was certain that whoever was in the approaching car must hear it.

And then the car was gone, passing her by, moving on, its taillights quickly vanishing in the fog.

She moved along, keeping to the shadows

and doing her best to make herself invisible.

The sidewalk ended abruptly at the edge of town, and she stopped short, looking ahead at the road that quickly disappeared into the thick fog. The dark mists could be concealing anything — Conner and his friends could be waiting for her, and she'd never even see them. And even if she could, what difference would it make? She couldn't run from them, and she didn't even have anything to defend herself with.

Maybe she should have stayed at home.

Except it wasn't home, and it never would be, and no matter how scared she was, she still had to talk to Bettina Philips.

She had to go to Shutters.

She stepped off the sidewalk onto the blacktop, taking one slow step at a time, feeling as if she herself was vanishing into the blackness.

What if she missed the driveway to the mansion? What if she walked right past it and kept walking in freezing fog all the way to —

To where? She didn't even know what lay beyond Shutters except the lake.

But she wouldn't miss it, she told herself. She'd see the gate.

She shoved her hands deep into her pockets and kept walking into the darkness.

CHAPTER SIXTEEN

Bettina Philips jerked awake, her heart pounding, her mind foggy.

What was happening?

Where was she?

Then the feeling of disorientation passed. She was home, in her studio, and she'd just fallen asleep on the chaise while she was reading.

Except she never fell asleep on the chaise, and as her mind focused, she realized that somehow, even now that she was awake, she didn't feel at home.

Something in the house was different; something had changed.

With Forlorn clutched tight in her arms and Cooper close at her heels, Bettina opened the big doors to the conservatory and stepped out into the massive foyer.

And stopped short.

The great crystal chandelier hanging from the ceiling was swinging slowly, like a giant pendulum, its slow and rhythmic motion making the large chamber seem to come alive with slowly moving shadows.

And now, from somewhere upstairs, Bettina could hear something.

Something like voices.

Maybe she should just leave and find somewhere else to spend the night.

Yet even as the thought entered her mind, she found herself moving toward the stairs, as if drawn by an unseen magnet.

On the first step, Forlorn tensed in her arms, then clawed his way free of her, leaping to the floor and disappearing through the dining room toward the bright light of the kitchen.

Maybe, she thought, instead of going upstairs, she should simply follow the cat. But what good would that do? If a window had indeed broken upstairs, the fog and rain or snow shouldn't be left to pour into the house just because she was feeling skittish.

"You still with me, Coop?" she asked the dog, which was now sitting at her feet, looking anxiously up at her. "Well, let's just get it over with then, okay?"

Slowly, with one hand gliding on the smooth banister, her steps muffled in the carpeting, Bettina ascended the curving staircase to the second-floor landing.

To the long hallway stretching out before her, which seemed to go on forever, with the stairs to the third floor at the far end.

And all along the hallway, standing either slightly ajar or wide open, were all the bedroom doors that had been closed for years.

That had been closed this morning, when she left the house.

And yet everything seemed quiet.

"Maybe it was nothing," she whispered to the dog, but even before her voice died away, she heard it again.

The same sound she'd heard downstairs a few moments ago.

The same soft babbling that was still coming from above, but at the far end of the house.

Cooper's upper lip curled and a low growl rumbled in his throat.

"Shhh," she said, touching the dog on the top of his head in reassurance. "C'mon."

They moved down the hall and mounted the servants' stairs to the third floor.

Halfway up, a waft of frigid air — air that smelled as musty as the basement — stopped her short, but it was gone so quickly that a moment later Bettina wondered if she'd actually felt it at all. "Okay," she whispered to Cooper, "we've done this before. It's just Pyewackett and Rocky up here making mischief, right?" But even as she uttered the words, she didn't believe them, and neither did Cooper.

As on the second floor, all the doors were standing open, some only a crack, others flung wide.

All except those to the huge old workroom at the far end of the hall where the staff had not only ironed and mended clothes, but hung laundry on days when it was too wet or cold to hang it outside, and performed all the other tasks Bettina's ancestor had demanded be done in the house rather than contracted out. Not only staff had worked in that room, but inmates of the prison as well. The doors to that room stood tightly closed, but from behind them came that same soft babble of voices.

As if, after decades of empty silence, the vast room was once again filled with the staff and inmates who had labored there so long ago. As she moved down the corridor, Bettina found herself half expecting to hear the hiss of an old steam mangle, or the muttering of angry voices grumbling at the work being demanded of them. As she moved toward the doors, Cooper hung back, and once more a low growl rose in his throat.

"It's all right," Bettina said, pausing for a

moment to look back at the dog. "Come on!"

She started once more toward the work-room, and a plume of thick white fog drifted into the hallway from under the door to the ballroom.

"See?" she said. "That's all it is — a window's broken, and the fog's drifting in."

Cooper only took a step backward.

"C'mon, sissy," Bettina said, squaring her shoulders and marching resolutely toward the workroom.

But as she was reaching for the handle, the open door to the room on her left suddenly slammed shut with a crash that made her jump and whirl around.

Then the door on the other side crashed closed, too, and Bettina moved instinctively back the way she'd come. Cooper was bark-ing loudly now, and from somewhere down below she could hear Rocky starting to howl.

Bettina quickened her step and in a mo-ment was running down the corridor as doors slammed shut on both sides.

Herded, she thought. It's like I'm being herded away.

She came to the top of the stairs as the last of the doors slammed shut, and began hurrying down, taking the steps two at a time, Cooper ahead of her. Halfway down, though, the dog stumbled, then rolled on down to the bottom. "Coopie!" Bettina cried, but even before the echo of her voice died away, the dog was back on his feet, racing away.

Bettina followed him down to the second-floor landing and hadn't taken more than two steps toward the main stairs when the doors on both sides of her slammed shut, the heavy oak panels banging their jambs so hard she couldn't believe the frames didn't shatter. Cooper was already at the next flight of stairs, looking back at her, his tail down even though his head was thrown back as he howled at her, and Bettina began running again. By the time she reached the stairs, her ears were ringing from the crashing of wood against wood, and she plunged down, no longer worrying about tripping, no longer even thinking about falling. All she wanted now was to get out.

The whole house seemed to have come alive, and she could hear doors slamming everywhere, and from above, the babble of voices was growing louder.

It wasn't the wind — whatever was in the house wasn't the wind at all. And whatever it was, it was coming for her now. She could feel it — an almost palpable force raging through the house.

What should she do? Where should she go?

She turned automatically toward the conservatory, but its door slammed shut even as she moved in that direction, and she turned away again.

The dining room! The dining room and the kitchen beyond! But those doors slammed shut, too, and finally there was no choice left. She raced toward the front door, the chandelier swinging madly above her, doors and windows slamming everywhere around her. Where was Cooper? And Rocky and Pyewackett?

But it didn't matter — all that mattered now was that she get out.

Get out while she still could.

If she still could.

She was still ten feet from the door when a new sound came.

Bells! Great, resounding bells, as if some monstrous clock were striking the darkest hour of the night. Bettina froze, and the bells kept pealing, but as they rose, the cacophony in the house began to die away.

The crash of slamming doors stopped.

The babble of voices fell silent.

The chandelier stopped swinging.

And the bells — the great pealing chimes

— softened, too.

The doorbell!

All she had heard was the doorbell.

Bettina stared at the door for a long moment.

The bell rang again, and then came a knocking sound, but a knocking that quickly grew into a terrible pounding.

And suddenly Bettina knew.

Whatever was outside was something the house was expecting.

It was as if the house had been preparing itself for this visitor.

As if the house *wanted* this visitor.

The pounding started again, growing until it sounded as if a battering ram were pummeling the wooden door. The very rafters of the house trembled with each slam that threatened to splinter the door and let whatever was out there inside, whether Bettina opened the door or not. But as the pounding grew steadily louder, Bettina also knew that it was no longer up to her whether she opened the door.

Moved by a force she was powerless to resist, she walked to the door, unbolted it, and pulled it open.

Sarah Crane stood shivering on the doorstep, her small fist raised for another rap on the doorjamb.

■ ■ ■ ■

An hour later Bettina and Sarah sat in the quiet of the conservatory. The house was silent around them, and the fog outside had cleared. A nearly full moon hung over the lake, whose watery surface glistened as if covered with a pavement of diamonds. Bettina had listened quietly to everything Sarah told her, only interrupting to occasionally ask a question. The fear Bettina had felt just before Sarah arrived — the utter terror that seized her as the house seemed to be trying to drive her out into the night — had vanished; the old house felt as safe and comforting as ever, as if it were dozing in a quiet somnolence.

Now, as the clock in the entry hall struck midnight, Sarah looked uncertainly at her. "What's happening?" she asked. "What does it mean?"

Instead of answering, Bettina countered with her own question. "Would you be comfortable sleeping here tonight?"

Without any hesitation, Sarah nodded. "I like this house. It feels —" She fell silent for a moment as she searched for the right word. "— it just feels good," she at last went on. "Like I belong here."

"Well, then, that's settled," Bettina said. "And considering what time it is, I think we'd better get both ourselves to bed."

Sarah shook her head. "I want to draw," she said. Then: "Is that weird? Wanting to draw even though I'm so tired I can hardly stay awake?"

"Not weird at all," Bettina replied. "I'd say it's more like talent. Talent that won't be denied. So if you want to draw, draw. And I'll put on another pot of tea."

Sarah shrugged out of the afghan she'd wrapped around her shoulders when she first came in, got up and walked over to the easel. She pinned a fresh sheet of paper to it and picked up a charcoal pencil.

Bettina waited until Sarah had made the first mark on the paper, then headed for the kitchen to set the water boiling. She had no idea what Sarah was going to draw tonight, but she knew that whatever it might be, it was important.

And in some way she didn't yet understand, it was connected to the house.

Her house.

This house.

Fire!

Nick Dunnigan was choking on the roiling billows of black, acrid smoke that seared

300

his lungs as flames charred the edges of his jeans, melted the rubber on his tennis shoes, and began licking up his legs. His nostrils filled with the stench of burning flesh and he lashed out at the flames with his foot, trying to kick himself free of the fire. Then he tried to turn and run, but his feet would no longer move.

He was going to die!

Die right here, die in flames, die with his breath burning inside his body as his skin peeled away and the thin layer of fat beneath started to melt and then burst into flames, and then he would actually *be* the fire and — and — He thrashed, thrashed as hard as he could to get his feet loose, and then, abruptly, everything changed.

He came awake, opened his eyes and saw white.

White everywhere.

Then it came back to him — he was in the hospital, and the bedcovers were tucked in too tight, and he couldn't get them free. He tried to reach down to pull the covers loose, and a wrenching pain tore through his side.

He reflexively tried to put his hand to the pain, but his forefinger had something taped to it and he got his hands entangled in a mess of tubes and wires. His head still hurt, too. In fact, it hurt worse than ever, pounding at him so hard that the blinding white of the room pulsated with each hammering heartbeat.

The painkiller they'd given him hadn't killed any pain at all; instead it had just given him nightmares.

Nick sank back into his pillow and closed his eyes against the blinding white of the room. Perspiration trickled down the side of his face and into his ear, and now his head was starting to feel like it was going to explode.

He felt around on the bed for the button that would call the nurse, but before he found it a different light — a bright orange light — flickered through his closed eyelids.

He squinted against the throbbing in his head and reopened his eyes.

Flames — *real flames!* — were burning at the bottom of the draperies. All the fear he'd felt in the nightmare flooded back over him as the fire climbed quickly to the ceiling, then started creeping toward him, blackening the acoustic tiles, then devouring them to feed its insatiable hunger.

Then one of the flaming ceiling tiles dropped away and Nick watched helplessly as it fell to the foot of his bed.

The white blanket burst into flames.

But this time he was awake.
This time it was no dream!

He tried to scream, tried to call out for help, but his voice was drowned out by the screaming voices that had suddenly risen in his head, all of them panicked, all of them shouting at him.

He tried to push himself up the bed, tried to pull his feet away from the flames, but the covers were pulled so tight he couldn't move. Now the fire was burning through the blanket and sheet and boring deep into the mattress.

"Help me!" he screamed, his strength already failing him, but it was too late — he knew it was too late. The flames were all around him now, rising up like some great beast, towering over him, and he could feel his face starting to burn.

Once again smoke and heat seared his lungs.

Once again he smelled the stench of his own burning flesh.

"F — Fire . . ." he gasped one last time, and as the cacophony of screams in his head began to die away, one voice rose above the rest.

Laughter.

It was the sound of laughter as the being in his head rejoiced at the inferno consuming him.

Nick let out a final anguished cry, praying for death.

And then a cool hand touched his forehead and he felt the prick of a needle in his arm.

Sarah Crane's face floated up in his mind's eye.

She smiled at him.

And then darkness.

Blessed darkness.

Angie Garvey lay flat on her back, staring up at the ceiling and listening to Mitch's loud snore beside her. But it wasn't Mitch's snoring that woke her — that was her cross to bear, and she'd learned to bear it years ago. No, something else had disturbed her sleep. But what?

She gently pushed on Mitch's shoulder. He rolled over, temporarily silencing his snores, and Angie listened carefully.

Nothing.

Except it was something, and until she found out what it was, she wouldn't be able to sleep at all. Sliding out from under the covers, she put her feet on the floor.

And knew what it was: a cold breeze swirled around her feet and legs.

Which was wrong.

She'd closed the house up tight before going to bed — she was sure she had. Had Zachary gone and left his bedroom window open?

That would be unlike him — Zachary was a good boy.

But God had shown her what was wrong — the draft coming under the door — so now it was up to her to fix it. She stood, picked up her robe from the foot of the bed, stuck her feet into her favorite felt scuffs, and quietly opened the door.

Out in the hall it wasn't just a draft — it was downright cold. Angie licked her forefinger and held it near the floor, then followed it until she came to its source: the breeze, feeling more like a cold wind now, was coming straight down the stairs from the attic.

That girl!

Did she think the money to pay for heat grew on trees? Angie marched up the narrow staircase to the attic door, pushed it open, and jerked the chain that turned on the light. The bulb swung on its wire, throwing shadows around the room, and she immediately spotted the source of the frigid breeze.

The window stood wide open.

Air as cold as if it were coming straight

305

down from the North Pole — which it probably was! — flowed in through the window and down the stairs while the furnace in the basement worked overtime to pump heat — heat she and Mitch were paying for! — right out the window. If she hadn't found it, this would have cost more than the county paid them to house the stupid girl.

A fireplace poker lay on the floor by the window, and Angie could see the gouge it had made in the sill as Sarah used it to pry the window open. Not enough to waste heat — she had to damage the window, too. She picked up the poker, clutching it tight. If she hadn't known that the Lord frowned on actually killing people, she might just have taken a whack or two at Sarah Crane, if only to teach her the value of money.

"Wake up, Sarah!" she commanded, a vein in her head starting to throb, which was a sure sign that her blood pressure was getting a lot higher than it should be.

Which was Sarah Crane's fault, too!

And the girl didn't even move.

Angie shoved the window down and locked it, then turned around and marched over to the cot Sarah was using as a bed.

It was empty.

Angie hefted the poker once more and realized it was a good thing God was keeping

Sarah out of her reach at precisely this moment. Then she threw the poker onto Sarah's bed and made her way back down the narrow stairs.

Maybe she should wake Mitch and tell him that the girl had sneaked out of the house.

Except that Mitch would just wake everybody up and then call Dan West and wake him up, too. There was no reason to get everybody in an uproar — not for someone like Sarah Crane.

Then what should she do?

But of course she already knew. Taking a deep breath, she dropped back down to her knees, bowed her head, and began to pray. And, as He always did, God quickly answered her prayers, telling her exactly what she must do.

She went downstairs to make certain the locks on both the front and the back doors were secure. Sarah might have snuck out of the house, but she would not be allowed to sneak back in. She'd *ask* to be let in, and she'd better hope that God was feeling a lot more merciful than Mitch when he found out how much heat had been wasted. But one way or another, Angie was determined to see to it that God's will be done. It was becoming increasingly clear that He had brought Sarah to their home for a reason, and one of those reasons was that He wanted her to teach the girl to take responsibility for herself.

And she would do precisely as God bid her, just as she always did.

The front door was securely locked, but Angie unlocked it and locked it again, just to make sure.

Then she threw the dead bolt.

God's will perfectly executed, Angie Garvey went back to bed.

Now she could sleep in peace.

CHAPTER SEVENTEEN

"Let me out here," Sarah said, her eyes fixed on the house that was still a block away, but was glowing like a beacon in the predawn darkness, which could only mean one thing. At least one of the Garveys — probably Angie — was awake. Awake, and waiting for her. "I'll walk the last block."

"I should go talk to Angie," Bettina said, "and let her know that you were safe at my house last night."

"That'll only make things worse," Sarah said, her voice starting to tremble. "Please?"

Reluctantly, Bettina pulled over and Sarah slid out of the car. "I'll see you at school," Bettina said. When Sarah barely even nodded, Bettina asked, "You're sure you're all right?"

"I'll be okay," Sarah sighed. She closed the door, waited until Bettina's car finally disappeared around the corner, then started toward the house, trying to figure out what she would say to Angie. What had she been thinking to spend the night at Bettina's? And why had Bettina let her sleep until 6:00 A.M.? But of course she knew the answer to that one — she'd hadn't finished her drawing until way after midnight. Besides, none of it was Bettina's fault — it was all her own, and now all she could do was stand up and face the music, as her mother used to say. Refusing to give in to her urge to turn around and walk the other way, she went up the front steps and tried the storm door.

Locked.

She rang the doorbell.

Angie opened the front door, then stood glowering at her. For a second Sarah thought she might just slam the door in her face, but at last she unlocked the storm door.

Sarah pulled it open, stepped inside, and smelled bacon frying in the kitchen. But instead of getting back to fixing breakfast, Angie held her cold eyes steady on Sarah. "You owe me an apology," she finally said.

"I'm —"

"And one to Mitch."

Sarah kept her eyes fixed on the floor.

"But mostly you need to pray to God that He forgives you for lying, cheating, and stealing."

Sarah's head snapped up. "I don't lie, and I don't cheat, and I don't steal!" she said with enough force that Angie's eyes glittered with fury.

"Shut your mouth," her foster mother spat. "You pretended to go to bed — that's lying! You pried that window open, gouging the sill instead of coming down the stairs and leaving through the front door like an honest person. So there's the cheating! And you let heat from our house run right out that window when you left it wide open, and that's taking our money as much as if you'd just stolen it out of my purse."

"I'm sorry," Sarah breathed, though she knew the words were going to be far too little and far too late.

"On your knees," Angie commanded. "Right here, and right now." Angie dropped to her knees on the living room floor and pulled Sarah down with her, ignoring the whimper Sarah couldn't choke off as a searing pain flashed through her bad hip and leg. "Ask God to forgive your sins and to show you how to live in His grace."

Sarah bowed her head. "I'm sorry," she whispered again. "I really am. But I'm just so confused —"

"The Lord has given us the Ten Com-

311

mandments so we don't *need* to be confused," Angie cut in. Her hands clasped at her breast, she bowed her head. "Teach me, O Lord. Show me the way to lead this child to the path of righteousness."

Sarah closed her eyes and tried to concentrate on the prayers Angie wanted her to offer up, but the pain in her body was so great that tears began trickling down her cheeks, and she knew that if she tried to say anything at all she would only start crying.

And that, she was certain, would only make things worse.

Seconds dragged into minutes, and each minute seemed to go on for an hour, but at last she heard Angie murmur one last word.

"Amen."

"Amen," Sarah quietly echoed. Then, as Angie rose to her feet, Sarah struggled to her own, her hip threatening to buckle under her.

"It is God's will that I deliver you to Mitch for whatever punishment he deems fit. He deals with the likes of you every day of his life, and he will certainly know what to do."

Sarah steeled herself against the wave of nausea that rose in her at the thought of what Mitch Garvey might consider a proper punishment, and then she bolted past Angie to the bathroom, barely making it to the toilet before she began throwing up. She was trying to rinse the bitter taste from her mouth when she caught a glimpse of Angie looming in the doorway, a look of triumph on her face.

"That's the evil in you," Angie said. "God is casting it out!" Sarah said nothing as she dried her face on a threadbare hand towel. "Mitch is upstairs putting a lock on the attic door," Angie went on. "And he's nailing that window shut." As Sarah hung the towel back on its bar, Angie's fingers closed on her arm, and a moment later she was being half led and half dragged up the stairs to the second floor, and as Angie shoved her up the steep narrow flight to the attic, Mitch smiled down at her.

But there was no warmth in his smile.

"Well, look who's back," he said. "The one who likes to stay out all night."

"I'm so sorry," Sarah whispered.

"Not as sorry as you're going to be," Mitch replied. His fingers clamping down on the flesh that his wife had already bruised, Mitch pulled her into the attic and closed the door. "But you can stop worrying," he went on as Sarah backed away from him. "If I put a mark on you, we'll lose our county money. So you're getting a pass this time."

Sarah's panic began to subside.

"But you listen to me and you listen to me good. The next time you cause me or my wife any kind of worry at all, I will hurt you." He hefted the hammer as if already weighing the damage it could do to her. "You think about that, understand? You stay up here today and you think about what you did. And I warn you — if I hear that you even tried to leave this room today, I'll fix you so you'll never leave it again." His lips curled into a smile as cold as his eyes. "And I'll fix your father, too. Understand?"

Sarah nodded again.

"Speak!" Mitch demanded, smashing the hammer down on the table that served as Sarah's desk.

Sarah jumped reflexively. "Yes, sir," she whispered. "I understand."

"Then when I come home from work tonight, I expect to see a different Sarah Crane. Understand?"

The hammer rose again, but this time Sarah didn't wait for it to crash down. "Yes, sir," she breathed.

Mitch left the room, locking the door behind him, and when she was finally alone, Sarah sank down onto the narrow cot, curled herself into a tight ball, and finally gave in to the tears she'd been struggling against for so long.

Ed Crane slowed to a walk as he finished his fifth lap around the prison yard, and used the sleeve of his prison-gray shirt to wipe away the sheen of sweat that covered his brow despite the chill of the air.

"Hey, Ed!" Little Mouse Mostella dropped his own pace as he caught up with Ed, falling in beside him for a moment. "Sonofabitch Mitch wants to talk to you."

Ed's eyes followed Little Mouse's tilting head, and sure enough — there was Mitch Garvey, lounging against the wall, his arms crossed over his chest, his eyes staring a hole right through him.

"He say anything?"

Little Mouse shrugged, then picked up his pace, leaving Ed behind.

Leaving the track, Ed cut across the yard, weaving through the clumps of prisoners who were huddled close together, their breath pluming in the cold morning air as they muttered among themselves. "You want to see me?" Ed asked. Having learned the hard way that it was always a mistake to come too close to any of the guards, he made sure to stay well beyond Mitch

Garvey's reach.

Garvey's lips twisted into a cold smile. "Just wanted to update you on your daughter's progress."

There was a glint in Garvey's eye that made Ed's belly start to churn, and he had to struggle to keep from letting his hands close into tight fists. "Oh?" Unfortunately he didn't quite succeed in keeping the single word as uninflected as he'd wanted, and he saw the pleasure his worry for Sarah gave the guard.

"Oh, yeah," Mitch said. "Just thought you'd like to know we're taking a few 'corrective measures' with your little princess. She's finally going to learn some respect for her parents. Not to mention taking responsibility for her actions."

Blood rose in Ed's cheeks, but he kept his arms and hands relaxed. Don't bite, he told himself. Just let it all go.

"She's a tough one, though," Mitch went on, seeing the angry flush in Ed Crane's face. "Gonna be a job to beat all your candy-ass crap out of her, but you can trust me." His twisted smile widened. "I'll get the job done. One way or another, I'll put the fear of God in her."

The word "beat" hit Ed like a sledgehammer. But what could he do? Even a single swing at Garvey would put him in the hole for a month. Besides, it was his own fault Sarah was where she was, and he wasn't about to do anything that would give Garvey an excuse to make her life even more miserable than it already was. Seething, he kept his tongue as well as his fists under control, but Ed knew Garvey could see his rising anger and was enjoying every second of it.

"I'm a different kind of daddy than you are," Garvey went on, dropping his voice to a pitch that held a far more dangerous note than the mocking tone of a moment ago. "She's going to learn a few things at our house." He leered at Ed. "Actually, that's not quite true. Fact is, she's going to learn a *lot* of things at my house."

Ed's jaw clenched and his hands finally clenched, too, but Garvey merely kept smiling. Don't do it, Ed told himself. Don't give him the satisfaction. But his anger was almost beyond his own control now, and he stepped forward.

And Garvey instinctively shrank back. He recovered almost instantly, though, and his expression darkened. "I wouldn't, if I were you," he snarled. "Do somethin' stupid, and it won't just go hard on you. It'll go hard on your girl, too." Turning away from Ed, Garvey disappeared back into the prison.

Ed Crane was left standing where he was, knowing there was absolutely nothing he could do to help his daughter. Maybe, he thought, it would have been better if he'd died that night, instead of the other guy.

Better for the other guy.

Maybe better for him.

And certainly better for Sarah.

CHAPTER EIGHTEEN

Bettina Philips found a spot in the overflowing prison parking lot, pulled into it and shut off the engine, but didn't get out of the car right away. Instead she sat behind the wheel, gazing at the guard towers, the high walls topped with glittering loops of concertina wire, and the uniformed officers going in and out of the front door. Maybe she was doing the wrong thing. Maybe she was taking this thing with Sarah Crane too seriously.

Maybe she was getting too involved.

But Bettina was a teacher, and every teacher she knew cared about their students, especially the ones who were getting a raw deal. And Sarah Crane was getting the rawest deal Bettina had ever seen. She hadn't been in class that afternoon, and a quick visit to the office told her that Sarah hadn't been at school all day.

Her gut told her that Sarah hadn't told

the Garveys where she'd been all night and was now being punished for it. And going to the Garveys herself would only make things worse for Sarah. Nor could she go to her principal; Joe Markham would only tell her that her relationship with Sarah was "inappropriate" and that she should mind her own business, which would be his way of telling her she was on the verge of giving the school board the reason they'd been looking for to fire her.

That left only Sarah's caseworker, and Bettina didn't know who that was. She could, of course, start wending her way through the county bureaucracy, but that might take days.

On the other hand, she could go see Sarah's father, who was bound to know who had legal responsibility for his daughter.

She checked the dashboard clock. Visiting hours at the prison would be over soon — if she was going through with this, she'd better get in there.

Shep Dunnigan packed the thick stack of financial printouts into his briefcase along with the budget projections the warden had asked him to review, and snapped the locks shut. He'd get more done on them in an hour in the quiet of his study at home than he would in two days at the office. He checked his e-mail one last time, shut down the computer, then stopped at Bonnie's desk to check any messages before heading for home.

She handed him a half-dozen pink slips. "Nothing that can't wait until tomorrow," she said. "And if you lose them, don't worry — I've got copies."

Shep gazed dourly at the stack of messages. "These," he pronounced, "are why I can't work these figures here." He flipped through them quickly and handed them back to her. "And I won't lose them, because I'm not even taking them home."

"Fine with me," Bonnie said. "Have a nice evening."

"Yeah," he said wryly. "Me, a bottle of wine, and the budget printouts. Very romantic."

He swiped his ID card through the security reader and waited as the barred door slid open. He was just about to step through it when a woman came through the outside doors, then pushed her way through the double doors leading to the visitors' check-in area.

A woman Shep instantly recognized.

Bettina Philips.

He stood where he was, letting the metal

door slide closed again in front of him.

What the hell is she doing here?

The last time that nut job had shown up at the prison, it was to propose art classes for the inmates, but he had put an end to that plan before it got started. It was bad enough that his own wife sometimes went out to have Bettina read the tea leaves — or whatever it was she read — without having the woman coming into the prison, too. So what was up? Was she trying again?

He reswiped his card, walked to the doors to the visitors' center, and peered through the glass window. Bettina Philips was still at the counter, but a moment later she surrendered her identification, took a badge from the guard behind the desk, and was let through the door leading to the actual visiting area. As soon as she was gone, Shep pushed through the double doors and asked the officer at the desk for a look at the visitor log.

And there she was, the last visitor of the day: Bettina Philips. Her printed name, signature, and driver's license number.

But she hadn't been here to see the warden or any of the staff.

She'd come to visit Ed Crane.

What possible business could she have with Crane? The man was in for murder, but what could that have to do with Bettina Philips? Then he remembered: Ed Crane was also the father of the crippled girl Nick had been hanging out with lately, the one Mitch and Angie Garvey had taken in.

But that still didn't explain why Bettina Philips had come to see Crane, unless she'd taken some kind of extra interest in his daughter. And if that was it, he'd see to it that Nick had nothing more to do with the girl — the last thing he needed was for his son to get mixed up with the one woman in town who everyone thought was crazier than he was.

Crap!

As he left the building, Shep added Bettina Philips to the list of things he had to deal with.

Fifteen minutes after she'd entered the prison, Bettina found herself sitting at a round Formica table in a barren room filled with inmates, their wives, mothers, and children, and the noise produced by all of them as they tried to hear each other. A moment later a tall, gaunt man whose tired eyes were filled with worry was escorted into the room and seated across the table from her.

"Mr. Crane?" Bettina said, reaching across

to shake his hand. "I'm Bettina Philips. Sarah's art teacher?"

At the mention of his daughter, Bettina saw Ed's eyes come to life, and he slid the plastic chair closer to the table and leaned forward. "She's good, isn't she?" he asked, his voice reflecting his pride in Sarah's talent. "I mean, really good — not just high school good."

"She is indeed," Bettina assured him. "I'm not sure I've ever seen another student with as much pure talent as Sarah." She paused for a moment, then decided to seize the opening Ed had offered her. "Which is one of the reasons I'm here, Mr. Crane."

"Call me Ed," Crane said. "Sarah's crazy about you, you know."

Bettina smiled. "And I'm pretty fond of her, too. But I'm not so sure her foster family's as supportive of her talent as you and I." The light in Ed's eyes when he talked about his daughter instantly faded, and Bettina knew she'd struck a nerve.

"What's she told you?" Ed asked, his voice dropping and his eyes flicking toward the closest guard. "What's Garvey done?"

"I'm not sure he's done anything at all. But do you know who Sarah's caseworker is? Perhaps I could talk with her."

Ed opened his mouth, then closed it

again, and a moment later his whole body seemed to sag in the chair and his eyes took on the same exhausted look they'd held when he first came into the visitor's room. "What kind of father am I?" he muttered more to himself than to Bettina. Then he tried to pull himself together. "Would you believe I only remember her first name? It's Kate Something-or-other," he said. "Can you believe that? I got so wrapped up in my own problems I can't even remember who's supposed to be looking after my daughter." His voice turned bitter. "Except that I know who's supposed to be looking after her — *I'm* supposed to be looking after her. But instead . . ." His voice trailed off, and when he finally met Bettina's gaze, she saw a sadness in his expression so deep that she wanted to reach across the table and hug him. "I'm sorry," he said. "I just —" He fell silent for a moment, then shook his head. "I'm sorry."

Feeling utterly helpless, Bettina put out a hand as if to touch him, but one of the guards shot her a look of warning so severe she yanked her hand back as if her fingers had just been scorched, and cast around in her mind for something — anything — to distract Ed Crane from his misery. But of course she knew what to talk about.

"You've raised a wonderful girl," she told him. "She's kind, and sweet, and obviously got a lot of talent from somewhere."

"Well, she sure didn't get it from me or my wife," Ed sighed.

Bettina cocked her head. "A grandparent, then?"

Now Ed shrugged. "Maybe so, but I wouldn't know." He looked at Bettina again. "The thing is, Marsha and I adopted Sarah when she was two days old." He cupped his big farmer's hands and held them out. "She fit right in there. I could hardly believe it. She was so tiny, and so helpless, and I swore right then —" Once again he faltered, but this time he forced himself to complete the statement, no matter how painful it was for him. "I swore I'd take care of her the rest of my life. Fine mess of that I made, huh?"

Bettina sat silent, waiting for him to speak again, and finally he did.

"Never knew who her folks were," Ed said. "Never heard from them at all."

"Sometimes that's for the best," Bettina replied as a two-minute warning came over the loudspeaker. She wrapped her scarf around her neck and slipped her arms into the sleeves of her coat. "I'm sorry," she said, leaning forward. "Maybe I shouldn't have come. But I'm glad I did — it was good to meet you, Ed."

Ed seemed not to have heard her, and Bettina rose to her feet as the other visitors began moving toward the door. But just as she was about to turn away, he spoke again.

"Keep an eye on her for me, okay?" he asked, his eyes brightening with tears. "And I'll try to remember Kate's last name, too."

"Don't worry about it," Bettina replied. "I'll find her name. And I'll see that Sarah's all right, too. Try not to worry."

"Can't help worrying," Ed said. "Not much else to do here. But I'm glad you came — at least I know someone besides me cares about my little girl."

Bettina, no longer trusting her voice, nodded at him, then quickly threaded her way between tables, chairs, and people, and through heavy security doors that led to the visitors' reception area. She signed out, then pushed through the doors into the fresh New England air, but the chill that suddenly seized her body was far colder than the day.

She had no idea how she was going to keep the promise she'd just made to Ed Crane, but she would find a way.

She had to.

CHAPTER NINETEEN

"They locked you in?" Nick said, pressing the phone so hard against his ear that it was starting to feel numb. He was perched on the edge of his bed, barely able to believe what Sarah was telling him. What if the house caught fire? How was she supposed to get out?

"Go help her," one of the voices in his head whispered. *"Go right now."*

"Kill them," another voice suggested. *"I can help you. I'm strong . . . stronger than you . . . just get me in there . . . we can do it . . . we can —"*

"No!" Nick tried not to voice the word, but didn't quite succeed. Now he squeezed his eyes closed in the vain hope that if he focused on nothing but Sarah's whispered voice, the ones in his head might fall silent. But they didn't.

"Ask her," one of them was saying now. *"What did she draw? Did she draw what I*

showed you? Ask her . . . ask her now or —"

Nick shuddered, trying to close his mind to the whispering voice, but it was too late. The demon inside him wanted to know.

"Nick?" Sarah said, her voice penetrating the din in his head. "You okay?"

"Wh — What did you draw last night?" he asked, his own voice now no more than a whisper. "The voices want to know." He waited, but when Sarah didn't reply, he said, "Fire. That's what it was, wasn't it? You drew fire."

Sarah's sharp intake of breath told him all he needed to know. Once again she had drawn what he was seeing.

Or had he seen what she was drawing?

"Someone's coming up the stairs," Sarah whispered, then the phone in his hand went dead.

"Go get her," one of the voices told him. *"Help her!"*

"I can't," Nick whispered, his voice breaking. "What am I supposed to do? I —"

"Something! Anything!" another voice insisted. *"Do something, or —"*

Suddenly Nick's bedroom door opened and his father strode in without so much as a knock. The voices instantly hushed, and Nick's heart hammered in the sudden stillness. Had his father heard him arguing with the voices? If he had —

"How are you feeling?"

Nick tried to analyze the question. Feeling how? Physically? Mentally? Nothing in his father's mien gave him even a hint. "I'm okay," he said carefully. "Sort of bruised, I guess." He touched the area of his chest that was wrapped in bandages under his shirt. "My ribs hurt. But I'm okay."

Shep sat down on the edge of the bed. "Your mom said you had another one of those —"

His father hesitated for a moment, and Nick knew why: as long as he could remember, his father had hated talking about what was wrong with him, as if not talking about it meant it wasn't real.

"Hallucinations, Dad," he said. "They're called —"

"I *know* what they're called," his father cut in. "So did you have another one?"

Crap, Nick thought. What am I supposed to say? If he already knows, why is he asking me? His father's eyes were boring into him, and he knew he had to say something. "It — It was not really a hallucination," he finally said.

"What do you mean, 'not really'?" his father said, his eyes narrowing. "Either it was or it wasn't."

"It — well, it was more like a . . . a vision."

"A vision?" his father repeated in a mocking voice. "You think that having a vision is better than having a hallucination?"

The voices began to mutter now. "No," Nick said quickly, hoping he could find a way to end this conversation before the voices got so loud he wouldn't be able to hear his father anymore. "I didn't say it was better. But it's different. Now I'm seeing things that mean something." He cringed the moment the words were out of his mouth; they made it sound like he was starting to believe the hallucinations were real.

"So it's getting worse," his father said, his voice as angry as the expression on his face. "And you know what? It's been getting worse since that girl came to town — the cripple you've been hanging around with."

A howl rose in Nick's mind. "No!" He stood up, glowering at his father. "That's not true. Sarah's my friend — she's the one who found me in the park! She saved my life!"

"Maybe she did," Shep said. "But maybe she's the one who got you into the park in the first place. All I know is, it looks to me like you've gotten worse since you met her."

"But —"

"So you're not going to see her anymore."

"No," Nick pleaded. "That's not the way it is at all. When I'm with her, it's better. The voices almost stop." He cast around in his mind, searching for the words that would convince his father. Then: "It's like I'm *normal* when I'm with her."

It was as if his father didn't even hear him. "Let me make this simple for you, Nick," he said. "Stop seeing the Crane girl or we'll have to send you back to the hospital."

The voices began to wail, and automatically Nick crossed his arms over his chest, wrapping them as far around his body as he could, trying to keep himself from yelling at the chorus in his head to shut up, knowing that would only make things worse than they already were. He searched his father's eyes, looking for any sign that his attitude might soften, but there was nothing. There would be no arguing with him, not on this point. But still, he had to try. "I'm trying to get better," he said, his voice cracking. "And I am. I really am."

"All I know is, I can't have you running around having visions with a girl whose father is in the prison I help run. So what'll it be? You want to quit hanging out with her or do you want to go back to the hospital?"

So there it was, and while the voices in his

head screamed in fury, Nick gave in to his father. "I'll do whatever you want me to do," he said. "Just don't send me back to the hospital."

Finally his father smiled, though Nick felt no hint of warmth from it. "Then keep away from the girl, and we'll see what happens, okay?"

Nick could not imagine staying away from Sarah, but he nodded anyway.

"Okay?" his father repeated.

"Okay," Nick whispered.

"Good. Then I guess we're done here. Dinner in a few minutes."

"I'll be down."

His father left the room, not bothering to close the door behind him, and it was all Nick could do to keep from going over and slamming it shut. But that would only make things worse, and he'd already started to think of ways around his father's order.

He could still see Sarah at school, especially if they arranged to "accidentally" bump into each other. What could his father do about that? How would he even know? It wasn't like his father paid that much attention to him anyway.

Besides, even if he wanted to stop seeing Sarah, he couldn't.

The voices in his head wouldn't let him.

CHAPTER TWENTY

Bettina Philips waited until the last of her students left the classroom before heading out into the crush of first period students and weaving her way through the crowded hallway to the administration office.

Enid Hogan, who had been the office secretary when Bettina herself had gone to high school — and might even have been there for her father as well, given that no one could remember Enid having changed at all over the last four decades — was doing exactly as she'd done every school day at this time: finishing entering the attendance records into the permanent files. The only thing that had changed in all the years Enid had been at her desk was that now she entered the records into a computer instead of the old ledgers she once used. It wasn't a change that came easily to Enid: pen and ink, she understood. Digits were a mystery, and a mystery she deeply distrusted, which was why, at Warwick High School, all the important records were still kept in a filing cabinet next to Enid's desk, as well as in the computer hidden away in a secure room in the basement. "If it's there at all," Enid had once sniffed. "And even if it is, what if it breaks? Then where are the records?"

Despite the fact that Enid had managed to double her own workload by doing things both "the new way and the right way," she still looked up from her work with her usual warm smile at the sound of the door opening.

"Hi, Enid," Bettina said. "Did Sarah Crane come to school today?"

Enid shook her head. "I called Angie Garvey yesterday, and apparently Sarah has the flu. Angie said she was throwing up most of the night. Not last night," Enid quickly added in her never-ending quest to make certain her records were perfect. "Night before last. So I didn't call this morning — I had that bug three weeks ago, and it kept me out for two days. So if Sarah doesn't show up tomorrow . . ."

But Bettina was no longer listening. Sarah Crane hadn't been throwing up the night before last — she'd been sound asleep on Bettina's own chaise, Cooper snuggled next to her and both of them covered with two warm blankets. Sarah wasn't sick at all.

Which meant something else was going on, and Bettina was pretty sure she knew what. She tilted her head toward the principal's office. "Is Joe in?"

Enid nodded. "Go right in."

Bettina tapped softly on Joe Markham's office door, then opened it and looked in.

"Bettina," the principal said, leaning back in his chair and looking far more tired than he should have, given how early in the day it was. "Come in."

"I'm a bit worried about Sarah Crane," the teacher said, stepping farther into the office and closing the door behind her. "She's not in school today, and she wasn't yesterday, either."

"Has Enid called?" he asked.

"Angie Garvey told Enid she has the flu, but that went around weeks ago. And if she does have it, she's the only one, which is also strange."

Markham's brows lifted slightly. "And because of that you want — what? For me to call Child Protective Services?" Then his voice turned serious. "I'm hearing some strange stories going around — I gather our Miss Crane is quite the little artist."

Bettina stiffened. "She's very talented, yes.

Which is certainly one of the reasons I'm interested in her. Talent like hers needs to be encouraged, but —"

"But the Garveys don't want her to have anything to do with you. Right?" Bettina nodded. "Which is why you want me to deal with them, right?" Bettina nodded again, and Joe Markham made a notation on his desk calendar. "Tell you what — let's see if she's here tomorrow, and if she's not, I'll see what I can find out. Okay?"

"Thanks." Bettina opened the door and was halfway out when she turned back. "Do we have the records from Sarah's last school yet?"

"Ask Enid," the principal replied, and Bettina could tell by the tone of his voice that he'd already turned his attention away from Sarah Crane and back to whatever he'd been doing before she came in.

Bettina closed the office door and turned to see Enid Hogan holding out a file folder. "Here it is," she said. "It was already out. Because of the sickness, you know." A mischievous smile played around the corners of her lips. "You know me — everything gets written down. And they'll probably burn it all the day I retire."

"Thanks," Bettina said, taking the file and perching on one of the chairs that were usually occupied by students waiting to answer to Joe Markham for whatever sins they'd committed. Apparently this morning had been sin-free, since all the other chairs were empty.

A glance at the clock told her she had about ninety seconds until the bell would ring and she'd have to be back downstairs in the art studio. She quickly flipped through the pages of transcripts from Sarah's last school — which had nothing to do with what she was looking for — and finally found what she wanted on the very last page: the name of the caseworker to whom Sarah Crane had been assigned.

Kate Williams.

She repeated the phone number to herself half a dozen times to make sure she wouldn't forget it before she was back in her classroom, and was about to close the file when something else caught her eye.

Sarah's birth date.

A terrible chill passed through her, and the folder slipped from her hands and fell to the floor.

"Bettina?" Enid said. "Are you all right?"

Bettina looked down at Sarah's file, then reached down to pick it up. "I'm fine," she said, not quite succeeding in keeping a slight tremble out of her voice. "Just clumsy."

Enid eyed her suspiciously. "You look pale. Did you have a decent breakfast? Low blood sugar can do that to you. There's some doughnuts in the teacher's lounge — why don't I send someone down to monitor your classroom while you go have one?"

Bettina shook her head. "I'll be fine," she insisted. Before Enid could object, she stood up, put the folder back on the assistant's desk, and left the office, repeating Kate Williams's phone number three times more.

There was no need to memorize Sarah's birth date though.

It was a date she'd never forget.

CHAPTER
TWENTY-ONE

Bettina slammed on the brakes, her car jerking to a stop just before it would have passed through Shutters' rusting wrought-iron gates.

Something had changed.

But what?

She sat motionless behind the steering wheel for a moment, telling herself that nothing at all had changed; that she'd simply seen Sarah Crane's birthday in the school records. Yet all through the day — a day that it seemed would never end — she'd felt a sense of some kind of shift taking place, a feeling that only grew stronger as she made her way home after school. And now, sitting in her car in front of the gates of the only home she'd ever known, she saw it.

But it was impossible, of course; the gates were no different than they'd ever been: sagging and rusty, the leaves of the original vine pattern long since fallen away as if the gates themselves knew that winter was fast approaching. Except that this afternoon the gates looked different.

Some of the rust seemed to have flaked off, and one or two of the corroding vines appeared to have sprouted tiny metal barbs. Which was ridiculous: metal — especially wrought iron — didn't do that. Once it rusted, it was gone, and no matter how real the vines may have looked a century and a half ago, they had never been anything but iron.

And yet . . .

The light. That had to be it — it was nothing more than a trick of the fall light, with the sun sinking so early now that the evening shadows were hiding the worst of the grinding damage of old age.

Taking her foot off the brake, she drove on. But as she emerged from the garage a few moments later, she once again stopped short.

She gazed up at the house.

And it, too, seemed somehow different. And yet what had changed? The paint was still peeling — at least the paint that hadn't already weathered away — and the roof still lacked the slates that had fallen over the years.

And yet . . .

Somehow the paint didn't look quite as bad as she'd thought when she inspected it a few months ago, and even the roof looked like it might make it through one more winter before she'd have to do something about it.

She went in through the back door just as she always did, but again found herself stopping just before stepping across the threshold. This time, though, she knew why.

She'd forgotten to turn the heat down in the kitchen, and it was the wave of heated — and expensively heated — air pouring forth that brought her to a halt. Not even bothering to shed her coat, she hurried to the electric heater and reached down to turn it off.

But it was already off. Nor was its fan blowing, nor was it any warmer than the kitchen itself.

Nor was Pyewackett curled up in front of it, warming himself while he slept the day away.

She left the kitchen, moving through the butler's pantry and pushing through the swinging door to the dining room.

It was as perfectly warm as the kitchen.

So was the great hall.

And so, she discovered as she passed its

open door, was the study. Not only was the door ajar, but heat was emanating from it, and so was the acrid smell of smoke.

Smoke?

Panic breaking over her, Bettina threw the door open, half expecting to find the room engulfed in flames. But all she found were dying embers in the fireplace.

And Pyewackett, curled up on the hearth, sound asleep.

But where had the fire come from? She hadn't built it — of that she was absolutely certain. And even if she had — even if she assumed she'd built it this morning before she went to work — how had it lasted all day? And how had it heated the whole house?

And if she hadn't started it, who had? She reached for the phone, about to call Dan West, but hesitated as her fingers closed around the receiver. If someone had broken in, why would they have left a fire burning? It made no sense.

Then her eyes fell on the yellowed manuscript that had been hidden away in the bottom drawer of the desk, but was now lying in the center of the desk's mahogany surface.

And she remembered the picture Sarah Crane drew two nights ago, the picture that still stood on the easel in the studio, propped up exactly as Sarah had left it.

Or was it?

Pyewackett woke up then, leaped from the hearth onto the desk, sniffed at the manuscript, then looked up at Bettina, his yellow eyes glowing more brightly than the fading embers on the hearth he'd just left. A second later he was gone, springing to the floor, dashing out the door and turning left.

Toward the studio.

Bettina was about to go after him, but first went to the desk and scooped up the manuscript. Then, with the ancient pages clutched tightly in her hand, she followed her pet.

By the time she got to the studio, Pyewackett was waiting for her on the chaise.

And the drawing on the easel, like the gates to the estate and even the house itself, had somehow changed.

The flames burned brighter than Bettina remembered, seeming almost to leap from the paper upon which they were limned.

Now Pyewackett was on his feet again, insistently nosing at the manuscript in Bettina's hand, then lashing out at it with his paw forcefully enough to knock half the pages loose. As Bettina clutched the remaining pages more tightly, her eyes fell on the words on the page that was now exposed:

344

I made a pile of all the papers from the file cabinets and arranged the wooden chairs around it. Beyond the chairs, I piled all the inflammable materials I could find in the office, and soaked the whole of it with kerosene from the maintenance shed. A little while later the whistle blew and I knew the spinners and the looms were in full production, all the workers at their stations.

Including Honoria.

Especially Honoria.

She would be at her loom, with my brother's bastard in her belly, her fingers weaving a fabric as loose as her own morals. But not for much longer. Already I could see the conflagration that would come once I touched a match to all my kindling. The lint in the air would catch a spark, and the very air would be aflame, engulfing the building and everyone in it.

I locked the two big warehouse doors from the outside and —

The phone rang.

Bettina jumped at the unexpected sound, dropping the rest of the pages to the floor as Pyewackett leaped off the chaise and skittered underneath it.

She picked up the phone and put the

345

receiver to her ear, but before she could utter even a word, a venomous voice lashed out at her. "Leave them alone," the voice said, soft and dangerous and trembling with fury. "You leave our kids alone."

The warmth of the house was washed away by a sudden flood of terrible cold. Bettina knew that voice, knew it perfectly, even though she'd never heard it over the telephone before.

Knew it from her past.

Knew it from her nightmares.

Her fingers gripped the phone as if frozen to it.

"I'm watching you," the voice said.

Then there was silence.

The terrible cold that had fallen over her a moment ago turned into fear, and she instinctively looked out the enormous conservatory windows. From the brightness inside, she could see nothing at all of the darkness beyond the walls of the house.

But from the blackness outside, anyone at all could be looking in.

Seized by a terror she had experienced only once before in her life, Bettina raced through the house, checking every door and every window to make certain everything was locked.

Locked, and bolted.

Yet still she didn't feel safe, and as if sensing her fear her animals had gathered around her, and when she finally turned off the lights on the lower floor and started up toward her bedroom on the second floor, they stayed close by her feet.

She listened to the house.

The animals listened, too.

Silence.

She led the animals into her bedroom, locked the door and climbed into bed, still fully dressed, still in the grip of the terrible fear the voice on the telephone had brought on. She pulled the covers tight around her neck and left the light on, and prayed that if sleep came it wouldn't bring more terror with it. . . .

She could feel the presence before she heard the sound. It felt like danger, and it was nearby, and she should run. But instead of running she stopped completely, waiting in the darkness, in the woods, in the loneliness of the night.

A twig snapped, the sound seeming to come from behind her.

She whirled, then heard it again.

Again from behind her.

When the third twig snapped she finally began to run, but her feet felt so heavy she could hardly move them.

And the presence in the darkness was getting closer.

She could almost see it, almost touch it, but somehow, even though it was very, very close, she couldn't quite find it.

Then something was around her neck, and she could feel it squeezing tighter, and now she could feel breathing on her ear, heavy breathing, and the thing around her neck grew tighter and now she was falling, falling, and falling until the ground rose around her and then the thing around her neck was gone, but now there was something on top of her — some terrible weight — and she wanted to scream but her voice was gone and when she opened her mouth nothing came out.

Fingers.

Rough fingers, all over her, pulling at her clothes, pulling them off, pushing their way inside her bra . . . inside her panties . . . inside her! *Now she did scream, but her voice was caught inside her and no matter how hard she tried nothing would come out except a strange grunting noise.*

She tried to bite, tried to claw, tried everything to get away, but her attacker was always just outside her reach, just beyond her flailing arms and legs.

The weight on her was even heavier, and

she was sinking into the forest floor, and her clothes were being ripped away and now something was pushing inside her, tearing at her, a searing pain slashing up from her groin and —

"I'll kill you," a voice whispered in her ear. The voice was low, and hard, and so cold its chill penetrated straight into her soul while at the same time it seared into her memory, never to be forgotten.

The voice penetrated into her memory even more deeply than the man penetrated her body.

She couldn't breathe, couldn't fight, couldn't do anything. But she had to — she had to do something or she would die. Die right here in the dark, in the forest, in the blackness of the night.

Darkness swirled inside the darkness of her vision, and just as she was about to give up, to let herself sink into it forever, she gathered herself for one last effort.

She filled her lungs, sucking her breath in as far as she could, then forced it out again in a scream that combined all the anguish and horror and pain she had just endured.

And sat straight up in her bed.

She wasn't in the woods, in the darkness and the cold.

She was safe in her bed, safe in her house,

safe with her animals.

She grabbed Rocky and hugged him close to her pounding heart.

But even with Rocky lapping at her face and the cats and Cooper snuggling close, Bettina knew that she was wrong.

She was not safe.

Something — everything — had changed, and she had to know why. And she had to know now. Steeling herself, she left her bed, unlocked the bedroom door, and started downstairs.

Sarah was perched on a rickety stool next to the attic window, angling her history text to catch the last of the daylight rather than turning on the attic's single light and risking another accusation of wasting electricity. A car turning the corner at the end of the block caught her eye, and she let the book drop to her lap as she watched it come down the block, slow, then pull to a stop in front of the house. Suddenly her heart raced as she recognized who it was: Kate Williams.

What was she doing here?

Had someone gotten worried when she wasn't in school and called the county? Or was it one of the drop-in visits Kate had told her would happen?

Or had Angie Garvey herself called, telling the county to put her somewhere else?

Even as the questions rose in her mind, she heard Angie Garvey pounding up the stairs, and instantly eliminated the third thought: if Angie had called to have her taken away, she'd have already told her to pack her things.

"That woman from the county is here," Angie said. "I've no idea why, but when I call you, you're to come down and tell her that we've provided you with everything you need." Her eyes bored into Sarah. "You say the wrong thing, and Mitch will take care of you when he gets home. But if you behave yourself, you'll go back to school tomorrow. Understand?" Sarah nodded, but Angie's expression hardened even further. "And you'd do well to remember exactly where Mitch works, and exactly how bad he can make life for your father. Got it?"

Sarah felt her face pale at the threat.

"Do I make myself clear?" Angie demanded.

"Yes, ma'am," Sarah replied, her voice little more than a whisper.

The doorbell rang and Pepper started barking.

"Then try to make yourself look decent," Angie said. "And I'll call you when I'm ready." She started out of the attic, then

351

turned back. "I told the school you've been out sick."

Once again Sarah nodded, and when Angie was finally gone, she left the history book on the makeshift desk and went down to the bathroom on the second floor to wash her face, brush her teeth, and comb her hair. But she wouldn't freshen up too much — if Angie had told the school she was sick, she might as well look the part. As she finished her hair, she heard Angie calling her, and began rehearsing what she would say that would keep Kate Williams from taking her away from Warwick. In just the short time she'd been here, Nick Dunnigan and Bettina Philips had become the two people in the world — besides her father — who mattered most to her, and she wasn't about to be separated from them the way she'd been separated from her father. With a last glance in the mirror, Sarah headed downstairs, doing her best to keep her limp under total control.

"Well, look at you," Kate Williams exclaimed as she came to the bottom of the stairs a moment later. "No crutches!" Then her smile faded. "But you look like you've lost some weight."

"She eats like a bird," Angie said. "And she's been a little under the weather the past few days. But don't you worry. We'll fatten her up."

Sarah smiled at Kate as Angie put her arm around her and gave her a squeeze. "Hi," she said, her voice barely audible. "It's nice to see you."

Bad match, Kate Williams thought as she left the Garvey house half an hour later. Although Sarah Crane had certainly looked wan, she hadn't actually looked *sick,* and more than once she thought the girl had cast a wary glance toward her foster mother, as if wondering whether she was saying the right things. Well, if she hadn't said everything Angie Garvey might have wanted her to, she certainly hadn't said any wrong things, either; certainly nothing that raised any huge alarms in her own mind. And, unfortunately, the sense that the Garveys and Sarah were a bad match wasn't enough to make her start looking for another place for Sarah, at least not yet. Any foster home was hard to come up with, and on the scale of foster parents, so far the Garveys seemed about in the middle: maybe not the best, but certainly far from the worst. And yet, even though Sarah insisted more than once that everything was fine, Kate had the distinct feeling that the girl wasn't telling her the truth.

At least not the whole truth.

As she got into her car and glanced at her schedule — she was going to be five minutes late for a meeting with a couple who were thinking about taking in a group of four children, all under the age of five, whose mother had died and whose father had abandoned them — she made a mental note to check back with Sarah Crane in another week or so. Maybe they'd have a little private time then, and if things looked all right, she might even be able to consider this placement permanent and move on to some of the more difficult ones — like the four children she hoped would, indeed, be taken in by the couple she was about to interview.

Starting the engine and checking the address of her next appointment, Kate put Sarah Crane out of her mind, at least for the moment.

Bettina moved once again through Shutters' downstairs rooms, trying to determine exactly what it was that had changed in the house. Coming home from school this afternoon, she'd paused not only at the worn gates to the estate, but outside the garage as well, trying to see if anything looked different. But it hadn't — not really.

Or at least that was what she told herself. After all, peeling paint and sagging shutters and falling roof slates couldn't just repair themselves. She'd just gotten used to it — that was all. She'd finally become inured to the steadily increasing decrepitude of the place, and it wasn't that it looked any better at all — she'd just stopped seeing all the damage she couldn't afford to repair.

Now, with Cooper and Rocky trotting ahead of her, she spent twenty minutes going through every room in the house one more time.

Nothing, until she came to the studio. And there it was: the yellowed manuscript still lay exactly where she dropped it when the phone rang a few hours ago and that terrible voice dredged up nightmares she'd hoped never to have again.

Now both dogs were sitting next to the manuscript like twin sentinels, and both were gazing expectantly up at her.

They know, Bettina thought. Whatever it is, it's in those pages.

Which, of course, she'd known all along. After all, since Sarah was drawing scenes from those pages without ever having read them, how could they not be connected to what was happening? She picked them up, straightened them out, then began going through them, not reading them, but looking for a pattern.

They read almost like case histories of the people who had once been inmates here, but histories written by the patients themselves rather than the doctors.

But her thrice-great-grandfather claimed they were fiction.

Tales from my imagination.

That's what he'd written.

But what if it wasn't true?

If the stories were truly fiction, why had her ancestor hidden the manuscript? Had he interviewed some of the inmates and then fictionalized their insanity?

But again, why?

The old filing cabinets in the basement — they were filled with old records. If she could match the stories to some of the inmates, then find the common factor among those inmates —

She shuddered at the thought of going down into the dank shadowy chambers under the house, but shook the feeling off. She'd never been afraid of anything down there before, so why should she now? But she already knew the answer to that, too. She should be afraid because now everything had changed. Everything about the house was different.

Everything.

But it's still just the basement, she told herself.

She went to the kitchen, found the big flashlight she always kept there, and called out for Cooper and Rocky. They came into the kitchen, but when they saw her opening the door to the basement, Cooper uttered a low growl while Rocky dropped to the floor in the open door to the butler's pantry, refusing to come a step closer.

The smell of mildew drifted into the kitchen, and now Cooper, too, dropped to the floor, pressing close to Rocky.

Bettina flipped the wall switch that turned on the string of ancient yellow lightbulbs. "C'mon, sissies," she said.

Neither of the dogs moved.

She started down the concrete steps, pausing halfway down to listen.

Silence.

Yet something was waiting for her — she could feel it.

She almost turned and fled back up the stairs to the bright lights and warmth of the kitchen, but then hesitated. She'd been down here thousands of times, and there was no reason to be afraid now. Taking a deep breath, Bettina descended the rest of the stairs and began shoving the decaying boxes of God only knew what from in front of the old file cabinets.

She opened the first drawer. Inmate files. Hundreds of them, all jammed together, and when she tried to pull one out, it crumbled in her fingers.

She closed the drawer again and stood still for a moment, gazing at the row of filing cabinets.

Where? She wondered. Where do I look? Where do I even start?

Then she heard a faint scratching sound from behind her, and instinctively whirled around, only to see Cooper, his head cocked, standing at the foot of the stairs, looking at her. Sighing, she turned back to the filing cabinets.

And something had changed.

But this time she knew right away what it was: one of the drawers — the bottom one in the cabinet farthest to the left — was open.

Not by much — just a crack — but she was certain that a moment ago, before she'd turned around, it had been closed.

Behind her, Cooper growled softly.

Bettina reached out, her fingers trembling, and pulled the drawer open.

At first it seemed empty, but then, when

she pulled the drawer all the way open, she saw them. Tucked away behind the metal slider designed to keep the files in front of it neatly upright, were a batch of large envelopes, perhaps thirty in all.

Bettina carefully lifted the first one out, opened it and slid the pages out, shining the flashlight onto the top sheet. The patient's name had been Tarbell: William G. Tarbell. All that was on that first sheet was a sort of time line, listing the date of admission and the various wards to which Tarbell had been assigned. The man had seemingly been well enough to act as a groundskeeper at Shutters during the last four months the time line included. Bettina carefully turned the pages, scanning the handwritten notes as quickly as she could. Over the course of a decade, Tarbell had apparently married three young women and fathered five children; only the last wife and one of the children survived. Tarbell, according to the notes, had *eaten* all the others.

Bettina was almost certain she remembered a similar story in the ancient manuscript. Taking all the envelopes from the drawer, and with Cooper at her heels, she went back upstairs to the light and warmth of the kitchen. She turned off the basement lights, locked the door, and carefully laid all the envelopes on the big wooden kitchen table. She went to the studio then, retrieved the manuscript, and returned with it to the kitchen.

Twenty minutes later she had correlated most of the stories in the manuscript to the files, and discovered that they had three things in common.

Each of the inmates had been in service here at the house; some as cooks, others as gardeners or housekeepers or stable hands.

Each had committed truly horrendous acts of violence and shown absolutely no remorse.

And finally, not one of them had a date of death listed in their records, let alone a date of release.

Not that anyone committed to Shutters Lake in its early days was ever released, and in only a very few cases had relatives claimed bodies when someone died. But most of Shutters' inmates never left at all; when they died, they were buried in the property's own cemetery, their names, dates of interments, and the location of their graves carefully recorded in a large ledger that was still in her grandfather's study. "Just in case," he said when he showed her the ledger so many years ago. "If someone came looking for a relative, my grandfather always wanted to be able to show them where the grave was, and he told me to keep the book handy, just in case any of their descendants showed up."

Bettina got up, went to the study, and found the ledger.

Not one of the people whose case histories had been tucked in the back of an otherwise empty file drawer were listed in the cemetery register.

But if they weren't buried in the cemetery — etery —

The memory of Sarah Crane's first drawing rose in Bettina's mind, and suddenly she knew where those people were.

The basement.

All of them were in the basement.

CHAPTER
TWENTY-TWO

Bettina was just about to take off her robe and crawl back into bed, which was already occupied by both dogs and all three cats, when Rocky stood up, stiffening as he went on point with his nose directed at the window. "What is it?" Bettina asked as she untied the belt. But the sweep of a pair of headlights across the ceiling answered her question even before Rocky — and then Cooper — began barking.

Someone had come up the driveway and was now stopping in front of the house.

Cooper's ears perked up and he stared at the bedroom door, waiting for the doorbell.

Bettina looked at the clock. Ten-thirty. Who would come at this time of night?

The voice on the phone.

The doorbell rang, the dogs began to bark, and Bettina opened the bedroom door to let them dash downstairs. She followed, more slowly, coming to a stop at the bottom of the stairs as an echo of last night's phone call rose out of her memory.

. . . I'll kill you . . .

What was she thinking? It wasn't time to open the door — it was time for an alarm system!

Except that anyone who wanted to kill her wouldn't ring the doorbell first.

Would they?

The bell rang again, but instead of going to the front door, she detoured into the study and picked up a heavy poker from the hearth. With it clutched tightly in her right hand, she finally approached the door, turned on the porch light, opened the small Judas door and peered out.

Lily Dunnigan stood on the porch, her face pale and her eyes darting nervously as she searched for anyone who might be hidden in the velvet darkness of the night.

Bettina dropped the poker into the umbrella stand, unlatched the dead bolts, and opened the door. "Lily?"

"Thank God you're here," Lily said as she slipped into the house and Bettina closed the door behind her. Then she noticed Bettina's bathrobe. "Did I get you out of bed?"

"Not even close," Bettina said. "I hadn't gotten my robe off yet." Then she saw the redness in Lily's eyes, and her tone turned serious. "Lily, what is it? What's happened?"

The dogs, apparently satisfied that whoever this was didn't mean their mistress any harm, sniffed eagerly around Lily's feet, and she reached down to give them each a scratch before blowing her nose on a well-used handkerchief. "It's Nick," she finally managed to say. "And Shep."

"Come into the kitchen," Bettina said. "I'll put on a fresh pot of tea."

Lily unbuttoned her coat and followed her to the kitchen. "Nick doesn't seem to be getting any better, and I'm —" She hesitated, and Bettina knew that whatever was coming next was something Lily wished she didn't have to say. After taking a deep breath, Lily went on. "Shep says that if Nick doesn't start getting better, he's going to send him back to the hospital."

Bettina frowned as she filled the teakettle. Though Nick wasn't in any of her classes this year, she'd seen him around the school, and he'd seemed all right, at least until he was jumped in the park. "Is he worse since he was beaten up?" she asked.

"It seems to come and go. We thought the new drug was working for his hallucinations, but now they're getting worse." Lily hesitated again, then: "And now he's calling them 'visions.' "

Bettina's frown deepened. "That doesn't sound good."

"I'm at my wit's end," Lily said, finally taking off her coat and dropping onto one of the chairs at the big oak table.

Now Bettina understood why Lily had come here in the dead of night. She put some tea in the pot, and while waiting for the water to boil, leaned against the counter, folded her arms across her chest, and waited on Lily Dunnigan. Whatever Lily wanted, she would have to ask for it.

It didn't take long.

"I — I've heard . . ." Lily began hesitantly. "Well, I've heard that you can do things . . ."

She looked so embarrassed that Bettina almost laughed out loud, but Lily also looked so miserable that she almost went over and hugged her. "Despite what you might have heard," she said gently, "I don't cast spells or tell fortunes or anything like that."

Now Lily looked like she wanted to fall through the floor. "I — I just wondered if there was anything — anything at all — you could do that might help Nick."

The kettle began to whistle, and Bettina poured water into the teapot, then took the pot and two mugs to the table. "I'm not a witch," she said.

"Oh, no, no, I'd never —"

Bettina smiled. "Come on, Lily — don't tell me you haven't heard the rumors." Lily reddened, answering her question. "Look, we both know I don't really fit into this town. I'm an artist — maybe not much of one — and I'm interested in all kinds of things. Herbs and natural medicines and things like that. That may make me a kook around here, but it doesn't make me a witch."

"I know," Lily insisted. "But I've heard you've given people things —"

"I've given a couple of people homeopathic remedies and mixed up a few herbal teas, and that's about it, Lily. But for problems like Nick's, I wouldn't have any idea what to do." Bettina poured tea into the mugs and pushed one of them across to Lily.

Lily eyed the mug suspiciously.

"It's nothing more than a little lemongrass, green tea, chamomile, and ginger," Bettina told her. "If I mixed it right, it should calm you down."

Lily hesitated, tasted the tea, then took a swallow, followed by another. She set the mug down and managed a smile, the color in her face already healthier. "I just don't know what to do," she sighed.

"Maybe Shep's right," Bettina offered. "I mean, I'm sure Nick's doctors are competent."

"But his drugs aren't working anymore. In the hospital, he had the most *terrible* hallucination —"

"Hospital?" Bettina said.

"After he was beaten up," Lily said. "They beat him up the day before yesterday, really badly. Cracked his ribs and gave him a concussion."

"Who did it?"

Lilly shook her head. "If he even knows, he's not saying. He says they attacked him from behind, and he never got a look at them."

Which told Bettina that Conner West went after Nick after blaming Nick and Sarah for his dog's death, and Nick was afraid that if he told on them, they'd just beat him up worse. Which, unfortunately, was probably true, given that Conner's father ran what passed for a police force in Warwick.

"Anyway," Lily went on, "Nick had a hallucination of his room in the hospital burning. He thought his bed was on fire and that he was going to be burned alive."

Bettina's mind raced. That was the night Sarah Crane had been here, drawing.

367

Drawing fire.

Drawing it at the same time Nick Dunnigan was seeing it?

Had it happened again? Did Nick see what Sarah was drawing, as Sarah told her he had when she'd drawn the butchered dog?

Lily took another swallow from her mug of tea. "The thing is, Nick's calling them visions now. He says they mean something, but he doesn't know what. Or at least he can't tell me what." She gazed bleakly at Bettina. "I'm sorry — I shouldn't have come. I don't know what I was thinking."

"You're just trying to help your son," Bettina told her. "Isn't that what mothers are supposed to do?"

Lily nodded. "I just feel so helpless, and Nick's so frightened. If he could just calm down —" Her expression abruptly brightened and she looked down at her mug. "Maybe this tea!"

"Lily, it's nothing but a few herbs. It —"

But Lily was suddenly excited. "You said it would calm me down, and it did. Why wouldn't it do the same for Nick?"

"I don't —"

"Isn't it at least worth a try? I'll pay you for it!"

Bettina laughed. "You don't need to pay

me. I can put it together in about five minutes, and I'll put some in a Baggie for you. But be careful: if Dan West stops you, he'll think it's marijuana."

Lily hesitated, her eyes widening. "It isn't, is it?"

"Of course not! Do you know what they'd do to me if I gave grass to a student?" Then her expression turned serious. "But don't tell anyone about this, all right? There are enough people in this town trying to get me fired already, and if they could accuse me of practicing medicine without a license, that might just do it."

"Would that be better or worse than witchcraft?" Lily asked, her voice as flat as her expression was deadpan. Then she giggled. "Probably worse — at least with witchcraft they could get the minister to pray for them."

As Lily poured herself another cup of the brew, Bettina set about mixing the tea and herbs. It might not do a thing for Nick, she thought, but at least giving it to him would make Lily feel better. As for Nick, whatever he was having, it wasn't visions.

It was communication.

Communication between him and Sarah Crane.

And whatever it was that was in this house.

CHAPTER
TWENTY-THREE

It seemed like the longest morning of Sarah's life. When she emerged from the Garveys' house a few minutes after seven-thirty, she'd started toward the corner as fast as she could, certain that Nick Dunnigan would be waiting for her. But there was no sign of Nick, not on the corner or anywhere else, and by the time she was half a block from the school, her mind was churning. He wasn't in the hospital — she was sure of that. And the last time she'd talked to him before the cell phone battery died, he said he was only going to be out for one day. But where was he? Why hadn't he been waiting for her?

By the time she reached the foot of the steps leading up to the school's front doors, she was so worried about Nick that she didn't even notice the way people were looking at her, but by the time she got inside and started making her way through the crowded hall toward her locker, she couldn't miss it. She couldn't miss the looks, and she couldn't miss the whispers, especially when the whisperers made sure they whispered loud enough so she could hear.

"*. . . heard she was putting out for Conner West . . .*"

"*. . . so nutty Nick tried to kick West's . . .*"

"*. . . Jolinda said she was doing three guys . . .*"

"*. . . I can't imagine even one guy wanting to do it with her. I mean, she's crip—*"

Sarah stopped listening then, and for the rest of the morning, through the first four classes, she'd done her best to look at no one, to hear nothing. Let them talk, she told herself over and over again. Just ignore them. All of them.

Once, between second and third period, she caught a glimpse of Nick at the far end of the hall, but he hadn't seen her, and just as she started toward him, the bell rang. But at least she knew he was there.

Now, at last, the clock was ticking down to the end of fourth period, and when the bell finally rang, she didn't stay in her seat the way she usually did, waiting for the crowd to thin out. Today she stood up, picked up her backpack, stuffed her history text into it and —

A hard shove knocked her back into her chair, and she looked up to see Jolene Parsons rolling her eyes. "Can't you wait until the rest of us are gone?" she hissed, keeping her voice low enough so only Sarah could hear her. "Why should we all have to wait just because you can't keep up?" Without waiting for an answer, Jolene turned away, and a few seconds later one of Jolene's friends looked back at her, snickering.

When the room was finally empty of everyone except the teacher, Sarah stood up again and walked out into the corridor. Looking at no one, refusing to hear anything, she clutched her backpack close to her chest and headed toward the cafeteria.

She saw Nick sitting at his usual place at the farthest table back.

Sarah smiled and waved, but just as in the hall earlier, he didn't seem to see her.

She bought a slice of pizza and a glass of lemonade and carried her tray over to him, but before she could sit down, he spoke, his voice low, his eyes fixed on the food in front of him.

"I need you to sit somewhere else."

"What?" Her hands weakened and her tray clattered to the table.

Nick still didn't look at her. "Someone

might see us together."

Sarah's heart was starting to pound, and she could feel the eyes of the rest of the people in the cafeteria watching what was happening. What was going on? Why was Nick acting like this? "What —" she began, but Nick shook his head.

"Don't talk to me. My father says if I don't stop seeing you, he's going to send me back to the hospital."

"Why?" Sarah demanded, sitting down in the chair opposite Nick. "Does he think *I* beat you up?"

Nick moved his tray away from her and slid into the next seat. "Just leave it alone, okay?"

She stared at him and tried not to hear the snickering rippling through the cafeteria. "Are you serious?" she demanded, lowering her voice in the hope that only Nick would hear her.

Finally he looked at her, his face twisted in misery. *"Please,"* he whispered back. "Just sit somewhere else. If you don't, someone will tell my dad. You know they will!"

Sarah held his gaze until he looked away. She opened her backpack, fished around in it until she found his cell phone, and set it down on the table. Then she stood up, picked up her tray, and looked for another place to sit.

But everywhere she turned, people either shook their heads at her or pretended they didn't see her at all. Not that it mattered — even if she found a table where they'd let her sit, her appetite was gone and her chest felt so tight she knew she wouldn't be able to swallow even a sip of lemonade, let alone choke down the pizza.

Leaving the tray on the busing table, she left the cafeteria and started back through the empty halls to her locker, struggling with every step against the tears that threatened to overwhelm her. By the time she found her locker, her eyes were so blurry she could barely see the lock, and it took her three tries before she finally got it open.

Sitting on top of her science book was a piece of notebook paper, folded twice.

No envelope. Not even her name written across it.

And even though she hadn't opened it yet, she was sure it wasn't signed, either.

In fact, why even bother to read it? It was probably some kind of death threat from Conner or one of his friends, or some disgusting picture someone had drawn of what they'd been whispering about all morning.

Maybe she should take it to the principal's office.

Or just throw it away.

But even as she tried to decide, she found herself picking the sheet of paper up and unfolding it.

Meet me at the library right after school.

Nick had scrawled his initial at the bottom, and as she gazed at the N, the tears she'd been fighting so long finally flowed.

Why had she doubted him, even for a minute?

Ten minutes, Sarah promised herself as she hurried down the sidewalk toward the old Carnegie Library that was still a block away. If I hurry, I'll still only be fifteen minutes late getting back to the Garveys. Maybe Angie wouldn't even notice. But as she waited for the light to change, she was already casting around in her mind for something that might deflect her foster mother's anger. But what did it matter, really? Even if she got home on time, Angie would still find something to punish her for.

The light changed and Sarah increased her pace to a lopsided trot. She was only about twenty yards from the library when a car horn blared, startling her so badly she lost her balance. As she grabbed at a lamp-post to steady herself, Conner West's car slammed to a stop next to her, and she saw Tiffany Garvey grinning at her.

"What do you think you're doing?" her foster sister demanded. "Our house is the other way!"

"I have to do a — a book report," Sarah blurted, snatching at the first excuse that came into her mind.

"Yeah, right," Tiffany drawled. "Going to meet your boyfriend, aren't you? Going to get it on in the history section?"

Sarah felt her own blush betraying her.

"Nutty Nicky can't get it on," Conner West chimed in. "After what I did to him, he won't even be able to get it on with himself for a week."

Sarah put her head down and started once again toward the library, but the car idled along beside her, keeping pace.

"Better be careful," Conner went on, his voice taking on a tone of menace that sent a chill through Sarah. "We're watching you. Not just me and Tiff — a whole bunch of us. And what we do to you'll be a whole lot worse than what happened to Dunnigan."

Sarah stopped short and turned to glare at Conner. "Why don't you just leave me alone? And Nick, too. What did we ever do to you?"

For a split second Conner West looked surprised that she'd actually talked back to him, but then his eyes narrowed in cold fury. "You killed my dog. And you're going to pay for it. You and Dunnigan both. I don't know how you did it, but I saw it, and I'm not forgetting it." He stepped on the gas and the car sped away, the screaming tires spitting a plume of rotting leaves over Sarah.

She looked around to see if anyone had seen what just happened, or even heard Conner's threat, but the sidewalk, as well as the street itself, was empty. Brushing the worst of the muck from the gutter off her clothes, Sarah climbed the marble steps of the library, pulled open the heavy doors, and instantly felt transported back to the days when her mother used to take her to the library back home for story time or to use her very own library card to check out as many books as she wanted. As the warmth of the building and the smell of old books began to seep into her, she looked around for Nick, but he wasn't sitting at any of the big wooden tables, nor could she see him standing in the stacks, waiting for her.

Then she remembered what he'd said at lunch and knew that wherever he was, it wasn't going to be where someone was likely to see him talking to her.

She scanned the children's area, empty except for a couple of little girls playing with puppets, then made her way between the tables and through the stacks to the back of the main room.

Nick sat at a reading carrel in the farthest corner, his back to her and his head in his hands. For a second Sarah thought he might be crying, but then she realized he was concentrating on a large book open in front of him. Slipping her backpack off her shoulders, she slid into the chair next to him.

He looked up, a relieved smile spreading across his face. "I was so afraid you wouldn't come," he whispered. "I was afraid maybe you wouldn't see my note, and that you'd think —"

"That you really didn't want to see me anymore?" Sarah broke in. "I might have — you put on a really good show at lunch."

Nick's smile faded. "I'm sorry. I was hoping you'd find my note before you went to the caf, but when I saw the look on your face after I told you to leave me alone, I knew you hadn't. But by then it was too late, and my dad really will send me back to the hospital."

"It's okay," Sarah assured him. "I found the note and I'm here. So what's going on?"

Nick was silent for almost a full minute, and when he finally spoke, he kept scanning the area around them for anyone who might be listening. "You're not going to believe this," he said, closing the book and turning it so Sarah could see the cover clearly. "I'm not even sure I believe it myself."

She gazed down at the old leather-bound book on the carrel desk. Its color had faded to a greenish shade, and the gold-leaf letters embossed into its surface had long since worn away. "What is it?" she breathed.

"It's about the place where Miss Philips lives. Not just the house — the whole thing, from back when there was a whole other building. They called it an 'institute,' but it was really a prison."

"For insane people," Sarah said. "Bettina — Miss Philips — told me."

Nick nodded. "Anyway, I used to spend a lot of time here, and one day I decided to see if I could find the oldest book here. And I found this." He looked up into her eyes. "And it scared me."

"Scared you how?"

Nick opened his mouth, then closed it again. What if Sarah thought he was as crazy as his father did? But she wouldn't — she couldn't. And he had to tell her, had to find exactly the right words. "I — well, it — I'm not sure. I know it sounds really weird, but it seemed like when I was looking through it, I could almost hear some of the people in it." His eyes shifted to the book for a moment, then came back to Sarah. "I think maybe that's when I first started hearing the voices. I don't really remember, but . . ." He waited, watching Sarah closely. If she got up and walked out . . . "I don't know — it just seemed like the way I've been seeing what you've been drawing . . . well, doesn't it seem like there's got to be some kind of connection there?"

He waited, afraid that Sarah was going to give him that look — the look the rest of the kids at school always gave him.

The look his father gave him.

But instead she reached out a finger and touched the fragile edges of the scarred leather binding. Finally, she opened the cover to expose the frontispiece, and Nick heard her gasp as she gazed at a photograph of a house with a man standing by the front door, then read the caption beneath it.

Warden Boone Philips at the New Residence, 1857

"I drew that house," she whispered. "*Ex-actly* like that, with charcoal!"

Nick stared at her.

"It was my first or second day here," she told him. "How could I have done that? How could I have drawn Bettina's house the way it used to be when I hadn't even seen it the way it is now?" Without waiting for Nick to answer, Sarah scanned the title page.

Shutters Lake Institute for the Criminally
Insane
A History
By Liam Clements

She turned the page.

The first photograph looked like a prison, but the caption said it was a hospital. It was still under construction, and the men working on it wore the black-and-white-striped garb of nineteenth-century prisoners as they leaned on their shovels next to newly planted saplings, with the building in the background.

Nick sat silently as Sarah turned the pages, and as he watched her, the murmurs in his head began to rise.

Rise, as if in anticipation.

She turned another page, exposing a plate

in which nearly a dozen inmates stood in front of the house, their placement looking deliberately posed and the smiles they displayed for the camera appearing forced even in the ancient photograph.

"Look!" said a voice so sharp and loud it made Nick jump. *"There I am!"*

"Wait," Nick said as Sarah started to turn another page. "Did you hear that?"

Her hand froze a few inches above the page and she looked up at him. "Hear what?"

Nick ran his finger over the photograph, and as he touched each face in turn, the voices in his mind rose and fell, almost as if he were running through the stations on a radio.

Select inmates with good behavior earn the privilege of working at the residence

"It's them," Nick whispered, his voice sounding haunted even to himself. "These are the people whose voices I hear." He waited, again half expecting Sarah to get up and walk out of the library, but instead she simply studied the picture for several more seconds, then looked up at him again.

"Are you sure?"

He nodded.

"You hear them now?"

Nick nodded again.

"Then let's try something. I'm going to turn the page."

A moment later they were gazing at a couple standing on the lawn in front of Shutters. The man wore a formal black suit, while the woman, clad in a white dress, was wearing an elaborate hat on her head and gloves that came past her elbows.

Boone Philips Married Astrid Moore On
August 13, 1868

"Do you still hear the voices?" Sarah asked.

Nick hesitated, then nodded. "But not as loud — they're just sort of whispering now."

Sarah turned more pages, and the voices in Nick's head faded, but then he reached out a hand to stop her. His eyes fixed on a photograph of Boone and Astrid and their two daughters and two sons. "Look," he said, pointing at one of the teenage girls. "She looks exactly like you."

Sarah leaned closer and gazed at the young woman's face.

The girl didn't look like her — didn't look like her at all.

It looked exactly like her mother, and she

383

didn't look anything like her mother. "No," she said, "it looks like —"

"It looks like *you,*" Nick insisted. "It looks *exactly* like you."

"Sarah?"

The single word was spoken so clearly in her mother's voice that Sarah's head jerked up and she looked around, half expecting to see her mother standing behind her.

But there was nobody.

"It's time, Sarah," her mother's voice said again. *"Time to go home. Time to go back where you belong."*

She gazed down at the picture. The image — the image of her mother — was smiling at her, but the voice wasn't coming from the pages of the book.

It was coming from inside her head.

Apparently, what had been happening to Nick for years was now happening to her, too. She tore her eyes away from the picture and looked at Nick. "I heard her," she said. "My mother — she said it's time for me to go home."

"Home?" Nick echoed. "The Garveys'?"

She shook her head. "Where I belong. She said I have to go back where I belong." Her eyes shifted to the book, and Nick understood in an instant.

"Shutters," he breathed.

Sarah nodded.

Nick closed the book. "We have to go out there, Sarah." The voices in his head began murmuring.

"I can't," Sarah said, her eyes pleading with him. "I have to go back to the Garveys'. I promised Angie —"

"Go home," her mother's voice said. *"Go back where you belong."*

"We have to go," Nick said. "It's where the people in my head are."

Sarah touched his arm. "Nick, they're all . . ." Her voice trailed off, but Nick completed her sentence.

"They're all dead," he said softly. "They must all be in the old cemetery." Inside his head, the murmuring grew louder. "I think I have to go up there. And I think you have to go with me."

Sarah looked deep into his eyes. "Are you sure?"

He nodded. "We have to go. Both of us. You know we do."

Sarah took a deep breath. "Okay," she said. "Let's go."

CHAPTER
TWENTY-FOUR

I should have stayed with Nick.

It wasn't the first time the thought had crossed Sarah's mind since the two of them left the library separately, neither one willing to risk being seen together. And Nick had insisted she couldn't miss the old graveyard — it was only two hundred yards off the road to Shutters, and the trail was both good and well-marked.

And the sun had still been high and the sky blue.

Now the sun was dropping fast and the sky had turned a steel gray, and the shadows of the forest fell across the road. Even though the trail was right there where Nick said it would be, the shiver that went through Sarah as she gazed at it was far colder than the afternoon. But she hadn't stayed with him, and it was too late to turn back now.

She stepped off the road and started along

the trail, and with every step she took the path seemed to grow narrower, the forest denser. She froze as something moved in the brush off to the right, unconsciously holding her breath as she listened.

Silence.

Slowly letting her breath out, but still straining to hear every sound, she took another step down the path.

And suddenly the brush just ahead seemed to explode as a deer burst from the bushes, crossed the path in a single leap, and vanished into the forest as Sarah's body burned with the shot of adrenaline the fleeing deer had triggered.

Quickening her step until her hip would let her go no faster, she came to the old cemetery less than a minute later. A misty fog drifting in from the lake was settling into the low areas of the weed-choked potter's field, tendrils of it swirling silently with each tiny breath of air, like tentacles seeking something to grasp.

Sarah shivered and pulled her coat more snugly around her throat.

But where was Nick? If he didn't get here in the next few minutes, it would be too dark to find anything at all.

What had they even been thinking of? What were they hoping to find? "Don't worry," Nick had told her just before they left the library. "The voices will tell me. I'm sure of it!" Which had seemed perfectly sensible in the bright light of the library. But now, with the afternoon light fading, the sky darkening, and the fog drifting in . . .

Bettina felt Pyewackett stiffen in her lap, and a second later first Rocky and then Cooper rose to their feet, their hackles rising.

"What is it?" she asked. "What's . . ."

Her voice died on her lips as she felt the house tremble.

She rose from her chair as Pyewackett jumped from her lap and disappeared through the door to the great central hall, but instead of following the cat, the dogs ran to the French doors leading to the terrace, and Cooper began barking. Frowning, Bettina went to the doors, too, and peered out into the gathering fog and darkness. "What is it, Coop?" she asked again. "Do you want to go out?" The dog's body began quivering, and a series of excited yelps emerged from his throat as he rose up and pawed at the door handles.

"All right," she said, turning the handle. But before she could push the door open, Cooper had hurled himself against it, throwing it wide, then plunged across the terrace and down to the lawn, Rocky following after him. "No!" Bettina called, but it was too late. Cooper had already bounded off into the fog.

Pulling on a jacket, she set out after him, following the sound of his barking.

"Sarah? Is that you?" It was Nick's voice, but it was no more than a harsh whisper floating through the swirling mist from the far side of the field. Then she saw him silhouetted against the glassy expanse of the lake beyond, and she started toward him, picking her way across the field. But the moment she was close enough to see him clearly, she knew they'd wasted their time, and his words confirmed it.

"I don't hear anything. No voices at all."

And suddenly the whole thing once again seemed like a terrible mistake. Even if she ran all the way back to the Garveys — which she couldn't — she'd still be so late they'd —

She didn't even want to think about what they might do.

"What are we going to do?" she whispered, as much to herself as to Nick. "I can't go back to the Garveys' now."

"I don't know," he said, kicking at a frozen

clump of grass. "I was so sure —"

He was interrupted by the howling of a dog, and an instant later they saw it — a great black shape charging out of the forest, coming straight at them. As Nick instinctively stepped in front of Sarah, the animal vanished into a patch of fog, but they could still hear its baying, and a moment later it reappeared, mouth gaping. The memory of Conner West's German shepherd rose in his mind, and along with it, the voices, too, came alive.

"Kill it!" one of them screamed. *"Kill it now!"*

The dog was almost upon them, and Nick raised his arm, ready to strike down the lunging animal, when Sarah pushed him aside.

"Coopie!" she cried as the dog, its tail wagging furiously, nearly rolled over in its effort to stop before ramming right into her. Then it rose up, put its forepaws against her chest and licked her face.

As Nick stared at her in stunned silence, Sarah grinned, and gave the dog a quick hug before pushing him back to the ground. "This is Cooper! One of Bettina's dogs."

Cooper dropped to his haunches in front of Nick and raised one of his forepaws. Without thinking, Nick took it, and found himself first shaking hands with and then being licked by the same animal he'd thought was going to kill him only a few seconds before. A moment later a much smaller dog came bouncing across the field, followed by a voice calling out from the direction of the house.

"Cooper? Rocky? Bad dogs! Come *back* here."

"Rocky?" Nick echoed, looking down at the little mutt that was now scratching at his leg, begging to be picked up. "His name is 'Rocky'? What kind of name is that for —"

But Sarah was no longer listening to him. "Bettina?" she called as she waved to the figure now emerging from the hedge that screened the old cemetery from the house. "They're over here!"

"Sarah?" Bettina replied as she hurried toward them. "Nick? What on earth are you two doing out here? It's almost dark, not to mention freezing!"

Nick glanced uncertainly at Sarah.

"We — We thought this was where Nick's voices were coming from," Sarah began. "I mean, we found a book in the library, and there was a picture in it, and we thought —"

"It was me," Nick broke in. "It was all my idea. I thought the voices belonged to the people in one of the pictures. They were inmates in the old asylum, but they worked in the house and —" He abruptly fell silent as his mistake dawned on him.

The house! That's where he should have gone. Not the graveyard. And Bettina Philips was nodding.

"They're not out here," Nick breathed, speaking as much to himself as to anyone else. "They're in the house — they've always been in the house."

And in his head the voices once more spoke, uttering a single word in quiet unison.

"Yesss . . ."

They started back toward Shutters, but instead of Bettina leading the way, it was Nick who strode ahead, Sarah beside him, with the dogs trailing along at their heels. And the closer he drew to the house, the more certain Nick became that the key to what had been going on in his mind ever since he was a boy lay inside the stone walls of the great house that now loomed in the twilight, barely visible through the fog, looking like something out of a nightmare.

Yet he felt no fear; rather, a great feeling of anticipation was coursing through him, and the voices in his head were no longer screaming at him, demanding terrible things of him.

Now they were whispering to him, guiding him, leading him on toward . . .

What?

Sarah, too, was gazing at the house, telling herself that the reason it looked different than the last time she was here was because the light was fading quickly, the darkness hiding much of its wear. And maybe the shutters on this side had never sagged as badly as the ones in front. But as she drew closer, her hand slipping into Nick's, the changes didn't seem to fade away; the paint on the shutters looked less weathered, and the mortar between the stones looked as if it had been pointed only months ago instead of a century and a half. But how was it possible? How could the house itself be changing?

Evil.

The word hung in Nick's mind, echoing and reechoing as he gazed at the house. He could feel a dark energy throbbing inside the ancient stone walls, as if all the terror and madness imprisoned here so long ago had never died at all, but was still contained inside the mansion, waiting.

Waiting for what?

Waiting for him . . .

Above the terrace, the glass walls of the old conservatory glowed with the brilliance of a lighthouse beacon. But this was no beacon to guide ships to safety. This was something else.

"A beacon to evil," the voices whispered inside Nick's head.

And he knew Sarah and Bettina felt it, too, for they both hung back as he mounted the steps to the terrace. Only when he was at the threshold of the French doors did he finally turn back. "I have to go in," he said. "We all have to."

Sarah looked up at him. "What is it?" she asked. "What's happening?"

Nick shook his head. "I — I don't know. But I know that whatever it is that's been happening to me for as long as I can remember started here. And it's still here, and there's something I have to do — something we all have to do."

They heard a sound then — a low, nearly inaudible moan that slowly devolved into a trembling sigh. Nick turned away from Sarah and Bettina and gazed up at the house, and suddenly he knew.

He understood!

It wasn't just what had happened in the

house, nor the people who had lived and died in the house.

It was the house itself, and everything and everyone within it.

"It's awakening," he said, barely aware that he was speaking out loud.

"Awakening?" Bettina repeated. "What do you mean?"

Nick shrugged uncertainly. "I — I'm not sure. I just . . . know. It's like the voices are telling me."

"Maybe we shouldn't go in," Bettina said.

Nick shook his head. "I have to go in. If I don't go in . . ." Once again his voice trailed off, but when he spoke again, it was strong. "It's all right. I have to do this."

A moment later they were inside the studio and Bettina had closed the door behind them, shutting out the cold and the gathering night.

And Sarah felt it. It wasn't just the outside of the house that had changed; now the whole house had an energy in it, an energy she hadn't felt before.

It was as if the very air inside it hummed.

The energy was everywhere. It came up through the soles of her feet. It made the hairs on her arms and the back of her neck stand up. Yet somehow it felt neither dark nor frightening. Rather, it felt more like

395

some kind of strange renewal was taking place around her.

Like the farm in the spring when all the bees and insects buzzed in the light of the sun.

"It's in the basement," Nick said, interrupting Sarah's reverie.

Staying close together, the three of them passed through the enormous marble foyer and then the dining room until finally they were in the kitchen.

Two cats were perched on the massive oak table, twitching their tails, but neither made a move to spring at Nick while Bettina dug through one of the drawers until she found three flashlights. When she passed two of them to Nick and Sarah and started toward the door to the basement stairs, both cats leapt to the floor and followed.

Bettina opened the door and switched on the light that illuminated the long flight of stone steps leading down into darkness.

Nick moved ahead of her, and a breath of something that felt to him like death drifted up from the vastness below.

"Ready?" he asked.

Without waiting for an answer, he started down the steps.

At the bottom of the stairs Bettina reached past him and found a switch, the blackness filling the basement ebbing as a few dim and ancient lightbulbs began to burn. They cast a yellowish glow onto the dusty oak file cabinets and piles of shrouded furniture and cardboard boxes.

Beyond that first room, though, lay darkness.

But somewhere in that darkness, Nick was certain, he could hear the voices urging him on.

Bettina turned her flashlight upward, playing it over the huge beams that supported the structure above. Even covered with dust and trailing a tangle of cobwebs, they looked familiar to Sarah.

"It looks like what I drew," she said. "Or at least what I drew had beams that look like this. But this one's too big."

Bettina moved the flashlight beam toward the darkness beyond the door in the wall to the left.

"That way," Nick said quietly.

"Why?" Sarah asked. "What's down there?"

Nick was silent for a moment. "I don't know. I just know this is the way we need to go."

With Bettina, Sarah, and the cats following him, Nick passed through the door and into another room. This one was empty except for a stack of old trunks against the far wall. Following the whispers in his head, he began moving the old trunks.

Behind them was another door, its panels warped and cracked, what little paint was still on it covered with mildew. The knob fell off in Nick's hand, but even had it worked, the door had swollen in the dank air of the basement.

He put his shoulder to it, and on the third shove it cracked, then broke away entirely, only a few fragments still clinging to the rusted hinges.

If there had ever been electricity in this section of the basement, it was long gone, and the three pale cones of illumination from the flashlights revealed only more passages, leading off in three different directions.

Then they heard it.

A noise — a faint creaking sound, as if someone had stepped on the loose tread of a staircase.

Nick froze as Sarah slipped her hand into his, and though Bettina played her light over not only the beams above, but the walls as well, all of them knew the sound had come not from this room, but from somewhere else.

They were not alone.

They could all feel it now, as if something unseen were watching from the darkness.

Yet none of them turned back, and Nick led them through one chamber after another. But where was he going? Where were the faint voices leading him? The farther they went, the stranger the maze of rooms seemed to be. Somehow the geometry itself seemed completely wrong, as if each door were leading not to another eerily empty storeroom, but somehow into a completely different dimension. Then they came to a corridor at the far end of which was yet another room, and though there was nowhere else to go without turning back the way they'd come, Nick hesitated.

Yet he had no choice — whatever force was in the house was driving him onward, and the voices were louder now, urging him to move faster. With Bettina and Sarah right behind him, he stepped through the last doorway and shined his light around.

People — more than a dozen people — were staring at him, their glittering eyes boring into him.

Sarah screamed.

But the people didn't move.

"Mannequins!" Bettina whispered.

Now her light, and Sarah's, too, played over the life-sized figures clad in ancient, rotting clothes from another time. They were arranged in a vague semicircle, all of them facing the door, standing like so many lifeless sentinels guarding —

Guarding what?

There were no other doors in the room, no other entrances or exits but the way they'd come.

"We can't go any farther," Bettina breathed. She played her light on the overhead beams. "This is it. Those are the beams Sarah drew — I'm sure of it. But . . ." Her voice trailed off as she searched for any sign of the grisly scene Sarah had sketched, but where Sarah had drawn bones and skulls, all Bettina saw around them were mannequins clad in rags.

Nick, though, moved toward one of the mannequins, the voices loud in his head now, and growing louder by the second.

He reached out, his hand trembling, and touched the jaw of the nearest of the strange figures.

And everything changed.

The mannequins collapsed, their ragged clothes vanishing, but instead of seeing the peculiar figures that looked like they could have served as tailor's models, something else was left.

Bones.

Everywhere they looked there were bones and skulls. The skeletons somehow stayed intact as they crashed down, and now they were spread across the floor, sprawled out as if they'd died while lying down, though others were propped up oddly against the wall, as though their bodies had been placed in a sitting position but collapsed as the decades passed and every speck of soft tissue disappeared, picked clean by nature's scavengers.

Cockroaches were skittering among the bones, darting away from the invading beams of the flashlights.

"It's just like Sarah drew it," Bettina whispered. "How many? How many are there, Nick?"

"Seventeen," a voice in Nick's head whispered. *"There were seventeen of us."*

"They say there were seventeen of them," Nick repeated as he played his flashlight over the skulls.

"That's how many stories are in the manuscript," Bettina whispered. "Dear God, what happened in this house?"

"Sarah," one of the voices whispered in Nick's head.

"Sarah can show you everything," said another.

A third voice joined the chorus, and then

a fourth.

"She can show you everything that happened to everyone."

"We'll help her . . . let us help her. . . ."

Nick turned to Sarah, but instead of looking back at him, her eyes were fixed on the macabre scene they'd found in the small chamber. "They want to help you," he whispered. "They say they can help you show us what happened." For a moment he wasn't sure if Sarah had even heard him, let alone understood his words. But finally she nodded.

Then, as Nick and Bettina silently watched, Sarah stooped down, the pain in her hip suddenly gone. Her fingers closed on one of the bones.

Then she picked up another, and another.

When there were too many for her to hold, she passed them back to Nick and Bettina, then went on with the grisly chore, following the unspoken instructions that came into her head from an unseen source.

And yet she understood and knew what she must do.

When at last she was done, all of them knew how many bones she'd gathered.

Seventeen.

Seventeen fragments from the seventeen people who had been brought down here so many decades ago.

Sarah looked first at Nick, then at Bettina. "I'm going to paint," she said, starting back through the maze of rooms in Shutters' basement. "I'm going paint it all."

CHAPTER
TWENTY-FIVE

Shep Dunnigan peeled off his overcoat, hung it on the tree by the front door, and rubbed his hands together to warm them. "Finally winter!" he called out. "It's freezing out there."

No answer came from the kitchen, even though he could hear Lily in there chopping something. And if she was working but not talking, something was wrong.

Crap. Just when he was figuring on pouring a good stiff drink, putting his feet up on the coffee table, and relaxing. *Double crap!*

He left his briefcase on the side table and walked into the kitchen. Sure enough, Lily wouldn't meet his eyes. No smile, let alone a kiss. Instead she just kept chopping celery into finer and finer pieces. The way she was going, there wasn't going to be anything left of it when she finally put it into whatever she was cooking.

Which meant one thing.

Nick.

"Okay," Shep sighed. "What is it this time? What's he done now?"

Lily sighed. "He didn't come home after school today." She turned toward him, her eyes cold, her lips set in a thin line that told him she blamed him for whatever trouble their son had gotten himself into. "What did you say to him last night?" Lily demanded. "Why wouldn't he even come home today?"

Shep tried to deflect the question. "Have you called his cell phone?"

But Lily was not to be put off. "What did you *say* to him, Shep?"

His jaw muscles starting to clench, Shep picked up the kitchen phone and dialed his son's cell number.

The call rolled instantly to Nick's voice mail. "This is Nick. Leave a message."

Shep's voice was hard when he spoke, his words like chips of ice. "You should be home, Nick. You know that. So wherever you are, you call us so we won't worry, and then get yourself home. Got it?" He clicked off and turned back to face his wife's accusing eyes.

"You said something," Lily repeated. "I know you did, and you know you did. What was it?"

Shep's eyes narrowed defensively. "I told him not to be hanging around with that crippled girl anymore."

Lily shook her head and rolled her eyes. "Oh, great," she said, her voice fairly dripping with sarcasm. "That was real smart, wasn't it? What do you think happens with teenagers when they're forbidden to do something?"

"If they've got any smarts at all, they do what their fathers tell them."

"Like you always did?" Lily countered, her eyes rolling a second time.

"Okay, so maybe I shouldn't have been so hard on him," Shep muttered. "But at least now we know who he's with." And he had a pretty good idea where the two of them were, too.

He pulled out the Warwick phone book, looked up Mitch Garvey's phone number, and dialed.

After two rings he heard Angie Garvey's voice. "Hello?"

"Hey, Angie, it's Shep Dunnigan. I don't suppose Nick is over at your place with —" He searched his mind for the name of the girl Mitch had taken in, but before he found it, Angie Garvey answered his question.

"Sarah hasn't come home from school yet." Though she was trying to keep the anger out of her voice, Shep could hear it clearly. "I'm starting to get a little worried about her."

Worried, or pissed off? Shep wondered, but then he tried to sound just as worried as Angie. "I have a feeling maybe the two of them are together somewhere," he said.

He could almost hear the cogs grinding as Angie turned this news over in her mind, but when she spoke again, she sounded as carefully bland as before. "Well, if I hear from her, I'll definitely give you a call."

"Thanks, Angie," Shep replied. "And I'll do the same." He put the phone back into the cradle.

"Should we call Dan West?" Lily asked.

Shep shook his head. "Not yet. Let's give them a little more time." He touched her shoulder, but the gesture didn't soften her anger. "I'm going to go change," he said, loosening his tie.

"Dinner in ten minutes," Lily said.

Plenty of time. He'd change clothes, wash up for dinner, and still have time to use the upstairs phone to make one more call. With Bettina Philips having visited Sarah's father, and Nick now hanging around with Sarah, he was pretty sure he knew exactly where they were.

■ ■ ■ ■

Sarah stood at the long table in Bettina's studio, all the pain in her hip forgotten as she began preparing paint. Had either Bettina or Nick asked her how she knew what to do, she wouldn't have been able to put it into words. All she could have said was that she *knew* some force coming from somewhere in the house was guiding her. She worked quickly, using Bettina's old stone mortar and pestle to grind one scrap of bone after another into a fine powder, keeping the small mound of powder from each bone separate from the others. When she began preparing her palette, she mixed a little of the powder into every color she blended, sometimes from one of the mounds, sometimes from two, three, or even four of them.

Finally satisfied with her palette, she took a clean canvas from the shelf beneath the worktable and set it up on an easel.

And then she stood, very still, in front of the empty canvas, her eyes fixed on it, not a muscle in her body seeming to move at all. As the seconds turned into minutes, Bettina finally stepped closer to Sarah, putting out a hand as if to touch her, but Nick stopped her.

"She's all right," he said. "She's — I think she's listening to the voices."

"I loved them all," the voice said. Though it was emerging from Nick Dunnigan's lips, it wasn't Nick's voice. It was older — much older — and had an empty tone to it, as if whoever was speaking was describing something that had happened to someone else and hadn't affected him at all. And as the voice droned on, Sarah stood at the easel, painting rapidly, the strokes of her brush illustrating the words falling from Nick's mouth. *"Ruth Lincoln was the first. She was beautiful — her eyes the blue of turquoise. And hair the color of flax. But the baby was ugly. We called her Florence, but she wasn't a comely lass. Not like her mother at all."*

Already two faces had appeared on the canvas: a beautiful Madonna-like figure, cradling a small child in her arms. But the child was not like the mother. Its features were uneven, its upper lip split.

"Ruth wanted me to do it," the voice went on. *"She sat perfectly still as I put the knife to her throat, cutting it deep and true so she would feel nothing."*

A great flood of red gushed across the

canvas as Sarah slashed at it with her brush.

"Her head dropped down, and when I cut the baby, too, Ruth was watching."

Sarah's brush moved again, and now the babe was bleeding also, blood pouring from its throat.

Bettina, transfixed, listened and watched as the voice kept speaking and Sarah's brush continued to move. She knew this story — it was in the old manuscript that now lay on her ancestor's desk.

The voice emanating from Nick's throat droned on, and more and more of the canvas was filled.

"And then I was done and Ruth was gone, and Florence, and my beautiful Laura and our little Freddie were gone and buried too, and I knew that Mary was next, and our little baby Mamie. . . ."

More faces appeared, two more beautiful women and the babies the man had sired, and Bettina watched in mute fascination as each of them died, their agony perfectly limned by Sarah's brush.

"But Mary knew. She knew, and brought me here, and left me and never came back. Mary and little Mamie. They never come and see me. They tell everyone I'm dead." The voice fell wistfully silent for a moment, then went on. *"After I finished my story and Dr. Philips*

asked me if there was any more and I told him there wasn't, he got up and went to his desk. I thought he was getting me more brandy — he always gave us brandy when we talked to him to loosen our tongues — but it wasn't brandy at all.

"It was a knife.

"A knife like I used on Ruth and Laura and would have used on Mary, too — my perfect Mary. But Dr. Philips used it on me, and then sent me down to the darkness to join the others. And he'd promised, too — promised that if I told him everything, he'd set me free. But he lied. He lied, and put me with the others. . . ."

The voice trailed off, and Bettina knew it would not speak again. A new face had appeared on a fresh canvas. The face of a man whose empty eyes seemed utterly unaware of the carnage he'd inflicted on the people he claimed to love, and as Sarah quickly finished the drawing, Nick spoke again. This time, though, it was his own voice that emerged from his lips.

"He was in the book," he said softly. "The one in the library. He was one of the men allowed to work in the house."

"And his story is in another book," Bettina replied. "I'll show it to you." She led Nick and Sarah into the study where the yellowed

411

manuscript still sat on Boone Philips's old mahogany desk. "My three-times-great-grandfather wrote it," Bettina said as Nick stared down at the ancient pages. "He called it 'Stories from My Imagination,' but I don't think they were from his imagination at all."

Nick reached out, his hand hovering over the stack of yellowed paper for an instant before he finally touched it. Then his eyes widened, his face paled, and Bettina heard a quick, gasping intake of air. "What is it?" she asked. "What happened?"

"He killed them all," Nick whispered, his eyes fixed on the manuscript. "He made them tell him everything they'd done, made them describe it to him." His voice faltered for a moment, then: "He killed them. He hid all their records, and he killed them and hid them down there." Now he looked up, his eyes meeting Bettina's. "For a book," he whispered. "Just so he could write a book." Nick began paging through the manuscript, scanning the pages quickly, recalling so many of the things he'd seen and heard since the voices and visions began when he was so young he hardly remembered some of them. He'd turned nearly half the pages of the manuscript when the jangle of the old-fashioned telephone on the desk tore his attention out of the past and back into the present, and when he heard Bettina Philips speak his father's name, he started to rise from the chair.

Bettina waved him back but held the phone just far enough away from her ear so Nick, too, could hear whatever his father was going to say.

"I'm thinking you've got Nick out there. And that girl the Garveys took in, too — the one who's father almost killed her."

"Why would you think they're out here?" Bettina countered.

"Don't play dumb with me!" Dunnigan shot back, his voice hardening and taking on a tone that sent a chill through Bettina. "Everybody knows —"

"Everybody knows a lot of things, Shep," Bettina cut in. But before she could say anything else the memory of that other call — the coldly anonymous call that had unearthed the old nightmares — suddenly rose in her mind.

Shep Dunnigan?

Had it been Shep Dunnigan who'd called her?

Now he was speaking again, and Bettina's knuckles whitened as she held the receiver. "So if I came up there to pay you a little visit, just to make absolutely sure Nick's not there —"

"I'm sure you'll do whatever you want to do," Bettina said, struggling to keep her voice from betraying the sudden panic rising in her. "I don't think I could stop you, could I?" Without waiting for him to answer, she hung up the phone.

Nick's face was pale and his eyes darted around the room as if his father might suddenly appear out of one of its darker corners. "I've got to go," he said. "If he finds me here, he'll send me back to the hospital."

"Why would he do tha—" Bettina began, but Nick was already heading for the door.

"I've got to get out of here. He can't find me here."

"Then let me drive you," Bettina said, following him out into the foyer, then back toward the conservatory. "You'll freeze out there!"

"No, I won't," Nick insisted, starting to pull his coat back on. "And even if I do, so what? It'd be better than going back to the hospital."

Now Sarah turned around, her back to the easel. "Nick? What's wrong? Where are you going?"

"My dad's coming out here!" he told her. "If he finds me here —"

He didn't have to finish his sentence — Sarah, too, had grabbed her coat and was

shoving her arms into the sleeves, then picking up her backpack from where it still lay
on the chaise. "I'm going with you —"

"No!" Nick protested, but she shook her
head.

"We shouldn't ever have come out here!
So let's just go back to the libra—"

"Sarah, listen to me!" Bettina said as they
both started toward the door. "I'll drive you
—"

Sarah shook her head, cutting Bettina off.
"If Nick's dad really does come out here,
you have to be here. Otherwise, he'll know!
We'll be okay. Come on, Nick!"

And they were gone, hurrying out the
French doors and across the terrace, then
down the steps to vanish into the darkness.
Bettina followed them out onto the terrace,
calling after them, but all she heard in
response was Sarah's voice, once more
insisting that they'd be all right.

Should she get into the car and go after
them? But they wouldn't take the driveway
— they'd go back through the woods, the
way they'd come. And Nick, she was sure,
knew every path and trail as well as every
other kid in Warwick. They wouldn't get
lost, but if they didn't want to be found,
there was no way she could do it.

Should she call Dan West?

That might make things even worse for Nick and Sarah when they finally got home.

But she had to do something — she couldn't just leave them out there in the dark. Turning away from the night, she closed the French doors behind her.

And her eyes fell on the canvas Sarah Crane had been working on.

The room began a slow spin, and she had to reach out to the worktable to catch herself as the wave of dizziness crested. Finally, she sank down on the stool she sometimes used when she painted, closed her eyes and slowly counted to ten.

The dizziness passed.

What she'd seen — thought she'd seen — had to be nothing more than some kind of bizarre hallucination.

Her heartbeat slowed, her breathing evened out.

She opened her eyes.

It had been no hallucination.

In the few minutes Sarah was at the easel, she had painted a clear, detailed image of a scene that had taken place in the forest outside this house before she'd even been born.

Bettina was gazing at a depiction of her own rape, except that in the picture Sarah had limned, Bettina could see something she hadn't been able to see on that terrible night.

Sarah had drawn not only her, but the man who had raped her as well.

Shep Dunnigan.

As she stared at the painting, she replayed what she'd just heard on the telephone.

The same threatening voice as the man who called yesterday, the voice that triggered the horrible dream about the brutal rape when she was only sixteen.

The rape that resulted in a child born on Sarah Crane's birthday, and which Bettina had immediately given up for adoption.

It was all impossible, but now, as she stared at the painting, it all made sense.

And right this minute, Sarah Crane's father — her real father — was on his way to Shutters.

Tiffany Garvey felt Conner West's hand caressing her breast and squirmed with pleasure under the weight of his body. Even though the backseat of Conner's car might not be the most comfortable place, she was enjoying what was happening enough that she didn't care that one of her legs was propped up on the back of the front seat.

His hand reached up her skirt, his fingers pulling at the elastic of her panties, and she began tugging at the buckle of his belt. It would have been a lot nicer — and a lot more comfortable — if they could have gone somewhere, but her mother was always home and so was Conner's, and neither one of them could afford a hotel room.

Conner's hands were all over her now, and he was pulling her panties off and —

A flicker of movement outside caught her eye.

Someone was out there! Someone had seen them!

With a sudden surge of strength fueled by a moment of panic, she shoved Conner, sat up, and peered out the window.

Sarah Crane was standing on the side of the old dirt road — the road Conner had sworn nobody ever came down.

And she was staring right at them, her eyes wide under her wool cap.

Their eyes met for a moment, and then Sarah — looking as startled as Tiffany felt — turned and stumbled away into the woods.

"Sarah!" Tiffany said, barely believing her eyes as she finally managed to get Conner's hands off her. "Do you believe it? Sarah Crane is out there, and she just saw us."

"You're nuts," Conner said, reaching out again, his hands groping at her.

"No!" Tiffany punched him on the chest hard enough to make Conner flinch back. "She's going to go home and tell my parents that we were parked out here."

Conner was looking at her warily now. "What are you — crazy? What would Sarah Crane be doing out here in the woods? She can barely even walk."

"Well, she was walking pretty good just now," Tiffany shot back, adjusting her bra and pulling her sweater down. "And I have to go. Now," she added pointedly when Conner made no move to return to the driver's seat.

"You saw a deer," Conner said.

"I know what I saw, so let's just go, okay? I'm already late."

"Come on, Tiff," he pleaded, "let's just —"

"*Let's go,* Conner!" She struggled her way back into the front seat and waited while Conner zipped his pants, buttoned his shirt, then got out of the car, slammed the back door hard enough to make Tiffany jump, jerked the driver's door open, got in behind the wheel, and slammed that door even harder.

Tiffany said nothing, knowing Conner well enough to know that if she pushed him too hard, he might very well throw her out of the car and just leave her there. Which wouldn't do at all. She needed to get home first, to be setting the table and doing her homework before Sarah got home. But Conner apparently wasn't convinced yet.

"Sarah Crane is not out here," he said quietly.

Tiffany could actually feel him getting ready to make another pass at her. "Can we just go?" she asked. "We'll come back here next time, okay?" Like there was ever going to be a next time, she silently added to herself.

Still Conner hesitated, and for a moment Tiffany was afraid the vague promise of something yet to come wasn't going to work. But then, letting out his breath in a long sigh, he shrugged.

"Yeah, sure. I guess I can wait."

He turned the key in the ignition, and the engine roared to life.

CHAPTER
TWENTY-SIX

"Maybe Tiffany didn't see you," Nick said, picking his way through the underbrush as fast as he could. It seemed to be getting colder by the minute, and though the canopy of the forest was catching most of the snow, enough was getting through that the flurries beginning when they left Shutters were now a steady fall.

"She saw me, all right," Sarah said, her voice as grim as the thoughts spinning through her mind. "She and Conner were in the backseat and she looked right at me. And she knew I saw her, too."

"So what?" Nick countered. "What's she going to do — tell her mom she was making out with Conner West and you saw her?"

"You don't know Tiffany," Sarah said, stopping to let the pain in her hip ease and to catch her breath. "She'll get home before I do and make up some story. And then they'll call Kate Williams and she'll send me away." Her bad leg suddenly threatened to give way, and she instinctively reached for Nick's hand to steady herself. "What am I going to do?"

"Right now, let's just concentrate on getting out of here," he replied. "The main road is that way," he went on, pointing to the right, "but if my dad comes out, that's the way he'll come. And Conner and Tiffany are on the old road. But if we keep going straight ahead, we'll run into an old construction road that connects those two. If we stay on it, it goes all the way into town. It'll take us longer to go that way, but at least we probably won't run into anyone."

"Okay," Sarah sighed, starting to walk again, but with her limp worse than it had been a few minutes ago. "Just tell me it's flat."

"It is," Nick assured her, and a few minutes later they emerged from the woods onto a narrow dirt road already covered with a thin layer of snow. An old stone retaining wall bordered the road to the north, and both sides of the worn track fell off into what was left of two drainage ditches.

"Know what you're going to say to the Garveys?" Nick asked.

Before Sarah could answer, headlights

flashed through the night from behind them, casting their long shadows onto the white road in front of them.

"Hide!" Nick yelled, dashing to one side of the road. But when he glanced back, Sarah had moved to the opposite side, where the ditch was shallower and the stone retaining wall offered no shelter at all.

"Sarah!" he yelled over the sound of the approaching car. "Over here!"

Sarah heard Nick's voice and turned to see him waist-deep in the ditch on the other side of the road and waving frantically at her.

What should she do?

The ditch next to her was barely deep enough to hide her even if she lay down. She looked down the road at the approaching headlights, and time slowed as her mind flashed back to another night. A night that seemed to be part of another life . . .

She was on her bicycle again, pumping the pedals hard, hunting for her father.

Headlights ahead of her — headlights coming toward her.

Just like now.

She was swerving toward the ditch, but there wasn't going to be time and —

"Sarah!" Nick screamed, climbing out of the ditch across the road and starting toward her.

But she didn't move. Caught in the grip of her memory, she stood frozen in the road.

It was going to happen again — she could feel it. She closed her eyes, unable to move, unable to do anything to save herself.

"I don't believe it!" Tiffany howled, staring through the windshield. "It's her! It's that skank, Sarah!"

"What?" Conner said, turning up his windshield wipers. "It can't be!"

"I told you she was out here," Tiffany shot back. "Want to give her a scare?"

But Conner wasn't listening. Instead he was hunched up over the steering wheel, peering intently through the windshield. "And there's Nutty Nick," he whispered more to himself than to Tiffany.

An idea came into Tiffany's head, and she started giggling. "Let's act like we're going to hit them!"

But Conner West was way ahead of her. "Oh, I'll do a lot better than that," he replied, an image of his dying dog rising out of his memory. He pressed down hard on the gas pedal, clicked on his high beams, and headed directly toward Sarah Crane and Nick Dunnigan.

■ ■ ■ ■

"It's Conner!" Nick yelled as the car accelerated. He grabbed Sarah's hand. "Come on!"

At Nick's touch, Sarah snapped back into the present, but as the headlights of her father's truck vanished from her mind, those of the oncoming car grew brighter and brighter, lighting up the night like some great blazing —

Fire!

A new memory leaped into her mind, this one of the picture she'd drawn while Nick was in the hospital. She could clearly see the flames it had depicted, hanging before her against the night sky.

Then one of the voices in Nick's head screamed out, and his mind exploded with the memory of the hallucination he'd had in the hospital.

Flames!

Flames everywhere!

But not just flames. Flames he could direct, flames he could control, flames he could use, just as he'd used the phantom weapon when Conner West's dog had been leaping at Sarah.

He raised his arm, as he'd raised it that

day . . .

The laughter died on Tiffany's lips as she realized what Conner was going to do. "Conner, don't," she cried, reaching for the wheel to try to turn the onrushing car aside before it struck Sarah and Nick. But just as her fingers touched the wheel, something happened.

Suddenly, the road was on fire.

Not just on fire, but blazing with a fury Tiffany had never witnessed before. It was as if Hell itself had appeared before her, and her cry of protest rose to a scream of pure terror.

As the flames seemed to rush toward him, Conner jerked his foot away from the accelerator and slammed on the brakes.

The car began to fishtail.

Tiffany grabbed at the door handle to steady herself before she was thrown into him, and the door flew open as the car went into a full spin. Before she even knew what had happened, she was hurled out of the car onto the dirt road, rolling into the ditch next to the retaining wall.

Trying to steer out of the skid, Conner jerked the steering wheel the other way. The car hit the ditch, glanced off the stone wall, bounced back, spun around, and stopped in the middle of the road.

Nick and Sarah still stood side by side and hand in hand. No more than five yards away, the flames still rose from the road as if the dirt track itself had caught fire, but they felt no heat from the roaring inferno.

No heat, and no fear, either.

And then Conner West's car exploded.

Tiffany ducked her head and covered it with her arms as both doors flew open. For an instant she felt herself being pelted with shards of broken glass and splashes of burning gasoline. She rose up, intent on trying to crawl to whatever shelter she could find, but before she could move any farther, her eyes met Conner West's.

He was still strapped in his seat belt behind the wheel, staring at her through the shattered windshield of his car. She could hear him screaming as the fire consuming his car began to consume him as well.

A moment later his screams faded as his face began to blacken, and then —

Her mind rejecting what she was seeing, Tiffany dropped back to the ground, rolled over into the ditch, and lay still.

Sarah stood frozen where she was, listening to Conner's screams until the heat seared his lungs and his throat and his howl of agony finally died away. Only when his cries were overwhelmed by the roaring of the flames engulfing his car did Sarah, still holding Nick's hand, stumble backward, away from the flames, away from the nightmarish sight.

"Let's go," Nick whispered, his fingers tightening as he pulled her away from the inferno. "There's nothing we can do."

Sarah was about to protest, but as the flames flared higher, she realized that he was right.

Whatever had happened — whatever actually caused the car to burst into flames — there was nothing either one of them could do now. But before she followed Nick back into the woods, she looked back one last time.

What was it?

What could have happened?

The flames she and Nick had seen weren't real — they couldn't have been.

And yet they must have been. Conner must have seen them, too. Seen them, and been so frightened that he tried to turn the car away before it hurtled directly into the fire.

Instead he'd succeeded only in spinning it around and slamming it into the stone wall and . . .

And dying in the fire the car crash had caused.

Shuddering, Sarah let Nick pull her deeper into the forest.

The faint glow from somewhere off to the left barely penetrated Mitch Garvey's consciousness. Though his body was steering his truck along the road from the correctional facility — a road so familiar that he could have made every turn blindfolded — in his mind he was already at home, stretching out in his Barcalounger with a beer in one hand and the remote to the new TV in the other.

But when the glow exploded into a tower of flames, he was jerked out of his reverie and pulled the truck to the side of the road. Getting out, he glanced around to get his bearings. Maybe he should just ignore it — there weren't any houses out here, so how bad could it be? He'd much rather just go home to Angie's supper and a quiet evening watching whatever was on the tube. But that impulse vanished almost the moment it arose. It wasn't that easy to see a fire and just walk away from it. At least it wasn't for him. As long as he could remember, he'd always loved fires. There was something about watching a house burn down, and listening to the roar of the flames as they consumed things you'd never think would burn at all, that aroused things in him that only Angie used to be able to rouse. Indeed, as he gazed at the flames now, the excitement began rising inside him.

But where was it?

And what was burning?

He looked around again, then spotted one of the mileposts. He was still two miles from Warwick, and given the way the road he was on turned through the next mile and a half, he knew where the fire had to be.

Somewhere near the old construction road.

Angie, supper, and TV could wait.

Just past the old inmate cemetery, Mitch turned left onto Fox Hollow Road, which was covered with an undisturbed layer of snow. He switched the windshield wipers onto high and slowed down — no need to end up in the ditch, especially with snow starting to come down steadily.

He reached for the cell phone that always lay on the passenger seat when he was driving and dialed 911.

"Do you have an emergency?" the 911 operator asked after she answered on the second ring.

"This is Mitch Garvey. I'm on my way

home on the main highway and there's something burning off to the north. I just turned onto Fox Hollow Road, and it looks a little bit east."

"A house?"

"Can't be — no houses out here. Think it's got to be on the old dirt road. Maybe a car or something."

"We'll send a truck right away."

Mitch closed his phone and slowed the pickup as he approached the turnoff onto the old construction road, then made the right turn onto the narrow road, which was already covered with snow. Mitch sighed — for years the town had been dithering about turning this into a jogging and biking path, but year after year nothing happened, and more kids came out here to get into mischief.

And practically every year, at least one of the girls came home pregnant. Still, at least he didn't need to worry about that — Tiffany was a good God-fearing girl.

The glow in the sky was getting brighter. Mitch slowed even more, came around a turn, and there it was. A car — or at least what started out as a car — was on fire. It was slewed crosswise, its front crushed against the retaining wall, the rest of it almost completely blocking the road. The windshield was shattered and the one door he could see was flung wide open, its window as ruined as the windshield.

He pulled as close as was safe, then got out of his truck.

And recognized the car.

Acid flowed into his belly and up his chest as he watched it burn, the usual excitement of seeing flames clawing at the night sky fading quickly away.

A bad feeling growing in the pit of his stomach, Mitch backed away from the intense heat, opened his phone again and dialed Dan West's home.

The first faint wailings of the fire engine's siren floated through the night as he leaned against the front fender of his truck while he waited for either Dan or Andrea West to answer.

Ed Crane couldn't get Mitch Garvey out of his mind.

More than an hour ago he'd put his empty chow tray onto the conveyor belt that took it back into the kitchen and started toward the common room. He was looking for nothing more than an empty seat to watch some television before going back to his cell for the night.

He caught a glimpse of a dark blue uniform out of the corner of his eye, but hadn't thought much about it until a hand landed hard on his shoulder and pulled him backward, spun him around, and slammed him into the wall.

It was Mitch Garvey, who put a palm on his chest, keeping him pinned to the wall. Prisoners filed by, and Ed didn't have to look at them to know their eyes were staring straight ahead, none of them willing to get involved with whatever was going on between him and the screw.

"Sarah's becoming a problem," Mitch said, his voice low and his face too close to Ed's. "And you're part of Sarah's problem. You and Bettina Philips."

"How could I be a —"

"I'm doing the talking here," Mitch interrupted, his face hard. "So listen up. Maybe I can't keep you from seeing Sarah, but I can damn well keep you from sceing Bettina Philips. Problem is, I don't want to have to fill out all that paperwork. So I'm telling you right now that if Bettina Philips comes here to see you again, you just refuse to see her. Got it?"

What the hell was he talking about? Ed wondered. How could Sarah's art teacher be part of whatever "problem" Sarah might be causing?

Then he'd gotten it: she wasn't a problem for Sarah — she was a problem for Mitch Garvey.

"I don't think I —" Ed began.

"Listen to me!" Mitch said through clenched teeth as he pressed Ed even harder into the wall. "Maybe we can't stop her from going to art class, but that's it! There's something wrong with the Philips woman. She's not Christian, and I won't have your brat having anything to do with her. Not as long as she's under my roof. Got it?"

Ed had gotten it, but his nod apparently hadn't satisfied Garvey.

"You want her safe and happy, right?"

Ed nodded again.

"Then you do as I say."

Ed nodded a third time, and after staring into Ed's eyes for a few more seconds, Garvey abruptly dropped his hand away from Ed's chest and sauntered down the hall.

Ed had watched him go, barely contained rage threatening to send him after the guard and at least take a shot at beating him senseless.

But that wouldn't be good for anyone.

Instead, he went to the common room, where a half-dozen inmates sat in a semicircle watching a sitcom. But whatever was on the set couldn't penetrate his fury. A few men were playing cards, and a chess game was going on over in the corner, but Ed couldn't get interested in either one.

So he'd sat in a chair at a table, alone, and stared at his hands, outwardly calm, waiting for his fury to subside.

It finally did, and then he knew exactly what he had to do.

Somehow, some way, he had to get Sarah out of the Garveys' house, and there was only one person who could do that.

He jumped up from the table, went back to his cell and retrieved the business card he'd forgotten he even had until yesterday when he'd found it stuffed in his Bible, the only book they'd let him keep in his cell. He grabbed the card, then walked down the hallway to the cubicle where the prisoners' phones were kept.

"Too late," the guard said as he pointed at the clock.

"What do you mean?" Ed asked, looking up at it.

7:01.

"I mean it's too late. Phones close at seven. Make your call tomorrow."

"But it's important," Ed said.

The guard snorted. "It's always important. It can be important tomorrow, too."

His shoulders slumped as, for at least the twentieth time that day, the full weight of life in prison descended on him. Yet again he felt the infuriating powerlessness, the absolute impotence, the complete lack of control he held over anything.

And now he couldn't even make a phone call to the one person who could make sure that his little girl was safe.

CHAPTER
TWENTY-SEVEN

"Nick, stop!" Sarah grabbed the sleeve of his jacket, gasping for breath. "I can't go this fast or I'll trip and fall."

"We've got to get out of here," Nick said. "C'mon, I'll help you."

"Slow down!" Sarah gulped air into her burning lungs. "Where are we going?"

"Away from there," Nick said, pointing back at the firelight still filtering through the trees. "We're going to be blamed for that, just like we were blamed for killing Conner's dog."

"But it wasn't our fault," Sarah argued. "Conner was going to run over us."

"We both saw what happened, Sarah," Nick said, his eyes fixing on hers.

She knew exactly what he meant, but shook her head. "He hit the wall," she insisted. "He went off the road and then his gas tank exploded or something."

Now it was Nick who shook his head. "If

anybody finds out we were there, nobody's going to be looking at his gas tank."

Sarah's voice took on a desperate note. "We can't just walk around in the woods all night. We need to go back to Bettina's."

"No way," Nick said. "My dad —"

Now they heard the faint sound of a siren in the distance, and Sarah knew in an instant what it meant. "Hear that? That's a fire truck, Nick. And there's going to be more. We have to go back to Bettina's. We'll tell her what happened, and she'll know what to do."

"But my dad —" Nick began again, and once more Sarah cut him off.

"We don't even know if your dad was really coming out here. At least we should go back to Bettina's and see. If his car's there, we'll decide what to do then."

Still Nick hesitated, but even as he tried to think of something that might be better than what Sarah wanted to do, he knew she was right. There wasn't any way they could get back to town now without being spotted, unless they tried to go all the way through the woods, and even though he knew where they were right now, he didn't have any real idea how to find the way back to town.

Shutters, yes — it wasn't that far away.

438

But home?

At least a mile through the forest, with no trail, and the wind-driven snow starting to sting their faces. Sarah was right.

Turning away from the glow of Conner's burning car, he started leading her back toward the old mansion overlooking the lake.

Shep Dunnigan opened the kitchen cabinet and pulled out two glasses.

"I'll get those," Lily said a little too quickly. "Just go sit down and I'll bring you your plate and a beer." She quickly added some sautéed string beans to the fried pork chop and a helping of mashed potatoes. If anything could improve Shep's mood, it was pork chops and mashed potatoes, but so far even the promise of his favorite meal hadn't cooled his simmering anger.

"I *got* them," he snapped, turning to glare at her. "What's going on with you, Lil? Is there something you're not telling me?" When she came up with no answer, he shook his head in a gesture that clearly told her he was resigned to having a wife so stupid she couldn't answer the simplest question. "Just put the plates on the table, Lily," he said. "Think you can do that? I'll be there in a sec."

Lily picked up their plates and went to the dining room, leaving the third plate, covered with plastic wrap, in the microwave, ready to be reheated when Nick finally came home. But she was beginning to think maybe it was time to call the police or the hospital or something, rather than just wait while Shep got madder and madder. Except any call she might make would only make him even angrier, and when he got mad —

She cut the thought short, not even wanting to think about what he might do.

Shep, left alone in the kitchen, set the glasses on the counter, opened the refrigerator, and was just reaching for a beer for him and a Coke for Lily when he saw the corner of a plastic bag sticking out from behind the coffee canister.

He frowned.

Lily knew he hated it when she left anything but the canisters on the counter. Closing the refrigerator again, he pulled the offending Ziploc bag clear of the canister and held it up.

Inside was about an inch of dried leafy green stuff.

What the hell? It almost looked like pot. But what would Lily be doing with something like that? "Lil!" he called out in a tone that left no doubt he wanted her in the kitchen and he wanted her there now. A moment later she appeared in the doorway, and he held up the plastic bag. "What the hell is this?"

Her eyes widened. "J-Just tea," she stammered, then went to the refrigerator herself to get the beer and Coke Shep had been after only a moment before.

Shep slammed the door shut before she had it more than halfway open and spun her around to face him. "Doesn't look like any tea I've ever seen. Where did you get it?"

"It's for Nick," she said, knowing if she tried to lie, Shep would recognize it right away. "It's just herbs to calm him down. I — I thought it might help with his . . . well, you know," she finished lamely.

Shep glowered down at her. "You and who else thought it might help?" he demanded. "You didn't just dream this up by yourself!"

She thought fast, but not fast enough.

"Don't make me ask you again, Lily." His voice was dangerously low and the vein in his forehead was throbbing.

"Th-There's nothing wrong with me wanting to help my son."

Shep leaned closer, towering over her, his clenched fist rising above her face. *"Who, Lily? Who gave you this stuff?"*

Her eyes widened with terror, and she saw no escape. "Bettina Philips," she whispered.

"You got this stuff from *that witch?*" Shep bellowed. "You go to that evil woman's house and talk about our *son* with her? You heard me telling *him* to stay away from her! Did you think I didn't mean you, too? Christ!" He opened the bag and smelled. "Do you even know what's in here?"

"She said —"

"I don't give a shit what *she* said." He wadded up the bag and threw it at her. It hit her in the face, then dropped to the kitchen floor. What the hell was she thinking? What if someone had seen her going out there? And what the hell was Bettina Philips doing, giving Lily drugs to give Nick? Well, enough was finally enough — he'd fix Bettina Philips right now!

Maybe he'd even fix her permanently.

Hurling Lily against the wall hard enough to make her cry out, Shep Dunnigan spun around, grabbed his keys and his coat, picked the Baggie up off the floor, and slammed the back door behind him.

When he'd called Bettina earlier, it had mostly been a bluff. But not this time.

This time it was serious.

Dead serious.

■ ■ ■ ■

The flashing red and blue lights of a fire truck and an ambulance lit up the snowy night and refracted off the layer of snow already accumulating on the dirt road. Dan West expertly braked to a stop without even a hint of a skid, turned off the ignition and jumped out of his patrol car, his heart pounding as he prayed that Mitch Garvey had been wrong, that whatever happened out here had nothing to do with Conner or his car. But even though the fire truck blocked his view of the burning car, the look on the fire chief's face as he grabbed Dan's arm to keep him from rounding the end of the truck was enough to tell him that Mitch hadn't been mistaken.

"Don't go over there, Dan," Harvey Miller said. "That's not something you need to see." Dan tried to shake Miller off, but the fire chief only shook his head. "Go home, Dan," Harvey said. "Go home to Andrea."

Dan searched Harvey's eyes for any hint, no matter how slight, that might give him hope, but there was nothing.

Nothing but sympathy.

"There's no possibility it's not Conner's car?" he choked out.

"It's his," Miller replied. "I double-checked the plates myself. As for Conner . . ." His voice trailed off for a moment, then: "The coroner won't get here for another hour."

Once again Dan tried to shake Miller's grip from his arm. "Let me go," he said. "I want to see — I *have* to see it myself."

"It's too late, Dan," Harvey countered, shaking his head. "There's nothing for you to do here. You need to be at home with Andrea."

"I'm the sheriff —" Dan protested, but his voice broke and he felt his knees weaken as the truth of what had happened began to sink in.

"Not tonight you're not," Miller replied. "Besides, there's no crime here, Dan. It was an accident, pure and simple." He shook his head sadly. "Kids," he muttered more to himself than to Dan West. "Kids and cars."

Dan West was no longer listening; instead, his son's name kept echoing in his mind.

Conner . . . Conner . . .

"I'm going to have someone drive you home," Harvey Miller said quietly, beckoning to one of his men.

Oh God, Conner . . .

A chill far colder than the night seized Dan, bringing with it a strange feeling of surrealism. None of this could be true. Whatever was happening was happening to someone else, not to Dan West. Dan West was the man who told people about things like this, told them that one of their kids was dead.

So it was wrong! Had to be wrong!

A team of EMTs appeared around the end of the fire truck, bringing a stretcher to the waiting ambulance, and at the sight of the white-shrouded form strapped to it — a form with an oxygen mask covering the face — Dan felt a flash of hope. But then he saw Mitch Garvey, his face pale as he watched the EMTs load the stretcher onto a gurney and slide the gurney into the ambulance, and his hope faded, and a moment later Harvey Miller crushed it completely.

"Tiffany Garvey," the fire chief told him. "She was in the ditch, unconscious."

Dan West's eyes remained fixed on the ambulance. "Anybody else? Any other vehicle?"

Harvey shook his head, and finally loosened his grip on Dan's arm.

Dan steeled himself against his shaky legs, refusing to give in to the emotions boiling inside him, focusing his mind on what had happened, rather than what had happened to his son.

A one-car accident in the middle of nowhere that burned so fast the driver couldn't even get out to save himself. How could that be?

The surrealism of the night tightened its grip on him, and for a moment Dan wasn't sure where he was or what he was doing there.

Then, as if of their own volition, his legs carried him two quick steps to the right, and he could see the blackened rear end of Conner's car.

Another two steps and he could see it all.

The remains of what only a little while ago had been his son were still behind the steering wheel, and even though he couldn't see his son's face, the full force of it finally hit him.

It was his son, and he was dead.

"Conner," he whispered, one arm coming up from his side, reaching out toward the car as if somehow he might help the boy from the wreckage.

But he couldn't.

All he could do was go home.

CHAPTER TWENTY-EIGHT

Nick hunched his shoulders against the wind and peered warily around the edge of Bettina's garage. An inch-thick layer of snow covered everything now, and in the dim yellow light of the sconces flanking the front door, the old house seemed to have lost even more of its age and ruination. He could almost imagine the old fountain filled with water, and horse-drawn sleighs, their bells ringing merrily, coming up the drive through the woods.

But there were no bells, and since the sirens that rent the night a little while ago were quiet now, a silence Nick had never experienced before had fallen over him.

He could hear nothing at all.

Nor was there anything to be seen.

No tire tracks, no car.

So far, at least, his father had not made good on his threat to come out here.

"He's not here!" he whispered. "C'mon."

But when he moved toward the front door, Sarah grabbed the sleeve of his coat and pulled him back into the shadows.

"They're going to be looking for us," she said.

"So?" Nick leaned against the garage wall to get out of the biting wind that had started to whip the leafless trees.

"So what if they come out here?" Sarah said. "Half the people in town already hate Bettina. If they find us here, they'll blame her for what happened."

Nick knew she was right, but even worse was the knowledge that if he hadn't panicked and left Bettina's house to begin with, Conner would still be alive. "What should we do?" he finally asked. "We can't stay out here all night — we'll freeze to death."

"I don't know," Sarah said. The cold was sinking deep into her now, and her hip was aching, and even though she knew she had to think, she couldn't. "Maybe we'd better just go back to town. After what happened —"

"What happened wasn't our fault," Nick broke in. "Conner was trying to kill us!"

"I didn't say it was our fault," Sarah protested. "But we don't even know what happened! Maybe —"

Abruptly, she fell silent as a pair of headlights swung across the side of the garage. Then Nick ducked back into the shadows behind the building, pulling her along with him. Holding her back in the sheltering darkness, he eased his head out just far enough to see a car emerge from the woods and stop. Whoever was in it doused its headlights before they hit the house.

His father.

It had to be his father.

"It's my dad," he whispered, though the car was 150 feet away and closed up tight, with its engine running.

Sarah's fingers closed on his arm.

"C'mon," he said. "We'll just get lost in the woods, and we can't go down the driveway. So we'll go in through the old coal chute and hide in the basement. Bettina won't even know we're there. And at least we won't freeze to death, and maybe we can figure out what to do."

"Where *is* the coal chute?" Sarah asked, too tired and cold to argue with him. Besides, he was right — if they stayed out too much longer, they just might actually freeze.

"It's got to be on this side of the house," Nick said. "Come on." Taking her hand, he led Sarah a few yards back into the forest behind the garage, then began working his way closer to the house. In less than a minute the house itself was blocking their view of Shep Dunnigan's car.

And Shep's view of them.

Nick tightened his grip on Sarah's hand. "I think I can see it!" He pointed toward the house with his free hand. "See that sort of slanting thing? That's got to be the door." Without waiting for her to reply, he started toward it, and a moment later Sarah found herself staring at what was indeed obviously the metal door to a coal chute.

With a badly rusted lock on it.

The wind was coming up, and the snow was falling faster, and Nick decided that even if he made a little noise, no one would hear. He reached down and gave the lock a tentative twist, but it held. Then he noticed that one of the hinges on the left panel was even rustier than the lock. Bending down, he slid his fingers under the door frame and jerked upward.

The screws snapped loose and the corner of the door lifted high enough so he could slip through. "I'll go first," he said.

While Sarah held the corner of the door up, he dropped to the ground, slid his legs through the gap, then rolled over on his stomach. A moment later his whole body was hanging over the edge of the chute, and

450

though his feet were touching nothing, he let himself drop into the darkness.

After no more than a couple of feet he landed on the concrete floor, flexing his knees to absorb the shock.

"Come on," he whispered up to Sarah. "It's easy — maybe two feet. I'll catch you."

Refusing to think about what might happen if Nick didn't catch her, Sarah wriggled through the gap and began lowering herself into the darkness.

Mitch Garvey stared numbly at the striped curtain in the small Warwick emergency clinic behind which his unconscious daughter now lay.

Unconscious.

The word resounded in his mind, but even though he kept hearing it, somehow it had lost its meaning. How could it be? How could his perfect Tiffany have been so damaged that she didn't even know he was there?

The doors opened and he turned to see Angie and Zach coming in. Her eyes met his, and he could see her pale face before she fell into his arms.

For a moment Mitch simply held her.

"Is Tiff okay, Dad?" Zach asked, his voice shaking enough to betray the fear he was doing his best to conceal.

Mitch's shoulders twitched in a faint shrug. "Don't know. She's unconscious — they're working on her."

"What happened?" Angie asked, finally stepping back from her husband and glancing around the waiting room as if embarrassed that someone might have seen her clinging to Mitch.

"Looked like she was thrown from Conner West's car. But until she wakes up . . ."

Mitch Garvey's words died on his lips as Tiffany's weak voice drifted out from behind the curtain. "Mama?"

Angie's eyes widened and she reached for Mitch with one hand as she pulled back the curtain with the other. Tiffany lay on a gurney, her face cut and bruised, an IV in her arm.

Relief flowed through Mitch, and he sagged into a chair near the gurney.

Angie wept silently.

"Wh-Where's C-Conner?" Tiffany whispered, her eyes barely visible in her swollen face.

"Conner?" Angie echoed. "Don't you worry about Conner West, sweetheart." She took her daughter's cold hand and tried to rub some warmth into it. "You just get yourself all better so we can get you home and take care of you right."

"Wh-What happened? We were —"

"There was an accident," Mitch told her. "You and Con—"

"No accident," she whispered, silencing her father as she shook her head as much as the pain in her neck would allow.

A doctor appeared, a metal-clad chart in his hands. "Mr. and Mrs. Garvey?"

Mitch nodded.

"We're waiting for X ray to check for broken bones, but I don't think the damage is too severe. She got quite a bump on the head, possibly a minor concussion. The fact that she's already awake is a good sign."

But Mitch was barely even listening to the doctor. "Tiff?" he said, taking his daughter's hand. "What do you mean it was no accident?"

His daughter did not answer, and the doctor pulled back an eyelid and shined a narrow beam of light into her eye.

Tiffany startled awake with a gasp.

"Princess?" Mitch began again. "What did you mean when you said it wasn't an accident?"

"They tried . . ." she whispered, and then her voice trailed off for a second before she pulled together the strength to finish the sentence. ". . . to kill us."

Her eyes closed again and her hand went limp in her father's.

Angie leaned over the gurney. "Tiffany? Honey?" When there was no response, Angie looked up at the doctor, her terror clear in her eyes.

He pulled the stethoscope from around his neck and scanned the meters displaying Tiffany's vital signs. "Maybe you folks ought to wait outside for now. Just give me a couple of minutes, all right?"

Mitch took Angie's arm and drew her away. "C'mon, honey. Let's let him do his job."

Back in the tiny waiting area, Tiffany's strange words finally sank in, and a cold fury began to build inside Angie. "She said it wasn't an accident, Mitch. You heard her. 'They tried to kill us!' That's what she said, Mitch."

He sat down in one of the plastic chairs and drew his wife down into the chair next to him, feeling her anger, along with the fury in his own heart. "Who, though?" he grated, directing the question to no one in particular. "Who'd do something like that?" But even as he asked the question, an answer was already forming in his own mind.

"Why doesn't someone ask Conner?"

Zach asked. "That's who she was with, wasn't it?" But when he looked at his father, he instantly knew the truth. "Oh, jeez . . ." he groaned, burying his face in his hands. "Conner can't be dead! He —"

"It was murder," Angie said, her fury finally erupting. "Whoever they were, they killed Conner, and they tried to kill Tiffany, too. You call Dan West, Mitch! You call him right now!"

But she didn't need to tell him; Mitch Garvey was already punching Dan West's home number into his cell phone. Whoever had done this was going to pay.

If he had to, he might very well kill them himself.

In fact, he'd like to do that.

He'd like that very, very much.

Bettina's eyes moved from the light and shadows on the wall to the window. A car was approaching, its running lights refracting in the snow, seeming to come from everywhere and nowhere at the same time.

The house trembled as a nearly subsonic rumble rolled through it, and a chill swept over her.

She backed away from the window.

Her hand closed on the iron poker from the fireplace.

She took a deep breath and let it out slowly.

The strange rumble in the house grew louder, but not quite loud enough to keep Bettina from hearing a car door slam.

Her grip tightened on her weapon.

There was a great pounding on the door, and before she could move either to open it or back away, the massive oaken door flew open.

Shep Dunnigan strode in, his face scarlet, his body shaking with barely contained fury.

Bettina unconsciously reached out to steady herself against the wall as she faced him.

"Where is he?" Dunnigan demanded, his voice low and dangerous. "What the hell have you done with my son?" He stepped toward Bettina, the front door slamming shut behind him and the locks falling into place. Shep spun around and tried to open the door.

It held, locked fast.

"Nick isn't here," Bettina said, struggling to keep her own voice under control, to betray nothing of the panic — and fury — welling up inside her.

Shep glowered. "You've done something to him," he snarled. "And to my wife, too. You're a witch."

And there it was.

The word that had been whispered about her for so long, finally flung in her face.

Bettina felt her legs weakening, and when she opened her mouth to speak, nothing came out. No, she told herself. You've done nothing to be ashamed of, and never have. She steeled herself, and found her voice. "I did nothing to them, and you know it." Her eyes bored into him, and she hurled one more word at him: "Nothing!"

Shep stepped closer. "Nothing?" he echoed, his voice as poisonous as the sneer on his lips. "Then what the hell is this?" He held up the bag of loose tea. "It's drugs!" he shouted, not giving her time to reply. "You think I don't recognize drugs when I see them?" He flung the bag of tea at Bettina's face, but before she could duck, a blast of air ripped through the huge foyer, snatched the Baggie and hurled it to the far end.

"What the hell was that?" Shep yelled at her. "What the hell are you doing?"

Again Bettina made no reply, but this time the house itself seemed to answer his question.

Bang!

Slam!

The outside window shutters slammed

shut and a guttural sound emanated from the base of the house.

Bettina froze.

Shep's eyes widened for a second, then narrowed as he focused on her. "You," he growled, starting toward her. "You think what I did to you last time —"

Bettina raised the poker, ready to defend herself, and then the whole house heaved violently, throwing Shep to the floor.

Bettina watched in shock as he tried to regain his feet, but he'd risen no farther than his knees when a burst of air buffeted him, throwing him down the hallway after the tea.

It was as if the whole house had suddenly come alive; there was electricity in the air, and all the energy the house was generating seemed to have focused on Shep Dunnigan.

A noise like thunder followed the stream of air that enveloped Shep, and he could neither get to his feet nor fight the force that drove him inexorably toward doors that led to the dining room, and then to the kitchen beyond.

And yet, though Bettina could hear the sounds — the thunder and what was now a howling wind — she could feel nothing of the tornado Shep Dunnigan appeared to be caught in. It was as if he were being drawn into some parallel universe, one that was close to hers, but different enough that she was not experiencing it.

She watched helplessly as Shep gasped for air and mouthed words she could barely hear.

"Stop it!" he was begging. "What are you doing?" But it was useless — though he could still see her, she was no longer in focus, as if she were fading away into some other place.

The wind strengthened further, propelling Shep through the dining room and into the kitchen. He reached for the pipes of the ancient porcelain sink, desperate to anchor himself against the energy pushing him, but just as his fingers were about to close on them, the faucets opened and a gush of black sludge — sludge that reeked of death itself — spewed over him and spread across the floor. A moment later Shep himself was thrashing on the floor, the slime burning his skin everywhere it touched him.

Bettina Philips, watching in stunned awe, stepped into the kitchen just as the door slammed shut behind her and the basement door burst open, crashing against the wall behind it.

Shep tried again to get to his feet, tried to reach for the table, or a chair, or anything else that might support him, but the black, burning, stinking sludge covered him now, and the unseen force that felt like the breath of Satan himself pushed him toward the open door to the basement and the steps beyond.

Bettina stood in the corner of the kitchen, her hand still clutching the iron poker as she watched Shep, his clothes torn now, his eyes blazing with impotent fury, tumble over and over, down the steps into the basement.

Then, as if coming from the bottom of some vast well, she heard his voice rise from the darkness of the basement: "I'll kill you! I swear I'll kill you and that evil brat, too!"

The words galvanized Bettina, and her muteness fell away as she dropped the iron poker and strode to the top of the stairs. "She's not evil!" she shouted into the darkness below. "She's our daughter, Shep! Yours and mine! You fathered her when you raped me!" And as if all the fury pent up inside her since that terrible night nearly fifteen years ago had finally been released, Bettina slumped to the floor. "Our daughter," she repeated over and over again. "our daughter . . . my daughter . . . my beautiful daughter . . ."

Then there was silence.

The howl of the wind died away.

The terrible stinking sludge was gone from the floor.

And all Bettina could hear was the beating of her own heart and the echo of her own words:

". . . my beautiful daughter . . ."

The whole world was reeling around Shep. His body ached from the fall and he could barely breathe. The maelstrom around him was even worse in the cold basement. Dim lights — lights that barely let him see at all — swirled in every direction, and then he was thrown against a wall, and then some kind of door opened and he was sucked through. The door slammed shut behind him and it was as if the opening had never been there at all.

And then it was over. The careening forces around him stilled.

He lay sprawled out on the cement floor, his chest heaving as he struggled to catch his breath, his mind reeling as he tried to make sense of what had happened.

He struggled to his feet. He was in a room — a room with concrete walls and heavy beams overhead.

And only one door.

Hesitantly, as if something were compelling him to do it, he opened the door, bracing himself against whatever might lie beyond it.

And the moment he cracked it open, he was sucked into another room.

The door slammed behind him and another appeared on another wall, but this time he tried to stay where he was.

It was impossible. As if his body were no longer controlled by his mind, he moved toward the opening in the wall to the right, and the nearer he drew to it, the stronger he felt the pull to the next room.

Doors opened and closed, vanished. Shep moved deeper into the maze, more lost with every twist and turn. It was as if he were lost in time and space itself, as if he were wandering a no-man's-land, being pushed, pulled, twisted, turned. He went up steps, down stairs, around corners, across thresholds. He tried to keep count, tried to keep his bearings, tried to remember where he'd been.

It was no use.

For just an instant Shep wondered if this was how Nick had felt his entire life, but in the next instant his mind turned once more to himself.

The hell into which he'd fallen took on a strange rhythm:

Over and over.

Round and round.

In a circle, around a bend.

First turn right, then turn left.

Over and over

Over and over . . .

He was lost now, hopelessly lost, but he stumbled on.

Over this threshold through this door.

This way, that way, over there.

New noises:

The slam of a door.

The clang of metal crashing against metal.

Shep whirled.

There was only one door — a door with a barred window. But this door didn't open as he approached.

He was locked in.

He backed up against the wall to steady himself, and now he heard a new sound. Footsteps — and voices! And they were coming closer!

There was jangling and a clattering of a key in a lock and then the door opened and three men, all wearing rubber aprons, entered the room.

"Where am I?" Shep whimpered as they approached him. "What's going on?"

"Just take it easy," one of the men replied. "You know what time it is."

"What? What are you talking about?"

"Let's get ahold of him, boys," another of the men said, sounding almost bored. Then he turned to Shep. "Why do you want to do this every time? You give us trouble, I'll have to call Warden Philips again."

Two of the men grasped Shep's arms and shoved him out of his cell.

Shep's mind reeled. Who were these people? Their shoes were tattered and their clothes looked like costumes. "Let go of me!" he demanded, but the men ignored him, half carrying and half dragging him down a dank corridor.

On the walls, gaslights in tarnished brass sconces flickered.

"Where the hell am I?" Shep demanded again.

The voice of the third man came from behind him. "Same place as always — Shutters Lake. Only question is who's crazier — the inmates or us guards." Then the man's voice took on a sarcastic edge. "Oh, sorry — Dr. Philips wants to call us 'attendants.' "

The names hung in Shep's mind. What were they talking about? Shutters Lake? Dr. Philips? The old prison — the place where they'd locked up the crazy people — had closed decades ago! Long before he was born; even before his parents had been born. And Dr. Philips —

"No!" Shep screamed, his mind rejecting the impossible idea it had just formed. "This is a joke, isn't it?" His voice rose, a note of hysteria creeping into it. "It has to be a joke!"

Instead of answering his question, one of the men swung open a door and the other two manhandled him through it. Faint light streamed in through a very high window, and in the center of the room, on the stone floor, sat a large tub.

They stripped Shep of his clothes, and for the first time he saw what he had been wearing. Instead of the clothes he'd had on when he came to Bettina's house, what they took off him now was something like a thin pajama.

Then he saw the chunk of ice floating in the bathtub.

And the truth of what they were about to do sank into Shep Dunnigan's mind.

"No," he pleaded. "Don't do that — don't put me in there." They lifted him up and he stretched his legs and put his feet on the edges of the tub like a dog fighting against a bath.

But it did no good. The attendants overpowered him and forced him into the tub, and while two of them held him down, the third put a heavy wooden lid on the tub, a thick lid with a cutout that allowed only his head to be out of the water.

A moment later the board was strapped down to keep his body completely submerged, and a cold such as he'd never before even dreamed of began to penetrate his body.

He screamed with agony and tried to thrash his way free, but it was no good — the thick leather straps held fast, and all he succeeded in doing was scrape off the skin of his knees against the rough underside of the tub's lid.

"Now calm down," one of the attendants said, his words barely penetrating Shep's agony. "You just think about why you're here, and I'll try not to forget you're in there."

Shep watched as they left the room, then closed and locked the door behind them. Then he filled his lungs with air and bellowed a single word: *"Bettina!"*

Her name only echoed back off the stone walls, and as the freezing cold of the water seeped into Shep Dunnigan's body, the truth slowly seeped into his mind.

Bettina Philips couldn't hear him. No one at all — at least no one he knew — could hear him. After all, how could they?

None of them would even be born for another century.

CHAPTER
TWENTY-NINE

"She's our daughter, Shep! Yours and mine! You fathered her when you raped me!" The words echoed in Sarah's head. She and Nick were crouched low to the floor next to the door that led from the coal bin to the main part of the basement.

She's our daughter . . . As Sarah recalled the words, the cacophony of fury raging through the ancient mansion faded into insignificance.

What was Bettina saying? Why would she say that?

"Sarah?" Nick whispered. "Sarah, we've got to find Bettina."

His voice jerked her back to the present, and she felt him holding her trembling hand. When she tried to stand, her legs turned to jelly and the pain from her hip nearly made her cry out.

Nick steadied her until she regained her footing. When the howling fury of a few moments before faded away, he slowly opened the door that led to the rest of the basement.

As they stepped out of the coal bin, the basement fell utterly silent.

Nothing had been disturbed.

It was as if nothing had happened at all.

But everything had changed.

Still holding Sarah's hand, Nick led her up the steep flight of stairs to the kitchen. It, too, looked exactly as it had before, and the only sound they could hear was the wind whistling outside and the snow hitting the windowpanes.

"Bettina?" Sarah called out. "Are you all right? Are you here?"

There was no answer.

They glanced uneasily at each other, then moved on through the dining room to the hallway, then into the old study. Bettina sat on a worn Victorian couch, her arms wrapped around herself, her dogs next to her. Her face was white and she was trembling.

Sarah approached her. "Are you all right?"

Though her face glistened with tears, Bettina nodded, and Sarah moved closer.

"Are you really my mother?" she asked so softly that her words seemed borne on no more than the faintest wisp of breeze.

Bettina nodded again. "I don't know why I didn't realize it the day I met you. From the first moment I saw you — and saw your talent — I should have known." Her eyes, wide and frightened, met Sarah's. "I couldn't keep you. Can you understand that? I had to do it — I had to give you up. I . . . I —" She couldn't finish, and choking back a sob, she buried her face in her hands.

Sarah sat next to Bettina and took one of her hands in her own.

Taking a deep breath, Bettina looked up again. "I'm so sorry, Sarah," she whispered. Then she turned to Nick. "I was —" She faltered, then: "It was your father, Nick," she said. "He found me one day and —" Again she fell silent. "I tried to get away from him," she whispered, almost as if to herself. "I tried so hard . . . so hard."

"It wasn't your fault," Nick said, his voice trembling. "Nobody gets away from my dad — not if he doesn't want you to. He just — he just —" His voice cracked, he fell silent for a moment, then found the strength to go on. "He's gone, isn't he? I mean, he's not coming back."

Bettina shook her head. "I don't think so."

"Do you know why?" Nick asked. "I mean, do you know where he went?"

Bettina's brows knit uncertainly. "I'm not

sure he's actually gone," she said, picking her words carefully. "I think he's somewhere close, but I don't think he can ever get back here." Sarah and Nick looked nervously at each other, and Bettina went on. "I don't think either of you needs to be frightened. But I think there are people who do, and I think your father was one of them, Nick. This was the first time he's been here since — well, since that night. And I think something in this house — some spirit, or force, or —" She shrugged helplessly. "I don't know what it is. But I think it understands people, and I think it deals with them."

Nick moved to the sofa and sat on the other side of Bettina. Pyewackett instantly leaped into his lap, settled in and began purring, and Bettina slipped an arm around Sarah and drew her close.

"Are you all right?"

Sarah hesitated, then nodded. "It's okay," she said. "I — I love my family. I mean, I loved my mom, and I still love my dad. I really do. Mom was really great, and I don't care what anyone else thinks, my dad's still great. But —" Her voice caught and her eyes glistened with tears. "I don't know — ever since I met you, and came to this house, I've felt — I don't know, different. Like I belonged here." Finally, she looked up at Bettina. "And maybe I do, don't I?"

Bettina put her other arm around Sarah, and drew her closer. "You certainly do," she whispered.

"So what's going to happen?" Nick asked. "I mean, what's going to happen to all of us?"

Bettina sat back and shrugged. "I don't know. But for the first time in a very long time, I'm not frightened. Not even a little bit." She looked first at Nick, then at Sarah. "And I don't think you need to be, either." A gust of wind howled outside and the lights flickered, went out, then came back on so quickly they barely noticed it. "See?" Bettina said, reaching out to give Nick's hand a squeeze. "The place is taking care of us."

As what was now a snowstorm raged outside, they sat quietly in the old house, waiting for whatever was to come, bound together by history, and bound together by fate.

And bound together by something else, something they knew they might never truly understand.

Dan West parked his patrol car in the clinic's parking lot but didn't immediately get out. Instead he sat perfectly still, willing

472

himself to move back into his role as head of the Warwick police department. But it wasn't possible. Tonight wasn't like any other night when he might be called to hear what someone had to say. Tonight it was about his son — his own son — and whatever Tiffany Garvey had to tell him, it better be good. For all he knew, Tiffany could have caused the wreck herself; God only knew what she might have been doing while Conner was trying to drive carefully along the narrow dirt road while snow fell. And what was Conner supposed to do? Push her away? Maybe Conner was barely old enough to drive, but he was still a man, and a man didn't push a woman away when she wanted to —

Her fault! That was it — it was her fault his son was dead, and now she would make up some story to get herself off the hook.

He pulled up the collar on his coat and stepped out of the car, bracing himself against the biting wind that blew stinging shards of sleet at his face and hands. Hunched against the cold, he hurried to the clinic's emergency entrance and through the big sliding door.

Mitch Garvey, flanked by Angie and Zach, were huddled together, praying, in the corner of the waiting room. Well, if his hunch was anywhere near right, they had a lot to pray about!

Mitch looked up when Dan entered, and stood when he saw the fury in his eyes. "Okay, where is she?" Dan demanded.

"Back there," Mitch said, tilting his head toward the curtained off area. "The doctor's working on her."

Dan West turned to the nurse at the reception desk, but she was on her feet even before he spoke. "I'll tell Dr. Nelson you're here, Dan," she said, and slipped behind the striped curtain.

A moment later the nurse drew it aside and waved Dan closer. Tiffany Garvey lay on a gurney, her face bruised and swollen. Ron Nelson, who'd gone all the way through high school with Dan West before heading off to college and then medical school, stood watching the monitors.

"Hey, Ron," Dan said, his eyes fixed on the injured girl. "Can I ask Tiffany a couple of questions?"

"You can ask," Nelson said. "She's been drifting in and out of consciousness, so I can't say how well she'll answer, but go ahead."

Feeling Mitch and Angie Garvey crowding behind him, Dan moved to the head of Tiffany's bed. "Tiffany?" he said. "Tiffany, can you hear me?"

Tiffany's eyelids parted, she squinted up for a second or two, then let her lids fall.

"Is she sedated?" Dan asked the doctor. If she were under the influence of drugs, interviewing her would be pointless — whatever she said would mean next to nothing.

"No way," Nelson assured him. "Nothing like that with a head injury until you know exactly what's going on."

Dan nodded. "Tiffany? It's Dan West. Conner's father. Can you tell me what happened tonight?" Her eyes fluttered and her brow creased, but she said nothing. "The accident out on the old road?" Dan pressed. "Can you tell me what happened?"

Finally, Tiffany's eyes opened, she blinked, then squinted in the bright light. Her eyes found her father, now standing at the foot of her bed. "Tried to kill us," she said, her voice weak and scratchy. She tried to clear her throat, only half succeeded, then repeated what she'd just said. "They tried to kill us."

"Who?" Dan demanded. What the hell was she talking about? According to Harvey Miller, it had been a one-car accident.

"Sarah," Tiffany breathed. Then: "Sarah Crane and Nick Dunnigan."

Dan West's eyes narrowed. What on earth would Sarah Crane and the Dunnigan kid have been doing out there? Everyone knew what kids were up to in that area — hell, he and Andrea had gone up there themselves before they got married. But the crippled girl and a kid everyone knew was nuts? Tiffany Garvey had to be lying.

Lying, and protecting herself. "Come on, Tiffany," Dan said, doing his best to keep both his suspicion and his growing fury out of his voice. "How could those two try to kill you?"

Her eyes met his. "Th-They saw us out by the lake," she said haltingly. "Th-Then they . . . followed us . . . and . . . and set the road . . . on fire."

Dan's fury grew. Set the road on fire? Was she nuts? Whatever actually happened — and he was surer by the second that he knew exactly what it was — couldn't she have made up a better story than that? But when he looked at her, she looked straight back at him, her eyes never wavering the way kids always did when they lied. It wasn't until they grew up that they learned to lie with a straight face.

"It's true," she insisted. "They set the road on fire. If you don't believe me, ask Conner."

Dan flinched at the sound of his son's name, and Tiffany's eyes widened as she realized what his reaction meant. "No," she whispered. "Oh, God . . . no . . ." Her eyes flooded with tears, and even in the grip of his fury, Dan West understood that not only had Tiffany not known Conner was dead, but truly believed he would back up what she said.

"I think that's enough," Ron Nelson said, moving closer, obviously ready to step between his patient and the sheriff.

Dan nodded once, took one last, and penetrating, look at Tiffany, who was now sobbing in her mother's arms, and walked through the curtain and back into the waiting room.

Rage was rising in him like a tidal wave now, and as he remembered the tale not only Conner, but Sarah and Nick, too, had told after King's belly was laid open, he felt his pulse throbbing in his veins. Well, they might have gotten away with killing his dog, but however they'd done it, Sarah Crane and Nick Dunnigan would pay for Conner's death. If it was the last thing he did, he would see to that.

"I *knew* it!" Angie Garvey spat a moment later as she came back into the waiting area, followed by her husband. "I knew that girl was evil! She's a tool of Satan, and it's not just her!"

Dan was already heading to the squad car.

"Stay with your sister," Angie told Zach, grabbing Mitch's arm and starting after Dan West. "Let's go."

She pulled him toward the squad car through the howling storm, yanked open the back door and climbed in.

"They're at Bettina Philips's house, Dan," Angie declared, her voice trembling with fury. "I'm sure of it. You're going to have to do something about that woman. She's destroying all of us! And what did we ever do to her?"

Dan heard only half of what Angie was saying. He, too, was sure he knew exactly where Sarah and Nick were: at Shutters. He put the car in gear and gunned the engine. Snow clouded the windshield and the wipers could barely keep up with it, but he stepped hard on the accelerator, his fury building with every second that passed, and by the time he reached the bottom of the driveway that led up the hill to Shutters, he was no longer functioning as Warwick's sheriff.

Now he was a father seeking vengeance for the death of his son.

He'd kill Nick and Sarah.

He'd kill them tonight.

And not one person would blame him.

He turned into the driveway and gunned the patrol car up the long hill.

At the top, he slammed on the breaks. The headlights revealed thc looming bulk of Shutters, its massive form seeming to loom even larger in the swirling snow. Getting out of the car, Dan strode toward the house, Angie and Mitch right behind him.

For all of them, the time of reckoning had come.

The heavy oak door swung slowly open even before Dan West could lift the knocker, the gusting wind sending flurries of snow into the foyer and the huge gallery beyond. The lights glowed brighter and then dimmed, and a rumble so low the sheriff barely noticed it emanated from somewhere deep within the old stone building.

His burning anger driving him, Dan strode inside, the storm swirling around him, his eyes stinging from the snow and sleet, his vision blurring, his ears all but deafened by the gale.

"Bettina Philips!" he roared, "I know you're here, and I know those kids are here, too!"

He heard muffled shouting behind him

but could make out the words no better than he could see into the depths of the house. He took another step forward, and suddenly the howling of a dog — a big dog — drowned out the sound of the wind, and then the stinging mist around him seemed to clear and he saw it.

King! It was King, and a few feet from him he saw Conner, and now Conner was shouting: *"Sic 'em, King! Get 'em!"* For an instant Dan caught a glimpse of Nick Dunnigan and Sarah Crane, but then everything changed and the dog — his *own* dog — was charging at him! Its jaws wide, its bared fangs dripping saliva, the dog was racing toward him. Instinctively, West took a step back, and heard the door slam shut behind him.

"What is it?" he heard Angie Garvey demanding, her voice shrill. "Why are you —"

But Dan West heard nothing else. All his attention was focused on the animal about to launch itself. But it was no longer the shepherd he'd raised from a pup. Instead it was a Rottweiler, but a Rottweiler far larger than any Dan West had ever seen before.

Instantaneously, Dan's rage dissolved into primal fear. His eyes locked on the dog's, and their eyes bore into each other.

Stay calm, he told himself. *It's a dog — it's just a dog.*

But he already knew it wasn't just a dog. This was a beast, and it was radiating an unholy fury, its eyes blazing with a burning light, an unearthly howl erupting from its throat. The animal was coiling itself for one final leap, and out of the corner of his eye Dan saw an open door. Not caring where the door might lead, he turned and fled, feeling the dog's breath on his neck and hearing its jaws snap shut where his face had been only a split second before.

Dan dove through the door, whirling as he entered the room, in order to slam the door shut behind him.

His hand touched the knob, and then it seemed every muscle in his body contracted as if he'd been shot through with a thousand volts of electricity.

The door remained open, and now the attacking animal was leaping through it.

Dan's arm came up to protect his face, and a second later he felt a searing pain shoot from his hand up into his shoulder, the enormous weight of the animal sending him tumbling back farther into the room.

The door slammed shut, though no one had touched it, at least no one that Dan West could see. His voice rising to a scream, he tried to shake his arm loose from the grip of the dog's jaws, but they held fast, and he began lashing out at the beast with his feet and one free arm.

It was as if he were thrashing at a void, as if he were in the grip of some monstrous creature he could see, and hear, and feel, but couldn't touch at all.

Then he felt the animal suddenly drop him, and he collapsed for an instant, only to howl in agony yet again a split second later as he felt the dog's jaws close on his neck, its fangs tearing deep into his flesh.

"Help me!" he screamed. *"For God's sake, help me! Get him off!"*

But there was no response.

Only the endless howl of a wind that seemed to be coming from somewhere inside the house, and the guttural sounds emanating from the Rottweiler as it tore at his body, ripping one of his arms from its socket, then settling down to gnaw at his belly.

Dan twitched, and tried to cry out again, but his larynx was torn away and no sound emerged from his throat as a gray fog slowly closed around him, muffling everything, even the pain of having his body torn apart.

A fog that Dan West prayed would never lift.

■ ■ ■ ■

Angie Garvey stared mutely into the room where Dan West had just fled.

Fled, and then disappeared.

For a brief second — so brief that she wasn't certain it had happened at all — she thought the door had shut, but when she'd looked again it was still standing open, just as it was right now. But the only living thing in the room was some kind of small dog — one of Bettina's pets — yapping away at nothing.

Nothing at all.

Then what happened to Dan West?

She wheeled around and found herself facing Bettina, flanked by Sarah and Nick, the three of them standing together just outside the door of what looked like some kind of library or study. Not that it mattered what kind of room it was — all that mattered was what was going on here. "Where is he?" she demanded, glowering at Bettina. "What have you done to Dan?"

"I've done noth—" Bettina began, but Angie's voice cut her off.

"Everyone knows you're a witch," she began, moving toward Bettina. "Everyone knows —"

"Stop it!" Sarah shouted, her voice trembling with anger. "Bettina isn't a witch, and she isn't evil, and she isn't any of the other things you say she is. She's my mother!" As if surprised at the sound of the last three words, Sarah fell silent for a moment. Then, far more quietly, she repeated them: "She's my mother." Her eyes glistened with tears. "She's good, and she's kind, and I love her."

Mitch Garvey moved forward, and once more the house trembled with a nearly inaudible rumble. "You keep a civil tongue in your head when you talk to my wife. You're no better than your father — you killed Conner and almost killed Tiffany."

He continued to move toward Sarah, then Nick Dunnigan stepped in front of him.

"Don't touch her," Nick said softly. Though his voice was low, there was a note of confidence in it that even he had never heard before, and as he faced Mitch Garvey, he felt not even a flicker of fear. "You don't know anything. You don't know anything about this house, and you don't know anything about us. So stay away. We haven't done anything wrong."

Mitch's eyes narrowed as his fury built. What was going on? Nick Dunnigan was telling *him* what to do? "Who the hell do you think you are?" he said, his eyes fixing on Nick with the cold look he used to stare down even the worst of the inmates at the prison. All of them knew what came after that look, and Nick Dunnigan was about to find out. His right hand clenching into a hard fist, he took a step toward the boy.

"Don't," Nick said softly.

But it was too late. Mitch's arm had already come up, and now he was swinging his fist toward Nick Dunnigan's jaw.

The low rumble that had energized the house before erupted into a crack of thunder, and Mitch felt the floor buckle beneath him. Struggling to keep his balance, he flailed at the air with his arms, but tumbled to the floor.

As Bettina put her arms around Sarah and Nick and drew them closer to her, Angie Garvey stared dumbstruck at her husband. It looked like Mitch had been seized by some kind of demon, and now he was thrashing on the floor fighting some enemy she could neither see nor hear. She watched mutely as he crawled toward the study as if trying to escape his invisible assailant. Then he was through the door and into the paneled room, and the door slammed shut, and Angie had a terrible feeling that she would never see Mitch again.

■ ■ ■ ■

The room was hot — hotter than anything Mitch had ever felt before. Once again he tried to regain his feet, but despite the carpeting, the floor felt slippery — so slippery he lost his footing and fell again. He tried to catch himself, but as soon as his hands touched the floor it felt as if he'd put them on a hot iron.

Then he saw it.

Ants — red ants — swarming over the floor, millions of them, so thick there was not a sign of the carpet beneath them.

Mitch opened his mouth to scream, but as soon as he did, the ants were in his mouth, swarming over his tongue, stinging the inside of his cheeks, moving down his throat like a searing flame, and in an instant he knew he would never scream again. Once again he thrashed, but the ants were everywhere, crawling down the walls, streaming over the furniture, pouring under the door from the hall. Only the fireplace seemed free of them, and he struggled toward it, his entire body burning not only with the heat, but the poison as well. He scrabbled across the floor, clawing his way, feeling his strength drain away in the burning heat.

And then he was there, dragging himself across the hearth and into the fireplace itself. His head was swimming and the ants were still swarming over him and the heat —

Flames burst all around him, and for a moment he felt a ray of hope. Even the ants couldn't withstand the fire blazing around him now. But in the next moment, as he watched his clothes burning away through eyes nearly swollen shut, he realized the truth.

It was himself — his own body — that had turned into a conflagration, and now his nostrils filled with the sweet odor of burning flesh.

He gasped for air, but his lungs were already on fire and he could no longer breathe.

He was dying — he knew he was dying, and he knew there was nothing he could do about it, and he knew with a terrible certainty where he was going.

He was going to Hell, and he was going to burn forever, burn like he was burning now, but the pain would never end, and he would never escape it and it would go on and on and on and on until —

"Stand back!" a voice ordered.

A voice? How could there be a voice? He

was in Hell and he was burning and —

"Back!" the voice commanded. "You hear me?"

Mitch Garvey's eyes snapped open, but all he saw was gray stone. His arms were still flailing, but there were no more ants.

And his body was still burning up, but there were no more flames.

He heard the jangle of metal on metal, the same jangle he heard every day when he opened a barred door.

The sound of a key.

A lock was opened.

Mitch stared at the heavy oak door whose planks were strapped together with thick wrought iron, and in a moment it began to swing open.

Two men appeared, holding a large fire hose.

"Didn't we tell you to stop hurting yourself?" one of them demanded.

Mitch's mind reeled. Where was he? How did he get here? What was going on? Then he looked down at himself.

Blood was dripping from his arms where he'd tried to scrape away the ants.

His nostrils were no longer filled with the stink of burning flesh, but with a far more foul stench, and then he could feel the mess he'd made in his own clothing.

He peered up at the men and reached out a trembling and supplicating hand. "Please," he whispered, his voice rasping through vocal cords worn raw from screaming. "Help me . . . please . . . help me."

"Oh, we'll help you, you crazy bastard," one of the men said. They tightened their grip on the hose's nozzle, and one of them nodded.

Before Mitch realized what was about to happen, a thick jet of ice-cold water slammed into him and he sprawled out on the floor. When he opened his mouth to beg them to stop, they hit him full in the face with the stream and he felt water forcing its way down his throat.

He was going to drown!

He was going to drown right here, with two people blasting him mercilessly with a stream of water that held him pinned to the floor.

And then it stopped.

"That'll keep 'im quiet for the rest of the day," one of the guards said.

Mitch rolled over in the puddle as the door was closed and relocked. Finally, he gathered enough strength to crawl over to the door and pull himself up to peer through a small barred window, to find himself gazing at the flickering mantel of an old-fashioned gas sconce. His eyes moved away from the light and he peered down a long narrow hallway, with more of the old gas lamps placed just close enough together to fill the corridor with dim light.

Between the sconces were more doors, doors with barred windows just like the one he was looking through.

From one or two of them Mitch thought he saw insane eyes peering back at him.

From the others there was nothing.

Nothing except the occasional scream, or a hopeless moan.

He sank back to the wet floor, the cries and whimpers of his future echoing through the corridors of the hell he knew he would never escape.

CHAPTER
THIRTY

Angie Garvey turned away from the reflection of herself she caught in the mirror that hung on the wall next to the coat tree, but it was too late. The image of her bloodless face, twisted with terror and fury, was seared into her mind. Even worse than her expression, though, was that what she'd seen in the mirror bore no resemblance to what Angie knew she looked like. The face in the mirror had aged; it was as if she were looking fifty years into the future. Her hair, thin and gray, hung lank around a face dominated by a pair of empty and hopeless eyes. Her skin was sagging and deeply creased, and though there was nothing in her reflection that she recognized, she knew it was her.

What was happening? Dan West had vanished and now Mitch —

Mitch! Panic rising, she moved to the door through which he had scrabbled. It swung open even as she reached for the knob, and Angie felt a surge of relief. Mitch was all right, and he was opening the door, and —

The door swung open to reveal the study just as it had been a few moments ago.

Empty.

Empty, and silent.

"M-Mitch?" Angie said, but now her utterance was heavy with her fading hope.

"He's gone," Nick Dunnigan said quietly, though his voice echoed in Angie's ears with the slow cadence of a funeral march.

. . . gone . . . gone . . . gone . . . gone . . .

She wheeled on Nick. "Where?" she screamed. "What did you do to him? Where did he go?"

"We don't know, Angie," Bettina said, reaching out as if to offer her hand to the distraught woman.

Out! She had to get out, and she had to get out before whatever had happened to Mitch and Dan West happened to her, too. Spurning Bettina Philips's outstretched hand, Angie turned to flee toward the front door, but after taking only a single step, she abruptly veered around and found herself lurching toward the staircase.

What was happening? She didn't want to go upstairs! She wanted to leave! Leave before —

She wheeled around, clinging to the banister as she raged at the three people who were looking up at her. "Let me go!" she screamed. "What have you done? What have you done to Mitch —" Her voice broke and she began sobbing as she lost her grip on the rail and started climbing the stairs once more, her hands still reaching for something to hang on to, her voice reduced to a nearly incoherent babble. "No . . . let me go . . . I'm sorry . . . sorry for everything . . . sorry for —" She was at the landing now, and as she made the turn to climb to the second floor, her eyes suddenly fastened on Sarah and her fury erupted. "You!" she screamed. "This is your doing! You're evil and you've always been evil and you should burn in —"

Her words were cut short and she felt herself being hurled up the stairs, her head slamming against the steps, her body crashing first against the wall to one side, then against the thick wooden balusters on the other.

Then she was at the top of the stairs. Regaining her footing, she fled down the corridor.

Doors!

There seemed to be doors everywhere. If she got through one of them — found a window —

Locked!

All of them, locked so tight they might as well have been nailed shut.

She came to the end of the corridor. There was only one door left now. She reached for the knob, but even before she touched it the door swung open and she hurtled into a second staircase, a narrow staircase.

Down!

If she could get down, maybe she could get out! But as she turned to start down the steep flight, she saw something move.

Something small, coming up the stairs.

A second later she recognized it.

A rat.

Huge, and gray, and coming right at her! Behind it was another.

And another and another and a —

Screaming, Angie turned back to the door, but it slammed shut even as she lunged toward it, and her right hip smashed against it, sending a terrible pain shooting down her leg.

The rats were coming closer now, and Angie stumbled up to the third floor, pulling herself on the banister, her right leg dragging limply, the pain from her shattered hip slashing through her body like a whip. She came to the top of the stairs and found herself at the end of another corridor, this one far narrower than the one on the floor below, but up ahead she saw a door.

An open door!

Behind her the rats were flooding up the last flight of stairs, and Angie forced herself to stand up.

Clumsily, bracing herself against the walls with both her outstretched arms, she began hopping toward the open door.

Now the rats were coming at her not only from the stairs behind her, but from under the closed doors on either side of the hallway.

She flung herself through the open door, slammed it shut behind her and collapsed on the floor, her heart pounding, her lungs straining to suck in enough air to let her catch her breath, her ruined hip burning beneath her.

Outside the closed door she could hear the rats chittering, and she crept a little farther into the room, which was so brightly lit it almost blinded her.

The noise changed, and for a moment she didn't know what was happening. Then it came to her: the rats were no longer chittering.

Now they were gnawing, and soon they would gnaw their way through the door.

She pulled herself a little farther from the door. *A way out! There had to be a way out — all she had to do was find it!*

Her eyes adjusted to the light, and then she saw it.

For a moment she couldn't believe her eyes: One whole wall was lined with French doors opening onto a terrace, and beyond the terrace she saw a broad lawn sweeping past a huge stone building — perfectly rectangular, with a black slate roof that looked like pictures she'd seen of the old institute that had been torn down so many years ago — down to the edge of a shimmering Shutters Lake. Leafed trees swayed in the breeze.

An illusion — it had to be an illusion!

Then she understood. An illusion was exactly what it was! It was nothing more than a painting. There was a name for it: tramp . . . tromp . . .

Trompe l'oeil!

That was it — a painting that looked perfectly real, so you felt like you were looking out windows even though it was only a wall.

A blank wall!

She heard the chittering then, and the scraping, as the rats began to penetrate the door behind her. She glanced back and saw them, coming through the door, and out of the walls, and —

Panic seized her, and without thinking, Angie pulled herself to her feet, ignoring the agony in her right leg and hip as a stream of adrenaline surged through her, spurring her onward.

Out! She had to get out before the rats could reach her. If she couldn't —

She could already feel them, biting into her legs, tearing her flesh from her bones, ripping at her until —

She hurled herself toward the image of the world outside, where the sun was shining and the flowers were in bloom and it was a perfect summer day and —

One of the French doors flew open before her, and Angie tumbled through it, falling into a swirling maelstrom of air and light.

Bright light, light that hurt her eyes.

Unearthly light.

She closed her eyes tight against the blinding light and tried to twist her body away from the pain of her broken bone.

"Okay, move her out," a woman said.

Angie opened her eyes. A heavyset woman in an ancient nurse's uniform stood over her, glowering down with furious eyes. "Are you going to behave now?" a harsh, guttural voice demanded.

Angie tried to move but couldn't. She could barely even breathe. "Let's go," the woman said sharply, clapping her hands.

Two men lifted Angie off a bed. Except it wasn't a bed at all — just a few wooden slats in a frame.

She could barely move her legs and her upper body was immobile.

She looked down and finally understood. With its large buckles and the heavy cloth, there was no mistaking what she was wearing.

It was a straitjacket.

Bound in a straitjacket, she was being half carried and half dragged by the two men through the door of a tiny cell and into a dark hallway, barely lit by the gaslights hung along its walls.

She tried to speak, tried to ask where she was, but even though she could work her lips, no sound came out. Now she looked frantically around for someone who might help her, but except for the two men flanking her and the stolid woman marching ahead, all she could see were glimpses of haunted-looking faces behind the barred windows that pierced each iron-strapped door she passed.

Muffled voices muttered.

A woman screamed.

Fingers came through a window, as if reaching for her.

They were near the end of the long corridor when Angie Garvey's eyes suddenly locked on to those of someone whose face was all but invisible in the darkness of his cell. But it didn't matter, for she recognized those eyes in an instant, and finally found her voice.

Her mouth opened and with all the energy she could muster she howled out the name of the man behind those eyes.

"MIIIITCH!"

Her husband's name echoed up and down the corridor for what seemed to Angie like an eternity, then faded away.

For her, though, eternity had just begun.

CHAPTER
THIRTY-ONE

Kate Williams drove slowly through the early morning rain as she turned off the highway toward Warwick. The morning had dawned unseasonably warm, and the heat along with the rain had dissolved almost all evidence of the snowstorm that blew in so suddenly last night.

Ed Crane's voice on the telephone this morning had struck a chord with the nagging feeling growing inside her that things might not be entirely right at the Garvey house. She had managed to shelve that feeling in the hope that she was wrong and that she wouldn't have to add Sarah Crane to her already crushing caseload. But Ed Crane had sounded not just worried, but actually frightened, and right after his call, she canceled her entire morning calendar and headed for Warwick.

Kate turned onto Quail Run and parked in front of the Garvey house. The draperies were still drawn, as if the household hadn't awakened yet.

She grabbed her shoulder bag, walked up to the door and pressed the bell. She heard the spaniel bark, but nobody came, and finally she opened the storm door and tried the knob.

It turned.

She hesitated. Should she go in? Or should she call the police? But what would she say? That she'd found a house left unlocked on a Saturday morning with nobody home but the dog? They'd think she was an idiot!

She pushed the front door open. "Hello?"

No answer, except the tail-wagging of the dog, who ran toward the back door, whining to be let out.

Kate paused in the living room. "Is anybody home?" she called. More silence, so she continued on through the small dining room into the kitchen.

Half-cooked chicken lay in a cold frying pan on the stove. Wilted salad sat in a bowl on the counter. And the dining room table was set for dinner. The Garveys had left last night, and they'd left in a hurry. She let the dog out to relieve himself, waited for him to come back in, then retraced her steps and left the house, closing the front door firmly behind her but leaving it unlocked, just the way she'd found it. She paused on the porch, surveying the Garveys' neighborhood.

It looked exactly as it should on a quiet Saturday morning.

The door to the house next door opened, and a man in his bathrobe stepped out to retrieve the morning paper. "Good morning," Kate called to him.

"Eh?" He looked startled, but then nodded. "Yuh — it *is* a good morning, isn't it?"

"I'm wondering if you might know where the Garveys are this morning?"

The man frowned, pursing his lips as if wondering just how much he should say to this person he'd never seen before in his life. But as Kate was reaching into her purse for her county identification card, he answered: "The wife said their girl was in some kind of accident last night. Saw it on the news."

"Which girl?" Kate asked, the quick breakfast she'd grabbed forty minutes ago suddenly congealing in her stomach.

" 'Ats all I know," the man said. "Some crazy weather, eh?" He waved his paper at her and went back inside.

Kate ran down the steps and got into her car. She'd been to the Warwick police station a couple of years ago, and now found it in less than two minutes. She parked in front and strode through the glass entry.

The uniformed deputy behind a desk glanced up at her. "Take a seat," he said. "I'll be with you in a minute." Before she could protest that she had an emergency — which might not exactly be true — he'd turned his attention back to a distraught woman who was sitting in a chair next to his desk.

"He didn't come home last night," the woman said, twisting a sodden handkerchief, then dabbing ineffectively at her eyes. "Dan always comes home. Always!"

The deputy spread his hands in a helpless gesture. "I'm really, really sorry, Andrea, but there's nothing I can tell you. We haven't heard from him, and believe me, we've been trying to get hold of him for hours."

But the woman wouldn't be put off. "Zach Garvey said Dan went with his parents to Bettina Philips's house. Have you been out there yet?"

Kate sat up straight.

"Bill Harney and I just got back from there half an hour ago," the deputy said. "Dan isn't there and neither are the Garveys."

"What about his car?" the woman demanded. "Where's his car?"

The deputy shook his head. "I don't know that, either, Andrea." His voice took on the kind of weary note Kate had often heard from police officers trying to respond to all the demands of distraught people whose spouses or children had vanished, often because they wanted to vanish rather than because they'd fallen victim to some sort of crime. "I know it's not at the Philips place, and I put out an APB on it, but I haven't heard anything. You've got to give it some time."

"Time?" the woman echoed, her voice rising and taking on a note of hysteria. "My son's been murdered and my husband is missing, and you say I have to give it 'time'?"

"Conner wasn't murdered, Andrea," the deputy said quietly. "It was an accident."

Kate stood up. "Excuse me," she said. "I'm Kate Williams with the Vermont Department of Social Services, and I'm here looking for the Garveys."

Andrea West turned a puffy-eyed face toward her. "We're all looking for the Garveys," she said. "And my husband," she added, her gaze shifting back to fix on the deputy again. "Who is the sheriff here!"

Kate saw the deputy redden. "I'm actually looking for Sarah Crane, the Garveys' foster child," she said.

Andrea's expression changed then, morphing into a mask of pure fury. "She's the one who murdered my son!" she burst out. "And almost killed Tiffany Garvey, too!"

The deputy stood up and started around his desk toward Kate. "Nobody murdered your son, Andrea," he repeated, then shifted his attention back to Kate. "I'm sorry," he said. "I'm Tim Ross. I —"

"The girl you're looking for is probably out there with that witch Bettina Philips," Andrea West cut in. "If you can call it living — they should have torn that wreck down years ago."

Tim Ross shot Kate a sympathetic look. "The Crane girl is out there," he said. "Actually, the next call I was going to make was to you, but . . ." His voice trailed off and his head tipped almost imperceptibly toward Andrea West. "You'll see the gates at the entrance to the property," the deputy said, "a little less than a mile out of town, off 157."

"Thanks," Kate said, then turned to offer her sympathy to the sheriff's wife, but Andrea West only glared at her.

"If the gates haven't rusted off by now," she muttered so quietly that Kate wasn't even sure the words were directed at her.

She left the sheriff's office and got into her car, her mind racing. Bettina Philips was the one who had gone to see Sarah's father, the art teacher concerned about Sarah's placement with the Garveys.

And Bettina Philips was the one who got Mitch Garvey so angry that he'd frightened Ed Crane enough to call her this morning and beg her to check on his daughter.

And now the sheriff's wife had called the teacher a witch? Or had she actually just substituted a W for a B before she'd spat out the word? Suddenly, Kate wished she'd paid more attention to that feeling she'd had that all was not as well with Sarah as both the girl and Angie Garvey had insisted.

As she turned left off Main Street onto Route 157, the rain stopped completely, and by the time she'd driven half a mile farther, the sun was starting to break through the clouds. As the sky turned bluer, she kept one eye on the odometer and searched for the gates with the other. And sure enough, just a little less than a mile out of town, she found them.

Except they weren't the kind of rusted, ruined gates the sheriff's wife had talked about. Instead she saw a pair of handsome — and massive — wrought-iron gates that hung perfectly straight on sturdy hinges.

Both the gates and the hinges looked freshly painted, and the gates stood open as if to welcome her.

She turned up a long curving drive, and the last of the clouds dispersed and the sun came out, shining brilliantly on the wet driveway, making it sparkle as if it were paved with diamonds rather than gravel. The drive curved gently through the forest for a couple hundred yards, then emerged into the grounds surrounding the house. The gravel drive formed a circle around an enormous maple tree; obviously, whatever else Bettina Philips was, she had a green thumb. The gardens were filled with asters and half a dozen other fall-blooming plants, and the lawns were green, well-mown, and — at least from what Kate could see — totally weedless.

Nor was the old stone mansion the "wreck" she had been led to expect. Rather, it was a handsome structure with heavy shutters at every window and the kind of slate roof she had always envied. The house appeared every bit as well-tended as the grounds surrounding it. The front door looked inviting, and even with winter coming on, there were perfectly matched topiaries in the massive stone urns that flanked the entry.

Kate pulled into the freshly graveled circular drive and parked next to a Mini Cooper that was the only other visible vehicle.

A lone bark greeted her when she rang the bell, and a moment later a woman who looked as if she hadn't slept all night opened the front door, with a little terrier wagging happily at her feet. The woman scooped it up so it wouldn't dart outside, but before either Kate or the woman could speak, a familiar voice called out Kate's name and a second later Sarah Crane appeared.

But this was not the subdued girl Kate had last seen at Mitch and Angie Garvey's house. This was the Sarah Crane she had grown to know, even love, during the months of her recuperation from the accident that crippled her. Kate dropped her shoulder bag and enfolded Sarah in an enormous, and relieved, hug. "Are you all right?"

Sarah nodded, wiping moisture from her eyes with her sleeve, then gesturing toward the woman who had opened the door. "This is Bettina Philips," she said, taking Kate's hand and pulling her into the foyer. "And this is Kate Williams, Bettina. She's my caseworker with the county. Except she's not just my caseworker — she's my friend, too."

"I know who Kate is, or at least I know of her," Bettina said, leading Kate into the huge entry gallery. "I think you'd better come and sit down," she said to the caseworker. "There's been a lot happening here." She led the way to the parlor, where morning sun was flooding through open windows. A pale woman and boy about the same age as Sarah were sitting on a small couch, both of them looking as tired as Bettina and Sarah.

The woman stood up as Bettina explained who Kate was, and offered her hand. "I'm Lily Dunnigan," she said, the words coming out in a nearly exhausted sigh. "This is my son, Nick."

Kate perched on the edge of an antique brocade wing chair as Sarah sank down next to Bettina on a second sofa.

"Sarah's father called me this morning," Kate said, deciding to approach Bettina Philips head-on. "Apparently Mitch Garvey was threatening Sarah about you."

"Well, that's not a surprise," Bettina observed, her brows forming a sardonic arch. "Was it the witch thing, or the 'tool of the devil' thing? Both are fairly common around here."

Kate decided at once that she liked Bettina Philips. "Actually, I heard the witch thing at the sheriff's office, but 'tool of the devil' is a new one." Then her voice turned serious. "But Ed Crane was very worried, and I've already heard that something happened last night. A boy was killed in an accident? And the Garveys are missing?" She saw Lily Dunnigan and Bettina Philips exchange a quick glance, but before either could say anything, Sarah answered at least one of her questions.

"There was an accident — Conner West's car caught on fire. He and Tiffany Garvey were trying to run us down — Nick and me. But he skidded or something and hit a wall, and his car caught on fire."

"Dear God," Kate breathed.

"The sheriff was here last night," Bettina said, and Kate had the feeling she was choosing her words with a great deal of care. "Actually, so were the Garveys, and Nick's father."

Kate waited, but instead of going on, Bettina's eyes moved from Sarah to Lily Dunnigan and her son, as if looking for some kind of signal. It was Lily Dunnigan who nodded so imperceptibly that Kate almost missed it.

"They were making threats," Bettina said.

"They seemed to think that somehow the accident was Sarah and Nick's fault. . . ."

Her voice trailed off, but Kate was sure there was more — much more — to the story. "And?" she prompted.

"And they left," Bettina said, her eyes never leaving Kate's.

"Left," Kate repeated. She glanced from Bettina to the other people in the room. "I'm not sure I'm following you. The sheriff and the Garveys came out here accusing Sarah and — Nick, is it? — of causing an accident that killed the sheriff's son, and they just . . . *left?* Where did they go?"

"I don't know," Bettina replied. "But I don't think they'll be back." Before Kate could say anything else, Lily Dunnigan spoke.

"There's something else you should know. Sarah is Bettina's daughter." She fell silent for a moment, then seemed to gather herself. "Bettina's and my husband's. She is Nick's half sister." Kate stared at Lily Dunnigan, stunned, but Lily wasn't finished. "Shep raped her," she said, her voice trembling with anger. "While I was pregnant with Nick, the man I was married to came out here and raped Bettina. Which I suppose at least explains why he always hated her."

"And you said he was here last night, too?"

Lily nodded. "He was going to take Nick back to the hospital." She took her son's hand protectively, almost as if afraid Kate might try to take him away. "Nick's had problems ever since he was little, and Shep —" She cut herself off, apparently deciding she might be saying too much. Then her voice hardened. "Shep wanted to have Nick committed again."

For a long moment Kate studied the four people around her. "And they all left and you don't know where they went?"

"Actually none of us really knows exactly what happened last night," Bettina said. "This is a strange house —"

"It's a *great* house," Nick broke in. "And I was never crazy. I just —" He hesitated, glanced at Sarah, then went on. "— I just have a sort of talent, kind of like Sarah. She can draw things, and I can . . . I don't know — sort of visualize and hear them, I guess."

Kate's mind was churning, trying to make sense of what she was hearing. It would be easy to prove whether Bettina was Sarah's mother — either adoption records or a DNA test would do it — but now that she was looking at both of them sitting side by side, she was sure what the outcome would be. As for the rest of it . . . "I understand two deputies have already been here this morning?"

Bettina nodded. "We told them exactly what we told you, that the people they were looking for were here, and they left. They searched the house and the garage and everywhere else."

"Looking for what?" Kate asked. "Surely they didn't think —"

"I have no idea what the deputies thought," Bettina broke in. "But I'm sure they'll be back, and there will be all kinds of other people with them. And I'm sure people will talk. But the fact of the matter is, none of us have any idea where Dan West and Shep Dunnigan and Mitch and Angie Garvey went." She paused for a moment, then went on. "And frankly, we don't really care, either, as long as they don't come back. And they won't — *that,* we're pretty sure of."

"How can you be so sure?" Kate countered. "If you don't know where they went, how can you be sure they won't be back?"

Before Bettina could answer Kate's question, Nick Dunnigan said, "This house. It didn't like them. It's a great house, and it likes us, but it didn't like them. It didn't like them at all. And there were reasons why."

Kate sat back in the chair, preparing herself for what she was certain was going to be a long story. "I'm listening," she said.

Epilogue

This was not how it was supposed to be!

Tiffany Garvey was not supposed to be standing in a hot kitchen, sweat dripping down her back as she tried to make the baby eat at least one spoonful of the disgusting pureed peas the brat's miserable mother insisted she feed it.

And Tiffany Garvey was certainly not supposed to be taking orders from anyone like Rowena Matheson, who'd only taken her and Zach in because instead of paying for staff, she'd found out the county would pay her to take in foster children.

Foster children!

Tiffany silently cursed her parents as Brian Matheson the Third spat more peas on the front of her blouse.

Brian Matheson the Third! What a pile of crap — Brian Matheson the *Turd* was more like it.

And it was all her parents' fault. If they

hadn't taken off while she was still in the hospital after Sarah Crane and Nick Dunnigan tried to kill her, she'd be home where she belonged.

And Sarah and Nick would be in Juvenile Hall, or wherever they sent people like them. But no — they'd gotten off scot-free, even though they'd killed Conner West, and probably Conner's dad and Nick's father, too.

Maybe even her own parents!

Well, it wasn't fair, and it wasn't right, and when she turned eighteen —

The baby's mouth opened then and a stream of vomit shot out, hitting Tiffany square in the chest. Her own gorge rising as the nauseating smell filled her nostrils, Tiffany ran to the sink, barely reaching it in time to throw up there rather than on the floor.

The sink, at least, was a lot easier to clean than the floor, which she'd already mopped once today.

She was just rinsing the vomit off her shirt when Zach walked into the kitchen through the back door.

"Oh, jeez," he groaned as he smelled not only the baby's puke but his sister's as well. "What did you do?"

"I didn't do *any*thing!" Tiffany shot back. "If —"

"Zachary?" a cold voice cut in.

They both turned to see Rowena Matheson framed in the door to the dining room, looking cool and fresh in a beige silk blouse and pants, despite the heat of the August day. Her feet were strapped into sandals Tiffany was sure had cost at least six hundred dollars, and every hair on her head was perfectly in place.

Why wouldn't it be, Tiffany thought, when she had to wash it for her every afternoon?

"Have you fed the dogs their supper and cleaned the kennels yet?"

Tiffany shot Zach a warning look as his face reddened and the vein in his forehead began to throb exactly the way their father's used to just before his temper exploded.

"No, ma'am," he said, struggling to keep his voice from betraying his fury.

But Rowena read his face perfectly, and her eyes narrowed. "You know we only wanted one foster child."

"Yes, ma'am," Zach said.

Tiffany watched him force himself to keep his eyes down. Mrs. Matheson had told them on the first day that they were never, under any circumstances, to make eye contact with her. *You are here to make my life easier. You are not my friends or my family, and you will not expect to be treated as such. You will be respectful at all times.*

"Keeping you two together was a gift," Mrs. Matheson went on now. "The least you can do is show your gratitude by keeping the kennels clean. Am I perfectly clear?"

"Yes, ma'am," Zach muttered.

"Then let's not stand around the kitchen keeping your sister from her chores. She'll keep a dinner plate warm for you."

Zach backed wordlessly out the back door, and all ten of Brian Matheson, Jr.'s German shorthair hunting dogs began to bark. Tiffany glanced out the window as Zach picked up the shovel, a bucket, and the hose.

Rowena Matheson smiled at her baby and gave him a little wave. "Isn't Trip the most perfect baby you've ever seen?" she said. "You're very fortunate to be able to take care of him — I don't know how many nannies applied for the job."

Who you couldn't have treated like slaves, Tiffany thought, keeping her expression carefully bland so Rowena couldn't see what was in her mind.

Then Rowena came to the real point of her visit to the kitchen. "We're ready for dinner, Tiffany," she said. "You may serve."

Dinner!

Was it even ready?

Tiffany glanced around the kitchen in a panic. "Right away," she said as Rowena Matheson turned and vanished into the dining room.

Tiffany pulled the salad she'd put together an hour ago out of the refrigerator and prayed that would hold them until she could finish garnishing the soup — a cold cucumber one that had taken her all morning to prepare — with the parsley the Mathesons always demanded.

"It just doesn't look right without it," Rowena had explained the one time Tiffany failed to add the parsley. "And it's not as if it's any trouble for you." It had been a statement, not a question, and Tiffany had already known better than to argue with either of the Mathesons about anything, even if she had the time, which she didn't.

In fact, she had no time for anything anymore. No time for friends — which she didn't have anymore anyway — and no time for homework and no time to be a girl.

No time, even, to call Kate Williams and complain about the home in which she and Zach had been placed.

But when she turned eighteen . . .

ABOUT THE AUTHOR

House of Reckoning is **John Saul**'s thirty-sixth novel. His first novel, *Suffer the Children,* published in 1977, was an immediate million-copy bestseller. His other bestselling suspense novels include *Faces of Fear, In the Dark of the Night, Perfect Nightmare, Black Creek Crossing, Midnight Voices, The Manhattan Hunt Club, Nightshade, The Right Hand of Evil, The Presence, Black Lightning, The Homing,* and *Guardian.* He is also the author of the *New York Times* bestselling serial thriller *The Blackstone Chronicles,* initially published in six installments but now available in one complete volume. Saul divides his time between Seattle, Washington, and Hawaii.